Minds
of
Winter

Also by Ed O'Loughlin

Not Untrue and Not Unkind
Toploader

Minds
of
Winter

Ed O'Loughlin

Quercus

New York • London

Quercus

New York • London

ISBN 978-1-68144-245-7

Library of Congress Cataloging-in-Publication Data

Names: O'Loughlin, Ed., author.
Title: Minds of winter / Ed O'Loughlin.
Description: New York : Quercus, 2017.
Identifiers: LCCN 2016033791 (print) | LCCN 2016041944 (ebook) | ISBN 9781681442457 (hardcover) | ISBN 9781681442440 (softcover) | ISBN 9781681442433 (ebook) | ISBN 9781681442426 (library ebook)
Subjects: LCSH: Polar regions–Discovery and exploration–Fiction. | Man-woman relationships–Fiction. | Family secrets–Fiction. | BISAC: FICTION / Historical. | FICTION / Literary. | FICTION / Mystery & Detective / Historical. | GSAFD: Romantic suspense fiction. | Mystery fiction.
Classification: LCC PR6115.L68 M56 2017 (print) | LCC PR6115.L68 (ebook) | DDC 823/.92–dc23
LC record available at https://lccn.loc.gov/2016033791

Distributed in the United States and Canada by
Hachette Book Group
1290 Avenue of the Americas
New York, NY 10104

Manufactured in the United States

10 9 8 7 6 5 4 3 2 1

www.quercus.com

For Simon

ARCTIC OCEAN

Edge of summer polar ice

*Beaufort
Sea*

ALASKA

PRINCE PATRICK
ISLAND

M'Clure Strait

MELVILLE
ISLAND

BATH
ISL

BANKS
ISLAND

*Viscount Melville
Sound*

Tuktoyaktuk

Aklavik

Arctic Circle

Inuvik

Fort McPherson

VICTORIA
ISLAND

McClintock Channel

PRIN
OF WAL
ISLAN

Mackenzie R.

Great Bear Lake

Coppermine

Coronation Gulf

Coppermine R.

KIN
WILL
ISLA

*Queen Maud
Gulf*

Great Fish R.

Great Slave Lake

Tree line

C   A   N   A   D   A

Lake Athabasca

The Snow Man

One must have a mind of winter
To regard the frost and the boughs
Of the pine-trees crusted with snow;

And have been cold a long time
To behold the junipers shagged with ice,
The spruces rough in the distant glitter

Of the January sun; and not to think
Of any misery in the sound of the wind,
In the sound of a few leaves,

Which is the sound of the land
Full of the same wind
That is blowing in the same bare place

For the listener, who listens in the snow,
And, nothing himself, beholds
Nothing that is not there and the nothing that is.

Wallace Stevens

One cannot map the sublime, or give it place names.

Chauncey Loomis, *Weird and Tragic Shores*

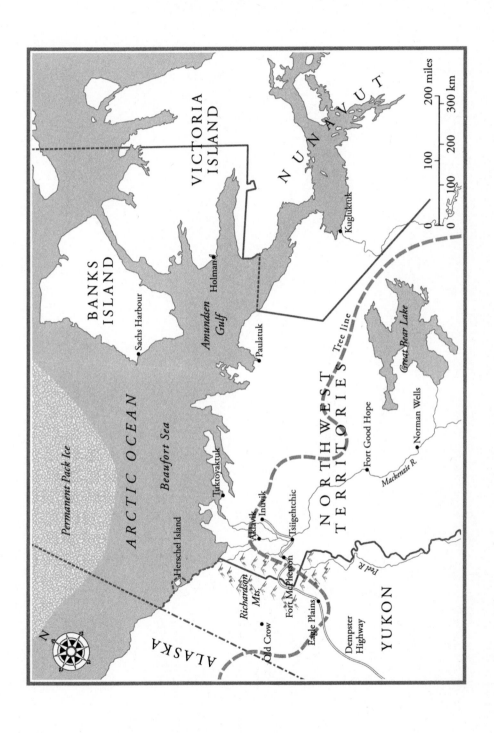

Prologue

HOROLOGISTS PONDER MYSTERY OF HOW
NINETEENTH-CENTURY CHRONOMETER SUR-
VIVED FATAL ARCTIC EXPEDITION

**Timepiece linked to Sir John Franklin's fatal Arctic expe-
dition returns to Britain disguised as a carriage clock**
By Maev Kennedy
Guardian, London
Wednesday, May 20, 2009, 15:26 BST

In a mystery worthy of Agatha Christie, a valuable marine chronometer sits on a workbench in London, crudely disguised as a
Victorian carriage clock, more than one hundred fifty years after
it was recorded as lost in the Arctic along with Sir John Franklin
and his crew in one of the most famous disasters in the history of
polar exploration.

"I have no answers, but the facts are completely extraordinary,"
said the senior specialist on horology at the Royal Observatory in
Greenwich, Jonathan Betts. "This is a genuine mystery."

When and how did the timepiece return to Britain, is it evidence
that somebody survived the disaster, or of a crime—even murder?

Betts has no idea—but he does know its shining brass mechanism could never have spent months in the ice, exposed to salt-laden

Arctic gales. It must have been stolen from the ship, or from a crew member who cared for it up to the moment of their death.

"This has never been lying around in the open air. I have handled a pocket watch recovered from the expedition, and it is so corroded it is not possible even to open the case. Conditions in the Arctic are so extreme this would have rusted within a day, and been a heap of rubbish within a month."

The chronometer returned to the same building—once the Admiralty store from which it was issued, now Betts's clocks workshop at the Royal Observatory.

The apparent fate of the superb timekeeper, made in London by John Arnold, after it was issued to Sir John's ship, is clear from the official ledger also on Betts's desk. Under "Arnold 294," the faded sepia ink reads: "Lost in the Arctic Regions with the 'Erebus.'" In the final entry, on June 26, 1886, more than forty years after it disappeared, it was officially written off.

The fate of Franklin in 1845, his two superbly equipped ships carrying two years' worth of supplies, including barrels of lemon juice to ward off scurvy, his one hundred twenty-nine men who starved, froze, and were poisoned to death in the ice and the suggestion that some survived for a time by cannibalism, haunted the Victorian imagination.

A record thirty-two rescue expeditions were sent, spurred on by his formidable widow, Jane.

Inuit witnesses described Englishmen dying where they fell in the ice, apparently without ever asking how the natives survived such extreme conditions.

Rescue expeditions brought back papers recording the death of Franklin, abandoned clothes and equipment, caches of supplies including poorly sealed tins of meat that may have killed many of the men, and eventually skeletons. Every scrap of evidence was recorded—but there is no record of anyone setting eyes on the chronometer again.

It is clear to Betts that whoever converted it into a carriage clock for a suburban mantelpiece knew they were dealing with stolen property. The evidence of a crime concealed is on the dial, where Arnold's name was beaten flat, and an invented maker's name substituted—and then changed back again when the clock was sold thirty years ago and a restorer spotted Arnold's name on the mechanism.

The Observatory bought it when it came up for sale again ten years ago, but its true history emerged when Betts dismantled it and matched it with the nineteenth-century records. None of those who handled it after conversion could have guessed its connection with the Franklin Expedition.

It will be on public display for the first time in an exhibition opening on Saturday at the National Maritime Museum, on Britain's obsessive quest to find the legendary Northwest Passage to the East through the Arctic ice, which over centuries cost the lives of Franklin, his men, and hundreds of other explorers and sailors.

Among poignant artifacts, including a sledge flag embroidered by his widow with the motto "Hope On Hope Ever," one of the still-sealed cans of meat and the revolting contents of another opened in the 1920s, visitors will see the rather dumpy carriage clock, with three fat little ball feet and a carrying handle crudely bolted onto the chronometer's original brass case.

Betts believes the only possible explanation for the conversion was to make Arnold 294 literally unrecognizable. Stealing a valuable piece of government property from an official expedition would have been a serious crime, punishable by transportation if not death. He yearns to know who dunnit.

North-West Passage: An Arctic Obsession, National Maritime Museum, Greenwich, May 23, 2009–January 3, 2010

Northwest Territories, Canada

They were driving on the sea ice a mile from the shore when a little brown creature ran out in front of them. It was heading out to sea, but the headlights confused it and it dithered in their beam. Nelson stood on the brakes and the car lurched to a stop, throwing Fay against her seat belt.

"What is it?" she said. And Nelson, who found he wanted to impress her, got out of the car and stood over the little animal. It had tried to hide under a tongue of drift snow but they could both see it plainly, the size of a hamster, its fur turned gray by the veneer of snow.

Nelson put on his gloves and picked it up.

"What is it?" she said again, and he turned and held it up to her.

"It's a lemming. They live under the snow."

She joined him in the funnel of the lights. I'm standing on the open sea, she thought. It's the Arctic winter, a month of night, and I'm standing on a frozen ocean, and that man is holding a lemming.

The little rodent stopped struggling and sat quiet in Nelson's palm, its nose twitching, staring at her with tiny black eyes. She reached out her hand then quickly withdrew it.

"What's it doing out here on the ice?"

"I don't know." He turned a full circle, studying the problem. A mile to the south the North American mainland came to its end,

a low snow-covered hump on the snow-covered sea. A timber
fishing cabin, shuttered for the winter, sat on its edge, the only visible detail. To the north the sea ice stretched off to infinity, its snow
carved by wind into motionless ripples. But there was no wind
today, just a tremendous cold, silent apart from their idling engine.

"It's come from the land, I guess," he said. "Heading due north,
right out to sea. I don't know what it wants out there."

To the west, from where they had come, the ice road curved
out of view between tongues of black stubble, the willows that
grew on the last sandy spits of the Mackenzie delta. To the east a
distant string of lights, hard in the dusk, revealed their destination:
the coastal hamlet of Tuktoyaktuk. Another ten minutes and we'd
have been there, thought Fay. Instead, this. She hugged herself
and shivered, already missing the warmth of the car. The sky was
a sad shade of silver, turning pink in the south where the sun had
tried and failed to clear the horizon. To the north, the stars held
firm against the civil twilight.

"Perhaps it's lost," she said.

Nelson cupped it in both hands. It sniffed between his fingers.

"Maybe," he said. "Or maybe it's trying to kill itself. They say
lemmings do that."

She had heard that too, of course. What else did anyone from
London know about lemmings? But she had never expected to
meet one. "I always assumed that thing about lemmings and suicide was just a legend."

Nelson didn't seem to hear her. Having transferred the lem-
ming to his left glove, he was stroking its back with one finger.
The little creature stretched out its neck as if liking the attention.
Nelson smiled to himself, then looked up at Fay.

"I'm going to turn it around," he said. "I'll let it go, pointing
back toward the mainland. With a bit of luck it'll find its way
back to the shore. It would only die out there." He jutted his chin
to the north. "Nothing to eat. Nothing to nest in."

That's interfering with nature, Fay thought. But it was none of her business. The lemming was his.

She watched Nelson cross the ice road. Bubbles of trapped air quivered like ghosts in the black depths beneath them. At the far side he knelt and pressed the back of his glove against the ice, uncurling his fingers so the lemming could escape. But now it wouldn't leave his glove, clinging to the bridge between index and thumb.

"It doesn't want to go," said Fay. "They must tame very easily."

"I don't know about that." Nelson scooped the lemming from his palm, propelling it head first toward the foot of the snow bank. Startled, it vanished into its element, burrowing back toward the shore. Nelson peeled off a glove, took out a pack of cigarettes.

"If you think about it," he said, "my hand is probably the only warm thing it's ever come across in winter. No wonder it liked it."

They stood there together, waiting to see if the lemming would double back, bound for the sea again, and when the cigarette was finished and it hadn't reappeared they got in the car and drove on to Tuktoyaktuk.

Cape Crozier

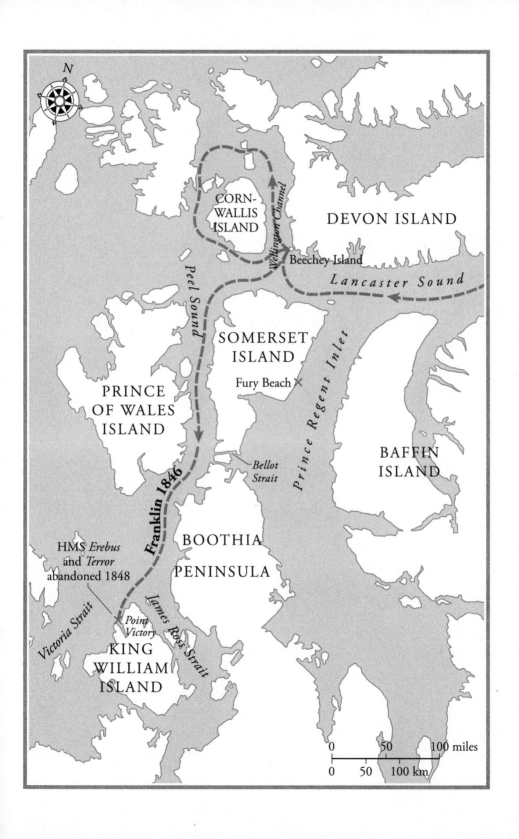

Van Diemen's Land, 1841

It had been intended that they would take the carriage all the way to the ball, but the evening was so mild that Sir John gave in to Sophia's pleading to finish the journey on foot. These are the lieutenant-governor's botanical gardens, Sir John reasoned; I am the lieutenant-governor: why must I take a carriage to the end of my own garden?

So the party alighted at the magnetic observatory, that curious new wooden building crowning the hill, and—defying convention—old Sir John Franklin, viceroy of Van Diemen's Land and famed Arctic explorer, set out on foot for a ball in his honor.

A footman with a lantern led them down the steep path to the Derwent, though it was still light enough to see through the trees. Sir John followed after him, a fat bouncing shadow on short sailor's legs. I ought to walk with Uncle, thought Sophia, who— her Aunt Jane being then absent, traveling in New Zealand—was accompanying Sir John tonight. But for now it did not matter. There would be time enough to adjust their order of march before they reached the ball, when the ladies would pause to unpin their dresses and change their shoes for satin slippers.

Checking her pace, Sophia moved close to her younger cousin Eleanor and took her by the arm. They had quarreled again that afternoon, and although Sophia was not yet quite ready to forgive her uncle's daughter she needed her company now. Otherwise she might find herself walking alongside Henry Elliot, her uncle's private secretary; it was to escape Elliot's unwelcome proximity in the carriage that Sophia had campaigned to finish the journey on foot.

Eleanor, feeling her cousin's touch, turned her head and smiled up at Sophia. Their dresses whispered together as they walked side by side. In the darkness behind them Lieutenant Kay, who had taken leave of his magnetic duties to attend the ball, was attempting to interest Elliot in his science, his phrases syncopated by the tramping of their shoes. And young Henry Elliot, son of the Earl of Minto and destined for high service, responded to the eager naval scientist with a lack of interest so beautifully polite, so drily amused, that Sophia had herself only teased out its meaning that morning.

It pained her still to think of that instant of revelation. It had occurred very close to where they were now, as she had walked in the gardens with Elliot, confiding to him her opinions of the novels of Sir Walter Scott, the winter sun bright on the Derwent, and she had glanced sideways for a moment, to assure herself of his enchantment, and had noticed for the first time, truly noticed, that he had long since fallen silent, and that, as he looked away from her, back toward the town itself and his place in the governor's office, there was a curiously droll turn to the corners of his lips. She had herself fallen quiet, and to his credit Elliot had made every appearance of alarm and consideration when she had stammered an excuse—that she had left her book on a bench by Commander Crozier's magnetic observatory, which stood in a clearing nearby—and went back to look for it. She *would* fetch it herself; Elliot's duties must be calling him.

What a cold little person he was. Quite insubstantial and unromantic compared to the officers of *Erebus* and *Terror*, lately returned from their glorious Antarctic cruise. But why should she concern herself with Elliot, or feel slighted in any way? It was not as if she had set her cap at him. He was known to have an understanding with a young lady in England.

They passed out of a grove of native Australian gum trees, which, not yet felled by the botanic custodians, screened the magnetic observatory from the river below. As one, Sophia and Eleanor came to a halt and even Lieutenant Kay fell silent. Sir John, taken aback, took off his cocked hat and wiped his forehead, which already glistened from the short walk. "Well, now," he said. "Well, now, indeed."

"They are on fire, Sophia!" whispered Eleanor, and she squeezed Sophia's arm.

Beneath them, lashed together in the estuary, the *Terror* and the *Erebus* blazed from stem to stern. They are bomb ships, recalled Sophia, who had studied her uncle's profession. That is why they were given such infernal names. Perhaps, being creatures of fire, that is why the Admiralty has opposed them to the ice.

Lieutenant Kay was beside them now, smiling. "It's a clever device, is it not? There are hundreds of mirrors fixed in the rigging, multiplying the lights of the lanterns and candles. I was aboard *Terror* this morning when the boatswain collected the men's shaving mirrors. The rest of the mirrors are trade goods, carried as gifts for any savages they should meet."

They stood a few moments longer, admiring the scene. The two little ships, dressed with every scrap from their flag lockers, were merely the brightest stars in a constellation of lights. Braced thirty yards offshore in a web of taut cables, they were approached by a pontoon made of rowboats lashed together, decked with planks, roofed with canvas and decorated with silver wattles. This floating bridge was set on either side with lines of burning torches that danced with their own reflections in the tide. The river too flickered with fireflies—the boats of guests who arrived by water, or of uninvited townsfolk who had come to watch and listen from outside the circle of light. Music was loud across the water: the band of the 51st Regiment of Foot striking up an air. Sophia, entranced, heard the notes step out boldly then artfully trip themselves, like a pretty girl with a clubfoot, at once jaunty, romantic and sad. She found herself fixed to the spot, listening, while her uncle and Lieutenant Kay hurried after the footman who had continued down the path. Perhaps it is just this occasion that moves me, Sophia thought, and the lights on the water. Perhaps it is not that music at all.

"Do come on, girls," urged Sir John, looking back at them. "That tune is our signal that it is time for us to show ourselves. Crozier arranged it. If I'd had my way they'd have fired a gun."

Starting after them, Sophia turned to Eleanor. "Nell, do you know the name of that charming air?" And Eleanor replied that she did not, though she was sure she had heard it before. Then young Elliot, whom Sophia had completely forgotten, spoke in the darkness at her side.

"I believe it is called 'The Brighton Camp.' A very old melody. It is the lament of a young man who must forsake his darling and sail off to war. It is very popular with soldiers and sailors, I believe."

Sophia drew her shawl a little tighter around her shoulders. "Thank you, Mr. Elliot. You are always so well informed."

She held Eleanor closer still and hurried on to join her uncle. And Elliot, left with only the second footman for company, smiled to himself unseen.

The band stopped playing as they crossed the pontoon, the boards rocking and flexing under their feet. Sir John led the way with Sophia while Elliot followed with Eleanor on his arm. A cool wind flowed down the river, bringing with it the smell of eucalyptus from the hills. They are all watching us, thought Sophia, adjusting her gray silk shawl. They are all watching me. She pushed back her shoulders and raised her chin, as she had seen her aunt do on such occasions, and she averted her gaze from the faces that crowded the rail of the ship. One of those faces, she knew, must belong to Captain James Clark Ross, captain of *Erebus* and commander of the Antarctic expedition.

A fit of dizziness assailed her. But if I look down at my feet I might stumble or trip, perhaps fall into the river. If that were to happen, she thought, I should not wish to be rescued. The only escape from such an embarrassment would be to do the correct thing and drown. And perhaps, to increase the effect of distraction, I ought to drag my famous uncle down with me. At that, she could not help smiling to herself. And several of those at the rail, seeing her smile, murmured together: such pleasant ease of character, to go with such beauty and poise!

The boatswains piped them aboard in a blur of light and faces, of whispered advice and discreet steering touches. Masts and rigging made a fairy roof above Sophia, gleaming with mirrors and lights. She saw Sir John touch his hat to the quarterdeck, and everyone fell silent as the band of the 51st Regiment, the King's Own Yorkshire Light Infantry, played the vice-regal salute. The ships' marines, drawn up on the quarterdeck, presented arms. Sir John paced their ranks in token of inspection and then he returned to Sophia's side. And now, she thought, I shall be presented to the officers, and Captain Ross shall be the first of all.

She saw him there, waiting on his quarterdeck, his blue uniform trimmed with gold braid. He was too slim and handsome for his forty hard years. The dark, hawk-like face was smiling at her. And as she started for the quarterdeck, in step with Sir John, she felt hundreds of eyes on her back, on the thin white silk of her dress, the black curls arranged at the nape of her neck, and she shivered with a strange new pleasure. No, I am not at all cold. She stopped before James Ross, the famed discoverer of magnetic north, veteran of seven Arctic expeditions and of the late glorious voyage to the fabled Antarctic, and she let her shawl slip down her bare shoulders, just a little, and gracefully extended her hand.

But someone had stepped between them. A heavyset officer with a homely face and bushy whiskers had moved into her path, leaning forward to whisper to the guest of honor. "If you'd care for a little refreshment, Sir John, before we set off the dancing, please step over for a minute to my cabin on *Terror*. James's cabin has been reserved for the ladies tonight, to serve them as a dressing room."

It seemed to Sophia that not many officers of the Royal Navy would have presumed, even in confidence, to address a lieutenant-governor as anything other than "excellency," or to refer to his immediate commander by his Christian name. But she ought to excuse Commander Crozier his impertinence. Though he did not enjoy their rank, birth, or wealth, he was, she knew, accepted by both Ross and Sir John as a friend and a peer, one of the navy's intimate circle of polar explorers.

Sir John released Sophia's arm so he could grasp the commander's hand. "Indeed, Frank, there's an idea for you! On a cool night like this it will be just the thing."

Crozier turned and smiled at Sophia. "Miss Cracroft," he said, "how delighted I am to welcome you aboard tonight. Your first dance must of course be reserved for Captain Ross, but I believe that as deputy commander I am entitled to the second. I now present my claim."

His soft Irish consonants were butchered by harsh Ulster vowels. Yet her Aunt Jane, Sophia knew, was charmed by Crozier's rustic way of speaking, and had become a great friend and champion of the *Terror*'s shy captain. That's quite a pretty speech for poor Crozier, thought Sophia. He must have practiced it ahead of time.

"I believe that the second dance is due to my uncle, as governor," she replied, "but I would be honored to pledge you the third." She was inwardly calculating, in spite of her better sense: after my first dance with Captain Ross, with how many other men must I dance before I might come to Ross again? But after all, what harm was there in that? It was merely for her own amusement; she knew very well that he was said to be engaged.

Sophia had, to her credit, done her best to avoid it, had wriggled and squirmed like a worm on a hook, but she could not escape it: she must open the dancing on the night of the ball.

But the ladies of Hobart will scorn me, she had protested. It is well known that I am helping to direct the preparations for the ball. If I stand up at the head of the dance, the ladies will flutter their fans to hide their mouths, and whisper together that it is a place of rare honor that I occupy, having appointed me to it myself.

Nonsense, said her uncle. The invitation is not yours, nor even mine, but comes from the hosts of the ball, Ross and Crozier. In any case, Lady Jane being absent, you are the mistress of my household and therefore take precedence; Eleanor may be my own daughter, but she is still too young. And to be quite frank, my dear Sophia, as we are both aware, Eleanor does not dance half so well as do you. Her education in such matters has been neglected since we left Lincolnshire. So let us send for a dancing master, if a respectable one can be found in this town.

Alas, there could not. Such dancing masters as there were then in Hobart Town were of a low character—men of the theater, or poets or journalists, most of them tickets-of-leave or emancipated convicts. Two very fine dance teachers had lately arrived from London and Bath, but neither could be engaged, as the one had been transported for poncing, the other for unnatural crime, and—the assignment system having been lately abolished by London—it was now quite impossible for the lieutenant-governor, as guardian of the law, to requisition their service, even in the character of gardener or groom.

This difficulty had scarcely presented itself before it was overcome by means unexpected and external. Within days of the ball's announcement an army of dancing masters had invaded the colony. So swift was their arrival that Captains Ross and Crozier, who were staying with Sir John at Government House, got out their charts and puzzled over the prodigious winds and currents that could have sped word of the ball so quickly to New South Wales. The newcomers were for the most part men of unknown character—a circumstance that must, in an Australian penal colony like New South Wales or Van Diemen's Land, have its advantages—and so were able to pass into the employment of the wealthiest colonial households and even those of the garrison and government.

By great exertion Sophia was able to find a man whose character was without proven blemish, having arrived into New South Wales two years before as a free settler. Before that, of course, his history was obscure, but whatever his origins, Mr. Snow was a very fine dancer and a patient teacher. Classes were held each day in the breakfast room of Government House, cleared of all furniture. Sir John's maids, a trio of transported prostitutes who still sometimes dabbled in that trade, would make excuses to sweep the veranda outside, peering in through the half-open windows, as Eleanor and Sophia and several other daughters of the colonial establishment practiced the country dance, the quadrille, the new schottische, and the daring waltz, with Mr. Snow and Sophia taking turns at the pianoforte.

Sophia had come out very well in London and had little to learn about dancing; indeed, she might have set up as an instructor herself, and saved Sir John a portion of his quite inadequate stipend, but for her want of patience and her habit, when angered, of revealing the sharpness of her tongue. This was apparent to no one more than to poor Captain Ainsworth of the 51st, who, having already had a marriage proposal rejected by Sophia, had attempted to join in the lessons himself, claiming—falsely, as Sophia well knew—that he had never learned to dance. Assuming the character of her aunt,

Sophia had coldly inquired of the lovestruck captain whether he considered it appropriate that he should be present, a gentleman in a red coat, at a gathering of girls who were there without chaperones, and had he not better wait until the night of the ball? He had departed, quite crestfallen, and Sophia, soon repenting of her scorn, had sent him a short but friendly note, advising him of the other times when Mr. Snow's services might be privately engaged. In reaching out to him thus, having already dismissed him, she believed in all innocence that she was being kind.

For weeks the dancing masters prospered in Hobarton and Launceston, instructing the sons and daughters of the colony in the latest points of the terpsichorean art, direct from the ballrooms of London and Paris. Even those with no hope of attending the ball were swept up in the fashion for hopping and stepping and bowing, until the lessons became an end in themselves, informal social occasions for which invitations were not the less ruthlessly sought and withheld.

Then came the week of the great disappointment, when a mere two hundred and fifty cards were sent out requesting the company of the recipients aboard *Terror* and *Erebus* on the first night of June 1841. The bubble was burst, and the disbanded host of dancing masters straggled back to Hobart port, counting its takings—all but a few who had found positions on the island, or who had fallen in love with their students, or resolved to go into business, and who would stay in Van Diemen's Land: for every army must have its deserters. Mr. Snow also remained, bringing his charges to the point of perfection, and then on the last day of May he too departed, intending to establish a school or hotel in the new mainland village of Melbourne. Like many who passed through Van Diemen's Land in those years of its decline he was never seen in Hobart Town again.

The ball would open with a country dance; the free settlers would expect it, most of them having quit England at a time when the quadrille was new and the waltz was still scandalous. And so, with a great deal of chatter and flirting (the officers and their partners) or grim-faced *froideur* (the free settlers, who were determined to be set in old ways half remembered) two lines were formed on the main deck of *Erebus*, the men facing the ladies.

At the head of the line stood Sophia Cracroft, fanning herself with her dance card, not because she was hot but to conceal the fact that her hand was atremble. She looked down the lines of dancers, the men in their coats of black or blue or red, the ladies in dresses of muslin or tulle, trimmed with silk flowers and ribbons, their slippers bright with hand-stitched roses, and she heard the musicians finish their tuning—a last few scrapes of a bow on a cello, a toot of the bassoon. The lights in the rigging, the lamps above the rails, shone on the jewels of the ladies, gleamed in the medals and orders of soldiers and sailors, and softened the harshest colonial faces, making them young again. The watchers fell silent around the ship's rail. All faces turned to Sophia, waiting for her to open the ball. And Captain Ross, at whom she hardly dared to look, her partner for the long, formal evolutions of this opening set, made his bow and addressed her.

"Now, Miss Cracroft, what is it to be? We have cleared our deck for action: please do us the honor of giving the word to commence the engagement. With what music would you have us begin?"

She was prepared for this. Her choice had not been difficult and the musicians were already informed. She smiled at Captain Ross, made her own curtsy. "On such a rare occasion as this," she said, "aboard two of Her Majesty's ships of war, there can only be one fitting commencement: let us please have 'Nelson's Victory'!"

Those close enough to hear her—the next in line were Sir John and his partner for this dance, a debutante daughter of the 51st Regiment, and then Commander Crozier, who stood up with Eleanor—warmly approved her decision. Captain Ross spoke to the band leader, then turned to his friends. "A most excellent choice, Miss Cracroft, particularly in our present company. For although I have heard it disputed whether the victory celebrated in that tune was Nelson's victory at Copenhagen or that of Trafalgar, His Excellency Sir John has very politely smoothed over the question tonight, by having had the foresight to serve gallantly in both."

There were laughs and a round of applause, and Sir John, wiping his forehead, called out: "I fear that the victory in question was that of the Nile, Captain Ross. From which I was absent."

How prettily Ross put things. Sophia would have to remember his words, stow them in a mind already confounded by lights and confused by impressions, so that she could recount them to her Aunt Jane who, like Sophia herself, admired nothing in a man so much as wit and learning. It was merely a superfluity of charm that made Captain Ross so handsome, so calm in command, so esteemed and graceful in his bearing. Yet it was said that he had a fiancée and that she was quite undistinguished, untraveled and unread, the child of a mere Yorkshire squire. In the course of his recent Antarctic voyage Ross had already named an icebound island and a stormy cape for this placid domestic, this tranquil Ann Coulman; to Sophia it seemed inappropriate: indeed, it was almost indecent. And she could not but wonder, who would name an island for Sophia Cracroft? Must she find one of her own?

All this, in an instant. Then the music began and Sophia, her gloved hands raised easily, her dance card hanging prettily from its ribbon around her wrist, stepped forward from her position and, watched by all eyes, paced out the pattern that all must observe and all must follow as the sets moved down the line. Forward, side, back, hand, turn—the decorous, detached self-absorption of doing things correctly, of doing them exactly as they ought to be done, rotating like clockwork, sometimes facing your partner, sometimes not.

Well, there would be waltzes later, in which a lady and her partner might turn away from the others and circle each other, their hands together, his right on her waist. She had by various stratagems and flutters of her dance card kept all her waltzes free thus far, although it was really not done to refuse a dance to one man and then to later be seen dancing it with another: she had been forced to invent phantom partners, official duties, even a fainting disposition, though she felt nothing but scorn for young ladies who fainted. Yet she could not have admitted, even to herself, for whom she was saving her waltzes; it is just, she told herself, that I must first be quite sure of my gentleman's dancing, to protect my dress and my slippers and to prevent the crushing of my toes.

She smiled at Captain Ross, with whom she had just crossed hands. He was not a tall man, scarcely taller than herself, and his eyes—the black, Scottish eyes that the ladies found so picturesque, for which he was known as the handsomest man in the navy—were not a foot away from hers.

"How very pleasant it is," she said, "to see naval officers dancing in their uniforms. I always thought it so unfair in England, that officers of the mere county militia are permitted to attend balls in their red coats while the gentlemen of the navy must wear civilian dress. It gives the army such an advantage with the ladies."

I am being bold, she thought. But I am known to have a bold character. I must be permitted to be myself. And he is engaged, of course.

They cast off around Sir John and his partner, who was too young and too shy to talk while they danced, to do anything but watch her own steps, and when Sophia and Ross came back into the set they gave hands, together again.

"Miss Cracroft," Ross said, "you have seen through our game. We have practiced a ruse. Our whole expedition—the Magnetic Union, the voyage to Antarctica, and the natural researches of

Mr. Hooker and Mr. McCormick—was conceived by Crozier and I, with the connivance of our old friend Sir John and the men of the Arctic Council, so that we might dance in our blue coats in Van Diemen's Land. How else are we to win the hearts of ladies, when in England we are shut out by the red coats?"

They passed by the right, performed a hey. I amuse him, she thought. That is why he is smiling.

"Cut out at home, Captain? Surely not. It is generally understood in the colony that you already have an understanding."

It was an indelicacy that she would never have permitted herself in England, or even ashore in Van Diemen's Land. But they were far from England, in a new country with manners of its own, and there was also the excitement of being on the deck of a ship of war, even if it was only at moorings in a stream. And there was also the light of the lamps and the candles, and the moon that now rose in the mouth of the Derwent. She had already drunk a full glass of champagne. Around the rail, people laughed and talked and stared at the dancers. Many men will be looking at me. They can see me dance, but they can't hear what I say.

They were to stand up, marking time, while Sir John and his partner cast off in turn. Ross's smile was still amused, it seemed to Sophia. "And it is also understood in the colony, Miss Cracroft, that you yourself are not entirely repelled by the sight of a red coat."

Captain Ainsworth. I ought to have been firmer with him. Oh, the vexation! How like people to misunderstand! She had confided to Eleanor that Ainsworth had proposed to her and that she had refused him. Surely Eleanor had not been so dull as to keep this secret to herself? And there was Ainsworth now, several places down the line, dancing with some overdressed colonial girl, a barrister's daughter whom Sophia did not know. But whenever the revolutions of the dance brought Ainsworth's eyes around to the head of the line they lingered on Sophia. And Ross, she saw, was well aware of Captain's Ainsworth's interest. Indeed, he was trying not to laugh.

She had already reached, perhaps passed, the outermost bounds of delicacy. And yet she made herself smile. "I find, Captain Ross, that this colony is often mistaken in its understanding of such matters."

They armed left, crossed hands again. "Indeed, Miss Cracroft, I find that myself."

It was time for them to go down the middle and change places with Sir John and his girl, the first evolution in a dance that would take Captain Ross and herself, turn by turn, dancing with every other couple, all the way down to the end of the line, which they would reach in about twenty minutes provided the musicians were brisk. They had passed the mizzenmast, were almost at the stern, with Sophia congratulating herself on the perfect indifference that she had shown to poor Ainsworth as the turn had come to dance with him, when the import of Captain Ross's remark came home to her; by accepting so freely, and indeed with such evident personal conviction, that the colony might misapprehend her own situation, and by avoiding any direct response to her own remark about his reputed engagement, might he not be implying that his own situation too was misunderstood? Perhaps he did not, after all, have an understanding with a young lady?

The first dance was almost over; they had reached the final set, and it was a good thing too, for the gradual loosening of the formation, extending the lines beyond the marked dance floor, had forced the last couples onto the quarterdeck, as far astern as the ship's wheel (because *Erebus* was a flush-deck ship, like many that were built as bombs). Sophia and Ross, in performing the last figures, had to dance around the binnacle, which, though idle in port, had its oil lamp lit to add to the festivity. The orange flame of the compass lit them both from beneath, throwing their eyes into shadow, a most singular effect that applied to them alone, as if they of all the company, and of all the dancers, had been chosen by the compass for its partners, and Sophia, catching her breath, looked into the pools of darkness that were Captain Ross's eyes, and saw there only what she wanted to see.

The music had grown indistinct—it may have been the distance from the band, and the blood that coursed in her ears, though the dance, if long, was not very energetic. She saw the moon in the rigging, the lamps in the mirrors, the gleam of buttons and jewels in the darkness by the rail, and she felt the tramp of scores of feet moving in time on the deck. She wished she could do as the sailors did, and kick off her slippers and dance barefoot on the holystoned planks. Turning away from her partner, she stepped sideways, came back into the middle, her arms gracefully extended, preparing to make hands before they moved into the final few steps. Instead, she found herself colliding with the standing form of Ross who, swayed by the shock, grasped her in his arms to steady them both, in the same instant that her own arms involuntarily wrapped themselves around him. Her face was in his neck, and his breath was in her ear. They stood there thus, embracing, for barely a moment, before Sophia pushed herself away from him. There was laughter, she could hear it now, and Captain Ross pulled a droll face and offered her his hand, which after a moment she accepted, though flushed with what, she told herself, must be mortification.

"Alas, Sophia, the music has already stopped." He spoke gently, so that no one else might hear him. "You were so lost in your dancing. Let me take you back to your uncle for the second dance."

Together, they walked back along the deck, applauded by all. The regimental band began to play again, a short, jaunty air to while away the interval, and Sophia, bright with pleasure, rejoined her uncle, accepted his compliments and smiled kindly at Eleanor who—being, it seemed, incapable of jealousy—was too wide-eyed even to smile at her cousin. Crozier beamed. "You have done it!" he exclaimed. "You have carried it off brilliantly! Was ever a ball in London opened so prettily? And to think that you were inclined to refuse the honor!"

But Sophia, accepting for a moment the use of her uncle's chair so that she might recover herself, was deaf to the voices that clamored around her. She wished only to hear again, rehearsed in the privacy of her own mind, the voice of Captain Ross, addressing her by her first name.

To retain the young people's interest the second dance would be a lively quadrille. Sir John was now his niece's partner, the head couple in their square, while Ross and Eleanor danced the sides. The dance was a sore test for Sir John, who was no longer the man who had tramped through the Arctic twenty years before. The stout lieutenant-governor, being now fifty-five years of age, had no breath to spare for conversation so there was little talk among their set. It was with visible relief that Sir John, hearing the last bars of the finale, retreated to a chair beside the foremast, where he charmed the ladies present by borrowing Eleanor's fan.

There was a brief interval, a sip of refreshment, and then the third dance was almost upon them, another country dance, and Sophia recalled she must dance it with Commander Crozier. There he was, already waiting for her as the musicians tuned their instruments, and she saw that Crozier had observed her watching him, and that she must therefore go and stand with him, exposed to the gaze of the ladies and the semaphore of their fans. She comforted herself that her next dance, another quadrille, was engaged to Joseph Hooker, the ship's naturalist and surgeon, who, though practically a civilian, was of her own age and both learned and quick. She had just engaged the following dance—the first waltz of the evening—to Lieutenant McMurdo, the first of the *Terror*, who looked very fine in his uniform and could easily be forgiven his soft Scottish brogue. Well, she would endure her present duty in anticipation of pleasures to come; she only hoped that Commander Crozier would not step on her dress or trample her toes.

She went and stood by him and gave him her hand. He stood there, looking down at her, and seemed as if about to speak, and then he thought better of it, or could not find his tongue, and bowed to her again. Of course! He is nervous. After thirty years at sea, and numerous polar expeditions, this professional seaman, esteemed by his peers for his coolness in danger, who had neatly threaded the *Terror* between two clashing icebergs in a southern ocean squall, was dumbstruck by fear, here, on this motionless deck in this safe moonlit harbor! It must be the dance, she concluded: he fears parading his clumsiness before so many eyes. Her pity moved, she resolved to assist her poor partner through his ordeal. She would whisper instructions, simplify the steps. So moved was she by her own kindness that it did not occur to her— not until later, after she had learned that Commander Crozier was in fact a perfectly sound dancer—that it was not the steps that frightened him but rather that he was to perform them with her.

Two violin bows sawed in unison, there was a final flourish of the bassoon, and the town's musicians, convicts to a man, reached for the beer glasses concealed behind their sheet music. It was over, the second of the country dances, and the ranks on the floor would thin out now as the older people, having discharged their duty, abandoned the deck to the youngsters. Sophia, anticipating the more fashionable dances to come, decided she must refresh herself, and as Joseph Hooker had yet to claim her she asked Commander Crozier to escort her to the dressing room. It pleased her to be able to favor him so: he had danced so bravely in the event, with so little help from herself; and if some of the other couples might have been discomfited by his lack of conversation, even when standing off, she herself had no objection to it: silence in such a man as Crozier might be taken as a virtue. How unlike the charming Ross he was, though they were known to be close as brothers: indeed, closer than most. It delighted her that she alone had fathomed the cause of his reticence, that the poor dear man was clearly engrossed in recalling and dancing his steps.

So Crozier, still mute, gave Sophia his arm and escorted her to the companionway that led to Ross's cabin, set aside for the night as a dressing room. And there near the companionway, in the crowd of chattering ladies and gentlemen, was her next partner, young Joseph Dalton Hooker, still in animated conversation with his fellow scientist and surgeon, Mr. McCormick. They must, Sophia surmised, have made up their recent quarrel, the talk of the two ships, over a certain friend of Hooker who had usurped McCormick's role as naturalist on a recent voyage of the *Beagle*.

Observing young Hooker, Crozier at last found his tongue.

"Miss Cracroft, I see my relief is at hand. But may I ask if you are already engaged for the final waltz of the night? I should be honored if you would dance it with me."

The last waltz of the night. It was still in her gift, and indeed she still had one other waltz free, the third, having just promised her second to her cousin Lieutenant Kay. Two waltzes, a reel, and a couple of quadrilles: these were the blanks that remained on her dance card, and none of them yet solicited by Captain James Clark Ross. There he was now by the rail, complacently talking to some men of the town, abandoning her to the trap she was in! She looked away from Crozier, searching for means of escape.

"The last waltz?" she said vaguely. "I believe that I have an engagement for that." She made no move to check her card; it was the shallowest of lies, and she despised herself for it. "But I have three other dances still free—you are welcome to any of them, Commander. It shall be a pleasure to stand up again with a gentleman who dances so well." And she gave him the smile—the beautiful smile, she knew—which she hoped might compensate

him for the disappointment on his broad, freckled face. And
though she reproved her own dishonesty (and took some comfort
from the fact that she had the evident good character to reprove
herself for it), a part of her also whispered: this is not my fault;
how does he presume to ask to dance with me twice?

"Alas," said Crozier, "the final waltz is the only dance for which
I myself am not already engaged." He surprised her by smiling.
"As captains of the expedition, Ross and I are much in demand
tonight; all the ladies of the town wish to dance with us, and we
have had quite a comical time of it, rebuffing all the outraged
gentlemen who wish to know why we don't ask their wives to
dance. Ross has appointed poor McCormick to act as our match-
maker, so as not to cause an incident each time we are obliged to
refuse. Now I have only the last dance left to me, and James has
no dance left at all."

Sophia looked away from him again, down the tunnel of
light that enclosed the main deck. How strange they all looked,
and small, in their best coats and ball dresses, their medals and
their fans. There was cousin Eleanor, that sad motherless little
creature with whom she lived, deep in talk with the Reverend
Gell, who was pompously in love with her. Here was Hooker, the
naturalist, who had spied her through the crowd, and was about
to accost her, to take possession. If I were to fall ill now, if I had to
go home . . . But they would send me down to the cabin, where
the ladies would surround me with their sympathy, and fan me
with their questions, until they had unpicked the cause of my
heartache, and then they would turn away from me and smile.

A gust of wind blew off the river. She thought she felt the deck
move beneath her feet, stirred by the last faint swell of the ocean,
that great southern ocean, which waited for *Erebus* off the mouth
of the Derwent.

She shivered and settled her shawl about her shoulders. She
was being silly. No: she had been silly and would be silly no more.

This was a ball after all. How many true balls were held in Van Diemen's Land? Would such a ball as this ever be held here again? "The Glorious First of June," the newspapers were calling it. She was unmarried, already twenty-four: society decreed that balls must be her business. And it would be such poor manners to refuse poor Crozier. She turned to him again, still smiling vaguely. "The last waltz, you say. That is the third, is it not?" She turned over her dance card, but still did not examine it.

He shook his head. "No, Miss Cracroft. The fourth. There are to be four waltzes tonight. The ball will conclude with the last of them."

She glanced at her dance card and brightened her smile. "Why, you are quite right, Commander! Here it is, a fourth! I had quite overlooked it!" She had, in fact, arranged the order of dancing herself. "And it is free. I had thought the third waltz was the last one." She turned over her card again, so that he might not see that the space for the third waltz was also left blank. "I am already engaged for the third with an officer of the garrison." She had little doubt that such a request would yet be forthcoming. "Of course I shall dance the fourth waltz with you. You are very kind, Commander."

And with that she left him and escaped to the dressing room, to avoid her own eyes in the mirror, while young Joseph Dalton Hooker, bewildered to see her thus flee from him, awaited her return at the top of the stair.

Her last dance before supper was with her cousin Lieutenant Kay, who must therefore by custom accompany her to supper with her party—which happened to be his own party as well.

The music, in stopping, had stranded them both near the mainmast, so that they were the first couple to cross the makeshift companionway, a kind of carpeted stile adorned with silver wattles, which joined the *Erebus* to the *Terror* where their hulls kissed amidships. And there on the other side, welcoming the stream of guests to his own vessel, stood the smiling Frank Crozier. He bowed to Sophia as her shoes met his deck.

"Here you see, Miss Cracroft, the result of all your labors. Without your assistance, we poor sailors would never have supplied such a feast as this." And with a sweep of his arm he showed her the supper that awaited the guests, set out on trestles that ranged the full length of the deck. There were platters and bowls of cold chicken and ham, of poached fish, salads, biscuits and cheese; of lobster, prawns, pies, pastries both sweet and savory, and raspberries and peaches from cold stores packed with Yankee ice. Servants bustled up through the main hatch—sailors and marines in their blue or red jackets—bringing with them the scent of roast beef and lamb and the almond smell of white soup. Surveying them all from his place by the mainmast, where he guarded a trestle crowded with bottles, was Mr. Hallett, the purser of *Erebus*, plying his corkscrew all the while.

Kay escorted her to her uncle's table, where they were joined by Sir John and Captain Ross, and by Lieutenant Bird of the *Erebus*, another close friend from their polar voyages with Parry. Next came McMurdo and Hooker, who was escorting Eleanor to supper. The Reverend Gell joined them uninvited, presuming on his status as unofficial chaplain to the lieutenant-governor's household; he sat on the other side of Eleanor, from where he looked darkly at Hooker, and sought to cow the young scientist with barbs of Latin and Greek, to which Hooker easily responded, until Gell topped him with a few caustic-sounding remarks in a language that Sophia, who was greatly amused, took to be Hebrew, or perhaps Aramaic.

It was time now for the toasts and speeches. Sophia had not thought there was so much crystal in all of the colony. The glasses, held high in readiness, splintered the light from the lanterns and mirrors, each facet and cut giving birth to a jewel.

The champagne, chilled by imported ice from the lakes of New England, sparkled within her. All eyes were now fixed on the quarterdeck, on Commander Crozier, who stood—for the naval officers, so as not to cause confusion with the guests, were waiving their privilege and would drink the loyal toast standing—with his own glass extended. How was it possible, Sophia wondered, for such a weathered old sailor to blush so deeply?

The loyal toast was given, and then the toast of the day, which, it being a Tuesday, was by custom "to our men," and then Crozier made a halting speech by way of introduction, a few words of Erse from the hills near his native Banbridge, *kade mealy faulty* (which many present, being untutored, mistook for Greek), and then it was the turn of Captain Ross to address the diners, and next the guest of honor, his excellency the lieutenant-governor of Van Diemen's Land, Rear-Admiral Sir John Franklin. And when all the thanks and congratulations and patriotic sentiment were quite run through, everyone could at last sit down and recharge their glasses and fill up their plates, and there was quiet for a while, because of the excellence of the supper, and the appetite born of dancing and talking in the cool air off the Derwent.

The meal having been consumed—or at least, the rate of its consumption having slowed enough to permit some polite interjection—the drone of voices could again be heard over the clink of glasses and forks.

As the interval progressed, the license was assumed to move from table to table. Joining the top table now was Mr. John Hepburn, the superintendent of Government House, a man whose humble origin—he had begun life as a Scotch cowherd before going to sea on a collier—was trumped by his heroic service to Sir John twenty years before. Hepburn had been his master's right-hand man when Sir John made his famous Arctic journey from the Great Slave Lake down the Coppermine River to the polar sea at Point Turnagain. He arrived at the table just as Captain Ross was discussing with his brother explorers his sailing orders from the Admiralty. These would soon send *Terror* and *Erebus* south of New Zealand, from where they were to follow the sixtieth parallel of latitude to the farther side of the Antarctic continent, attempting as they went to fix the true position of the Nimrod and Aurora islands. Having reached the vicinity of fifty-five degrees west, they were then to turn south and attempt to pass through the pack ice for a second time, to see what lay beyond it at that longitude.

Returning from this exploration of the far south—God willing—the ships were then to touch at the Falkland Islands to perform a hydrological survey and then visit Tierra del Fuego for magnetic observations. After that, if the ships were still sound, they were directed to brave the southern ice for a third summer season, to search for Bouvet Island and Thompson Island before finally returning to Greenwich. Nor were they likely to rest there for long, Captain Ross confided: there was talk in his mail from the Admiralty of sending the two ships out again as soon as they could be refitted, this time to the other end of the earth, where they would attempt to traverse the fabled Northwest Passage.

"They offer me command of this next expedition," he told his friends, "though I confess I have seen enough ice for one lifetime."

"As have we all," said Sir John.

"Aye, indeed," said Crozier.

But how could one tire of the ice, thought Sophia, enraptured by the names on Ross's itinerary. The Nimrod Islands. Aurora. Cold beauty that waited, shrouded from knowledge, in secret vaults of ice. If she could only cut off her hair, dress as a boy, and run off with the ships, like the famous Grace O'Malley, the pirate queen of old Ireland, who had dared to present herself, a wanted rebel, at the royal palace at Greenwich, where she had treated with the great Elizabeth as if she were her peer.

Sir John spoke again, though his voice was kept low, so that his words might not carry beyond this private circle.

"I confess," he said, "that I am aggrieved for myself, that the Admiralty's orders must send away the dearest friends to have passed through Van Diemen's Land since I took up my post here. Yet I am even more aggrieved for yourselves, that their lordships have seen fit to order your ships to attempt the pack ice twice more in this same expedition. What more can you do than you have already done in your last season? You have passed clear through the southern pack ice, which has never been done before. You have determined the location of the south magnetic pole. You have discovered new lands and prodigious wonders, like the Great Ice Barrier that guards the southern continent, and the volcano that burns at your farthest south, your marvelous Mount Erebus. And all this without losing a single man to scurvy! To try more than this is to tempt fate."

Captain Ross answered his old friend with a smile.

"Your care for us makes you overstate our peril, Sir John. Our little bomb ships may be poor sailors in the open sea, but they are built strongly for their calling and have proven well-suited to enduring the ice. All that can be done has been done, and we are in the hands of God, now as ever."

"Amen," said Sir John, who was a deeply pious man for all his seamanly concern for pagan fate. "Yet I cannot help but fret. Hepburn and I know all too well the horrors that can befall an expedition that goes awry. When I think of that brute Terohaute, and the meat that he fed to Hepburn here, saying it was wolf meat, but which we later learned was the flesh of his fellow voyageurs, whom he had murdered in the Barrens . . ."

Hepburn shook his head dutifully, though he did not seem much put out at this revelation of his unwitting cannibal past. Sir John continued: "Dr. Richardson had to put a bullet in Terohaute's head after he murdered poor Midshipman Hood. That was no job for a physician."

Sophia scarcely dared to breathe. Such tales of horror were not told in the books of adventure and travel that she inhaled like fresh air, and which formed such a staple of her conversation with her aunt. Let him only speak on, she thought. Then she noticed that Crozier was watching her. She lowered her eyes, then raised them again in mute appeal. Don't reveal me as a spy, she thought. Crozier cleared his throat and looked away from her, addressing Sir John. "Your concern for us does you credit, Sir John, especially in light of your Arctic experiences. But you had to travel by land from the interior of the Canadas, in boats and on foot, whereas we are supplied with two fully victualed ships and a wide sea to sail them on. Should one of our ships be stricken, it is to be hoped that the other would be on hand to take off its crew." He made a diffident bow to Hepburn, as if seeking his forgiveness for this exposition. But, Sophia realized, he is explaining this to me.

"Perhaps," countered Sir John. "But I fear you speak ingenuously, Frank, in order to make light of your danger in this present charming company." He turned and smiled at his niece, who thought, oh, so he has not forgotten me! Sir John continued: "When *Erebus* and *Terror* leave here they must cross again the Roaring Forties and the great southern ocean, where they were already separated on their voyage here from the Cape. In the event of a shipwreck I do not think that any small boat could weather such waters for long."

There was a moment's silence as all in the circle considered the evident truth of Sir John's words. Then Captain Ross reached across the table to clap his friend Crozier on the shoulder. "There, my dear Frank. The Madeira is sitting before you. Pass it around and let us drink to our good fortune, that she may remain constant to us. And tomorrow, when the wine has worn off, we shall make amends for our superstition and commend ourselves properly to our Maker, who holds us in His hand."

The talk continued on happier subjects until the sawing of bows signaled the musicians' intention to resume their work. One by one, the officers went off to claim their partners for the next dance, but Lieutenant Bird, who was to dance with Sophia, was detained at the rail by Captain Ross on some ship's business, leaving Sophia alone with her uncle. Sir John sat back in his chair and watched the revelers flee from the ruins of their supper.

"What a great shame it is, Sophia," he said, "that your aunt could not be here. She has worked so hard for the people of this colony, convict and settler alike, and with so little thanks. The officials plot against her campaign for humane reform and would have me dismissed if they could. Tonight, at least, she might have had some reward for her troubles."

Sophia, distracted by confused thoughts of eternal love and of dire extremity, ventured to say what she had heard said by others, and of others, but which she could not yet conceive to be true also of herself: that it was a sad fact of life that people do not always get what they deserve.

She regretted her remark immediately. It was too offhand, too casual; it was unworthy of Lady Jane's tireless philanthropy and improving zeal to consign her to the category of mere "people." Yet her uncle surprised her by solemnly nodding.

"You are quite right," he said. "People do not always get what they seem to deserve in this life, and must await their true reward or punishment in the next. The ways of God are not laid bare to us and are quite beyond our moral judgment."

Sophia, who knew of her uncle's great piety, readied herself for a sermon on the Divine Will. Yet her uncle surprised her again.

"That being the case," he continued, "it is all the more pleasant to observe the good fortune of a friend who is about to receive his deserved reward on this side of heaven. Our dear friend Frank Crozier—" and here he seemed to fix her with his eye—"has never been given the credit he deserves for his distinguished service. He is known as one of the finest seamen in the navy, and a keen scientist too. And yet Frank has little private interest at the court or in Parliament, so promotions and posts have often eluded him. His father left him nothing—he has not even a house of his own."

"What a great pity," said Sophia. It was a cause of some embarrassment to her that she knew all this already; did Sir John not understand that the ladies of the town had assayed to the last ounce the wealth and prospects of each unmarried officer of the squadron, almost as soon as his feet touched the shore? Sophia, a romantic of the heroic stamp, considered such gossip indelicate. She believed—no, she *felt*, for her reason was sound enough and tried to tell her otherwise—that the worth of a man could be read in his eyes.

"All that will change now," said Sir John. His gaze was still on her. "If it pleases God that the ships should return to England, Frank Crozier will finally get what he deserves. Ross will be knighted and Frank made post captain, and they will offer Frank command of the Northwest Passage voyage should James refuse it, as I think likely. And when God willing he returns from that expedition, Frank will have earned a salaried post at Greenwich. I have heard him say how much he loves to stand by the observatory, astride the prime meridian like a fanciful schoolboy, and to placidly observe the ships and boats that pass up and down the Thames. To have a little house nearby and to walk each day on the Black Heath is his notion of heaven. He even talks of bringing his unmarried sisters there from Dublin. If he cannot get a wife."

She was looking beyond her uncle, to where Ross and Lieutenant Bird conversed at the windward rail of *Terror*. Across on the *Erebus* the tuning of instruments was now complete. If Bird did not hasten to claim her they would have to join the dance late, at the end of the line. Ross, glancing across, saw her and smiled.

"It sounds a charming prospect," Sophia said distractedly. "I am sure that Commander Crozier will be most deserving of his future happiness." Her memory stirred within her. "And is it not fixed that Captain Ross will also live at Greenwich once his voyaging is done?"

"It is. He has had enough of polar sailing. Unless there is a war this may be his last voyage. So he has bought a house on the Black Heath that is big enough for himself and Miss Coulman. And God willing their children as well."

She turned away from her uncle, in the vague direction of the bows.

Sophia knew the Black Heath well, and all of Greenwich and its environs. She had often gone there with her uncle and aunt, paying calls on the tribe of serving and retired navy men who had settled near the naval college, braced between London and the sea. Yet now, on the deck of the *Terror* in this cold hour of night, her recollection of those genteel districts, their parks and their hills and their houses, was infused with a sudden dread. The houses and the terraces, the squares of the naval college and the old Greenwich palace, seemed newly strange and sorrowful: like offerings, old and new, large and small, arranged beneath the shrine of the observatory, where time was transubstantiated from the sky and consecrated in chronometers, then served to the ships that passed down the reach. It was in Greenwich that days were born and there that they returned to die.

She shuddered. Was this to have been the scene of her triumph? Men had wives there, and children, and problems with servants. Their houses, she had noticed, were often a little too small, their furniture not quite of the best manufacture, showing the scars of too-frequent removal from one rented home to the next. And here and there, in odd corners of dusty upstairs rooms, she saw the great sturdy sea chests that called to her softly like a shell held to the ear. How could they stand it, men who had sailed into battle, who had dared the unknown and written their names there, to settle down here on this hill by an estuary, with what comfort and love they could gather around them, and wait for death, whom they knew well already, to find and reclaim them? How could they bear to sit still?

It was a little after three when the last waltz was called. Many of the older guests had long since departed, the exceptions being those with marriageable daughters or those who were lucky or reckless at cards.

The floor now belonged to the youngsters. Which is to say, it belonged to the young ladies and to those gentlemen who, in this most unbalanced of colonies, where men outnumbered women several times over, were charming or ruthless or lucky enough to have secured partners for the very last waltz of the Glorious First, an occasion that would be talked of in Hobart Town life-times from now: long after *Erebus* and *Terror* had vanished in the frozen Arctic labyrinth; after the shameful name of Van Diemen's Land was replaced with the blameless Tasmania; after Sophia's own travels had finally ended, fifty-one years later, on a rainy June evening in Phillimore Gardens, Kensington; after both the poles were conquered, and the last blank spaces on the map had been claimed by the aerial photographers.

And yet even the next day Sophia herself could remember almost nothing of that final entry on her dance card. Crozier must have been silent again. He must have danced well, although she was sure he would have looked very tired. His hand had not been too heavy on her waist, his fingers had not sweated through her glove and he had not stepped on her feet. He had left her, in short, to dance by herself, as she had done since suppertime, alone with the music and the forms of the dance, forms that included the steps and the partner and whatever small-talk she was required to make, which she did quite mechanically, hearing herself speak while the music flowed through her, shaping itself to her need. She was borne upward by her weariness, exalted in her loneliness. She no longer cared whom she danced with or who might be watching her. The white planks of the deck were a snowfield; the dancers were swirls in a blizzard, figments of a winter dream. What a fine thing it was to be tired and heartsore and wise beyond one's years. If she could only stay that way forever.

The music stopped and she heard the hum of voices. Commander Crozier asked her to take a turn with him by the stern rail. She stood, looking out to the mouth of the river where fading stars gave notice of the dawn, and half listened to the honest sailor as he talked of his prospects. Was she caught in a circular dream? She had already heard the same talk from her uncle tonight, although it seemed like long ages before. The six men of the quadrille orchestra, their instruments cased on the deck at their feet, stood by the mainmast exchanging tired conversation. They wore blanket-cloth coats and their breaths smoked in the air. Every few moments one head or the other would turn in her direction, and she thought: They are waiting for me to be finished with Crozier, so Crozier can pay them, and then they can go on their way.

Then the bandsmen of the 51st Regiment took up their instruments to play the last guests off the ships, and at once Sophia was awake again. It was that tune, the same that had moved her the evening before, when she had descended through magical gardens and marveled at ships on the river, ships that were burning with light. Hearing it now, she understood the beauty of that moment; it was her own beauty, and she pitied it and mourned it, although for the rest of her life it could be summoned by that tune.

All this turmoil of regret and understanding, and yet Sophia still had to stifle a yawn. She pulled her shawl tightly about her. Crozier was coming to his point. She ought in kindness to stop him before he reached it. But how could she decently divert him? He stood beside her at the rail, clasping it with both hands as if waiting for a wave to break over him, his face braced for the cold slap, and he was telling her that of course it was by no means certain that the next two seasons of the voyage would be crowned with success, or that he himself would be spared from the hazards of the sea, but that if, upon returning to England . . .

She put her hand on his sleeve, stilling him. "My dear Frank," she said, "things will be as they shall be, and I will pray for your safety until we see you again. But please tell me now, in case it should slip me to ask you, and then later come back to trouble me, as it has troubled me all night—what is the name, do you know, of that tune they are playing? It is lodged like a thorn in my memory and I cannot pluck it out. Mr. Elliot said earlier that it might be 'The Brighton Camp.' Do you know if he is right?"

Crozier seemed taken aback by her interruption. Yet he mastered himself quickly. He does have manners, she thought; I am sure he will forgive me. "'The Brighton Camp'?" he pondered. "Why no, Sophia, it is no such thing as far as I know. It is one of our old Irish songs—surely the lilt of it betrays its origin. We call it 'The Girl I Left Behind Me.'"

"'The Girl I Left Behind Me,'" she repeated, weighing herself with the words.

Hers would be a life of departures, but it was not she who would be left behind. And a life of departures must also be a life of quiet renunciations: it was things such as these—old friends half forgotten, cold wind on your face, rain on a London window as the light fades in June—that made you feel alive.

She linked his arm and led him away from the rail, back to where her uncle awaited them. "Thank you, Frank. It is a very lovely air. I shall send for the broadsheet. 'The Girl I Left Behind Me.' We shall play it in our drawing room and think of you and your ships."

And Francis Crozier, quite mistaking her meaning, squeezed her hand to his side with his elbow then quickly released it once more.

Northwest Territories, Canada

If there had ever been a sign, then Nelson had missed it. Instead of taking the highway south he found himself in the car park of Inuvik's small airport, built on its own dead-end road on the south side of town. He was about to turn and drive on, but then he remembered that he needed cigarettes, and that Fort McPherson, the next township to the south, was about two hours' drive away.

He parked his car and went into the terminal, and by the time he understood his mistake—that the airport was too small to have its own store—it was already too late.

She was alone on the plastic seats inside the door. Her bag lay on the floor beside her. Voices murmured from a distant backroom but the hall itself was empty. The paleness of her face, the shadows under her eyes, suggested a long journey. Her hair was short and too dark, too lacking in gray, not to be at least a little bit dyed.

She got to her feet and smoothed down the knees of her jeans. "Taxi?"

"No. I'm sorry." He turned to go.

"Then could I ask you for a lift into town? I've been here for ages and no one's come or gone."

He could see a couple of small planes through the glass doors at the back of the hall, their engines wrapped in canvas. Grounded by weather, he guessed: the radio had said there were storms to the south over Whitehorse and Yellowknife and Norman Wells.

The snow front was headed this way; if he didn't get out now he could be blocked in the mountains.

"I'm not going back to Inuvik. I'm headed the other way. Out."

The door swooshed behind him and he stood in the cold, seeing the way that her face had looked, lost and dazed, as if she'd been traveling forever. He walked back to his car, boots crunching in an inch of new snow. Then he remembered the cigarettes. The stores would be open in town.

He found her again at the back of the terminal, staring up at a stuffed polar bear. She didn't seem to notice him until he was right by her side.

"I can give you a ride after all," he said. "I have to go back into town."

"That's very kind of you." She didn't seem surprised to see him again. "My name's Fay."

Her hand was quite cold though the building was well heated.

"Nelson," he said. "Let me help you with your bag."

She gasped as the January air burned her lungs. The cold turned her face pink, brought it to life again. Nelson put her bag in the trunk of his old Ford Taurus. When he closed it again she was waiting on the driver's side: she must have come here straight from England, he guessed.

"Lady? You're on the wrong side of the car."

She was staring at the willows that grew beside the parking lot. They were curdled with snow, bowed by the weight of it. She turned and frowned at him, as if she'd forgotten he was there, then came around the hood while he crossed behind the back, keeping the car between them.

"That's stupid of me." She got in the passenger seat. "I've been traveling for ages. I can't believe that I'm finally here."

She said she had a booking at the Eskimo Inn so he parked outside and carried her bag up to the lobby and then he said good-bye.

Crossing Mackenzie Road, he bought a carton of cigarettes at the Mid-Town Market, and because he'd be late on the road, and you never knew up here, you might get stuck, he also bought some nuts and raisins and chocolate and potato chips, and a couple of bottles of water and two three-packs of Red Bull to keep him awake at the wheel. Outside, he lit a cigarette and watched cars come and go from the NorthMart, lights flaring across its windowless wall. A group of boys and girls came out of the food court, their oversize snow boots clomping down the metal stairs. They bunched together on the pavement's dirty snow and he heard them laughing though he couldn't make out words. Their eyes passed over Nelson without seeming to notice him. They won't see me, he thought, because they think I don't belong here. They're right about that.

He tossed the cigarette, ready to go. Then he looked across the street and saw her again, standing on the stoop of the Eskimo Inn, her bag beside her, looking hopefully about. Oh Christ, he thought. Will I ever get out of here?

"I'm really sorry to impose on you again," she said, as he carried her bag down the steps. "They say that when they tried to confirm my reservation last week the computer wouldn't accept my credit card. So they just canceled the booking without letting me know. Now the hotel is booked out for some engineering conference. Something to do with a new road they're building."

The Mackenzie Hotel was also booked out, for the same reason. But a desk clerk mentioned another place, an off-season tourist resort. Nelson drove her back out of town, past boxy public buildings and snow-shrouded truck lots and new subdivisions of small vinyl houses, all built up on stilts to stop the ground melting. It was five in the evening, the twilight long gone, and traffic was quiet. They met a snowplow on the outskirts, grading the verge between the road and the trees. Their headlights made rainbows as they passed through its plume.

The sign they were looking for said "Northern Villas." It pointed down a side road to a clearing in the spruces. A few log cabins stood around the clearing, also mounted on stilts above the permafrost. There were lights in a couple of them, trucks parked outside, but the rest were dark and empty. A larger house stood by the entrance, evidently a residence, but with a reception room built to one side.

Pulling up the car, Nelson felt his front wheels crunch pleasingly into a snowdrift. The woman, Fay, was asleep now, her chin tucked into her chest. Her face was blue from the lights in the clearing.

Maybe, he thought, I should leave her to sleep for a bit, go in there myself to see if they have a room. But he thought better of it: If they say no, then I'll still be stuck with her. He knew from experience that they'd be more likely to say no to him than to someone like her. And he ached to drive south without stopping. He touched her shoulder to wake her up.

A buzzer on the counter summoned a big, rugged-faced man from the back of the house. Nelson guessed he'd been eating his dinner in back.

"I can help you tonight," said the owner. "Tomorrow and the next day too, most likely. After that I don't know. I have bookings for all the cabins—engineers for the new overland road from here to Tuktoyaktuk. But I'm not sure when they'll turn up."

"Two or three nights is all I need," she said.

The owner woke up his computer, began to jab it with two fingers. "I'm not saying you'll definitely have to check out in three days, if you don't want to. It just depends how long the flights are grounded and the highway stays closed."

Nelson, who had been waiting for a chance to say good-bye, stepped back to the counter. "The highway's closed?"

The owner didn't look up. "Fresh snow in the Richardson Mountains. Storms came earlier than they predicted. My engineers just called from Eagle Plains to say they got stopped at the boom. It went down about a quarter-hour ago, just as they were leaving. Otherwise they'd have been here late tonight." He looked up at Fay. "I'm giving you their chalet. Name, please?"

"It's Morgan, Fay. Fay Morgan."

"Sam Ringnes." They shook hands. "And your friend's name?"

"He's not staying. He was kind enough to give me a lift."

Nelson did his calculations. The booms had gone down only fifteen minutes ago. If I'd've taken the right road, or if I'd've left her at the airport, I would have made it past Fort McPherson before they closed the boom there. I could have crossed the Arctic Circle tonight and seen the sun come up tomorrow.

He wanted to curse, to turn and walk out of there, but her bags were still in his car.

The owner stopped typing. "I can't get this registration form to load. I guess I'll do it later." He looked up at Fay. "Do you have a ride of your own? We're two miles out of town here."

"I was going to ask you about that. I want to go north to Tuk-toyaktuk tomorrow, but I don't drive. Could you recommend a taxi?"

"Want to drive the famous ice road, huh? It's usually guys who come here for that. They see it on TV."

"It's not that. I just want to look around."

Ringnes set both hands on the counter. "There's the minibus taxis, I guess. They run back and forth on the ice road when they can fill enough seats. I could give you a couple of numbers."

"I was hoping for a private hire."

"Norcan Hire is just across the road there. But you say you don't drive." Ringnes took a slow look at Nelson. "You need someone who's got some free time on his hands. And who could possibly use a little cash."

Her back was turned to him, but Nelson could tell from the tilt of her head that she was waiting. She doesn't want to ask me herself. She's embarrassed, or afraid of me. She thinks she made me miss my chance to get out of here. So she'd rather I'd just leave now, so she can find someone else.

The office was a lean-to built onto the side of the house, with triple-glazed sides and a glass pane in the roof. Looking up, Nelson saw the wind stir patterns in the snow dust on the glass. The tank in his old Taurus was a quarter full. He had in his pocket three hundred seventy dollars, the last of the money he'd found in his brother's apartment. Three thousand kilometers, at say thirteen kilometers per liter; it might just get him to Edmonton if he drove really smoothly and slept in the car. But what would he do when he got there?

"I can drive you for a couple of days. At least until the highway's clear." He needed an out so he reached for a lie. "As soon as the road's clear I have to go south . . . I have a job interview down in Whitehorse."

Nelson dragged his bag across the threshold of his brother's apartment, then stopped, the hall door still open. When he'd left this place that afternoon he'd had no intention of ever coming back here.

The town's hospital stood across the road from the apartment and its lights shone through the curtains, the same nylon curtains, printed with bright summer flowers, that hung in every window of his brother's short-lease building. The light seeped onto the cheap nylon couch, the beige nylon carpet, the cluttered desk and the maps on the wall.

It came to this, thought Nelson. Any way you looked at it, this is what it came to. Swimming in Saskatoon Lake as boys in the summer. Piano lessons. The five-day drive across the whole country, him and his parents, all the way from Grande Prairie to Montreal to see Bert graduate college. As kids, Bert and Nelson had dreamed of making that drive across the country, the forests and silos and wheat fields. It hadn't worked out as planned. His brother hadn't driven with them. He had been waiting for them at McGill University, in that other life he was now going to have. And that too must not have worked out as planned, because the scholarships, the prizes, the good looks, and the girlfriends should have led to something better than a lonely place like this.

And yet, Nelson thought, remembering himself with a hard sense of relief, for me this is pretty sweet. There was cable and Internet, heat and light and hot water, his brother's bed to sleep in, clean sheets, until or unless his brother came back from wherever he'd gone. There was the money his brother had left for him, waiting in an envelope on the coffee table. He hadn't asked for it but there it was, and he certainly needed it.

He had the keys to the apartment and to his brother's SUV— "If Im not home when u get there keys in tailpipe burgundy equinox ab plates back of basement." They had been there in the tailpipe, just as the text said. He had the driver's license, the credit cards, the library passes, all the odds and ends that Bert had left in his wallet on the shelf beside the door.

Why had Bert left his wallet on the shelf beside the door?

But no roommates, no cold, no sleeping on couches or in the back of his car, making excuses, behind with the bills . . . Nelson was in a home here, a retreat, sheltered accommodation. The only problem was that he had no idea where his big brother was, or why he had invited Nelson to come and stay with him on the Mackenzie delta, as far north in Canada as it was possible to drive. Bert had been gone for over a week now without an explanation; he'd already been gone when Nelson had got here. But his cell phone still sat on the desk, fully charged and plugged into the wall.

Nelson meant to call the cops to tell them Bert was missing. He had meant to call them days ago. But there were a few unpaid traffic tickets, and a long-ago fight in Fort McMurray might still be a problem. One day turned into the next. He watched TV, drank Bert's whiskey, asked about work, went to the town's only bar. He told himself he was waiting for Bert to come back. And as time went on the task grew in its enormity. Nelson came to believe, or half believe, that to tell the cops about his brother would be a kind of betrayal: as long as Bert was missing, Bert was still alive.

Nelson turned on the light and went over to the desk. Bert had set it in a corner facing the wall, beneath a corkboard covered in letters and Post-its and printouts and notes.

On either side of the corkboard were maps of the Yukon and the Mackenzie delta, showing relief and drainage and roads and old trails. Both maps were covered with cellophane overlays, a trick their granddad had taught them from his time in the signal corps: you wrote on the overlay with pencil or felt-tip, traced your routes and objectives, made observations, then when you were done you could wipe the map clean again. You could cover your tracks, their granddad had joked. Or at least Nelson had assumed he'd been joking. These particular overlays were still scribbled with crosses and arrows, illegible notes, scrawled dates from the 1920s and 1930s, winding up the Yukon valley then across the divide to the edge of the sea.

There was a black-and-white photograph too, reproduced from some old newspaper or magazine, blown up so much that you could see each fuzzy grain. It showed two men in winter clothing standing at the door of an old-fashioned ski-plane. It was not these men who had interested Bert, it seemed, but two shadows, one on either side of them, cast by figures just out of the frame. Bert had circled both shadows several times with a marker pen.

None of this made any sense to Nelson. But then his brother had long been a stranger, and his interests had long been obscure.

He pulled out the swivel chair and sat facing away from the desk. The furniture, the shelves of books, the TV, and the coffee table, all were now exactly as he'd found them when he came into the north ten days before. He'd made a point of tidying up before he'd fled the place that afternoon, meaning never to return. It would look as if he'd never been there, except for the note that he'd left on the coffee table.

> Dear Bert. I waited ten days but no sign of you. I have to go south again. I couldn't find work up here—it's not like they say it is. Please call: I'm worried about you. Thanks for the money—I'll pay you back. Love, Nelson.

How he had torn himself over that word "love," though no doubt it was true.

Nelson swung the chair around to face the desk. This too he had left as he'd found it, more or less; the sleeping laptop computer, the heaps of books and notes and cardboard boxes of files, the Post-its and chewed-up old pens. He found it hard to believe that Bert would have kept his desk that way. Maybe the desk had been tidy the last time his brother had sat there. Maybe this disorder was itself a kind of clue. Bert might have had some sudden fit of rage or despair, thrown everything about the desk, then stormed out the door.

Carefully, so as not to disturb the layers of scattered papers, Nelson peeled them apart and took out the note he'd only found that afternoon. Maybe Bert had originally meant for the note to be lying on top of the other folders and papers, not hidden among them, where Nelson had found it.

It was addressed to no one, signed by no one.

> When you hold this note please don't be angry or sad. I'll sleep on it tonight—I always have before—the lure of a warm sleep. I know it's selfish. I'm sorry—it's been a long time coming but the notion has come calling many times

before. I can't imagine moving forward in life and for as long as I can remember I haven't been able to. There have been pipe dreams that offered an imaginative buzz from time to time but they don't translate to reality. When that's a state of being with no avenues out, best to close the chapter.

And then on the back, in a different ink:

I may, however, have some real life ahead of me. Alaska through the mountains—set up where you can dogsled into Alaska from the Canadian side in the heart of winter. Build igloos and sleep with the dogs for warmth. VHF/short wave for communication. Grow a beard. Night-lights. Allsorts.

Night-lights: their glow. Radio pulses across the cold distance. Allsorts: their mother loved licorice candy, but Nelson wouldn't eat it. Bert always took his share.

Alaska. Bert's last dream was to search for lost warmth in the wilderness. Was Alaska any wilder than here? It seemed to Nelson, the first time that he read that note, that his brother was out in the woods somewhere, snug in a snowdrift, where the ravens would find him in spring.

So Nelson had packed his bag and fled, then somehow missed the turnoff, and now he was back here, for another day, maybe two or three, until the road crews from Fort McPherson and Eagle Plains had cleared the passes in the mountains. Then he really would pull the plug on his brother. Meanwhile, he would work for that lady for gas money, drive her wherever she wanted to go. And he would use Bert's car, the newish SUV in the basement with the nice high ride and the all-wheel drive. Better that on the ice roads than his own clapped-out Taurus. Bert owed him the use of that car. The cash in the envelope wasn't payment enough for what he was doing to Nelson.

Nelson closed his eyes for a long moment, squeezing them tight until the dancing grains turned red. When he was sure that he wouldn't cry again he looked at the books and papers scattered on the desk. At the top of the heap was a manila folder filled with blue-lined pages of Bert's penciled writing. The cover sheet was blank apart from some kind of reference number and a single line of writing, also in Bert's tidy hand. Nelson had time on his hands again. He might as well start here: "Francis Rawdon Moira Crozier: from Room 38."

Tuktoyaktuk, Northwest Territories

It was at Margate Sands, in a pedal boat with her mother, that Fay first learned she was prone to motion sickness. Her mother had noticed the change in her even before she did so herself. At six years of age, all Fay knew was that the best day of her life had sunk into dismay, and that she was no longer excited by the ice cream she'd been promised when this, her first sea voyage, was over. Her mother stopped pedaling, letting the little swan-shaped craft bob on the oily skin of the windless estuary. She wrapped her bare arms around her only child. Her dark hair, still wet from swimming, plastered itself to Fay's face.

"You've been watching your feet on the pedals and it's making you ill," Alice whispered. "Keep your eyes out of the cockpit. That's what my dad learned in the air force. Fix your eyes on the horizon. It always worked for him."

Fay had tried it and it had worked, long enough for them both to get back to the beach. She had enjoyed her ice cream.

Keep your eyes out of the cockpit. Well, it didn't work up here on the ice road, a mile out from the shore. A haze had softened the stars and now Fay could see neither coast nor horizon; she couldn't tell where the sky met the frozen sea or where the sea met the frozen land. It was this lack of reference that dizzied her; the car hardly seemed to be moving, its wheels humming evenly over the graded sea ice. She shut her eyes for a moment, trying to stop the sickness from rising in her stomach, and when she opened them again she was looking at her feet. Funny. The snow she had walked into the footwell two hours earlier, when Nelson had picked her up from her chalet on the outskirts of Inuvik, still hadn't melted though the heater was on full. When she looked at the dashboard it said ninety kilometers per and thirty below. The sickness eased as she looked at the numbers. So keep your eyes *inside* the cockpit. It's upside down up here.

The ice road curved around a low cape to reveal lights strung along a bluff like an artificial horizon. Fay stared at the lights gratefully, restoring her balance.

"Tuktoyaktuk," Nelson said needlessly. "End of the road."

It was the first time he'd spoken since he'd stopped the car for that wrong-headed lemming. That was fine with her: he was her driver, not her guide, and she guessed from his clothes and his way of talking that he hadn't had much education. He was a tall man who walked with a stoop. His stubble, almost a beard now, was a shade of red she hadn't seen before, like fresh-cut copper wire. He might have seemed handsome if he could have looked her in the eye.

"Shit," he announced suddenly, and braked hard. The lights of the village blinked out, all at once, as the car hit something very hard, bounced, then flew upward at a sharp angle. But Fay, grabbing the dashboard, had the paradoxical sensation of falling: ahead of her, the land seemed to drop steeply toward a dark ocean, now only yards away. There's no way we can stop before we splash into it. With a presence of mind that surprised herself she grabbed for the door handle: if I can get out before the car sinks I might still survive.

The ground disappeared, and the car seemed to fly through the air before landing again, this time without bouncing. Now the sea was where the sky should be. The sea *was* the sky, she realized. Perspective had failed her again.

"Snow ramp," explained Nelson apologetically. "From the sea ice up to the shore. In this light, with everything white, it's hard to see until you're right on top of it. Kind of makes your head swim, right?"

"We were going very fast."

"Sorry about that." But he seemed a little pleased with himself. "It's a good job we're in this Equinox and not my old Ford. I doubt her axles would have taken that whack."

He wants to talk about cars now. "I suppose not," she said, and turned her face to her window. They were on a street of sorts, in a sort of village. A few dozen wood-frame houses were scattered across the flat tundra, brightly painted and plastered with snow. Curtains glowed and stovepipes smoked. Plywood sheds, dead trucks and bits of odd gear peeped from the snow that lay deep in the yards. A dog came out of a lean-to kennel and watched the car roll past, its breath curling around it. There were cables everywhere, strung crazily between the houses and propped up by poles. Off to the south, on the edge of town, two red lights blinked in and out of existence between the last row of houses: the tail lights of a snowmobile, or maybe a truck. Apart from that and the smoke from the chimneys, Fay saw nothing that moved.

"Now that we're here, where do you want to go?"

She could already see the military radar station east of the settlement, low in the sky, a white sphere on a gantry. It glowed in the lights that shone at its base. Two other radar domes sat beneath it, growing from the ground like puffballs in a bog. A single red light, unblinking, shone in the darkness above it. I'll get to you later, she thought. I mustn't seem too eager. "Do you know where we could get something to eat?"

They were passing an old sailing boat set up on timbers as some kind of a monument. Its mast and its rigging were coated with ice. Across the road from it stood a little wooden church with a Roman steeple at one end and a Byzantine dome at the other; a tarpaulin covered the roofless schism between them.

"There's the Northern Store, I guess. They'll sell you a burger or a pizza. But it's no kind of restaurant."

"You know this place well?"

"I drove up here once before. A few days ago."

She was happy to leave it at that. But he must have felt a need to explain himself. "I was looking for work, but there isn't any. There used to be, when they were doing the energy exploration, but it's all on hold now, on account of the government wouldn't pay for a pipeline, and now the price of gasoline has dropped. And there's all this new shale gas in the south."

He braked beside a roadside monument. It was shaped like three human figures with their hands in the air. "That's the marker for the northernmost point of the North American road network—at least in winter, when the ice road is in. In summer you can't drive any farther north than Inuvik, and you have to come up here by plane or boat. But now they're building a new all-weather road between here and Inuvik, to link up year-round. That's why you couldn't get a room in town, I guess."

"When the new road is built there'll be no more ice road in the winter?"

"I guess not. But this place will still be the end of the line."

The Northern Store was a windowless vinyl box set on a metal frame above the permafrost. It stood, Fay guessed, on a spit of land beside a harbor, though with all the snow and ice it was hard to tell for sure. A couple of snowmobiles were parked beside the store, their engines still running, the exhaust vapor pooling in the still evening air. They left their own motor running and climbed the steps that led to the side door. At the top Nelson stopped to smoke a cigarette. They stood in silence for a moment, looking over the icebound harbor, its snow crisscrossed with old snowmobile tracks. The radar station loomed larger here; it seemed to be standing on a spit of its own on the far side of the harbor, away from all the homes.

"That thing over there—that's a radar station, is it?"

He sucked smoke and freezing air. "Distant Early Warning."

"And it's still in use?"

"I guess so. The Russians are still out there, or whatever else they're watching for."

"Distant Early Warning." She let the phrase sit there between them. It was getting colder, too cold for a haze. To the south, the refracted rays of a sub-Arctic day silhouetted the little dome-shaped hills that rose from the tundra. Those are pingos, Fay thought. She'd read about them in her guidebook.

"You want to go over there?" he said.

"I beg your pardon?"

He tossed away his cigarette. "You want to look at the radar station?"

"Oh." She pretended to consider it. "Do you think we could? Is it not army property?"

"It's automated and unmanned, and I don't see any fences. And I don't know what else there is to look at up here." She saw his teeth in the red stubble. "You've come a long way just for lunch." He put his glove on the door handle. "It won't be the best lunch you've ever had either. Not that I'm fussy."

When they'd eaten their microwaved burgers and wiped their fingers clean with napkins they went back to the car. Nelson drove Fay slowly around the settlement, then turned eastward on a track across the tundra. The lights from the Distant Early Warning station were to their left; I'll get to you last, thought Fay.

They passed the little airport, its flare path extinguished, its two-story terminal lightless and dead, then carried on beyond the last houses. Mothballed trucks and drill rigs stood in lines in a snow-covered lot. Farther on there were rows of prefabricated dormitories from the golden days of exploration, elevated modules with airlock doors and lightless slit windows, jacked up on steel rams and joined by sealed tubes. They looked like moon bases, or undersea habitats.

Soon they ran out of track and turned back toward the settlement.

"You ever see the northern lights?"

"No."

"Let me pull over and switch off the lights."

She zipped up her coat and put on her gloves and walked around the back of the car, past the gurgling exhaust pipe, to join him on the driver's side. To the south, but high in the sky, a gauzy yellow band of light curled and straightened and curled again like weed in a slow-moving stream. It stretched from one horizon to the other, a wandering cousin to the Milky Way. Seeing the aurora for the first time, Fay understood its fascination: it was moved by a wind that did not come from earth.

"You can get other colors," he said. "Green, blue, sometimes red."

"Could I ask you a favor? Could you turn off the engine for a minute or two? It won't freeze up if you do, will it?"

He killed the ignition. The silence crashed over her like a cold wave. She settled back until she was leaning against the side of the car, the chill of the metal burning through her clothes. The stars were so fierce that she feared they might hurt her.

A second band of light had formed beside the first, roughly parallel to it, spooning its curves. Directly below it, a couple of miles away, a pingo glowed in the light from the sky; its dome relieved and revealed the tundra's desolation. These are the Barren Lands, she thought. They go like this all the way to Hudson Bay and beyond. People disappear in them and are never seen again.

She listened for the fabled hiss of the aurora. There was a vehicle moving in the settlement, and she could hear the moan of a generator. When Nelson shifted his feet they crunched through shallow drift snow, and then a lighter rasped and she smelled fresh smoke. The air was cold and hard as steel. She couldn't feel her feet.

Nelson gave a whistle, so loud and so shrill that she jumped in her shoes. Black shapes peeled away from the snowy waste in front of them and rose into the air. The stillness was torn by the cries of angry ravens.

"What are you doing?"

He seemed startled by her anger. "I'm whistling at the lights. They say up here that if you whistle at them they'll start dancing."

"Oh . . . Is that what they say?"

The aurora was if anything paler than before, slower in its evolutions. She pointed to where the ravens were settling again, fifty yards away, on a mound of dirty snow. "What are those birds doing out here?"

"This must be the dump."

The cold had worked its way into her coat and was clamping her kidneys. She had to clench and unclench her gloved fists to keep her fingers from freezing. Inside the car it would still be quite warm. But she would stay out here a minute or two more, watching the aurora.

"In Norway they believed that you should never whistle at the lights," she said. "I read that somewhere. They thought it makes them angry. They'll swoop down and take you away."

"That's not what they say up here."

"Try whistling again."

The ravens squawked in protest, but this time they stayed put. The lights, unheeding, continued with their self-absorbed proceedings. To Greenlanders they were the souls of lost children, playing in the sky. Fay had read that in a book. But she kept it to herself.

"You still want to look at the Distant Early Warning base?"

★ ★ ★

The radar station stood on a rise at the end of a promontory half a mile east of the town. To reach it, they had to drive along a spit of land not much wider than the road itself with the frozen sea on either side of them. The wind had licked the snow into a stucco pattern. To the west were the lights of Tuktoyaktuk, to the east nothing but stars. This close, Fay could see the other buildings in the complex—a small hangar or garage, an office or workshop, a couple of small huts. The windows were unlit. It would have been bigger back in the early days, she thought, when it was still manned, and her grandfather had been here.

"I guess we can go all the way up to it," said Nelson. He glanced at her sideways. He was driving very slowly.

"Why not?"

Their headlights swept across the geodesic radar domes. Fay saw them flare in the beams then die back to a glow. Then, a moment later, they lit up again, but less brightly this time. She was still trying to figure that out when Nelson slowed the car.

"There's someone behind us."

Fay turned, saw headlights on low beam. "Would anyone live out here?"

"I doubt it. The station's unmanned."

The vehicle behind them did not seem to be moving very fast. "What shall we do?"

"This road's too narrow to turn without maybe getting stuck in the snow. There's no room to let them pass. We might as well go on up to the radar station and wait for them there."

There was a clear space, a sort of courtyard, between the two lower domes and the workshop. Nelson drove into it, made a half-circle and stopped in the middle, pointing back the way they'd come. A sign on a wall, illuminated by a caged bulb, declared that this was military property and that trespass was a serious offense. Nelson dimmed the lights and sat waiting, his hands between his knees, as the other car pulled into the yard and halted in the entrance, blocking their way out. Now Fay could see lights mounted on its roof and "RCMP" on its hood.

"Shall we get out and talk to them?"

"Cops don't like that. They want you to stay in your car unless they tell you to get out."

A spotlight flicked on and dazzled her. She was still holding her eyes, trying to regain her night vision, when a gloved hand knocked on the window.

The policeman stood a little to the rear of the door where he could see her better than she could see him. She wound down the window.

"Hello," she said. Then, from force of English habit, "It's very cold, isn't it?"

He wore a muskrat hat that matched his brown mustache. Both were filmed silver from his frozen breath. "Did you read the signs?"

"I did, yes. Sorry. Just a minute ago. When we got here. We didn't know we weren't allowed to come out here. We just wanted to take a look."

He leaned closer to study her. "You're from overseas?"

"I'm from England." She smiled apologetically. "I'm here on holiday. Just traveling around Canada. I didn't think there'd be any harm just having a look."

"What's your name, madam?"

"It's Morgan. Fay Morgan . . . I can show you my passport."

"Please do."

He took a torch from his pocket and looked through her passport. "You said you were English. This passport is Canadian."

"Yes. But it's new. I was born in England, but my mother was Canadian. I thought I'd get a Canadian passport when I came on this trip." She smiled at him. "So they'd have to let me in." He showed no reaction to her joke. So she found herself doubling down on it. "Besides, who knows? If I like it up here I might stay."

He handed her passport back. "You'd be welcome. But it gets pretty cold."

He leaned down to the window so he could look across at Nelson. "What do you say, Mr. Nilsson? You've been up here long enough to know that this is government property."

Fay saw the expression on Nelson's face, half suspicious, half puzzled. "I'm sorry," he said. "We weren't going to get out or anything. We were just having a look."

The policeman stared at him a moment more. He had dry gray eyes. "You hear about old Moses Isaac from Aklavik? He had to go into hospital in Inuvik last week. Must have been a couple of days after I sent you to see him."

Nelson shifted uncomfortably. "Oh yeah? That's too bad."

"At his age, he might not get out again. But they've got a really good seniors program in Inuvik, so maybe it's for the best. He can sure talk still, but it wasn't right him living on his own in Aklavik."

"I guess not."

"Did he help you with what you wanted to know? I told him he should talk to you."

"Pretty much."

"Well, if you need to talk to him again, go see Eunice at the hospital. She's in charge of the seniors' program. You can tell her Sergeant Peake sent you."

The sergeant turned to Fay again. "To be honest, Ms. Morgan, I'm not too worried if people want to take a look at this place, but when I saw your lights I had to check on you. The Americans own half of this facility, and they can get uptight about visitors. So please don't take any pictures."

"I wasn't going to. We're heading back to Inuvik now."

"You staying at the Mackenzie or the Eskimo Inn?"

"Northern Villas. The others are full."

"I'll bet they are. There's construction people everywhere because of the new road." The sergeant took a step backward and beckoned to the police truck. It moved up beside them, unblocking the exit. Fay couldn't see the driver. The sergeant tapped the roof of their car to formally release them. "We'll follow you back down the track. Have a safe trip back to town."

The police truck followed them past the airport, through the settlement, and right to the edge of the ice road. Then it stopped, its lights perched above the frozen ocean, seeing them on their way. They drove on until the lights of the settlement were blocked by a headland. Then Nelson looked at Fay.

"Do you mind if we stop? I could use a smoke."

We could have done this back in the town, where it wasn't so dark and so lonely. But perhaps he has his reasons. He seems shy of that policeman.

Nelson got out. Fay sat for a few moments, thinking things over, before she joined him. It was beyond cold now; even the aurora had frozen. If I didn't have this car, she thought, if I took off these clothes, I'd be dead in a couple of minutes. The glaring stars, the diamond grain of the galaxy, confirmed her situation: she might as well be floating in space.

"Could I have a cigarette, please?"

He had already half finished his own cigarette, but he took out another. Between drags she put her hands together and blew into her palms to stop her fingers freezing. The smoke made her light-headed, almost ill. She decided to ask him.

"How do you know that Sergeant Peake?"

He tossed away his cigarette. "I've never seen him before in my life."

You were right, she told herself. You shouldn't have asked him. The nicotine had made her feel sick. God knows what this man has done that you don't want to know about. And now he's having to lie to you, and you have to go along with it. He's clearly had dealings with police. You're out here alone with him.

But she took another drag on the cigarette. "He thinks he knows you. He said he met you in Aklavik."

"I've never been there."

"He knows your name."

"Okay." He said it quietly, as if he was tired. "Okay," he said again. "He just thinks that he knows me. He's mixing me up with my brother." He leaned back against the car, waiting.

"Your brother."

"My brother whose car this is. My brother whose apartment I'm staying in. We look alike."

"Right . . ." This would probably be a good place to let things lie. "You didn't put him straight?"

"No."

"You could get in trouble, lying to police like that."

He took out another cigarette. "He lied to himself."

"You're not wanted, are you?" She said it facetiously, as if she didn't care. She'd known all sorts in her younger days in south London, and at college, before her life had tamed her.

"No. I just didn't want him to know that I wasn't my brother, because the next thing he'd ask me is how my brother is, and then I'd have to tell him that I don't know how my brother is." He lit the cigarette.

Fay thought, That doesn't make a blind bit of sense. Has he killed his own brother and hidden the body? Is that really so out of the question? Why else was he so desperate to get away from Inuvik yesterday, before the passes were closed?

He must have been able to see her face better than she could see his. He gave a sour laugh.

"My brother's gone missing. He told me he needed to see me, so I drove all the way up from Alberta and when I got here he was gone. But he'd left me this car and the keys to his apartment.

And now I'm beginning to think that he might have done something . . . He left all these crazy notes and stuff on his desk."

Fay decided that she didn't want to care about this man's brother and the rubbish on his desk. So she said nothing. He waited, then went on.

"Like, there was this letter I was reading last night. I think Bert must have copied it from somewhere, because it's written in his hand-writing, but it's really long, and the language is really old-fashioned."

"Really." She got back into the car.

He got in beside her, put the car in drive. "There's this guy called Crozier, who was on the famous Franklin expedition, the one that got lost in Baffin Bay or wherever. He's writing to another guy to tell him why they abandoned their ships and what he did after." He glanced across at her. "It's almost like a suicide note."

"It's fake. Your brother must have written it himself."

"How can you be so sure?"

"Because right now the Canadian government is putting on a big underwater search for Franklin's lost ships. It's all over the TV and newspapers. And the articles all say they never found any let-ters or journals or logs from that voyage. They only found bones, and one short note."

"Really? . . . You want to take a look at the letter? It's in that folder on the backseat."

Before she could refuse he had reached back and dropped a folder in her lap. It was made of plain manila cardboard, the same sort of folder they use for suspension files. Written on it in neat ballpoint letters was "Francis Rawdon Moira Crozier: from Room 38." She looked at it distastefully.

"I get sick if I read in a car."

"Oh . . . That's okay then. Don't worry."

He reached for the folder to put it back in the rear seat. But he picked it up clumsily, distracted by the driving, and one of its pages slid out on her lap.

Fay couldn't help looking at it. It was a copy of an article from the *Guardian* of London, a newspaper that she often read herself. But she must have missed this issue, which dated from several years before. If she had seen it she would definitely have remembered it.

The piece concerned the mysterious reappearance of a Royal Navy chronometer that had been lost with Franklin's ships. She had never seen the article, but she recognized the clock in the photograph, a little brass instrument with a round white face and spiky black numerals.

She had seen that clock before.

"This does look interesting, I suppose . . . Maybe I'll take a look at it when we're back in Inuvik . . . I suppose I could read it overnight."

Lancaster Sound, 1848

Private and personal:
To Sir James Clark Ross
Number Two, Eliot Place
The Black Heath, Kent

Captain F.R.M. Crozier RN
at Beechey Island, Lancaster Sound
20th of August 1848

My dear James,

It is more than two years since I last set foot on this island, an interval so filled with dire incident that I scarcely know where to begin this account.

Of all the officers and men who wintered on Beechey Island three years ago I alone have returned here alive. I last saw the other men of the expedition this spring, far to the south of here when, after two winters locked in the ice, they abandoned *Erebus* and *Terror* and fled south on foot.

As their lawful commander (poor Sir John died of old age in June of last year, when all still seemed quite well) I had urged them to take the contrary course and head north to Fury Beach, where there are stores and boats that might bring them safe to the whalers that visit Baffin Bay. But they would not accept my orders, or heed my warnings on the sodden nature of the mainland, its vast and lifeless extent and its shallow impassible rivers. I do not think any will survive the attempt to flee in that direction. Alas, I have failed in my first true command.

This private letter is intended only for your eyes, and for our friends in Room 38, so I shall not trouble here with any detailed account of the ruin of the Northwest Passage Expedition. You will find all you need on this point in the papers of *Erebus* and *Terror*, which I ordered Captain FitzJames to inter in the cairn at Point Victory after we gave up our ships. I also include with this letter some surplus instruments that I took from the ships and that I believe might be useful to Room 38. It is to be hoped that my whimsical cairn, built of food tins and gravel, will preserve them intact from the cold and the damp. I have little doubt, James, that you will be the first to come and search for us, and thus the first to open my cairn on Beechey Island. Perhaps you are already near, leading the search for your old friends and shipmates. I wish that I could wait for you, but an opportunity is afforded to me to make a great journey, and if I do not seize it now it will not come again.

To explain myself I must begin with a singular event that occurred in April of this year, but of which you will find no mention in the logs of either ship: I was careful to omit it from my own records, and by that time Captain FitzJames, having become as disordered as most of the men, had ceased keeping his own. We had just passed our second winter beset in the ice off King William Land, stores were running low, game could not be found for hunting, and the crews despaired of the ice ever breaking. The men were near mutiny, and disease and scurvy had reduced our numbers to only one hundred. Our ships no longer kept naval watch, except for a few good men who could still be trusted to stay on deck to keep a lookout. Thus my boatswain was alone on deck on the evening of April 18th when I heard him hail me as I worked below on my magnetic records.

Ascending from the cabin, I saw that the sun had already set and its light was giving way to a most active aurora. By its pale light, and the light of the stars hard above us, the boatswain had observed what he thought to be reindeer crossing the ice to our north. I ordered him to fetch my hunting pieces, but before he could bring them up it became apparent that these were not animals but men.

You may imagine our joy. We had not seen others of our kind since we lost sight of the last whalers in Davis Strait; at such a remove from civilization even the company of natives would be like opening a window in a small and lightless cell. Moreover, it seemed to many, still watching at a distance, that these might even be Englishmen, or at least Europeans, since they man-hauled their sledges, lacking the dogs of the Esquimaux. Perhaps this was some far-flung expedition of the Hudson's Bay Company, or even Danes from Greenland or Russians from Alaska. Yet as they drew nearer, observing them through my telescope, it became clear to me that these were natives, their faces having much the same cast as the Esquimaux or Innuits.

I resolved to go out to meet them unarmed so that they might not take fright (though because of the mutinous state of the men I carried concealed the engraved Colt pistol that you so kindly gave me). So as not to alarm the newcomers I brought with me only Johannes, our Greenlandic interpreter.

The newcomers were half a dozen in number. When we joined them they returned our greetings with apparent cordiality. To my surprise, they spoke a dialect that was

at first quite unintelligible to Johannes, though the Esquimaux tongue is known to be consistent from Alaska to
Greenland. They were also much taller than the common
Esquimaux—as tall as the tallest man aboard our ships and
broad in proportion.

Most striking, though, was their ornament: each wore a
polished disc of bone around his neck, scored with radial
lines like the points of a compass. Their coats were fastened
with toggles and buttons carved with the most minute and
finely conceived figures of spirits and animals. One of these
men, who seemed to be their chief, wore in addition a
string of strange amulets—ivory bears and walruses carved
as if they were almost rotted to skeletons. To his chest was
attached a mask cut from whale bone: a human face contorted in a hideous scream of terror and pain.

Johannes, observing this fetish, became dumbstruck from
fear. It was I therefore who was forced to begin the conversation, using the Esquimaux phrases I had learned when
we spent our winter at Igloolik under Parry's command.
Meanwhile Johannes seemed anxious to keep my person
interposed between himself and the strangers.

After much repetition and gesture, it gradually became
clear to me that their language was indeed a cousin of the
Innuit tongue, though primitive in form and pronuncia-
tion. I learned that they had traveled a great distance from
their starting point, which lay somewhere in the east or
north. Their leader, finally deigning to address me, said that
they had come to view "their sun," but when I pointed
to the south, where the sunset showed above the ice, he
shook his head and pointed to the northeast, whence they
had been observed to come. It thus became apparent to me
that they must have observed traces of our passing along
the west coast of Boothia, not far from the magnetic pole,

and have hastened to follow us southward, as is the habit of Esquimaux eager to trade with white men.

Yet now, having found us, they declined my invitation to come aboard our vessels, preferring instead to camp on the shore some distance away. We agreed to meet again there the following morning, and I turned in some perplexity back to the ships where they lay in the ice.

As I walked back, pondering the encounter, Johannes told me in great agitation that he recognized the amulets and fetishes of the newcomers, having seen similar dug from the floors of ancient stone circles in his native Greenland. He said these circles once held down the skin tents of the Tunit, a fantastical race of giants who faded from the north with the coming of the Esquimaux. Their masks and carvings, with their contorted faces and silent screams, are objects of dread whenever they are found. He begged me not to trust my life again to such a savage race.

I too had heard of these Tunits. You will recall that when we wintered at Igloolik with *Hecla* and *Fury* I spent many nights in the house of the old sorceress Iligliuk, who told me that these old ones persisted in regions too bleak for the Esquimaux. A few were said to linger still to the east of Igloolik, in fog-shrouded islands that she drew for me on a map, though she said it would be death for any man to go there.

When I left the ships the next morning the men had commenced stripping them of all the useless junk they would bring with them in their flight. Boxes and barrels crashed onto the ice, scattering their contents, and men argued and fought over choice pieces of clothing and fine silver cutlery and porcelain place settings. Turning my back on this scene of degradation, I saw a trickle of smoke on the shore which guided me to the strangers' camp.

Angak, their leader, waited for me outside their tent, seated alone on the sledge. The others were within, cooking seal meat and talking in low voices. No sooner had I stopped before him, having nowhere to sit myself, than the old man pointed to the bulge in my coat that concealed my Colt revolver, your parting gift to me at Greenhithe.

Overcoming my misgivings, I took out the revolver and showed it to him. He made no effort to touch it, but only nodded, satisfied, then pointed to himself. Next he indicated the hunting piece that I carried in its skin case, and then pointed five times at the snowhouse, as if enumerating the men within. And I realized at once, without any word being spoken, that he wanted five hunting pieces for his men and my pistol for himself. The guns would be payment. But payment for what? They had nothing with them that I wished to buy; I was already well furnished with reindeer clothing and sealskin boots from our visit to the Greenland settlements. Then Angak stood up and— gazing at me from his flat and expressionless face—raised his hand and pointed north.

At once I understood his proposal. They were offering to guide me! And what a fine offer this was! Traveling in the company of such natives, living as they did off the land and the sea, who knew what journeys I might compass? The Northwest Passage might lie within my reach, the secrets that lie beyond Parry's furthest north. I might even set eyes on Sir John Barrow's grail, his open polar sea, and add it to our science!

Two days later, when the crews of *Erebus* and *Terror* set out for the south, heaving the ships' heavy boats across buckled ice on groaning wooden sledges, I went with FitzJames to add a note of the expedition's intentions to the cairn at Point Victory. Then I returned to my magnetic observatory on the shore nearby, telling poor FitzJames that I would follow in a day or two when my observations were complete. Instead, I turned into the north with my new companions.

They are outside my tent now as I write on Beechey Island, once again lashing down gear on their sledges. I must hasten to join them, so I will be brief.

Leaving the forlorn ships behind us, we traveled along the coast of King William Land until we came to Ross Strait, where we turned north up the west shore of Boothia. What a pleasure it was, after two years confined in the ship, to journey with such hardy companions, who thought nothing of making twenty miles or more a day, moving swift and light-footed along the smoothest of the shore ice. And though I struggled at first, unused to such hard exercise, I soon felt my spirits and strength revive. My muscles knitted and my appetite adjusted to its new diet of seal meat and blubber (for the Tunit would not eat our naval rations, nor permit me to bring any for myself). After the first week I took my place in the traces, hauling with the best of them.

Our route here passed close to that happy spot where in 1831 you were the first to attain the north magnetic pole. Yet to my surprise my new observations showed that the pole now lay elsewhere, having moved northward some twenty miles or more along the shore of Boothia. The magnetic pole wanders, James, as if it were alive! If I could trace its journey, predict its future path, I might at last find some glory in James Ross's footsteps!

Forgive me, James. I know that you too would like to see that old jibe thrown back at those who have made it at my expense—I may not even call them my enemies, because of enemies I have none. And that is its own kind of poverty.

Where we are bound next I do not know; Angak says only that he will take me to places never yet seen by

Europeans, but when I ask him to look at my maps and place these new lands for me he refuses: they are his homeland, the few remaining refuges of his dwindling tribe, protected by strong taboos and perpetual fogs. But he is clear on one thing: their journey will take them far to the north and then the west, perhaps even—I tell myself—across the unknown region of the north pole itself!

I am done now with writing. It is very late, and almost dark outside, though we are still in the term of the midnight sun. An hour ago I took a turn on the beach and saw a flight of Ross's gulls—your gulls—winging northward, as if fleeing the south for the winter. Do they really spend winter in the furthest north, as the whalers and Esquimaux say? And if that is the case, and they perversely fly south in the summer, what is it that drives them there? Is it love of darkness that sends them southward when their polar home is bathed in perpetual light? Well, I shall follow them now to places beyond knowledge. Perhaps I shall learn where your little gulls nest.

I had thought to enclose with this letter a short message for Sophia but I have decided against. Her aunt would surely come to hear of it, and dear Lady Jane, as one of the first women of our time, is not to be sullied with knowledge of a secret correspondence. Nor do I have any desire to trouble Sophia's youth and tranquility, if trouble them I could. Look for my message cairns in the far north, toward the pole, where our maps remain untouched. There, perhaps, I shall find something fit to honor with the name of Cracroft.

Your friend now and always,
Frank Crozier

PART TWO

Bellot Strait

72°00′N 94°30′W

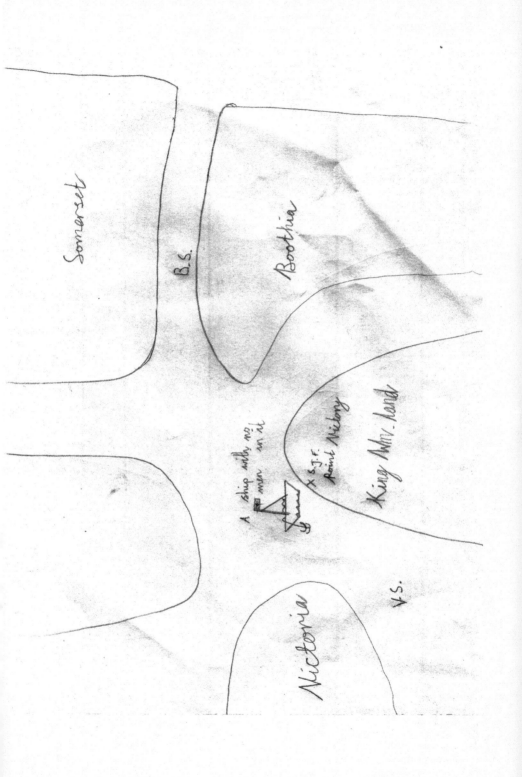

Somerset

B.s.

Boothia

A ship with no man in it

x S.J.F.
Point Victory

King Wm. land

Victoria

V.s.

Northwest Territories, Canada

Fay forgot to ask Nelson to stop by a food store on the way home from Tuktoyaktuk. Her kitchenette in the chalet had only tea and coffee and little catering tubs of long-life cream and butter, but she found a box of old crackers at the back of a cupboard so she dined alone on that. As she ate she looked through the contents of Nelson's strange folder, reading the letter three times. The third time, she took out her smartphone and tried to cross-check its details online. Her Wi-Fi came from the reception room on the other side of the clearing, so the connection was slow and weak, but from what she could see the letter contained many plausible details.

She looked at the *Guardian* article again and thought of her grandfather.

When Fay was very young she had seen a picture of Christmas presents scattered in the wreckage of a plane. The plane hadn't caught fire so the presents were still in their colored wrappers, scattered across a snowfield among shreds of aluminum. It so happened that she had seen the photograph on the same day that she learned from her mother that her mother's father, until then a hypothetical figure, was a Canadian airman who'd been killed—or rather, he had disappeared—somewhere near the North Pole. After that, Fay sometimes thought of him at Christmas.

Sometimes, when she was sad or short of money, Alice would hug her daughter and tell her how different things would have been if she'd never left Canada. There was so much room over there, forests and mountains and lakes. Alice had run barefoot all summer with the other kids on the air force base. All winter long she had played in deep snow. Transported to County Down by her widowed mother, the twelve-year-old Alice didn't take to the dripping hedgerows and gray winter mud, the chapels and the churches. She had fled to London as soon as she could and made the most of its freedoms. One of them had turned into Fay.

Fay met Alice's mother Elizabeth only a few times, and only in London. She later guessed that these meetings had been kept secret from Elizabeth's brothers, who were unmarried, stern, and religious, and whom Fay met only once, on her first and only visit to their hometown of Banbridge.

There was a history of strokes in Alice's family. Elizabeth lay in a coffin in the front room of the house where she'd lived with her brothers. Her anxious face, which was so like Fay's own, was loosened in death. Fay, who was then very small, had kept watch at the door while Alice, who assumed she would be shut out of the will by her uncles, stole a last memento of her mother.

Alice chose a framed black-and-white photo that had been taken in that same Ulster parlor. It showed Elizabeth and her Canadian groom on the day they were married during the war. They stood at this very fireplace, the one over which the photograph was displayed: she in a sensible jacket and skirt, he in his number-one uniform. Her grandmother must have been pretty, Fay thought, but the rigid clothes and padded shoulders, the stiff, unnatural hair and the posing of the photograph made her face seem long and horse-like and much sterner than in life. The 1940s weren't kind to women's faces. Her new husband would have been older than she, already in his thirties, but he looked older still, as people did back then. He was stocky and clean-shaven, which always seemed odd to Fay. She thought of World War II pilots as languid men with pointy mustaches. Her grandfather didn't have the face of a warrior; his eyes had a shy, distracted look, as if he half wanted to be somewhere else. So, thought Fay, looking at the picture that her mother was stealing, that's the Christmas Man. It was the first time she'd ever laid eyes on Dead Santa.

The newlyweds held hands stiffly, as if under orders from the photographer. Behind them on the mantelpiece sat a little brass carriage clock, a beautiful instrument with spiky black numerals on a plain white face.

Flight Lieutenant Morgan had put it there early in the war in case he did not return from his submarine-hunting patrols. If I'd left it at Castle Archdale, he told the young Alice once, some bugger might have swiped it when they came to clean out my kit. When the war ended he took his pregnant wife back to Canada and the little clock went with them. Twelve years later, after Group Captain Morgan vanished, the clock returned to Banbridge with his widow and his child.

Fay had fallen in love with the clock at her first and only sight of it. She had picked it up to feel its clever weight, breathed on its brass to watch clouds form and sublimate. And Alice, seeing her daughter's disappointment when she chose to pinch the photo instead, had pointed to the clock's black-and-white image in the back of the photograph and said, look, this way we get to keep the clock too! She stuffed the photo in her handbag just as an angry tea tray rattled in the hall.

But here was the clock again, pictured over the news piece in the *Guardian*. Fay's uncles must have sold it as soon as Elizabeth was gone. Fay was quite sure it was the same clock: the photograph of her grandparents had hung on the wall over her mother's favorite armchair, where Alice sat up most days since her own stroke had crippled her. Fay, who nursed her mother herself, had seen it every day for twenty years.

The coincidence alone was shocking, and then there were all the questions that it raised. Had her grandfather known what his clock really was? And by what freak of chance had this mystery fallen into her lap on the ice road from Tuktoyaktuk? Was it really just coincidence, or was someone playing a trick? But no one could know who she was or why she had come here. Least of all someone like Nelson. But he did know, she supposed, where this supposed letter had come from. Which was something she wanted to know for herself.

More snow had fallen in the passes in the night, undoing the work of the graders, but to Nelson this no longer mattered. He had sat up late reading the papers on Bert's desk, and he thought he could see a solution at hand. The Englishwoman, Fay, seemed to be taking an interest. She had borrowed the Crozier file to read in her chalet. Now he was on his way to pick her up to drive her to the airport. But he knew from the radio that the storms in the south were still grounding all flights. She seemed to have had some college; as long as her exit was blocked he might enlist her to his search for meaning.

The weather was overcast, not as cold as it had been. His headlights revealed a rain of fine crystals, too small to call flakes or to see in the dark. They fell slant in a breeze that came off the mountains, sticking to the windshield where the wipers did not reach. The crystals grew larger. As he drove though the last pool of streetlight they were falling more slowly; by the time he reached Fay's lodgings it was snowing as it should. The flakes whirled in the breeze like a murmuration of starlings, billions of fleeting pixels that formed then dissolved dark trees by the road. Opening the car door, he heard the hiss of new snow brushing over old crust.

Ringnes had given Fay a chalet of her own, a log cabin on stilts on the edge of the clearing. Wooden steps led up to its porch. Her door had opened before he was halfway up the steps. She was fully dressed, with Bert's folder under her arm.

"I can take you to the airport," he said. "But I think that it's still closed."

She came down the steps, watching her feet in case she might slip. Reaching the ground, she looked up at him doubtfully. "It is," she said. "Mr. Ringnes just told me. Perhaps we can get some coffee, then have a look around the town."

They had breakfast in a café on the main street, sitting by the window where they could watch the cars. She ordered the biggest breakfast on the menu, with bacon and eggs and sausage and pancakes. And then he remembered that he had dropped her straight back to her chalet the night before, and that she had probably gone without dinner.

She ate her food absently, looking out the window. It was still snowing. Trucks and cars hissed past infrequently, announced by gold light that flared on the road. He saw her blink a couple of times, as if in disbelief. There were deep shadows under her eyes.

"You look like you've been awake all night." He nodded at the folder set beside her on the bench seat. "Did that file keep you up?" He had been waiting for her to mention it herself.

"Not really." She became interested in a piece of bacon. "It's jet lag, I suppose. I haven't been able to sleep since I left London."

"I've never had jet lag. I never went farther than the States, and I drove all the way . . . They say that after a day or two your body resets its clock by the sun."

"There is no sun here."

"There will be next week. But by then we'll both be gone."

The new snow had forgiven the town for most of its flaws. It settled on roofs, on service lots, on Dumpsters and highway signs. It clung to the roof of the igloo-shaped church, waiting for the first breath of wind to send it sliding to the ground, and it powdered the pavement, crunching underfoot as they walked to the car. Nelson drove slowly around the small grid of streets, showing her what there was to see: the legion post, the police station, the stores and garages, the view out across the river where the ice road drove into the north.

"Let's go a bit farther," said Fay.

A gravel road ran a little way into the trees. Out there, thought Fay, just beyond those low hills, was the tree line, where North America turned into something else. But the tree line wasn't really a line; she had learned that on the ice road the day before. The trees had merely dwindled in size, wandered away from the river-bank, until somewhere between here and Tuktoyaktuk they had found themselves in the Barren Lands. She hadn't even noticed until it was too late. On the way back it had been too dark to see.

"I'm not quite sure," she said, "that the Crozier letter is fake."

"Yeah?" He drove slowly, absorbed in the landscape. The ground was lower here, perhaps prone to flooding, the spruces replaced by willows and birches bent under the snow. The road was a gray strip between them, torn from the vacant gray sky. "You said last night that nobody ever found any word of those ships."

"That's what I thought . . ." Did she need to tell him about her grandfather, or his chronometer? No, she did not. "I looked it up on my phone in the chalet. No written record was ever found from that expedition, apart from one short note that didn't say much."

"So then the Crozier letter can't be real."

"You would think so. But I read it several times and I checked the details as well as I could. If that letter is a fiction it's a pretty good one. This Crozier had been deputy commander of the first voyage of exploration by those two ships. It was a scientific voyage to Antarctica. When they got back to England the government decided to send the ships out again to try and find the Northwest Passage. Crozier was meant to lead this second expedition. But then Sir John Franklin, who was senior to him in the navy, took the job instead. He'd been sacked as governor of Tasmania and wanted to restore his reputation. So Crozier had to sail as his number two. To make things worse, Crozier had also had a proposal refused by Franklin's niece. She's also mentioned in that letter."

"It ties in, then."

"It does. But I can't work out why there's no mention of a letter like this anywhere on the Internet. It would have caused a sensation."

"Where do you think Bert got it?"

"I was going to ask you that. What did your brother do for a living?"

If he thought about it honestly, Nelson had never been sure. But he had to give her something. "Bert came up here a while back to teach in the local high school. But he hadn't started yet. He's due to begin next semester."

"A teacher? That's all?"

"He wasn't always a teacher. At least, not a high school teacher. He used to be a college professor and do research and stuff. He did work for the government. He had a PhD from McGill."

"In what?"

"He was a geographer." He seemed to expect her to find this funny. "Apparently that's still a thing. You'd think they'd be done with that by now, right?"

"Did he have access to any special archives?"

"I wouldn't know. If the letter is real, why is it written in his own handwriting? Why didn't he just make a photocopy or whatever of the original?"

"I was thinking about that last night, when I couldn't sleep, and after a while I had an idea."

On the right, a lane through the trees led to a mesh of poles and wires standing in a glade. "That's for the northern lights," said Nelson. "Some kind of detector. So what was your idea?"

"Well . . . I don't know much about the Canadian government archives." Apart, that is, from all that she had learned about archives while studying for her library degree, and in her recent search for her grandfather's lost service record. But this, like the chronometer, was none of Nelson's business. "But I trained and worked as a librarian, and I can say for sure that this reference code on the folder isn't from the Ottawa archives. In fact, it doesn't make sense in terms of any of the existing international archival standards: no information about the material's date, author, description, or size."

The road narrowed as the willows closed in, finger-like twigs reaching clear of the snow. Fay was reminded of a trip she had once made to Lincolnshire in winter. The fens had been flooded and only the tips of the hedgerows, stark above the water, had guided their car through a fog.

"Meaning?"

"Meaning, he could have come across this letter in a public archive, but he's trying to disguise where he found it. Or else he has access to some other archive with its own system of filing that I don't know about. Either way, I can guess why he might have wanted to write it all out by hand rather than photocopy it. I suspect that he couldn't afford to have it copied."

"He had plenty of money. He'd always been well paid."

"No, what I mean is that he couldn't afford to get someone else to make the copy for him—it wouldn't have been private. In most archives, if you want something copied or scanned you have to fill out a form and get the librarians to do it for you, assuming permission is granted. But by doing that you leave a record of what you were looking at. Which is not a good idea if you've stumbled across something that you want to keep to yourself. Something very sensitive or secret."

"He could have used a spy camera. Saved himself a lot of writing."

"Was your brother a spy?" She was joking when she said it.

"Of course not . . . He wasn't a very practical man."

Not like you, she thought. But this nice car belongs to him, not you.

"I wonder," Fay said carefully, "if your brother had any more stuff like this letter. Stuff that could be a help in working out if the letter is genuine. Or if he was just making things up." She saw Nelson's face, and hurried on. "I mean, he could have been working on a novel or something."

They had come to the end of the road. It widened into a small clearing with a clump of willows in the middle. Ahead was a miniature forest of birches and willow twigs, some still wearing the dead leaves of summer. A track too narrow for their car, a firebreak or trapline, continued on north. Nelson drove slowly around the clump of willows until the car was facing back toward town. Then he stopped. The lights of Inuvik were hidden by a low rise in the land.

"I doubt very much that Bert was a writer." He looked at her. "What about you? What's your interest in this?"

She studied the willows, frowning. "Nothing really. I just thought I might help you. There's not much else to do until I can leave."

She waited for him to speak again. After a pause he did. "There's plenty more stuff like that letter. I can't read all of it."

No. That's not your thing, is it? Aloud she said, "It sounds like there's a lot of it."

"There sure is. And some of it's in French."

"I can read French. If I have to. With the help of on online translator. Why don't you let me take a look?"

Orkney, June 3, 1851

The little town of Stromness turns its back on the harbor from which it was born. Gray stone houses face a single long street, showing blind gables to the sea. Between the houses, narrow alleys sneak down to the private piers and slips that are hidden behind them, as if the sea were a family secret that everyone knows but no one acknowledges.

This arrangement confused Ensign Bellot the first time he saw it. It had been a lovely summer evening. The low green slopes of Orkney, the rugged hills of Hoy, were mirrored in the still waters of Stromness harbor as *Prince Albert*, Lady Franklin's private search vessel, picked up her moorings off Mr. Clouston's pier. Why, the young French volunteer wondered, would these houses shun such a beautiful view?

His answer had come the next day, and was repeated on every day since; for a week the Orkney Islands had been battered by southerly storms. Ensign Bellot had never been this far north before. He knew the Biscay gales of Rochefort-sur-Mer, his native home, and he had weathered a hurricane at sea during the Anglo-French raid on Madagascar. Such winds were intense but soon blew themselves out: he had not experienced the prolonged, cold, unwavering spite of a North Atlantic storm, the frigid, driving rain, the wind that jabbed and weaved from south to west for days at a time like a boxer seeking a weakness. It drove sheets of stinging spray off the sheltered harbor, stirred a short but angry slop that pounded the ship as she loaded her stores from the Hudson's Bay depot. Shivering on deck in a suit of borrowed oilskins, Bellot now knew why the town turned its back to the wind.

If it is like this here, he thought, in the middle of summer, how will it be in winter in the channels of the north? How will I cope with the Arctic dark and cold? He had won the Legion of Honor five years before, at the age of nineteen, shot in the thigh in the raid on Madagascar, but he was a sensitive young man, and a tendency to doubt his own worth had not been helped by his recent meetings in London.

John Barrow the younger, chief of mapping at the Admiralty, had looked down his nose at him. I can't think why Lady Franklin would appoint a French naval ensign as her cartographer. She could have her pick of the Royal Navy. And what does a Frenchman know about ice?

Colonel Sabine had made similar noises, as had Sir Francis Beaufort and the other British polar grandees whom Bellot tried to cultivate. But Lady Franklin knew her own mind better than Bellot knew himself: he would do for the north, she told him, and that was the end of it. So now here he was, waiting to sail off in search of her husband. If the storm would only slacken and release the windbound ship.

Prince Albert was not much bigger than a pleasure yacht, built for the Azores fruit trade, but now strengthened for the ice. Despite the late hour there were dockers still aboard her, using a tripod and boom to load her last stores. It had been left to Bellot, who slept aboard, to watch over them: most of the eighteen-strong officers and crew were Orkneymen, who would stay with their families until the last minute; their leader William Kennedy, although born in Saskatchewan, was the son of a Hudson's Bay trader who, like so many who worked for the Company, had been hired from Orkney: he too had been staying with family ashore. So when the workmen were done and Bellot went below, meaning to write in his new explorer's journal, he was surprised to hear voices behind the cabin door. He stood in the dark passage, taking off his oilskins, and after some hesitation decided to knock: he would like to go ashore if someone could relieve him; there was to be dancing tonight in Miss Robertson's parlor. Dancing was his secret joy.

The door swung open, leaking light into the passage. Captain Kennedy squinted in the darkness, adjusting his eyes.

"Yes?" Then he turned and called to someone within. "It's the boy from the post office. Were you wishing to send something?"

"I had not asked for him." It was the voice of a young woman. Bellot recognized Miss Cracroft, Lady Franklin's niece and companion. "You can send him away."

It's my lack of height, Bellot told himself, mortified. And my blue uniform jacket, and the shine of my gold buttons. He wished he had not knocked. "Excuse me," he managed. "It's me. Ensign Bellot."

There was an embarrassed silence and then Kennedy stepped back to let him in. "Ensign Bellot. I do apologize—I don't see well in the dark. Please come in."

Sophia Cracroft sat at the table under the skylight. She was facing the door. A lamp shone on the table, and Bellot could see she was still in her cloak, a cape of local manufacture, made of brown-and-green wool silvered with rain. The lamp made shadows of eyes that were, Bellot knew, almost as dark as his own. Kennedy too still wore his damp street clothes, the black suit and coat that often had strangers mistake him for a clergyman, as if his great piety were not enough. His black beard was beaded by rain or by spray.

They must have only just come aboard, Bellot thought, and yet I did not see them. Perhaps my back was turned.

"Good evening, Ensign Bellot." Miss Cracroft tried to stand up, but she was as tall as the cabin was low. She made do with a half-bow over the table on which her hands were spread.

His eyes drawn downward in sympathy, Bellot noticed the paper held flat by her hands. It was a crude map, more like a child's drawing, showing islands and channels with handwritten names. His eyes, never good, struggled to focus in the light of the lamp. Near the middle of the map was a drawing of a boat—a tiny stick ship, as an infant would draw it, one-masted, flying a flag. Beside it, in firm childish letters, someone had written "A ship with no men in it."

Miss Cracroft saw where he was looking and lifted her hands from the table. Freed of their weight, the little map rolled itself up with a snap. She picked it up and placed it behind her.

"Forgive me," she said. "I had just come aboard to confer with Mr. Kennedy on a minor matter. Please ignore me. Or if you have private business I can wait up on deck."

"Not at all," said Bellot. "I was only wondering if I might go ashore for a spell. I have an engagement at Miss Robertson's house."

Kennedy, who normally stood a head taller than Bellot, had been brought to the same level as he stooped for the roof. Now he sank into a chair.

"Of course, my dear Bellot. By all means go ashore. I shall be here anyway. I have some work to do at my desk."

Taking his leave of them, Bellot went to the converted pantry that served as his cabin amidships (it is well you are small, Mr. Kennedy had said, when Bellot joined the crowded little ship at Aberdeen—we need only take out the pantry shelves and install a small cot for you). Closing the door, he lit a candle and fetched his journal from his chest. It was his plan to keep a plain and honest record of his daily adventures, ornamented with splashes of prose and philosophy, so that someday, God willing, he could make it into a book. If the book was successful—and his agent assured him that there was then a great shortage of French polar explorers on the literary market, and therefore a latent demand—it might provide him with the name and fortune that he would not inherit from his father, a hard-working blacksmith from Rochefort. He had been told he wrote very well. He need only put down a little each day.

But now, pen in hand, he had to ask himself: What exactly had happened today? He had eaten breakfast and lunch, and watched the ship being loaded. He had walked the narrow street of Stromness and tipped his hat to passers-by. He had gone below and heard voices in the cabin . . . Perhaps, he thought, I should write about that strange business with the map. Leave nothing out, that's what he'd promised himself.

But it was late, and there would be dancing in Miss Robertson's parlor. He could write up his journal tomorrow. By the look of the weather there'd be nothing else to do. So he put on his best trousers, swapped his seaboots for shoes, wiped the salt off his buttons, and put his hat under his arm. Passing the cabin, he heard the murmur of several more voices.

Bellot danced that night with the cleverest girls of Stromness, stepping to a fiddle in Miss Robertson's house. He taught them the schottische, already a favorite in France yet unknown in Orkney. They reeled and jigged and clapped and formed fours, whirling sparks in the dance of the candles. They were lovely, the glowing daughters of the manses and farms and the Hudson Bay factors, each one determined to claim her turn with the soft-eyed young sailor in his dashing French uniform, the hero bound for places where the Company dared not go. When a break in the music allowed him to ease his thirst—buttermilk, alas, was all that was served in an Orcadian parlor—he saw Miss Cracroft watching from inside the door, her cloak dark from the rain that drummed on the windows.

She must have come up from the ship, he thought. Perhaps she has come for me.

The bow sawed at the fiddle, a couple of strokes to make sure it was in tune. Bellot, gathering his courage, walked to the doorway and held out his hand. She was taller than him, and only a little older.

"Miss Cracroft. Will you honor me?" He knew he had stammered the "Cracroft," but he trusted his accent to lay a false trail.

She paused for a moment before she answered, as if she were considering his invitation. Then she smiled and shook her head. "You are very kind, monsieur. But I'm not one for dancing."

I ought to retreat now, he thought. But I'm halfway across this bullet-swept ground—there is as much risk from retreating as there is from charging on. And this conversation might never come again.

His smile hurt his face. "Then I must mistake you for another lady. On our passage here from Aberdeen old Mr. Hepburn spoke of a great ball that was held aboard *Terror* and *Erebus* ten years ago, when Hepburn was an official at Van Diemen's Land. He said that a Miss Sophia Cracroft led the dance with Captain Ross. She was the pride of the ball."

He waited, his hand still extended, feeling the blood rush to his face. But it is quite gloomy here, in this parlor without gaslight. I can always retreat under cover of darkness.

"You are not mistaken, Ensign Bellot—I was indeed another lady then. Since my uncle was lost I have had little time for dancing. Even so, I might be tempted tonight." She smiled at him, and he felt his heart leap. "But alas, I was sent here on business. Captain Kennedy has asked me to find you. He and Mr. Leask and Mr. Hepburn have just conferred with my aunt aboard the ship. Mr. Leask expects the wind to ease tonight, and if it does you will sail for Greenland tomorrow."

He no longer had any thought for dancing. So there had been a conference on the ship after he had left it. Lady Franklin had consulted with Mr. Kennedy, the expedition's leader; with Mr. Leask, the ice master; with Miss Cracroft, the expedition secretary; and even with Mr. Hepburn, the elderly volunteer who had given up a sinecure to look for his old friend. But Bellot himself, the expedition's only scientific navigator, had not been invited or informed.

"Well then," he said at last, "I will follow you over in a few minutes. I can't leave these kind ladies without saying good-bye."

He watched her leave. She had reached the door, had a hand raised to open it, when the fiddler abruptly launched into a tune. It was a reel of some kind, lilting and skipping, yet he felt it a little more sad, a little less jaunty, than the sturdy Scottish fare that had been served so far tonight. He saw Sophia's hand pause at the door latch, her frame frozen, as if listening, unable to move. So, he thought, she is not yet entirely lost to our world of dancing. Then she roused herself and was gone.

Baffin Bay, July 16, 1851

A day out of Upernavik, her last landfall in Greenland, *Prince Albert* entered the ice. Leask, the ice master, steered her into a lead of open water between two drifting bergs, translucent castles of white and blue that were buttressed and arched and crenellated, polished by cascading meltwaters.

The ship drove on with a fair breeze behind her, seeking the North Water passage to Lancaster Sound. Dovekies and gulls wheeled and cried through her topmasts, hoping the ship was a sealer with slaughter in mind. But the seals on the pack ice, wary of potshots, slipped into the water before she drew near.

Bellot, as was often his habit, stayed on deck when his own watch had ended. The evening was cool but not cuttingly so. Summer was ending in the high Arctic and everywhere he looked life hurried to conclude its business for yet another year. Flocks of purposeful seabirds—fulmars, guillemots, Arctic terns, auks—flew back to their roosts on the skerries and cliffs of the Upernavik Islands. Higher up, chevrons of brent geese arrowed into the south. Flurries of eiders and petrels skimmed low on the water, making patters of spray where the sprats swam too close to the sun. Once, looking over the side, Bellot saw a party of white ghosts gliding under the ship—belugas or narwhals, they were too deep for him to tell—diving from one open pool to another. Probing ever westward, maneuvering with foresails and ice-poles, the little ship threaded through loose cakes of sea ice. The floes moved ponderously northward in the West Greenland Current, bearing on their backs the rubble of other, smaller floes that they had conquered on their tour of Baffin Bay. Bellot, watching them recede from the deck of *Prince Albert*, longed to understand their cold and lonely progress.

The sun did not set but only dipped to the horizon, burning red above the ice, yet the sky was now dark enough for Venus to make her first appearance of the year. Soon the stars and aurora would join her. Bellot waited until he could barely keep his eyes open, then went below to his cabin in the pantry.

Sometime later—there was no light or window, so how could he be sure?—he was woken by giant claws scraping both sides of the ship. He had heard that noise before, when *Berceau* had grounded in the Madagascar campaign. But he knew it meant something different up here: he had been waiting a long time to hear it. Instead of rushing on deck he lay there and listened. He had better get used to it. Timbers groaned and heaved the whole length of the ship, which shuddered and lurched and came to a halt. When he went on deck the lead had vanished, the pack had closed, and *the ship* was alone in a desert of ice.

Prince Albert had been caught in the pack for more than a week when two strange brigs were sighted on the northern horizon. At intervals the topsails of these ships were seen to billow and set to a breeze that did not stir *Prince Albert*. Their topmasts heeled and slowly grew taller, then their mainsails appeared in the glass of Bellot's telescope. The brigs had found both water and wind and were working their way slowly south to *Prince Albert*. By the morning of the second day, when Bellot came on watch, they were only three miles away, jammed into the same close pack that held *Prince Albert* in its grip. They both hoisted their ensigns: two bursts of stars and stripes. Then two little dots detached themselves and crossed the ice toward his ship.

The leader of this pair of visitors—and the smaller of the two—was not much older than Bellot himself and not an inch taller. He was dressed in a plain sailor's peacoat and a hat and boots of Eskimo sealskin, and he had a large leather satchel strapped to his back. Reaching the *Prince Albert*, the stranger scrambled nimbly up the side, threw one leg across the gunwale and then stopped, his grin frozen on his face, looking confusedly about the deck.

"Where is Mr. Snow?" he demanded. "Where is Captain Forsyth?"

Captain Kennedy was a tall man with a dark beard and a wide, honest brow. Although dressed in plain seafaring clothes his authority could not easily have been mistaken, standing as he did alone on the quarterdeck. But he took the impertinence in good part.

"I am William Kennedy. I command this vessel with my ice master, Mr. Leask—" he indicated the old Orkney whaler who stood by the wheel—"and also Ensign Bellot, my deputy, seconded from the French Navy."

Bellot, the sole naval officer among this crew of whalers and sealers and Hudson Bay veterans, was the only one to bow.

Still the stranger did not move, his foot comically cocked just clear of the deck. It was as if, having picked his way across three miles of shifting sea ice, he was unwilling to trust his weight to anything so unsubstantial as a ship.

"But this *is* the *Prince Albert*," the stranger insisted. "I visited aboard her last year. She came to our rescue when we grounded in Lancaster Sound. She is the private search yacht of Lady Franklin. Her commander is Captain Forsyth of the Royal Navy, with Mr. Parker Snow as his mate."

He shook his head, like a man detained in a dream. Beneath him, still standing on the ice, his companion shifted about to keep warm. He was also quite young, but wore an old man's fierce whiskers. The gold buttons on his peacoat showed that he was, like Bellot, a naval deck officer.

"You are correct about the ship," said Mr. Kennedy affably, "but not about the men. Captain Forsyth and Mr. Snow were replaced after they returned the ship to England prematurely last fall. Lady Franklin has sent us out in their place to continue the search."

"Ah." The stranger digested this information. "Then you are coming, not going. When I saw *Prince Albert* again I thought she might have been caught, like us, for a second winter in the ice."

"As to whether we are coming or going," said Mr. Kennedy, "I hardly know myself, thanks to the drift of the floes. But we are six weeks out of Stromness in Lady Franklin's service, searching for her husband and the men of *Erebus* and *Terror*. And may I ask, sir, who are you?"

The stranger, recollecting himself, stepped down on the deck and gave Kennedy his hand.

"Please excuse me. But one forgets one's manners after a winter up here. I am Elisha Kent Kane, surgeon, United States Navy. This—" he indicated his friend, now climbing the ship's side— "is Mr. William Murdaugh, passed midshipman and first officer of the United States Ship *Advance*, which you see yonder with her consort, the *Rescue*. We too have been engaged in the search for Sir John Franklin. We sail under the command of Lieutenant Edwin de Haven, United States Navy."

To Bellot, a change seemed to come over Mr. Kennedy's normally open face, as if his Canadian friend had heard some delicate matter mentioned and wanted to hush it away.

"Dr. Kane," he said vaguely. "I have heard that name. You are Mr. Grinnell's friend, I recollect? And Mr. Snow's?"

Kane still held Kennedy's hand, but with a new watchfulness in his face and his bearing. "I am," he said, and looked quickly around the faces of the men of the *Prince Albert*, all nineteen of whom were now on the deck, eager for news from the fabulous labyrinth to the west. "Mr. Grinnell is the private sponsor of our mission. The United States government offered its men while Mr. Grinnell has provided the funds and the ships."

"I too am a friend of Mr. Grinnell. I stayed at his house in New York on my way to England to take up this present position—" Kennedy indicated the ship, the ice. "If you please, come to my cabin."

Bellot followed them to the companionway, as did Murdaugh and Leask, assuming the invitation applied to all the officers present. To his surprise, Kennedy stopped in the door after Kane had descended, barring any further entry.

"If you please, Ensign Bellot, be so kind as to show Mr. Murdaugh around our little ship. There have been several changes to her since he last boarded her. You may join us when I send for you."

He was gone. And Bellot was left to wonder, as he gave the young American a tour of the *Prince Albert*, what private business Mr. Kennedy could have with an obscure Yankee doctor— business from which Mr. Murdaugh, a sailing officer, who outranked any mere surgeon, was excluded.

The Americans brought sensational news. The summer before they had penetrated deep into the maze of channels that wriggles westward from Lancaster Sound. They had been caught in the ice, dragged up Wellington Channel then spat back into Baffin Bay. Their ships were sprung, leaking, and short of stores, their crews so mutinous that the officers went armed. But the summer before, at the western end of Lancaster Sound, the Americans had shared in a momentous discovery: the last known trace of Franklin's ships on the gravel strands of forlorn Beechey Island.

Their own landing party, along with those of several other search expeditions that chanced on the scene at the same time, had found the shore of Beechey Island littered with food tins and discarded naval gear, proving that British sailors had recently spent time there. The chance discovery—by Dr. Kane himself—of three graves on the beach, marked with the names of men of *Erebus* and *Terror* and dated winter 1845, confirmed the supposition: the Northwest Passage expedition had spent its first winter on Beechey Island before sailing on to its unknown end.

This was remarkable news: the ships had not vanished entirely. But where had they gone next? On this point the mystery only deepened. For although Sir John Franklin's men had built a stone message cairn on the crest of the island, marked with a cross to attract passing ships, when the searchers opened it they found not a word from *Erebus* and *Terror*. It seemed that, contrary to all accepted rules and custom of exploration, Sir John had omitted to leave a note of his intentions before he moved on.

An urgent dispatch for Lady Franklin was immediately fastened to the leg of *Prince Albert*'s best pigeon, the prodigious Sir John Ross, to be sped to the bird's native Ayrshire. Alas, the bewildered pigeon flew three times around the ship, landed on deck, and was eaten by a dog.

"And then," said Dr. Kane, "after I discovered the graves, I came across another mystery on Beechey Island. Erected above the beach on the eastern tip of the island was a second cairn, much the same size as the empty stone cairn on the cliff. Only this one was made not of stone but of empty food tins, some six or seven hundred of them, filled with gravel and arranged in a pyramid. And when I searched inside . . ."

He looked about him at the faces crowded around the table in the cabin of *Prince Albert*—Kennedy, Bellot, Leask, Murdaugh, and the American commander, Lieutenant de Haven, a gloomy, thickset man of about thirty-five. Nearest the door sat old John

Hepburn, Franklin's former seaman-servant, who had come as supercargo to search for his old friend.

"Inside?" prompted Bellot, impatient.

Kane was enjoying his moment of suspense. He took a sip of the strong tea, which—Mr. Kennedy being an abstainer—was all that was served aboard ship.

"Inside," he said, "this cairn proved just as empty as the first! It was beyond all explanation. I took it apart there and then, tin by tin, and found nothing inside it. Some other men then chanced on the scene, and together we dug into the tundra beneath the tin cairn until we met the frozen soil below. There was nothing. Nothing at all."

"When you say 'we,' Dr. Kane, I presume you mean the Americans of your *Advance* and *Rescue*?"

"Well, yes, Ensign Bellot . . . although there may well have been men of other ships present by then; by this time several different expeditions had also arrived at Beechey Island and sent parties ashore. They all appeared there, as if by magic, within the space of two days at the end of August last year."

"A remarkable coincidence," remarked Mr. Kennedy. "Unless we take it as a sign of guidance from a higher power."

"One might take it as such," said Dr. Kane, smiling, "but other explanations can also be found. The map will show you that Beechey Island lies at a crossroads for the high Arctic, where five great channels diverge from the Lancaster Sound—Prince Regent Inlet, Peel Sound, Wellington Channel, Barrow Strait, McDougall Sound. It also has a large harbor protected from the currents and the ice. Little wonder that Sir John and his men selected it for their first winter quarters.

"We ourselves came to the island in consort with *Felix*, a steam yacht under the private command of the famous Sir John Ross. With us also were the *Lady Franklin* and *Sophia*, both under the renowned whaling captain William Penny. Then the following day Captain Austin of the Royal Navy bought his *Resolute* and *Pioneer* into the harbor. His colleague Captain Ommanney, who had inspected the empty stone cairn on Beechey but missed the graves, was still only fifteen files away with the *Assistance* and *Intrepid*, detained in the ice of Barrow Strait. That makes nine ships, from five different expeditions, all in the same anchorage or its immediate neighborhood. And your own *Prince Albert*, then under Captain Forsyth, cannot have been far away."

Now old Hepburn spoke, which was a rare enough occurrence. He talked with the precise, spidery accent of his Scottish boyhood, a manner of speaking that allowed him—although by birth a cowherd—to sound when he wished like an Edinburgh lawyer, one whose statements take the form of carefully barbed questions.

"When you say that nothing was found on the island, Dr. Kane, no written note or record, you can only speak for yourself. There must have been many sailors roaming ashore on those days in late August. And there is, I believe, twenty thousand pound offered for the men who rescue Sir John Franklin, or discover his fate." He let his meaning sink in, then continued: "Captain Ommanney and his men were alone when they inspected the stone cairn and found it empty?"

Poor Bellot, shocked at Hepburn's suggestion, could only turn and look at Kane, hoping to hear him refute it.

But Kane was silent for a while, tapping his fingers on the table. "This is true, Mr. Hepburn," he said at last, "as far as the general run of the island is concerned. But as for Captain Ommanney, I do not believe that an officer of the Royal Navy would do such a thing. In any case, he was not alone when the stone cairn on the cliff was inspected. The master of our own consort the USS *Rescue*, Mr. Griffin, was present when the stones were removed."

"And you are as sure," said Hepburn quietly, "of all the men of your American ships?"

"I am as sure of that," replied Dr. Kane, "as I am sure of the honesty of my own dear fiancée back home in Philadelphia."

"Well then," said Bellot stoutly, looking from one man to another, "we need say no more of that."

"What a miracle," said Mr. Kennedy, who had seemed distracted while all this went on, gazing up at the soft white glow in the skylight. "What a miracle, that so many ships and men should have been present last year, brought together in that extreme desolation, to bear witness when such a discovery was made. It passeth all understanding, except that we trust in the ways of the Lord. Let us pray now, gentlemen, that He will continue to guide us, and lead us through this icy maze, that we may succor our brothers who have commended themselves into His hands . . . And let that prayer be our grace before eating as well, for supper is about to be served."

"Amen," said all, and bowed their heads.

Prince Albert had killed her last sheep for this special occasion. The allure of fresh mutton, combined with the news from Beechey Island (and the absence of wine from the menu), made for a silent and thoughtful mood at table. Little more was said until the meal was over and Mr. Leask proposed—as Mr. Kennedy abstained also from tobacco—to go on deck to smoke a pipe. There followed a general exit from the cabin, with only Dr. Kane and Mr. Kennedy—who had hinted at a private medical concern—remaining together below.

The evening was clear and windless, the air almost mild. The officers lounged amidships, looking across a wasteland of pack to the stark peaks of Greenland. The mountains swam on a haze above the sea ice. Above and beyond them gleamed the dome of the ice cap, also floating in blue air. The sun, now nearing the horizon, wore a halo that was set, at its cardinal points, with smaller, sharper copies of itself.

"It is very beautiful," Bellot said, waving his hand at the shimmering peaks, the geometric wonder of the gleaming parhelia.

"All these tricks of the polar light. I wonder if one could ever grow tired of them."

Lieutenant de Haven, to whom he had addressed the remark, puffed his pipe a couple of times in quick succession, as if getting up steam. Then he spat over the side.

"They're beautiful, alright. But treacherous too."

Young Mr. Murdaugh, who seemed relieved to hear the silence broken, now joined in the conversation. "It's all very well on a clear day," he told Bellot, "when the sun throws plain shadows and shows you the horizon and which way is up. But an overcast sky can play painful tricks. If you are crossing fast ice or an open snow-field you may think you are setting foot on a hillock then step into a hole instead. You hop down from a little hummock and fall ten feet onto your face. You lose your bearings and all sense of distance, then see a friend across the way, large as life, waving his arms at you. But when you approach him he turns into a bird and flies away, leaving you more lost than ever. In a fog or a blizzard it is all too easy to wander and die."

It was Lieutenant de Haven who next spoke. To Bellot, watching the pensive, wondering look on his face, the American seemed to be talking as much to himself as anyone present.

"The light has its tricks, and so does the perception, and I am not scientist enough to swear that there is not some other prankster at work in the polar latitudes." He waved at the mountains to the east. "These are the mountains of western Greenland. The Vikings knew them a thousand years ago. It is two hundred years since this coast was charted by whalers, and we know from our navigational science exactly where we lie in relation to it. These mountains are known to us. They are real."

Still no one else spoke. Bellot saw Kennedy and Kane come out of the cabin, discussing a little wooden case that Kane was showing Kennedy. The case's hinged glass lid, together with a glimpse of a round white dial, revealed the object to be a commonplace marine chronometer. Seeing how rapt the other men were, the newcomers fell silent as they joined them, and Kane stowed the clock inside his leather satchel. De Haven paid no heed to their arrival.

"Before I ever came to Baffin Bay I knew what I would find from looking at the maps. And I had already seen these mountains." After a pause he went on: "Or rather, mountains just like them. Their mirror image, in fact, because I saw them at the antipode to where we lie now, on the exact opposite end of the planet." His face moved as he sorted his memories into words. "Ten years ago I was a midshipman with the United States South Seas Exploring Expedition. Pressing deep into the Antarctic pack we saw new lands to the south of us, a range of high mountains and glaciers and bays. I stood beside my commander, Lieutenant Wilkes, and wrote down the bearings he took with his instruments, transcribing the new coast onto our map. The yards and ratlines of *Vincennes* were lined with staring sailors. And every man aboard, including myself, would have sworn on the Book that our new lands were as real as any landfall we made in our circumnavigation, as real as Madeira, Tierra del Fuego, the Sandwich Islands, the Heads of Port Jackson, or the bay of San Francisco."

He stopped again, to knock out his pipe over the side of the ship. And Bellot understood why the others stayed silent. The scandal of Wilkes was generally known.

Lieutenant de Haven turned back to his listeners, whose gazes—all except for that of young Bellot—were now averted.

"A few weeks after we mapped that new coast Commander Crozier of the Royal Navy—" he nodded to the west—"who is now himself missing in the ice, sailed HMS *Terror* through that very same spot, at sixty-six degrees south, one-sixty-five east. He saw there only open waters. His six-hundred-fathom line could find no bottom. There was no new continent there, not even an island or shoal. Alas, this news did not reach Washington until long after we ourselves did, and by then Wilkes's new coast, claimed for the United States, was already printed on our maps." De Haven spat over the side. "Many of our Washington politicians, who hated Wilkes almost as much as he despised them, tried to turn his error into a fraud. It greatly damaged his career and those of his officers. That is why I volunteered for this mission. It is not for any great love of the ice."

He leaned back against the gunwale and folded his arms. It was Kennedy who broke the heavy silence.

"I have seen a few such phantoms myself in the Bay service, and heard of many others. When I first shipped to Orkney as a boy, to be schooled at Saint Margaret's Hope, an old sailor swore to me he had once seen Hy-Brasil, the magic island west of Ireland from which no man has ever returned."

"Once," said Dr. Kane, "when I was traveling though Italy, I saw the Fata Morgana. It appeared as a fabulous city of towers and arches looming over the Strait of Messina. I even saw people walk on its battlements. It is said to be a glimpse of lost Camelot."

They are trying to comfort de Haven, thought Bellot. They mean to be kind.

Old Leask cleared his throat. "We whalers have our own names for such will-o'-the-wisps. Sometimes in the Spitsbergen or Chilean fisheries you will spy on the horizon a mountain range or headland, but however long you steer for it and however fair your wind, it will always flee before you. We call it 'Cape Flyaway,' or 'the Coast of Cloud Land.'"

Bellot, seeing that Lieutenant de Haven still stared gloomily out to sea, decided to join in. "Such honest mistakes are easily explained. We know from science that they are caused by simple optics, by the reflection or refraction of light through atmospheric ice crystals or layers of air of different temperatures. I am sure it was a similar mirage that deceived Sir John Ross thirty years ago when he thought he saw mountains blocking Lancaster

Sound, and turned his ships early for home to the great hurt of his reputation."

"The fabulous Croker Mountains," said de Haven. "I sailed through their position twice last year and never noticed a thing."

No one replied to him. And in that silence Bellot was seized by a queer kind of vertigo, an inward spinning and trembling. He saw at last that this journey might prove treacherous in ways that he had not previously understood. Well, he would chart his islands carefully. He would check and recheck his instruments, take diligent temperatures and bearings, be doubly and trebly sure of his path by ship and boat and sledge. And he would resist in himself and in others that siren's lure of empty fame, the lust to have one's name attached to some cape or frozen sound. His journal would be his scientific Bible, his instruments his Redeemers. They would guide him through the dark.

London, 1853

Lieutenant de vaisseau Joseph René Bellot held his hands up to the bedroom mirror, inspecting the insignia of his new rank. There they were: three golden rings beneath a fouled anchor, bright on the ends of his sleeves. He had just taken delivery of a bespoke dress uniform: his unspent pay, backdated to his promotion in absentia the previous spring, when he'd still been wandering the Arctic behind a team of dying dogs, had covered the fees of a good London tailor. I am not overdoing it, he told the face in the mirror. It is not every day that a French officer is made a fellow of the Royal Geographical Society. I owe it to my country to show myself well.

But the face in the mirror (older now than its years, scarred badly by frostbite) would not let him off so easily. Your old uniform, it reminded him, was good enough for Queen Victoria last month. It was good enough for the Minister of the Marine in Paris, and for the Emperor himself. It would have been good enough for Sophia Cracroft, when she and Lady Franklin finally return from New York.

He turned away from the mirror and went over to the window. It was already dark outside his Islington lodgings, the gloom deepened by one of those ghastly London fogs. A boy in a messenger's uniform flitted through the globe of sick light that stifled a gas lamp; he vanished in the darkness at the front of the house.

Bellot heard the clack of the knocker, the sound of the front door. Perhaps it's for me. Perhaps . . . He pushed the thought away from him. It was not yet time to feel hollow; his latest wave of triumph still had not broken, and he must rehearse the words he would say tonight to the Royal Geographical, the extempore little speech—a touch bashful, perhaps a little halting, though in fact his English was very good—in which he would accept this humbling honor and give his own brief account of those terrible months on the ice. It was only a shame that Lady Franklin, and Miss Cracroft, would not be there.

He shut his eyes and leaned his head against the grimy window, hoping the cold would shock him out of his melancholic mood. It did not work, and he opened his eyes to see his own face in the window. Why, his eyes asked him, must you always second-guess your luck?

Footsteps came up the stairs from the hallway. They passed the sitting room on the first floor and the two suites of grand rooms off the second-floor landing. They continued past the goodish rooms on the third floor, where Kennedy would stay whenever he was in London. Now they took on a hollower tone, mounting the narrow, uncarpeted steps that led to the corridor under the eaves, that row of cheap little rooms, formerly servants' quarters, in the cheapest of which Bellot lodged alone.

He opened the door before the servant could knock. The houseboy stood with a lantern and a brown paper parcel, smiling obsequiously. He was only twelve or fourteen but his teeth were stained by tobacco and porter. "Package for you, sir. Heavy it is too, up all them stairs."

Bellot felt his heart sink within him. He knew what it was. He'd been told to expect it earlier in the week, but he had begun to hope that it wouldn't come at all. If he did not have to look at it then maybe it would not exist. Now here it was. He took the parcel reluctantly.

The houseboy stood his ground. "I had to tip the messenger, sir. He wouldn't leave it otherwise."

"Really? You had to pay the boy from Mr. Kennedy's publisher to do his own job?"

The porter did not so much as blink. "I gave him tuppence from my own pocket, sir. You can ask him if you like."

"Where is he?"

"I can go after him, sir. I saw which way he went."

Bellot gave up and handed him tuppence. He would soon have to swallow bigger ones than that.

He untied the string that fastened the parcel and took out a book smelling fresh from the press. *A Short Narrative of the Second Voyage of the "Prince Albert" in Search of Sir John Franklin. By William Kennedy.*

A note from the publisher asked him if perhaps he would be so kind, for Captain Kennedy's sake, as to bring the book with him to the Royal Geographical Society and mention it in his talk. The resulting publicity in the newspapers would be most welcome, especially since Mr. Kennedy was already en route to the Bering Strait in Lady Franklin's new ship, *Isabel*, and could do nothing to promote his book for himself. Compliments and thanks from Dalton Publishers, Cockspur Street, Trafalgar Square.

Trafalgar. That was a good one. And the book in his hands was not even from the deluxe edition, the leather-bound volumes with engravings and maps got up for rich subscribers. Instead, he had been given one of the cheap, mass-market hardbacks that would soon be in the shops. Its pages had already been cut for him, although he did not want or need to open it: he had already read the damned thing in proof.

He tossed the book on the bed and went back to the window. The fog had thickened so much that he could no longer see the street lamp, only its diseased glow.

The agony of snow-blindness. The screaming haze of exhaustion and scurvy. Whiteout fogs that dazzled and disoriented you until you felt so sick that you had to lie down in the snow and close your eyes so you wouldn't puke up the last of your pemmican. He remembered all this, but memory was merciful, so he could not say honestly that he remembered it well.

He stuck out his chin and addressed the window. "Your Royal Highness. My Lords and Ladies. Fellows and learned members of the Royal Geographical Society. Honored guests and gentlemen . . ."

Was that the right form? He would have to check with the secretary before he was introduced. He would have to write it down and memorize it. You knew where you were when you wrote it all down. Or so he'd used to think.

Kennedy's book lay on the bed behind him. He could see its candlelit reflection in the windowpane, a spectral projection on the swirling fog.

He was seized by a desperate hope. Perhaps he'd imagined the offending passages. Or perhaps Kennedy, a good man, a good friend, who surely was no liar, had realized his mistake and excised them before the proof went to press. Perhaps he'd seen sense at the last minute. Perhaps the crisis had melted away.

Bellot seized the book from the bed and desperately skimmed through it.

But it was still there, on page 131.

April 7, 1852: From a high hill near our encampment at this spot, we observed a broad channel running NNE and SSW, true (variation 140), which was at first taken for a continuation of Brentford Bay, until its great extent convinced us that we had fallen upon a western sea or channel, and that the passage we had just gone through was in reality a strait, leading out of Prince Regent Inlet. It appears on the map of our discoveries as Bellot Strait—a just tribute to the important services rendered to our Expedition by Lieutenant Bellot.

Their greatest and indeed only discovery: a new Northwest Passage, the northernmost shore of the American mainland.

Bellot's Strait.

But Bellot had walked with William Kennedy every step of that terrible journey, eleven hundred miles on foot behind a team of foundering dogs, blundering through flat uncharted waste-lands, lost, snow-blinded, starving, dazed by sleeplessness, thirst, and scurvy. And if there was one thing of which Bellot was sure, one thing on which his journal and his memory perfectly agreed, it was that he had seen no "Bellot Strait" between Somerset Land and Boothia, no new Northwest Passage at all, only a low isthmus and a large frozen lake.

But why would Kennedy insist on seeing something that was not there?

Bellot had searched through his journal to look for the answer. He had found only more questions.

Why, a week into their sledging trip, had Kennedy borrowed Bellot's private compass, then kept it for himself, even though he already had another?

Why had Kennedy insisted on minding their sledging chro-nometer himself—even though he was not qualified to use it—and then forgotten to wind it, causing it to stop?

Why, when Bellot was preparing to observe the lunar distances that would allow him to reset the chronometer—their only reli-able means of fixing their longitude west of Greenwich—had Kennedy accidentally knocked over and broken their artificial horizon? Why, on Kennedy's orders, had their mercury horizon and their magnetic dip circle been left on board the ship?

Bellot, the mapmaker and scientist, had been stripped of his tools one after the other until Kennedy was the uncontested guide of their sledging expedition. And Kennedy never even bothered writing a journal. He said he could keep it all in his head.

Working at night with frozen fingers, thawing the ink inside his clothes, Bellot had doggedly kept up his own journal, the book that he meant to publish one day to earn dowries for his beautiful, penniless sisters. But a journal meant nothing without angles and numbers to pin it to the map.

Now Kennedy had given Bellot's name to his greatest—his only—discovery and Bellot could not refute it. Instead, Bellot's reputation was tied to its existence. Why didn't he call it Kennedy Strait? Then perhaps I could denounce him.

And what, Bellot asked himself again, staring into that creeping London fog, do I really remember about those months on the ice?

He remembered Kennedy staring hopelessly at his compass, its needle swimming listlessly around the dial, after it had once again steered them in circles through fog and waist-deep snow. A compass was useless so close to the magnetic pole.

He remembered hills that were low islands and islands that might have been hills.

He remembered being too weak and thirsty to drill through ice for water, and trying to shoot holes in it with a musket instead. If the water was fresh they were crossing a lake. If not they were crossing the ocean.

He remembered bears and reindeer looming in the fog, not thirty yards away, and shooting and missing. Short rations and gnawing hunger. The black gums and stinking breath of scurvy. Healthy teeth that came out in your pemmican if you tried to eat it cold.

The exquisite agony of sleeplessness, the urge to lie down in the snow.

He remembered the terrible scene when they finally turned back. They were on the edge of a vast white plain stretching north and west to an obscure horizon. Tears were freezing in his lashes, and he was bawling at Kennedy that he was wrong, that this was not Prince of Wales Land but some undiscovered sea beyond it, that they must have wandered all the way across Peel Sound without even noticing it, and that they were now facing west and not south. Kennedy and his useless compass had led them far off their course. They would not reach King William Land. Not this year or the next.

I told you so, Bellot had shouted at Kennedy, while the starving dogs whined in their traces and the other exhausted men looked on. If we'd had the right instruments, if you hadn't broken them all, we'd have reached King William Land long before now. If Franklin was there we'd have found him, or signs of his ships. We'd have discharged our mission. Instead, we've achieved nothing at all.

The ships may yet be there, mumbled Kennedy, shamefaced, not meeting his eye, but I am sure that by now they are long since abandoned. And we haven't achieved nothing. We've confirmed the new strait's existence. It was exactly where I looked for it. It was where it was set on the child's map.

Bellot had turned away so the others could not see him weeping. "What strait? What child? What whore of a map?"

And so Kennedy had told him.

Derry City, Ireland, two years before

The front parlor of number 34 Strand Road in Londonderry was, like the "good rooms" of most Irish houses, a shrine to the family that lived hidden behind it. There, in a silence broken only by the ticking of the clock, reposed jugs and portraits and china and ornaments, parchments and heirlooms, brooding on their mantels or hanging from their nails. They abided there in solemn state, patiently awaiting the opening of the door, the timid approach of the maid who dusted and polished, or the firm tread of the high priest of this cult, master shipwright William Coppin, who came in once a week to wind and correct the family clock. And it was there, not two years before, that little Louise Coppin had been laid on her trestle, her hands clasped on her chest, dressed in her sister Ann's hand-me-down church clothes, having never—and she was now frozen for all eternity, her clock stopped forever at the tender age of four—been given a new dress of her own.

That sad event, as we say, had come to pass almost two years before this spring evening of 1851, and the scent of tuberoses had long since faded from the room. To Mr. William Kennedy, waiting alone on a couch by the window, the air smelled only of wax and metal polish. Yet the family clock, an ancient wooden upright with a yellowed ivory face, seemed to knock inside its case like a soul trapped in a coffin, a hollow, despairing, mechanical sound, until Kennedy, who was sensitive to such things, rose abruptly from the couch and took a walk around the room.

Here on a table by the wall was a model of Coppin's most famous design, the steamship *Great Northern*, the biggest screwship in the world on the day, nine years before, that she glided down his slipway and into the Foyle. Here were framed certificates from the London Board of Trade and the registrars of shipping. Here was a framed drawing of the first screw propeller, which Captain Coppin had championed, and whose patent he had disastrously failed to exploit. And here too, retaining Kennedy's interest the longest, was a portrait of the Coppin family, a calotype image dated two years before. This portrait, or *photograph*, showed Captain Coppin and his wife Dora with their five children, the four older children standing in front, the parents behind, with Mrs. Coppin holding her newborn in her arms. The older children stood with their hands limp by their sides, gazing hither and thither, some looking at the apparatus, some to one side, with the stupid, self-absorbed faces of those who did not yet understand that new form of magic called "drawing in light," who did not comprehend that in facing the lens they were facing eternity. Only one of them, the second youngest, a sturdy little girl in a dress that was too big for her, a child of perhaps four years, seemed to notice the camera's existence; she gazed into the lens with a frank curiosity and on her lips was the trace of a smile.

Mr. Kennedy remembered his strange mission, the letter in his pocket. Louise, he thought. Little Weesy. It must be her. And he, being also unused to photography, gazed with wonder and grief at the face of a child returned from the grave. His eyes welled with tears.

There were loud steps in the hallway, and Kennedy had just time to steady himself before the door opened. Captain Coppin, an old friend from the Canada coasting trade, was the first to come in, his frown hidden in his beard, his beard buried in his frock coat. He was speaking impatiently to someone behind him.

"Come, child," he said, "we have kept Mr. Kennedy waiting long enough." Then, as if pushed from behind, little Ann Coppin, the girl he had traveled from London to interview, came hurrying after her father. Last to enter was the girl's aunt, Miss Smith, who—her sister Mrs. Coppin being again indisposed—was supplying the place of a mother. She was a handsome woman, with a strong broad face and hair that was still brown, but her staring eyes had, for Kennedy, an unsettling intensity. He noticed it again now as she glanced around the room, as if searching in its corners for something he could not see.

"Come, Mr. Kennedy," said Coppin, who made an effort to smile at his friend. "Let us both sit and you may question the girl."

Ann Coppin was a thin child of about nine years of age with stiff red hair pulled back from her forehead and pale white skin through which veins showed like marble. Her eyes were green yet red-rimmed from crying, or want of sleep, or excess of nerves; they had a distracted, feverish look as they darted around the room. It is more than eighteen months since Louise died, thought Kennedy. Can her grief be still so fresh?

The child was introduced to Kennedy and made her curtsy, though she did not meet his eye. Then she stood there and waited, swaying from side to side with an almost imperceptible motion, as if intent on some distant, private music, her eyes turned to the carpet. Looking more closely, Captain Kennedy observed a faint smile on her lips—the same knowing smile he had seen on the face of her dead little sister in the portrait on the wall. Louise was the first, he understood: this one will be second. She is already halfway there. He turned his head for a moment, to steady his feelings, and saw the rags of gray cloud that tore past the window, the smoke from Coppin's shipyard across the Strand, the rain on the glass pane. They all move before the wind; they ought not to beat back against it. An immense sense of sorrow momentarily seized him, as if his soul were bared to the universe, as if he must feel compassion for every dead soul, every lost child, every grain of dust in all creation: as if he were God, all-knowing yet powerless.

Is this what the child knows? Is that the wind that sways her? He had a list of questions he had wanted to put to her about the letter that Captain Coppin had sent to Lady Franklin. He could dispense with most of them now.

"Do you still see her, Ann?" he asked softly. "Is your little sister Louise here in this room with us now?"

The girl looked up at him sharply, as if she had suddenly awoken to his presence. After a moment's pause she shook her head.

"No, sir. She is not here."

He nodded and smiled to encourage her. "If she were here now, in this room with us, would you be able to see her?"

She answered quite frankly, without affectation, as if she were merely settling some detail of her previous day's activity. "Sometimes I see her, sometimes I don't. But when she is here, even if I do not see her I would always feel she was present. So would the other children, sir. But only I would see her."

Her aunt, who stood behind her, spoke up. "We set a place at the table for Weesy every night, Captain. She sits between myself and little Ann."

Reluctantly, Kennedy gave Miss Smith his attention. He did not trust this woman's quiet exultation. "Have you seen her too, Miss Smith?"

"Oh no. I am not sensitive enough, alas. But I feel her presence. So do the other children, and Captain Coppin himself." Her brother-in-law moved in his chair and looked embarrassed, but kept his silence. "Little Willie is more sensitive than the rest of us, though less sensitive than Ann. Sometimes he glimpses Weesy as a ball of blue light and rushes over to embrace his little sister, who was his great darling. That is why he hits his head against the wall."

"I see." She was smiling tightly, though not at him or anyone else in the room. Her eyes looked past his shoulder at the gray sky and the rain. "So, you say that it is his grief for his sister that makes the child William harm himself?"

"Not grief, Mr. Kennedy, but love. Little Weesy is still with us. There is nothing for Willy to grieve."

Ann made a loud sigh and her aunt, interpreting the sound as an indication of agreement, patted the child's thin shoulder. Standing behind her niece, Miss Smith could not see the expression that flitted across the child's face, an eye-rolling grimace of scorn and impatience. But Kennedy saw it, and sank heavily back in his chair, stunned at the child's silent insolence, and more, at this glimpse of a secret knowingness, even a bitterness, far beyond the girl's years. He turned and looked at his friend, seeking confirmation that he had not imagined it, but Coppin was evidently in the grip of deep emotion and sat leaning forward with his face in his hands, his eyes covered and his shoulders stiff, as if his whole frame had been frozen in the act of a sob. When Kennedy turned back to the girl her face had resumed its previous serene expression. He watched her sway in her invisible wind.

"Do you know your letters, Ann? Can you read and write?"

She screwed up her face again, but this time it was with the innocent frown of a child. "I know the letters. But I am not good with them. Often when I write them they come out backward or wrong. I am behind my class at school and the teacher often beats me."

"You do not like your school, Ann?"

"No, sir. But of course I must go."

Her aunt spoke again. "She is a good child, Mr. Kennedy. She does her best at all her lessons and is very good at her sums. I always tell her that when her teachers oppress her or her classmates bully her that she must remind herself that God has given her another book to read, one that is beyond her tormentors' sight."

Kennedy waited until she was finished and then he spoke to the child. "And Louise," he said, "could she read and write?"

Miss Smith interrupted again. "Weesy was only four years old when she passed over, on the Whitsun before last. She had not started her letters. But she was a quick child and would have done well at lessons."

Glancing sideways, Kennedy saw that his friend remained stiff and silent, but he had pulled his hands halfway down his face, so that his eyes, dull and dry, stared at the far wall. How I wish, thought Kennedy, that poor Coppin were not here. But he addressed the child again.

"Little Weesy could not write, and you yourself have trouble reading. Yet the message you received was in the form of writing, appearing on the floor?"

"Yes, sir."

"And the map has several names on it. Were they in writing too?"

"Yes, sir."

"I see . . . Had you, or your little sister, seen any such maps, or read any accounts of the search for *Erebus* and *Terror*? I mean, before Louise passed on?"

"They had not," interrupted Miss Smith. "These were not matters to interest little girls."

"But there might have been newspapers lying about the drawing room, perhaps? Or perhaps they might have heard Captain Coppin discuss the missing expedition with his visitors? Seafaring men have spoken of little else these past three years."

Coppin stirred, and at last he spoke. His voice was hoarse and taut with feeling.

"No map such as ours ever appeared in a newspaper. It shows places and things that have never been charted. And I do not see why Little Weesy would deceive us now when she never told us a lie in her lifetime."

Again Captain Kennedy saw that look of scorn and disbelief flash across the face of little Ann, unobserved by anyone but he. It was a look he remembered from his own boyhood, the expression of a child who must endure hearing a rival wrongly praised. The look remained on the child's face even as Miss Smith, who could not see it, brushed her fingers lovingly on her niece's hair.

"Are you quite sure, Ann," said Kennedy, speaking very gently, and with as much delicacy as he could, "that it was Weesy who brought you these messages, and not some other source or power? Are you sure that it was she?"

The little girl stared back at him, now expressionless, for what seemed like many seconds. She does not blink, thought Kennedy, and began to feel uneasy. One moment she was a child, the next she was like an old woman made bitter by a lifetime of suffering. He tried again. "Are you sure it was little Louise, Ann?"

It was her aunt who broke the silence with a sudden cry of scorn. "Of course it was Louise, Mr. Kennedy! How can you doubt it? She was a dutiful child, and this is a good Christian household! To suggest anything else—"

"I have my duty to discharge, madam. I am sent by Lady Jane to question the child, and I must play devil's advocate."

Miss Smith clutched the child's shoulders so tightly her fingers dug into the flesh. Ann cried out and wriggled but she could not shake herself free of her aunt, who continued in a high, angry voice: "Playing devil's advocate? That is another name for lying. We are plain-speaking people here, Mr. Kennedy, and we say what we mean."

"Harriet," warned Captain Coppin, who had been recalled from his private misery by the sound of raised voices. But his sister-in-law ignored his interjection, glaring at their visitor. Two bright spots burned on her cheeks.

"We say what we mean, Mr. Kennedy, and we know in our hearts what is right. Dear little Weesy is always with us in this house. We feel her everywhere. She is with us all the time!"

Captain Coppin began to sob, the harsh, agonized convulsions of abject grief. Observing his friend's distress, Kennedy himself felt close to tears.

Miss Smith was shouting at the finish of her speech and its conclusion left a silence in the room. But this was quickly broken by a new sound, the wailing of the child. She buried her face in her hands and her knees began to give, until she was only supported by her aunt's hands on her shoulders. Tears ran onto her dress. Her aunt, calming enough to observe her distress, spun her little niece around and clasped her in her arms, patting her back and smoothing her hair, all the while glaring at Kennedy, whose mortification was now complete.

"There, there, little Annie," soothed Miss Smith, though the expression she showed Kennedy was one of contempt. "There is no need to grieve for little Weesy. She will never leave us."

And now of a sudden the child writhed in her aunt's arms, kicking and scratching, trying to break free of her grasp. Her face, pulled away from Miss Smith's bosom, was contorted with passion, though whether her emotion was grief or rage or terror Kennedy could not have said.

"Let me go!" screamed the child, in a voice so lost and so hollow that it made Kennedy's skin crawl. "Let go of me! You know nothing!"

She pulled a hand free and struck blindly at her aunt. And Miss Smith, injured and shaken, sank back against the wall with horror on her face. Little Ann, thus freed, took a step toward the door, looking wildly about her, and then all strength seemed to leave her and she fell to the floor and lay sobbing.

Kennedy was first to her aid; he picked her up in his arms and brought her over to a little sofa under a window. Captain Coppin rang for a maid to bring salts and water. But before the maid returned the child had stopped weeping as abruptly as she had begun. She sat up on the couch and smoothed down her skirts, and blew her nose in a handkerchief her father had given her. When she spoke her voice was quiet, although her eyes were still wide with shock or with terror and she seemed to stare through the wall where her aunt cowered.

"You are wrong, Aunty Harriet. Weesy is gone."

Miss Smith slumped onto the floor, a child herself again, her back to the wall, and began to weep noiselessly.

Kennedy took the child's hand but still she did not look at him. "Where has she gone?"

"Wherever they go." It was almost a whisper. "She is gone. I didn't tell my family, because it would upset them all so. But it is several weeks now since I have felt her in this house."

And then the child turned on her side on the couch, closed her eyes, and went to sleep.

It was now quite dark outside. Nevertheless, Kennedy suggested that he and his host might take a turn on the Strand to work up their appetite for dinner.

It was a cold night, and clear, with the stars hard above them. A mist rose from the low places and covered the river; it swallowed two ships moored in the narrows until only their masts protruded from the sheet of ghostly white. Across the Strand road, Coppin's shipyard was dark and silent, all lights extinguished in its offices and sheds. A fire burned near the wrought iron gate—the brazier that warmed the watchman huddled inside his hut.

The friends turned left along the shore, past the last scattered houses. Behind them the lights of the unconquered city burned on their hill, defying the darkness that bided in the north.

"I don't know how I missed you at the ship this afternoon," began Captain Coppin, but then, as if startled by the loudness of his voice, because they were already in the countryside, where anyone or no one might hear them, he checked himself and lowered his tone. "I cannot understand it. I was at the foot of the gangway when the first passenger came off the *Maiden City*."

"Perhaps," said Kennedy, "you were at the wrong gangway. I traveled second class."

His friend caught his sleeve and pulled him to a halt. "But my dear Kennedy, you should have told me in advance! I could easily have asked the North West of Ireland Union to take you gratis! It was I who built the *Maiden City* for them, you know."

Kennedy pressed his friend's shoulder. "It was not a question of expense. Lady Jane implored me to travel discreetly. My face is quite well-known, since she gave me command of her *Prince Albert*, and there are reporters who make it their business to watch ships arrive and to study the passenger lists. But they seldom bother with the second class."

Their heels, which had rung on the cobbles, fell silent, though they continued to stride side by side. Dark shapes loomed up on either hand, absences of starlight and of mist, and Kennedy guessed that their road had devolved into an unpaved country lane with hedges on each side of it.

Coppin spoke again. "Lady Jane has therefore abandoned her notion of seeking publicity? When I last met her, she talked of inviting Mr. Dickens, or Miss Cracroft's cousin Tennyson, to write an account to raise interest for her cause."

Kennedy chose his words carefully. "Lady Jane had become concerned . . . on the advice, I believe, of her niece Miss Cracroft . . . that news of her interest in the *events* here might well be misconstrued by elements in the press and the scientific establishment— and indeed the Church—in ways that might harm her reputation."

"I see." Coppin looked away, across the white sheet of fog that covered the Foyle. "I had thought she believed me. When I sent her my message she responded like one who is truly convinced."

"She does believe. But for the present we must be discreet."

"And what of you, William? Do you believe?"

Kennedy had met an old Innuit woman on Baffin Island who had drawn for him maps of islands and channels that neither she nor any of her tribe had ever visited. He had recently had the opportunity to compare some of these maps to the first scientific charts made by that prodigious overland traveler Dr. Rae, his fellow Orkneyman, and found them alike in almost every detail. But the Kirk had taught Kennedy that while there was only one God there were yet many demons; that God, having sent His son to complete His revelation, no longer had use for auguries and miracles, which must therefore be viewed in a sinister light, as the work of powers that are not of heaven.

He resolved to change the subject. "Your business is good? I heard you have five hundred men in your shipyard."

"I perhaps had that when I built the *Great Northern*, but that is nine years ago. The market has since passed us by—our river is too shallow for the big new designs. But I have other interests."

"Your marine inspectorate?"

"Yes, that. And I am also an agent for the Canada mails. But I find that lately I am most engrossed in the science of salvage. It has become my great passion."

Kennedy ventured to say that he had never known his friend to be without a passion, and that yet whenever they met, which was at intervals down the long years, he invariably found that this passion had changed.

"You are right," replied Coppin, turning away from the river. "But I am older now and settled, and I think that this particular hobbyhorse will see me out. Just think: all this great fuss and cost of designing and building new ships, yet as soon as they founder, even in inshore waters, we give them up for lost. Yet such ships can often be raised again and their hulls and cargoes saved."

"And is there profit in this salvage?"

"There is profit, of course, but more than that." Coppin stopped again. He put his hand on Kennedy's sleeve and stared soberly into his face, trying to see it through the gloom. "I do not do this for Sir John, or Captain Crozier, or the men of the *Terror* and *Erebus*. I do it for Weesy. I believe that she is with them, and that if they are found she will be at rest."

"Lady Jane believes," repeated Kennedy. "She has had other signs." He found himself lowering his voice and looking around him, though they were quite alone. "Mr. Parker Snow, who went as Forsyth's deputy on last year's voyage of the *Prince Albert*, also claims to have had visions of Sir John and his men near the magnetic pole. I met Parker Snow myself in New York, on my way to join Lady Franklin in England—he was at Mr. Grinnell's house when I stayed there.

"But Captain Forsyth is one of FitzRoy's followers in the navy—a rationalist and scientist. When Parker Snow let slip to him the basis for their mission, Forsyth declared that he had been sent on a fool's errand by mystics and charlatans. He then turned the ship for home. That is why Lady Jane has appointed me to lead this second voyage."

Coppin clasped his friend's hand. "Then Weesy's map will be your guide? You will confirm her information?"

"I am no navigator, William, nor a mapmaker. I've never been more than a Hudson's Bay trader. There is pressure from the Admiralty on Lady Jane to appoint another Royal Navy man as her cartographer and scientist. Instead, Lady Jane intends to recruit a young French officer who wrote to her out of the blue. After what happened with Captain Forsyth, she feels that an ardent young foreigner will be easier to steer."

Paris, 1854

Ministry of the Navy
Hôtel de la Marine
Rue Royale
Paris
October 14, 1854
at 2:35 p.m.

MEMORANDUM: MOST CONFIDENTIAL

My dear P.

The latest dispatch from the Admiralty in London, arrived this morning, informs us of the lamentable loss of Lieutenant Joseph René Bellot in the course of his second Arctic voyage with the British.

Having returned from his first voyage on Lady Franklin's *Prince Albert*, Lt Bellot had, as you will know, made interest in Paris to lead a purely French naval expedition to the Arctic. Failing in this objective, he then accepted a place as a volunteer on HMS *Phoenix*, which was resupplying a squadron of Royal Navy search vessels in the region of Lancaster Sound.

Alas, in the course of a sledging expedition young Bellot was carried away with two other men on a detached ice floe. The other two castaways, ordinary British seamen, were later recovered and furnished what details they could, though neither observed the moment of his demise. He walked away from the snowhouse they were building on the floe and was not seen again. He is therefore presumed to have gone through a crack in the ice.

The loss of so fine an officer at so young an age must be deeply regretted; though only twenty-seven, he had won the Legion of Honor at Tamatave and performed prodigious service on the *Prince Albert* two years ago. It is certain that the good lieutenant will enjoy a posthumous fame in France commensurate with his popularity in England, where they are already taking up a public subscription for a memorial to him at Greenwich.

Clearly the ministry will have to do something fine to commemorate such a gallant French officer. But matters of ceremony are for other officials: we in the intelligence department have other concerns now that Bellot has vanished.

News of his loss spread quickly through the department this morning, and it was scarcely an hour after I read the dispatch myself that M. Julien Lemer, a journalist and author, presented himself at my office. M. Lemer is a friend to our service, and happened to be in the building when he heard the news about Bellot, whom he counted as a friend. It is well that Lemer was here: from what he tells me, we will have to move quickly to prevent the lieutenant's death having a most damaging sequel.

The problem is this: on his *Prince Albert* voyage Lt Bellot started a journal in which he wrote frankly of all that he saw and did in the course of the expedition, and to which he confided his hopes, fears, and opinions. It was his intention to edit and shape this journal into a book that he could publish to further his cause and to earn him some money—he is from a very poor family, and has several siblings to provide for as well as his parents.

According to M. Lemer, whom Bellot engaged as his editor and agent, and whom he allowed to read the full journal, there are several passages and episodes therein that would cause great scandal and sensation were they to become publicly known.

Chief among these is Lt Bellot's belief that Lady Franklin was influenced by clairvoyants when she directed the *Prince Albert's* crew to search southward to King William Land, ignoring the advice of the Admiralty, whose searches are directed to the north. He also writes that M. Kennedy was influenced by a "spirit map" when he recorded a new Northwest Passage between Somerset Land and Boothia—a channel that Bellot (after whom Kennedy has named it Bellot Strait) himself denies having seen. It is for this reason, it seems, that Bellot was so keen to return to the north, to prove or disprove the existence of this phantom strait.

I need hardly say that any such public revelations, coming from the pen of a French officer whom the British had taken to their hearts, would be grievously damaging not only to Lady Franklin but also to our relations with the Royal Navy—and this at a time when we must make common cause against Russia in the Crimea.

Another of Lt Bellot's stated suspicions, that the American naval surgeon Elisha Kent Kane might have removed items from a message cairn built by Franklin's men on Beechey Island, would likely strain our relations with the United States.

Lemer says that Lt Bellot was aware of these considerations and—in the interests of his country and his service—intended to remove any sensitive passages before he published his journal. When he sailed north again on the *Phoenix* he left the journals in the keeping of his sisters in Rochefort, to be safe until he returned.

We now arrive at the heart of the matter: being recently in Rochefort, M. Lemer paid his respects to his friend's family and expressed a desire to see the journal so he could prepare samples to circulate among publishers to cultivate their interest. Instead, the sisters told him that their brother had decreed that the valuable journals should not be given into the keeping of any third party. They also believed that he intended them to publish the journals themselves should he fail to return from the Arctic. Now that Bellot is lost it is to be feared that the sisters will show the unedited journal around the newspapers and publishing houses of Paris. And that would put an end to all hope of discretion.

All may not yet be quite lost, however. M. Lemer believes that the sisters might yet be persuaded to entrust the journals to himself if they are assured that they will be indemnified against their possible loss. I therefore propose that we make immediate interest with the Imperial court to have a special pension granted to the late lieutenant's family, contingent on the sisters giving the journal into our keeping. This being done, I see no objection to subsequent publication once the appropriate adjustments have been made. The lieutenant enjoyed, it seems, not a little literary ability.

I have no doubt, my dear director, that you will see the merits of this plan, which would work to the benefit of all concerned. Thus the family might have its security while the deceased might enjoy a last tilt at glory. The public might have its hero, while M. Lemer might have the satisfaction of doing one last act of kindness for his friend, and doubtless also of earning an editor's fee (his service to our department is patriotic and unpaid). The Emperor, in stooping to raise up the distressed family of a decorated martyr, might worship again at the Bonaparte shrine of meritocracy. And we, my dear director, might quietly proceed with our humble daily duty, to preserve and protect our homeland from its foes and its heroes alike.

Please accept my kindest wishes,

R.

PART THREE
Joe Island

81°15′N 63°28′W

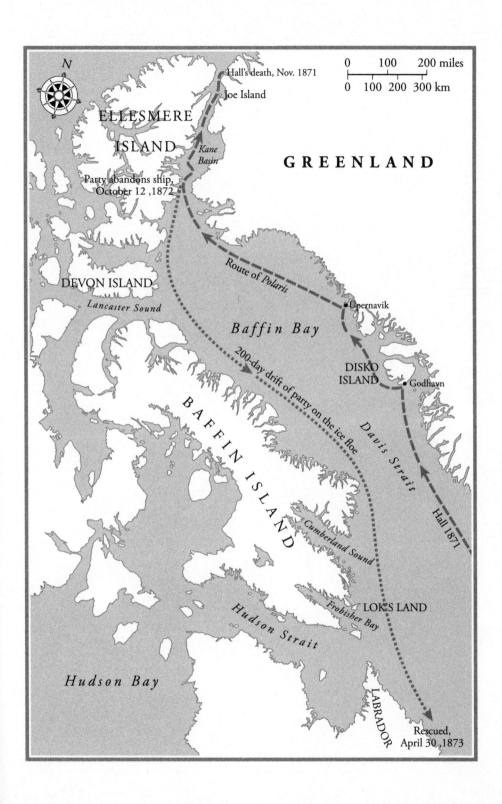

N

Hall's death, Nov. 1871

Joe Island

0   100   200 miles

0   100   200   300 km

ELLESMERE ISLAND

Kane Basin

GREENLAND

Party abandons ship, October 12, 1872

Route of *Polaris*

DEVON ISLAND

Lancaster Sound

Baffin Bay

•Upernavik

200-day drift of party on the ice floe

DISKO ISLAND

•Godhavn

BAFFIN ISLAND

Davis Strait

Cumberland Sound

Hall 1871

Frobisher Bay

LOKS LAND

Hudson Strait

Hudson Bay

LABRADOR

Rescued, April 30, 1873

Inuvik, Northwest Territories

Nelson opened his eyes and found himself lying fully clothed on the comforter of Bert's bed. The door was closed but the curtains were open. It was still night outside. Of course it was still night outside. He was still in Inuvik and it was still January. The parking lot lights still seeped through the curtains. Bert was still missing. But he'd seen him in his sleep again. They were back in Grande Prairie, at the Nite Owls ski slope, and he was trying to teach Bert to snowboard. You should have learned this when we were kids, he told Bert. But Bert just smiled sadly and looked away. Of course, we didn't call them snowboards back then, said Nelson. We called them Snurfers, remember? I'd have helped you learn if you'd let me. I'll help you now. It's easy. It's never too late.

He had meant that when he said it in his dream. But Bert wasn't listening. He had never learned to snowboard. Bert was scared of the kids who ran the spoonlift and the chairlift and who bullied him at school. Don't worry about them, insisted Nelson, and in his dream he tried to hug his big brother, who stood there stiffly, his arms by his sides, still looking away. I'll make sure those assholes don't mess with you. But he remembered, even now, when he was almost fully awake, how this had bothered him when he was dreaming it: why did he still have to take care of that business? Hadn't he done it already? Didn't Michael Rudenko have a scar on his eyebrow where Nelson had punched him?

Hadn't Nelson been blamed for starting that fight, one of several counts that, eventually, led to his expulsion? Did he have to do all this again? Would there ever be an end to it?

From where he lay he could see Bert's red Canada Goose parka hanging on the back of the door. He knew that Bert had worn that coat in Antarctica, because Bert had sent Nelson a photograph—a proper old-fashioned printed photograph—in a letter mailed from McMurdo Sound. When it reached Nelson's old place on Vancouver Island, the nice place that he'd once had with Donna, they had shown it to little Lizzie and said, "That's your Uncle Bert, the scientist. Look: he's at the South Pole!" It was the closest Lizzie ever came to meeting her uncle. She would be eight years old by now.

He wanted to go back into his dream again but it was already closed to him. All that was left was Bert's smile, the sad, patient smile of somebody who knows something that you don't, and a stupid dead word: "Snurfer."

There was a tapping sound beyond the bedroom door. Was that what had woken him? That's right: the Englishwoman, Fay, was out in the sitting room. She'd come back here to look at Bert's French-language folder; she had wanted to use Bert's computer to translate the words she didn't know. He had only meant to lie down for a minute, leaving her to it: how long had he slept? His phone was his clock, but it didn't connect to the eccentric old cell network they still had up here so he'd let the battery run down.

He got up and went over to the door. It was open a crack. Fay sat at the desk with the computer in front of her, hunched and staring at the screen. He watched her read for a while, then type some more, then read.

Her face was creased in pain and concentration. She still hasn't slept since she got here. If I throw open the door it might frighten her.

He retreated from the door, silent in his bare feet, then made a point of coughing noisily. The tapping stopped. He walked once around the room, stepping heavily, then opened the door.

"I guess I fell asleep," he said. "Want some coffee?"

She was standing by the desk, putting on her coat. She already had her boots on. He stared at her groggily. "What are you doing?"

"Who are you?"

"What?"

"I said, who are you?" Louder this time. She eased sideways past the desk, keeping her back to the wall. Nelson realized that she was inching for the door.

"I'm Nelson." It was all he could think of.

She slid another couple of feet along the wall. "Nelson. Your brother's surname is Nilsson. So you're Nelson Nilsson? Did your parents play a joke on you?"

My parents loved us both. You couldn't say that they didn't. "My surname is also Nilsson. People just call me Nelson. It stuck a long time ago."

"How do you know all these things about me?"

He saw that she was trembling. She was ready to run. Her eyes were red and staring. She was angry or terrified or both. Maybe, thought Nelson, it really was time to call in the cops.

"What things?" He took a step backward to try and take the pressure off her, like you would with an animal, and he felt the couch bump the back of his legs. "What am I doing? Just tell me."

She jabbed a finger at the desk. "How do you know about that?"

"What?"

"That note there. The one included with that French officer's journals."

"I can't read French."

"The note's in English."

I'd better humor her, he thought desperately. He picked it up and looked at it. It was another blue-lined page of his brother's handwriting. It read:

These documents were retrieved from the archives of Abwehr 1-M, German naval intelligence, by Squadron Leader Hugh Morgan RCAF, attached GHQ Liaison Unit Regiment (Phantom Signals). An element of Phantom entered Hamburg May 1, 1945, two days before the city's surrender, to retrieve Abwehr files on Operation Holzauge, the Weather War in Greenland. Included in the German file were these French documents, believed to have been seized by the Abwehr from the naval ministry at the Hôtel de la Marine, Paris, following the fall of France in 1940.

Nelson put it back where he had found it. "I don't know what that means and I've never seen it before in my life."

She ignored him. "How do you know about my grandfather?"

He was glad he had stayed on his feet. She was clearly quite nuts. "Your grandfather? What the hell are you talking about?"

She slid closer to the door. "Squadron Leader Hugh Morgan. His name is written right there at the end of those French journals. You must have put it there. Why are you pretending to be someone you're not?"

He was tired of this. Whatever was eating her, she could go when she liked. "And who am I pretending to be?"

She reached the door and stopped. "You're not Nelson. You're Bert Nilsson. The mad geography teacher. You're the one who's been making this whole thing up."

"That's a good one. How do you make that out?"

"Because I don't think a loser with a name like Nelson Nilsson would have the brains to cook up a story like this. I don't think he'd have even heard of Franklin or Crozier or Bellot. And

I don't think he'd have found a way to go online and work out who my grandfather was and write him into his batshit fantasy." She opened the door. The hallway was a blur of yellow light.

"I didn't write it," he said. And although his primary concern was, of course, the crazy lady in his apartment, he began to worry that something strange really might be going on. "And I'm not Bert. I'm Nelson."

"That police sergeant in Tuktoyaktuk didn't think so."

"He made a mistake."

"You're driving Bert Nilsson's car. You're living in his apart-ment. You have this story that's he's missing, but you're the only one who knows. I'm going back to my room now."

He rubbed his eyes vigorously. "I'll drive you, if you like."

"No, I don't like." She took off down the hall.

He followed her, stopping on the threshold. She was already halfway to the stairwell. This could end even worse than it seemed to be ending right now. "How are you going to get a taxi?" he called after her. "You don't have a phone. You can't just hail a cab here at . . ." What time was it anyway? He had no way to tell. "It must be thirty below out there. Let me call you a taxi."

She stopped by the door of the stairwell. He watched her think it over.

"Okay," she said. "I'll wait at the door of the flat while you call me a taxi. But I want to hear you give them this address and my name."

Is there any point, he wondered, in telling her that she's crazy, or that I'm not going to hurt her? He decided there was not. "Okay," he said. "Whatever you like."

He retreated back into the apartment as she came to the door. She watched him pick up the cordless landline phone that lay on the coffee table. "Put it on speaker," she said.

The taxi said it would be there in twenty minutes. It would call when it was outside. Nelson put the phone down and looked at her. "You can wait there," he said. "Or you can come in and sit down."

She sat on a chair by the door, perched on the edge of the cushion, her legs half turned under her, knees toward the door. She was ready to bolt.

"What time is it?" It was really just something for him to say.

She looked at her wristwatch. "It's ten past seven."

"Morning or night?"

"Jesus Christ. Give it up."

"I swear," he said, "I'm not messing with you. I don't know how long I slept. It's hard to keep track."

"It's night."

"Thanks . . ." He needed this to end on friendlier terms. He was afraid of what she might say about him. "You want to take some cigarettes with you?"

The idea seemed to appeal to her. But then she shook her head. The silence that followed seemed less fraught than before, so he decided to try again. "I don't know anything about your granddad. If his name is in those papers, it has nothing to do with me. I haven't read that French stuff."

"So you say." Her face grew pinched again. "You know what? I think I'll go and wait outside. That taxi won't be long now."

He sat where he was and watched her leave. I did my best, he thought. The door closed, a sound followed a few moments later by the swish of the spring-loaded door in the corridor. And then he remembered: she never paid me for those rides.

The chalet was so hot that Fay kicked the duvet to the foot of the bed where she lay. Then the air grew cooler and she pulled it back up again. She still couldn't sleep. She opened her eyes and stared at the knotty pine ceiling. The bedroom was lit by a bulb that shone through the door of the bathroom: she didn't want to lie in the dark.

The knots on the ceiling formed into patterns, constellations, that hinted at meanings that melted away again. I could count the knots, she thought, plank by plank, until I fall asleep. But now the knots were lakes, the million unnamed lakes of the circumpolar tundra, as futile a landscape as the surface of the moon. She let her eyes widen in horror, then noticed the edges of the planks themselves, parallel meridians stamped across the chaos. They reminded her of a different image, one she had found on the Internet in Nilsson/Nelson's flat while he slept: an aerial photograph, overlaid by a reticule grid, of the sea of craters made by Allied bombers on German lines in Normandy. A penciled arc, drawn across the bottom of the photograph, indicated the Bomb Line, the ne plus ultra traced on the map to prevent Allied planes and gunners from harming friendly forces. Beyond it, they could bomb and strafe and shell as they liked.

This particular Bomb Line, the caption noted, had been drawn by the unit responsible for mapping the shifting front line, a secret interservice organization known variously as Number 3 British Air Unit, GHQ Reconnaissance Unit, GHQ Liaison Unit, or—unofficially, from its radio call sign—as Phantom Signals.

Phantom's most famous member, Fay read, had been the Hollywood star David Niven. She knew of David Niven, but she had never before heard of Phantom Signals. She had no interest in such things. But earlier that evening, searching the Internet for clues about her grandfather, she had learned that Phantom was a picked group of scouts, linguists, radio operators, drivers, and code experts who probed ahead of the most advanced Allied units to find and fix the ever-shifting front. Wherever they found it, they drew the Bomb Line on the map.

Had her grandfather really been a part of something that dashing? She thought of the shy, slightly plump man in her mother's stolen photograph. He didn't look like David Niven. He didn't seem the type to rub burned cork on his face and slit someone's throat with a commando knife. She knew from her mum that he'd been some kind of boffin, that early in the war he'd been based in Northern Ireland hunting for submarines. That was how he'd met her grandmother. He'd been an expert on wireless and radar. Maybe his job was to fix Phantom's radios? Yet the note in Nilsson's folder suggested he'd done more than that: he had entered Nazi Hamburg before it even fell . . .

But that mention of her grandfather was beyond belief—a hand-written note on the end of a file that itself made little sense to her.

On the one hand, she knew that Bellot had been wrong about his strait's nonexistence—Fay could see it on the map above the desk, a thin blue line between Somerset Island and Boothia Peninsula. But on the other hand, he had been right about something even more fantastical—his allegations that a "spirit map" had secretly guided the expedition. According to an old academic paper she found on the Internet—"The Paranormal Arctic," by Ralph Lloyd-Jones—there was evidence that spiritualists really did persuade Lady Franklin to search for her husband at King William Island, where no one else had looked for him. Their map really did show a new secret strait where none had been charted—Bellot Strait. William Kennedy, the commander of Lady Franklin's ship, really had made a last-minute trip to Ireland to see the child who drew that map.

Strangest of all, six years later Captain Leopold McClintock had taken his *Fox* through the Bellot Strait, confirming its existence. That was written in the history books; it had really happened. Reaching King William Island, McClintock's sledge teams found a short message in a cairn at Point Victory—where little Ann Coppin had drawn the "ship with no men in it"—confirming the death of Sir John Franklin and the abandonment of the two ships. Bellot, the idealistic young rationalist, had rejected the strait's existence and scorned the advice of the spiritualists, yet he had been wrong on both counts. Then he himself had vanished . . .

It couldn't all be fake. And who would want to fake it, and why? To trick a random tourist who was only passing through?

She made the wood knots on the ceiling blur before her eyes, then set the blurs dancing with a flutter of her lids. She had binged on the web until, dazed by not enough sleep and too much information, she had barely known where she was.

Wood knot: *holzauge* in German. Operation Holzauge: the Weather War. With the outbreak of war Germany lost access to international meteorological reports. So it sent its own ships and submarines to transmit weather bulletins to guide its air and surface operations. But the British, homing in on their radio signals, quickly captured or sank them. So then the German navy conceived Operation Holzauge, which inserted secret teams of weathermen into the fjords of eastern Greenland to transmit weather reports for as long as they could. In time the Allies detected these transmissions too. One by one the German weather stations were located and put out of action. Her grandfather had somehow been involved in that too.

It made her head hurt to think of it: all afternoon she had looked for glimpses of Hugh Morgan on the World Wide Web, moving click by click away from her starting point until she no longer knew where she had been or how she had got where she was. What sequence of links had brought her to an obscure white supremacist site, no longer active, that talked of a legendary team of German weathermen who, knowing themselves detected, had fled into Greenland's ice cap interior? Legend had it they were still transmitting voice messages—long chains of numbers, some kind of unbreakable code—from somewhere in Peary Land when the war ended. Then they signed off and vanished forever.

What else had she seen or imagined on the Internet? She remembered an American militia officer called John Cleves Symmes who could scientifically prove that the earth was hollow, with openings at both poles. Symmes's disciples had won the support of Harvard

University, and persuaded Congress to fund Lieutenant Charles Wilkes's South Sea expedition, the US government's first scientific venture, with secret orders to look for "Symmes's Hole."

She had encountered the wealthy New York merchant and occultist Henry Grinnell, who acquired Wilkes's flag and passed it to Elisha Kent Kane, an American traveler and naval surgeon, who then took it far up the west coast of Greenland, farther north than any white man had ever gone before. Kane, she learned from a mouse-click, was by then secretly married to Margaret Fox, one of the famous Fox Sisters, who had been introduced to him by Henry Grinnell. The sisters' famous ability to speak with the dead had inspired the global belief in Spiritualism, a cult that did not fade even after Margaret confessed their productions were fake.

Now the knots in the ceiling melted together. They made Fay feel dizzy, as if she might faint. She narrowed her eyes and brought them back into focus.

Who was this Nelson? If he was not a dangerous creep and a liar, and perhaps even if he was, he was surely an artist in bullshit and time. He hadn't seemed dangerous. He only seemed sad.

She closed her eyes and listened to the night outside the chalet. The breeze had dropped away, but every now and then she heard a breath on the veranda and the hiss of drifting snow. The heater in the corner started ticking, which meant the thermostat had shut off for now, and that for a while the room would grow cooler. Fay stretched her arms and legs under the comforter, felt the clean cotton slide on her skin. And so, spread-eagled on her back, she closed her eyes and, to her own surprise, felt herself falling asleep. I mustn't think about sleep, she told herself: I'll only jinx it again. And then, like the last swirl of water sucked down a plughole, she disappeared.

After Fay left the apartment Nelson put on his coat and went out back for a cigarette. Bert didn't smoke, and Nelson didn't want to stink up his rooms.

At the back of the building was a concrete loading platform that stood by the service road for the underground car park. Concrete steps led down to the snow-covered tarmac. There was a bulb over the door, and the ice on the platform was dirty with ash and spent cigarettes. A chain-link fence gleamed in the light from the bulb. Beyond that was the forest. The cold air and nicotine drove the sleep from his head. All he could see, as he shivered and smoked, was the fence out back of the apartment block and the silent trees beyond it. But he could hear the seesaw noise of traffic on the road out front, people going about their lives.

He could plainly see the weak links in Fay's crazy story. How could she know for sure that this Hugh Morgan, whose mention in that file had so upset her, really was her grandfather? They shared a name, but Morgan was hardly uncommon. What's more, how did he himself know that Morgan really was her grandfather's name? She could have made that up. Maybe she'd even written that note herself, the note that she had tried to blame on him. He knew that he hadn't written it. When he examined the handwriting it appeared to be Bert's, like all the rest of it, but some people are good at forgery: she could have written it herself—he'd been asleep quite a while. And as far as he knew it was that note, and that alone, that linked Fay's own supposed family history to Bert's weird obsessions.

Nelson knew something about delusions. Toward the end of her life his mother had told her doctors—although not her own sons, whom she no longer trusted—that she was really Princess Anastasia, the missing daughter of the last czar of Russia, whose body couldn't be found after the Bolsheviks butchered the royal family.

This was, the doctor told Nelson and Bert, a surprisingly common delusion among troubled women. Nelson hadn't really understood the doctor's explanation, but he himself thought that it might have something to do with swapping sorrow for tragedy.

Tragedy would be kind of an upgrade. It, at least, could be said to have some sort of point.

Who are you? His mother had asked him that too, and then she stopped talking to him. She thought that he and Bert worked for the communists and she was terrified that they would kill her, the last of the Romanov princesses. Or even worse, that they would annihilate her story and force her back to her own life.

Who are you? He should have asked Fay that question. World War II. Lost explorers. What an interesting person she was in those yarns.

He remembered how he had found her, waiting alone in a deserted airport whose planes were all grounded. How long had she been sitting there? How long had it been since the last flight came in? Had she really flown in that day, or had she been haunting the place, waiting for someone to share in her madness? Had she been waiting for *him*?

But that was impossible. He'd missed his sign, his turnoff. Otherwise he would never have gone to the airport that evening, would never have met her at all. Then the storm had closed the passes. If it hadn't been for that random delay—two hours would have seen him past the boom at Fort McPherson—he would have left her in Inuvik, forgotten already. Right about now he'd be driving into Edmonton.

It was only coincidence that brought them together. He felt again, just for an instant, the stab of grief and loss that had staggered him, a few weeks after the death of his mother, when Russian scientists announced that Anastasia's DNA had been found in the ashes of her family. She had never been lost, would always be dead now. His mother too had once been a girl.

He made himself think of driving on a clear winter day in Alberta, distant sunlight through the birches on the banks of the Peace River. It was beautiful, it was black and white, it was thirty-five years ago, and it was still there before his eyes, but how could that highway still be an escape?

He foresaw himself buying gas in Dawson Creek so that he wouldn't have to stop in Grande Prairie, the town where he'd been fairly happy, he had thought, with his parents and his brother and his grandfather.

He saw himself driving Bert's Equinox and being randomly stopped by the cops.

There was no getting away from it. He'd have to talk to the Mounties before they talked to him. But he felt very tired. He would wait until tomorrow and then he'd go and see them. He had until then. Meantime, there were still several folders piled up on Bert's desk. He picked up the top-most. "Eskimo Joe" it said.

King William Island, Northwest Passage, 1903

My name is Ipiirviq, which was also the name of my father's brother who died just before I was born. He went hunting for seals on the edge of the ice and his dogs came back without him. When I was born the angakkuq examined me and said that Ipiirviq had returned to his family. I was given his name, and my father and mother called me their brother and my sisters called me their uncle. My uncle was a very good hunter, and so am I.

The English whalers called me Joe, though why they chose this name I don't know. In the Gospels Joseph was a kindly man who raised a child that wasn't his own. I too became a stepfather, but that was much later and the child didn't live.

When Captain Bowlby took Taqulittuq and I to England on his whaling ship he tried to call me by my Inuk name, but he could only say "Ebierbing," which I thought was close enough. Then when we were in England I became Joseph Ebierbing, because it was thought proper that I offer two names, like a white man, when we went to meet the Queen.

The Queen was named Victoria, like the island to the west of here that the Copper people call Kitlineq. She was very polite to me, but she spoke mostly to my wife Taqulittuq, who wore the fine clothes of an English lady, as handsome as any of them, and took her tea with the best English manners. I had to sit still and keep my mouth shut and watch what Taqulittuq did with the cups and the forks so that I wouldn't embarrass her. The Queen's husband was also there. He had to keep his mouth shut too, which I thought was rather funny. He caught my eye while the women were talking, all of us there in our stiff clothes and buttons, and it was all that the two of us could do not to laugh.

Taqulittuq was the only wife I ever had. We chose each other when we were little more than children in Cumberland Sound and I never shared her with another man. I remember our wedding in Captain Bowlby's house in Hull in England. They said we should be married by a Christian priest if we were going to be presented to the Queen as man and wife. We'd already been married with our own people in Cumberland Sound, but Taqulittuq was a great Christian when we were in England, and I thought to myself, what harm was there in another feast? After the prayers were said there was a wonderful dinner, with fresh beef and pork and mutton and cakes, as much as you could eat, and Mrs. Bowlby played the piano for us. Taqulittuq wore a blue silk dress that Mrs. Bowlby had given her, one that had belonged to her own daughter, and we danced a Scottish and other dances whose names I don't remember. There were many people there and all were kind to us. Taqulittuq amazed them with the grace of her dancing, but I wasn't surprised. I knew how well she had danced in our own country.

Taqulittuq had been known to the whalers in Cumberland Sound as Tookoolito, but in England, and later in America, people called her Hannah, which is a name she took for herself after reading the Bible. In the Bible, Hannah was a woman who couldn't have children, and prayed to God, and was eventually rewarded with a baby of her own. Taqulittuq also had much sorrow with children, and that is I believe why she started to pray to the Christian god when we were both in England. After we returned to

Cumberland Sound she kept many of her English dresses in a sea chest and would wear them when the whaling ships came. She made tea for the whalers and served it in china cups, and wouldn't allow them to use bad language in our house. Nor did she sleep with any of those who arrived on the whaling ships, not even Captain Hall.

Captain Charles Francis Hall was from Cincinnati in the United States. He first came to Cumberland Sound aboard the *George Henry*, a whaler of New London, with Captain Budington, who we knew from his previous voyages to our home. When we first went aboard his ship that summer, having ourselves come back from a journey up the coast, Captain Budington drew Taqulittuq aside and pointed to a man who stood on the deck by himself. He wore city clothes and had thick arms and legs and a very dark beard, and he stared across the deck at us as if he knew us from before.

Budington said that this man Hall was not a whaler but a traveler. He needed someone to interpret for him and to guide him, and if we agreed to work for him Hall would pay us well, having already read about our expedition to England. And so we agreed to help him. Captain Hall was not like the other white men who came to Cumberland Sound in the whaling ships. He didn't swear, seldom drank, and didn't try to sleep with the women. This made people suspicious of him, especially as he showed no interest in whales or in hunting, unlike the other white men in the ships.

It was easy for our people to understand why white men would come in search of whales, even if they took only the blubber and whalebone and threw the precious meat to the blind eqalussuaqs, the giant Greenland sharks, which became very numerous when the whaling ships were in the sound, moving like shadows under our kayaks. Like us, the whalers loved hunting and were happy when they succeeded. When opportunity afforded they abandoned all other activity to kill as many whales as they could, and when there was nothing else to do they rested and ate, as did we.

But Hall was an explorer who wanted to make new maps. To accomplish this, he needed always to travel quickly onward, and he was always angry whenever we natives broke our journey to hunt or fish and he was forced to stop with us until we had eaten our fill and rested and repaired our clothing and gear and cached whatever food was left over. He didn't understand that for us there was no reason to travel except to find better hunting, or that haste is very dangerous: when it is very cold, a person who sweats will soon freeze, and a person who wastes their strength will not easily regain it. But Hall was always in a hurry, always wanting to be somewhere else before the ice melted and made sledging impossible, or before the ice froze and stranded the boats.

Taqulittuq and I, unlike the others, had been to England and seen all the bustle and industry, and how people there were in so much of a hurry that they built railways and rivers that cut into the land. We therefore understood the curiosity that drove Hall to search for new places and put them on his map. I think that is why we became such friends with him. We even invited Hall to stay with us at our camp ashore, to learn to speak and travel like an Inuit himself, instead of wintering on the ship with the whalers.

Hall had brought with him several books with very old maps. One of these maps showed that the long inlet to the south of Cumberland Sound was really a strait, a shortcut through our island to the farther sea beyond it. Hall hoped that he could sail down this strait to reach Repulse Bay, which the people there call Naujaat, and thence make his way overland to King William Island many weeks away in the west. He was sure that on King William Island he would find news of Lord Franklin, the famous

English captain who had gone missing many years before. This was then his greatest goal.

Now, it was well known to us that the inlet in question was not a strait but a very long bay. So to spare Hall a wasted journey I brought him to see my grandmother, Ookijoxy Ninoo, who was famous for her stories of the old days and who could draw maps of all the islands for many weeks around. She talked with Hall and in time he became convinced of her truth. He was on the point of abandoning his plan to visit that inlet when she mentioned that long before her grandmother's time many white men had left piles of coal there amid the ruins of stone houses.

Hall became excited when he heard this. He said that my grandmother's account resembled a story told hundreds of years before by Martin Frobisher, an English captain. Frobisher had come to our country looking for a passage to another great sea to the west.

But Frobisher found gold in the inlet and instead of exploring he stopped to build mines. After much digging the gold was found to be a different metal, without any value, and they all sailed back to England, keeping the location of the inlet a secret: Frobisher had meant to return there one day and claim the secret passage for himself.

According to Hall's book, Frobisher had left messages and cairns on an island at the mouth of the strait that he had called Lok's Land. But when Hall asked my grandmother about that place she said that it was a very bad place and that he shouldn't go there. A strange tribe had once lived there, a people called the Tunits, who were cousins of our own people but older in their ways. One day in spring they all went onto the ice foot to celebrate a seal hunt and the tide broke the ice from the land and all the people were taken out to sea and never seen again. Since then our people wouldn't go to Lok's Land for fear of their ghosts.

Nevertheless, Hall took me aside and asked me if I would go there with him. Taqulittuq was away visiting her family and she wouldn't know that I had gone to Lok's Land, he said. Besides, there was nothing for Christians to fear from old stories. He told me that he would pay me well. And when I still didn't agree he made me another promise: that if I went with him to Lok's Land he would take Taqulittuq and I with him when he returned to America.

And at that I gave in to him, because I was restless. Since I'd come back from England I found I could no longer be happy just to travel to hunt, and to hunt only to eat, and to eat so I could rest, and to rest only to be able to travel again. In England I'd seen roads diverge from me in all directions and the trains rushing back and forth and the smoke from all the ships that docked in Hull and London. Where were they all going? I'd been told about Jesus, and that life was a journey from one thing to another. If I stayed at Cumberland Sound I would roam around the same shores all my life until one day I didn't come back from the hunt, or I grew sick and died, or else I grew too old to feed myself and, having no children to care for me, the young people might leave me alone in my last house. Perhaps if I'd had children then, if I could have seen their lives moving onward from my own, I might have answered Hall differently.

We set out for Lok's Land with two dog-sledges, accompanied by another man whose name was Koodloo. He'd been promised a rifled musket if he would come. It was June, never dark, and we traveled over smooth ice for a day and a night until we came to Lok's Land, where we found a little shingle beach on which to drag up the sledges. There were many bearded seals farther up the beach nursing new pups. These seals had never been hunted by men, and only tried to swim off when we were already within striking distance. Koodloo and I speared and clubbed so many cows and pups that the sea turned red. And then to add to our happiness a bear came around the point, attracted by the distress calls of the seals, and we brought it to bay with our dogs. I killed it with a single shot from my gun.

And it was only then, still hot from the pleasure of killing, that we paused to look around us and realized that Hall had disappeared. I saw the great slaughter that we had committed on the beach and an emptiness came into me and then a great fear. The seals looked like dead people—women and children washed up on the sand.

Koodloo too was filled with horror, and we debated what to do next. We wanted to leave at once, but we couldn't abandon Hall there. So we followed his trail up a steep rocky ridge until we came to the top of the island—rocks and old snow and the odd tuft of sedges shaking in the wind.

It wasn't long before we caught up with Hall. He was walking very slowly, casting from one side to another like a dog seeking a scent. Although we hailed him from a distance he didn't look at us until we were almost upon him.

Many seabirds nested on the island—gannets, terns, and gulls—and these attacked us as we walked, shrieking about our heads and striking our shoulders with their wings and their beaks. Koodloo was frightened. Although he was a famous bird-nester, who would creep down the sheerest cliff just to take a single gull's egg, he swore to me that he had never encountered an onslaught such as this.

At last the birds relented and we came to the far side of the island, where steep cliffs dropped into the open sea. There, perched on the edge of the cliff, we saw an odd heap of stones, the height of a man, made of slabs of flat rock piled up on one another. There were two large pieces sticking out from the sides so that it made the shape of a cross facing out to sea. Now Hall slowed his pace at the sight of this strange thing, which was surely man-made, and when I looked at his face I saw how intently he stared at it.

But of course it was only a heap of old stones, and when Koodloo and I ran toward it Hall shook off his strange mood and came after us. We walked around it a few times and when he was satisfied Hall said to us that we had made a great discovery, that this was a cairn that had been left by Frobisher as a sign to those who came after him, and that if we opened it up we would surely find a message from hundreds of years ago.

But it seemed to me that the stones were set together more loosely than the cairns built by white sailors, and when I moved around to the seaward side, to the edge of the cliff itself, the stones no longer resembled a cross but rather the figure of a human, arms outstretched to the sea. I thought of inuksuks, the stone statues built by our people as markers or decoys, and I remembered the story of the strangers who had all been taken by the ice. Or perhaps not all: someone had built this stone thing to mourn for them.

I told Hall that we had made a mistake in coming to Lok's Land, and it would be a much greater error still to tamper with these old stones. But he wouldn't listen to me. I stood apart and turned my back as Hall and Koodloo took the cairn apart stone by stone, setting the pieces around them in an ever-widening circle. There was nothing inside it—no paper, no metal, no cache of old food.

The waves crashed unseen in the mist at the foot of the cliff, hurling chunks of broken ice against the rocks. The gusts carried spray that froze on our sealskins.

I told Hall that we should rebuild the cairn so that it would look as it had before we disturbed it. But again he wouldn't listen: he was hungry and cold and very downcast at not having found any sign of his Frobisher. He wanted only to leave that place at once.

We went back to our sledges and drove off some bears that had been feeding on the dead seals. We could easily have killed some of them, but Koodloo and I had already got much more meat than we could carry away, so we butchered the dead bear and cut up several of the fatter seals and put the best meat on our sledges. Last of all, to propitiate the bear's spirit, we inflated its bladder and fixed it to a pole that we tied to my sledge.

When we neared our camp the people came running out to greet us, because they could see the bear's bladder and knew that there would be a feast. And before they could come up to us I turned to Koodloo and said something that had been on my mind for much of the journey. I told him that it would be as well if we didn't tell our friends where we had killed these seals, as there was a taboo on visiting Lok's Land and they might shun us or attack us for breaking the taboo. Nor should we tell them about the cairn, and what we had done to it, because surely it had been left there by the old ones who lived here before us. And then Koodloo was angry at me, saying I had led him first into breaking a taboo and now into a lie, and that both crimes would surely be punished.

Koodloo agreed to stay silent, but he was never friendly toward me again. In fact, he disappeared several weeks later, leaving his new rifle on his sledge. His dogs came back without him.

There was a feast that night and for several days afterward. When Taqulittuq came back from her journey she was very pleased with my success in the hunt and my good service to Hall. She told me that at last she was pregnant. After that, we spent much of our time in her tupik and Hall didn't disturb us.

Taqulittuq gave birth to Tukerliktu, our first son, while Hall was off exploring Frobisher Bay. When he returned he was very pleased because he had found many proofs that Martin Frobisher had been there lifetimes before. He was also delighted to see the healthy little boy carried in his mother's hood. He called him "Little Butterfly," which was the English for his name.

True to his promise, when he went back to New York, Hall took all three of us with him. There I was given another English name: "Eskimo Joe." That was what they wrote on the posters for Barnum's museum. Hall had asked us to attend lectures and circuses and stand in our sealskins with our harpoons and implements and also some dogs we brought from Baffin Island. People would pay to look at us and touch us and ask us questions. And although it was very hot in the summer in our sealskins, and although the dogs were sick because of the wrong food and the heat and the noise and made a horrible stink with their shit and their vomit, until eventually they died, we did this for Captain Hall. He said that he needed the money to go back into the north to Qiqiktaq, which the English call King William Island—where we are now. He was still anxious to look for news of the famous Lord Franklin, who had been missing then for twenty years already. And he told us that when he went to look for Franklin we would go with him as his guides. This suited Taqulittuq and I, as we still had a desire to travel and to see places we had never been before.

On the circus posters in New York and Boston our Little Butterfly was called "Eskimo Johnny." I made a toy harpoon for him, although my son was not yet two years old. But he got sick during the circus tour because of the heat and the people, and he died. They buried him at Groton in Connecticut, where we lived near Captain Budington. I believe it was his Inuk name that they put on the gravestone, or something quite like it.

Taqulittuq was very bad for a long time after Butterfly went. She wouldn't eat, and wanted only to die so she could be with little Johnny. We put his harpoon and all his toys on his grave and she went to visit it every day to watch over him. People used to come and look at her as she sat by the graveside. One man told me that he was surprised to see her there, as he had read in a book that Eskimos were hard people and didn't grieve for their lost children. One day, just as she was getting a little better, she saw that someone had stolen from the grave a little tin bucket, painted bright red, that Captain Budington had given Johnny. That made her very bad again. If Captain Hall hadn't taken us away to Repulse Bay I think she would have died at that time. It would have been her wish.

Our second son was born during our first winter at Repulse Bay. Captain Hall told us to call the boy "King William" for good luck, as we were trying to get to King William Island to look for Franklin. We decided we would choose our own secret name for the child, but that this time, to be prudent, we wouldn't share it with the white man. Even among ourselves we never called him anything but King William, or Little King William, to keep his real name hidden. In that way we hoped to keep him alive.

In the spring we set off across the Barren Lands toward King William Island. But we soon met a big storm of sleet and rain, such as I have never encountered so early in the year. Afterward Little King William fell sick. The angakkuq who accompanied us, Nukershu, performed a divination, and saw that Taqulittuq had secretly been giving the child medicine that she got from Captain Hall. The angakkuq made her promise to stop this.

We continued on our way and every day the child grew worse. Then Nukershu suggested another well-known cure, that the child should be given to another couple who were traveling with us so they could change his name and raise him as their own. This was done so that any curse that was following his mother and me wouldn't know where to find him. Yet the child grew even worse, and Captain Hall said that he would die without his mother's milk. So she took him back and carried him in her own arms.

When the baby went quiet she wouldn't put him down. She carried him on for a day before Captain Hall and Nukershu could make her understand that we must leave him there. I made a small inuksuk, like a stone child, to stand over his grave, and Captain Hall was pleased because, as he had done on Lok's Land, he wrongly assumed that the thing was a cross. He wrote a note on a piece of paper and left it in the stones, saying that the note would inform anyone who might read it what the child's name had been and the names of its parents. But even he did not know the child's name.

We walked on a few days more until we met some of the people who lived at Pelly Bay. They traded with Captain Hall for many things that were left in the tundra by Franklin's men, such as spoons and buttons and the like. They also had stories from their old people, who had found two wooden ships deserted off King William Island, and many bones of white men on the mainland nearby, who had died where they fell or eaten one another.

Hall wanted to press on to the island itself, but the people warned us of a strange band that had been seen in that area, whom no one dared to approach or to talk with, but who were said to have made several people disappear. Nukershu decided to turn back, and Captain Hall had no choice but to return to Repulse Bay in the hope of coming back the following year.

On the way back, Taqulittuq wanted to see Little King William again, but the snow had since thawed and the land was flooded and confused, and even I could find no trace of his grave.

Our third child we called Panik, which means only "daughter," because we wanted to be cautious. Her mother was one of our friends from Repulse Bay. I gave her a sled and some shirts so that Taqulittuq and I could have our own child. That is how I became a stepfather.

Captain Hall said we must name our new child Silvia, which was the name of the daughter of Mr. Grinnell, the rich man in

New York who had paid for our travels. Later, when she went to school in Groton, her written name was Silvia Ebierbing, but people heard us call her Panik, and so she became Punny at school and then at home.

Some whaling ships arrived in Repulse Bay shortly after we returned there, and now Hall had the idea of hiring white men to stay through the winter and act as his helpers. In the summer, when the ships returned, they would hunt whales again.

The five Americans were called Frank and Pat and Peter, and I don't remember the other two. Pat was their leader, but only Frank was any use for traveling or hunting, so it was he who came away with Hall and Taqulittuq and Punny and I when we traveled north in the spring. The others stayed behind to mind our camp and to cure the caribou and musk oxen that had been cached over the winter.

This time Hall did not wish to go west to King William Island, but north, to the country of Igloolik. The summer before he had heard stories about strangely shaped inuksuks that had been found in that region and about a party of silent Europeans seen passing in the night some years before. Hall believed these might be the last of Franklin's men, and that he should go north in search of them.

We didn't find them. But I came across an old tent site in which the anchor stones had been laid in a square, as only the white men do, and Hall said this was a sign that Franklin's men had been there recently. But I saw from the way the stones were settled in the turf that they had been there for many years. The people at Igloolik told me that parties of white men had passed that way safely several times before us, even before Franklin's time, and so these stones could have been left by any of them.

But I didn't tell Hall this. I thought, What does it matter to me what he believes? If any of Franklin's men had survived in this

region, they would have reached Repulse Bay many years ago
and been rescued by the whalers. What curse could hold living
men prisoner in an open country, free to wander and hunt, yet
detained forever from their homes and their families? It seemed to
me that Captain Hall was looking for ghosts, and that Hall knew
this himself but would not admit it. As he brooded upon their
fate he became closer to them and withdrew from his friends, and
I became worried, because only an angakkuq should have dealings with spirits.

One morning when our Igloolik friends were slow in breaking camp Hall got even angrier than usual and showed them his
revolver. After that I called Taqulittuq aside and suggested that we
should leave Hall and take our child back to Repulse Bay: if Hall
attempted violence against our escorts they would be obliged
to kill him, and us too. Instead Taqulittuq went and talked to
Hall alone in his tent, and when she came out again she handed
me the gun and said that Hall had asked me to keep it until we
returned to Repulse Bay.

While we were away the American sailors had heard a story that
was new to us: it was that the captain of the lost English ships,
Lord Franklin, had been buried ashore in a little house made
of a liquid that turned into stone. By this I suppose they meant
concrete, which I have seen poured and set hard in half of a day.
In another such house nearby, the people said, the English had
left papers and instruments, and when they were all dead and the
Netsilik people tried to break into this cache it proved too strong
for them to open.

Pat, who was the sailors' leader because he was a harpooner by
trade, was very pleased with this story. As soon as we returned he
told it to Captain Hall. But instead of praising him, Hall became
abusive and accused Pat of gossiping. This dispute took place
at the entrance to the sailors' tent with the other men standing

close by. The people of Repulse Bay, who were camped within earshot, came a short way toward us, standing and watching.

Hall shouted at Pat that he had a mind to box Pat for his insolence and for trying to steal stories that belonged to Hall alone. And Pat shook his fist in Hall's face and said he was as good a man as he was and had as much right to talk to the Eskimos. If he wished to tell his own stories when he got back to America then it was his own business to do so. If Hall struck him, he said, he would quickly regret it.

Now Hall turned away and went back to his own tent. I went over to talk to Pat and the Americans, who were laughing together at Hall's embarrassment. Then Hall returned, and before Pat could even raise his hands Hall shot him in the chest.

Well, everyone ran away then, apart from Hall and Taqulittuq and myself and the baby. I too would have run had Taqulittuq not stayed. The Repulse Bay people immediately broke camp and moved to a lake a day's march inland. The American sailors went with them for a few days then came back to the beach one by one, because they were frightened of missing their ships. They were all there on the beach when Pat died; the bullet had missed his heart and only nicked his lung, and although the wound went bad it was two weeks before it killed him. He was a big man and young and strong.

It was Hall who nursed Pat and who talked to him and prayed with him, demanding his forgiveness and offering forgiveness in turn. Forgiveness: what sort of kindness is that? If Hall had wanted to help Pat he should have shot him again right away.

Pat was awake most of the time and talked of his home and his mother. Toward the end, when his veins turned green and his mind was fevered and he was in great pain, he spoke of Hall as his friend.

The other Americans, deprived of Pat's leadership, followed Hall around and competed for his favor. They agreed that they had wronged him and that Pat had been about to attack him when Hall had been forced to fire his shot. They were like a team of dogs whose leader has been bested by a rival. Yet when the first topsail of summer appeared on the horizon every one of them deserted. We never saw them again.

Later, after we returned to America, Hall tried to give his account of the killing. He sent letters to the American government, since Hall and Pat were both Americans, and to the English, who were said to give the law in Repulse Bay, though I never saw them there. The Americans said the English should decide whether Hall should be punished. The English said the Americans should do it. Nothing was done in the end.

But it is my belief that Hall couldn't rest easy after that. He had lived among our people long enough to know that it is a very big thing to kill a person, even a rival or an enemy; that it is not enough to say, as the whites do, that if the act is not condemned by others then you may walk clean away from it. Hall should have atoned for Pat's death, yet his own laws denied him this, and of course he wouldn't follow the Inuit customs. He should have sought out Pat's relatives and bared himself to them, offering reparations, and he should have performed the necessary acts of self-mortification until he knew that he'd been released from his crime. Or he should have been killed for his crime there and then. Either way, he should have thrown away that pistol, because it is a great mistake to keep a gun that has killed a man, or to feed your family with meat taken by such a weapon.

Hall spent that summer persuading the people of Repulse Bay that he had committed no crime and that they shouldn't be afraid to help him. He had decided that he would not go home yet and risk being punished for murder, but would stay another winter and make one last effort to reach King William Island.

And that is what we did. This time the spring weather was as fine as you could wish for—cold enough for the sleds to run well, yet not so cold that we or the dogs grew tired and sluggish. We sped across the Barren Lands and when we reached the farther sea the ice was smooth and sound.

Captain Hall was at first delighted when he set foot here, because King William Island had been his only goal for many years. We found numerous signs of the lost ships, even about here, this little bay where we are talking now, and also bones of the missing men. Wherever he found these bones Captain Hall stopped to bury them and say prayers. Yet we couldn't find the stone house that was Franklin's grave, or the other stone house with the ships' papers in it.

Hall became gloomy again. He was also angered by a story we heard from the Netsilik people, that many years before some of their elders had met a band of starving white men dragging a heavy boat across the gravel. Instead of helping them, the Inuit had run away in the night, having only enough food for themselves. Hall was now convinced that all of the English sailors were dead and that our people were to blame.

It was in this black mood, I believe, that Hall conceived the idea that was to prove the death of him, the desire to go into the far north, farther north than anyone had ever been before, where the sun doesn't show itself for half the year. Maybe this was to be his atonement. He hoped to find a secret there, an open sea with warm waters and many whales, and in that sea a deeper secret, one that he never discussed with me, though once or twice I heard him hint at it in private talks with Mr. Grinnell. If my English had been better perhaps I would have understood.

Hall took us back to Groton in Connecticut, close to Captain Budington and his wife. Taqulittuq and I did farm work to pay for our keep. We didn't like the farm, as the work was hard and boring and didn't pay well. It was no kind of living for a hunter and his wife.

Sometimes Hall still brought us with him on his lecture tours to demonstrate our clothes and our implements. We went to New York, where we stayed with Mr. Grinnell, and to Washington, where we attended the White House and shook hands with President Grant. After that we went to Cincinnati, which was Hall's home, though he seldom ever went there. It was there that we met the famous Lady Franklin.

She had come all the way from England to ask Hall what he had learned the summer before on King William Island. The people of Cincinnati were very pleased to have her visit their city, as she had become very famous for her efforts to find the lost ships. Our meeting took place at the Burnet House hotel on the evening she arrived. As we waited in the lobby we could hear the crowd cheering her carriage. English and American flags hung together from the street lamps, and there was a line of soldiers outside doing tricks with their rifles. A band played the English and American songs, and also another pretty tune that I have heard the whalers whistle whenever they slip moorings.

When at last Lady Franklin and Hall came into the lobby the mayor was with them in his gold chain and there were lots of other fine-looking ladies and gentlemen, and with all the big hats and tall, stout people crowding into the lobby Taqulittuq and I had to climb halfway up the stairs so we could see Lady Franklin. She was a small lady and very old and round. Her clothes were very bright—a green dress and a red shawl. She was a cheerful sight among all those important men in gray and black. They jostled her so much, shouting and waving at her, that her lady companion, who held her by the elbow, had to push them all away from her and take her to her room.

After a while we were sent for, and found Lady Franklin in her parlor with Hall and the other lady, Miss Sophia, who was her niece. The story that interested them most was the one that Pat had told us, that Lord Franklin's body had been sealed by his men in a grave made of concrete, and that later, when the men began to starve and the ships were abandoned, various records and other things were put in a cache made of the same substance. Lady Franklin begged to know if Captain Hall had searched for this grave and this cache. When he replied that he had done all he could in the time he had on the island, she asked him if he would make one more trip to King William Island on her behalf to search for them some more.

Hall said he couldn't do as she asked because he had recently received orders from the President of the United States to take an American navy ship to the North Pole. All the English sailors had been lost in the Barrens a long time ago. It would be vain to search any further, he said.

It was strange to hear Hall speak so carelessly of King William Island, having lived with him for so many years when it was his only goal in life. As for me, I had always thought that Franklin's ships were an odd kind of quarry: when men vanish in the ice they seldom come back again, and what does it matter how they were lost? You freeze or you starve or you drown, or you are killed by a bear or a walrus or perhaps by your own kind. This woman was very old—even her niece was almost an old woman now, older than Hall—and yet she still talked of her husband as if he could return to her. You mourn your dead but you must go on living: to do otherwise is impious. Lady Franklin ought to have married another man years ago rather than cling to this corpse, this old man who would have been dead by now even if he had never sailed from his home. As for her niece, who went quietly about the room serving tea to us, she was still a very handsome woman, graceful and dark, yet Taqulittuq told me afterward that Miss Sophia had never been with any man but merely traveled the world with Lady Franklin. And when I heard that, I thought I understood her better.

Having again begged Hall to lead another expedition to King William Island, and again been refused, Lady Franklin then asked him if he would consent to go as paid guide with an English expedition. Hall told Lady Franklin that he had been made an officer of the United States Navy by the president himself and could not be hired for money. Lady Franklin then suggested that he let her have Taqulittuq and I to guide her expedition, since we had already been to the island. Now instead of being hot Hall grew very cold, and told Lady Franklin that he needed us himself for his next journey. Besides, we were not his property, he said, but his friends. We were as dear to him as his own children.

Hall had two young children, I believe, and a wife as well. But he seldom saw them and I never met them, not even in Cincinnati.

Then Lady Franklin said that she hadn't wanted to purchase us but to hire us, and that we would be very well paid and that afterward she would undertake to return us to America or Cumberland Sound or wherever we wanted to go. She said she didn't see how Hall, if he really was our friend, could prevent her from making such a generous offer.

They were standing face to face now, and Captain Hall was very pale, and she was quite red, so that the contrast almost made me laugh. Miss Sophia tried to intervene, standing between them and saying soothing words, but nothing would calm them. Then Taqulittuq stood up from the couch and said in a loud voice that she and Joe thanked them very much, but that Captain Hall was our friend and we would go with him wherever he went and had no desire to return to King William Island or even to Cumberland Sound. And so that was settled. But I wish she'd consulted me before she spoke. I'd have accepted Lady Franklin's offer.

The navy gave Hall a ship called the *Periwinkle*, which I thought was a good hard name for a ship that must serve in the ice. Hall renamed her *Polaris*, the North Star, by which she would steer. Our old friend Captain Budington was appointed to command her.

While the ship was fitting out at the Brooklyn Navy Yard we stayed with Mr. Grinnell in his big house in Manhattan. Taqulittuq was happy there, but I was very restless, and I took to wandering the shores of the island and talking to the sailors and dockers whom I found about the piers. Often enough we would go to a bar together, because I was now drawing navy pay, and money would be of little use where I was going. Nor did I worry that I was now drinking alcohol, a weakness that I had been careful to avoid since coming to America: I would very soon be out of temptation's way. And it was fun to sit in these American bars, with their colored glass and brass rails and smoke and pianos, and listen to stories about racehorses and wars and boxing and countries I hadn't visited yet. Sometimes there were fights, and I once saw a man beaten half to death until the police came and rescued him. But no one ever harmed or hindered me. Whenever I wished I could walk into the street and the people who passed by wouldn't even see me.

Before we sailed for Greenland we attended one last big meeting in New York. Mr. Grinnell organized it, and we were asked to go in our sealskins. At the meeting everyone praised Captain Hall and prayed for his success. And they gave him a special surprise, which was an American flag that had been sent out before on other great journeys. A captain called Wilkes had taken it with him when he'd tried to reach the furthest place south, the South Pole, where it is said to be as cold as our own country. Ten years after that this same flag had gone north with another friend of Mr. Grinnell, Dr. Kane, when he tried to find an open ocean in the north. Now it would go north again with us. Hall was so pleased with this honor that he wept in front of all the people.

After the meeting I sat in Mr. Grinnell's drawing room and watched as he gave Hall a small wooden box. This, I heard him say, had been left in his keeping by Kane himself. He would now entrust it to Captain Hall for his journey. Hall couldn't speak, but he took the box and opened it, looked inside, then took out a smaller box with a glass lid. He weighed it in his hands, with fresh tears in his eyes, then he put the smaller box back in the larger one, closed it, and put it in his portable writing case. I was sitting there with Taqulittuq and Mrs. Grinnell, waiting to be allowed to go up to bed, and although I was curious to see Captain Hall so dumbstruck I didn't want to ask Taqulittuq to explain the situation to me. I had been bored at the big meeting and had slipped away for a while, and I didn't want Taqulittuq to hear me speak and know that I was drunk.

If you ask me, Dr. Bessels murdered Captain Hall, and I believe that he did it with poison. Captain Hall believed this too, because he told us so himself, me and Taqulittuq, as we tried to nurse him in his cabin on *Polaris*. Later, when we all had to appear before the navy court in Washington, I heard Dr. Bessels swear that he hadn't even been aboard the ship when Hall drank the coffee and became very ill, but was ashore in his magnetic observatory on the beach at Thank God Harbor—which is what we called the place in the far north of Greenland where the ship was trapped by winter. But Bessels was lying, because I had seen him myself near the door of the galley where the coffee was prepared.

Dr. Bessels looked down on the American officers and sailors and anyone else who hadn't studied in books. I believe he looked down most of all on Hall, whom he considered stupid, and on Budington and Tyson, the captain and first mate, whom he regarded as common fishermen. He thought he should command the expedition, as it was a scientific mission, and he was a scientist. Perhaps that is why he did it. I'll never know.

After he was poisoned poor Hall sometimes had convulsions, while at other times he suffered from paralysis and vomiting. He thought he saw blue flames coming from our mouths, and clouds of blue poison in the cabin air. He was mad at times, at other times cunning. Often, pain seized him and shook him until he became senseless and shouted strange words in his daze. I never heard him speak of his wife or his children. Sometimes he crawled around the cabin looking for his pistol, but I'd stolen it from him and hidden it, because I couldn't be sure that he wouldn't shoot one of us with it, and not merely Bessels or himself. Hall lasted two weeks before he died, as had Pat. And so Hall atoned for Pat's murder.

They dressed Hall's corpse in his new navy uniform, put him in a coffin and covered him with Mr. Grinnell's special flag. The crew carried him from the ship across the sea ice and buried him in a shallow hole that the men had dug into the frozen ground with crowbars and pickaxes.

We were so far north that it was as black as midnight, though it was not quite noon by the clock, and Mr. Tyson the mate held a lantern so the chaplain could read the prayers for the dead. After that, rocks were piled on the grave to keep off the bears. Everyone else went back to the ship, because it was terribly cold up there in the north of Greenland where the sun didn't rise for months on end. But Taqulittuq and I stayed by the grave to say good-bye to our old friend.

They had buried him with his feet facing southeast, which is where the Christians have their holy place, so he lay with his back half turned from the north and from the frozen bay where the ship lay beset. Taqulittuq and I said nothing, because there was nothing to say to each other, and then we turned and walked for a little way north up the beach. An aurora had appeared in the south, giving enough light for us to see the rings of stones that protruded from the snow. These were tent-rings, left by people like the old ones who had lived on Lok's Land, perhaps a long time ago, perhaps only recently. I was glad that Hall had died before he noticed them: when he and I had sledged northward ahead of the ship the previous autumn, just before he was poisoned, and we had climbed the furthest mountain ridge and seen only a frozen sea beyond it—no new lands stretching ahead of us into the north, nothing green or living, no warm blue waters or spouting whales—Hall had been very disappointed; his consolation was to tell himself, falsely, that he had at least gone farther north than any human had ever been before.

There was aboard ship another of our people, Hans Hendrik, a Greenlander, and his wife and children. As the winter drew on we took our families away from the ship and built our own snowhouses ashore. We were safe there should the ship's hull give way in the ice and sink. And we were kept apart from the madness of the crew. At night, when it was quiet, we could hear them aboard the *Polaris*, howling and fighting and singing their songs. They were often drunk, brewing their own liquor from sugar and tinned fruit or stealing the alcohol that Dr. Bessels had brought to preserve his dead animals. It was this latter stuff that maddened them most.

One night in December Captain Budington, who was the drunkest of them all, became terrified of something he thought he had seen on the ice in the moonlight. He ordered that all the rifles and pistols aboard be shared out to repel an attack. Of course, once the sailors were armed he couldn't disarm them. Half of the crew weren't Americans by birth, but Germans. Now factions began to form, with Dr. Bessels, who was also a German, stirring up trouble, so that neither side would agree to hand in their guns. Sometimes the white men came out on deck and shot at the sky or at phantoms they saw on the floes; after a while Hans and I had to move farther up the beach so that our children were safe from the bullets skipping off the ice.

We moved back to the ship when the sun returned and birds and seals reappeared in the strait and the crew became less crazy.

But the ice in the bay didn't break when it should have. We didn't see a clear lead until August, and no sooner had the ship passed into the strait then the ice closed on us again and bore us away. The ship was moving south, but only at the speed of the drifting pack, and there was now no way to break free and find another winter harbor: we were in the middle of the strait, at the mercy of the first autumn storm.

It hit us in the night far out to sea. The storm broke the ship free of the ice and sent her whirling through a lead of black water until she crashed into an old floe on the other side. The waves smashed most of the boats and part of the aft hatch. Water flooded the stokehold so the engineers couldn't raise steam. Then the ice closed on us again, driven before the great storm, and we heard the timbers and braces groan and then crack until the ship heeled right over. It seemed sure that her ribs were broken and that only the ice now held her afloat.

Hans and I and our families were the first onto the ice, taking all our best gear with us: we trusted the ice more than we did any ship. Tyson the first mate was with us, and a few of the others. We got the last two whale boats over the side, and Hans's kayak, and some tents and some food. The wind-blown snow blinded and numbed us as we stumbled about on the floe, trying to stop our gear sliding into the black water.

Then the wind veered and the floes parted once more. But the ship didn't sink. Instead, the wind and waves drove her, without power or sails, into the night. And though we were frozen and terrified, stranded on the ice in a storm in the sea, it was we who felt sorry for Captain Budington and the others who were still aboard *Polaris*: the ship would surely sink soon, and we on the floe had both of her surviving boats.

The floe that we lived on was quite large at first. On the second day I shot two ringed seals and Hans got another. We had taken some tinned food and bread from the ship, and if we could only drift a little farther south we could hope for a calm spell that would allow us to rig the two whale boats and make for the eastern shore, where we might fall in with some Greenland people.

We were nineteen in number—seven Germans, two Americans, one Englishman and nine Inuks of whom five were only children. Captain Tyson, the first mate, was the senior officer.

While we awaited our chance to escape we built snowhouses to shelter us all. The men seized most of the canvas and packing crates that we had with us to make their own house comfortable. And when it grew colder, and their small supply of coal and wood ran out, they burned one of the boats to keep warm.

Tyson tried to stop them, but they had pistols and rifles and shotguns and Tyson had brought none for himself from the ship, having worked through the night of the storm with no thought of himself. Unlike the Germans he was a whaling man, a skipper in his own right, and he knew the ice well, and that one whale boat couldn't take all of us safely with all the food and gear we would need for a sea crossing. The waves would wash into it and it would founder and sink. When they burned that first whale boat we lost our best chance of escape.

As the winter deepened there were hardly any seals to hunt, not nearly enough to feed both ourselves and our dogs, so we ate the dogs one by one until there was none left and then Hans and I had to go hunting without them. It's an eerie thing to be out on the sea ice in the black night of winter without a dog to smell the air for you. When the mist scatters the moonlight, or when there is no moon and only the light of the stars or the aurora, every hummock and ridge in the ice becomes a stalking bear, and indeed might conceal one. When a swell lifts the floe and the water sucks beneath its edge you hear the snort of a bear breaking cover and charging you. And when the temperature drops and ice flowers form on the leads of open water, rustling on the waves, it sounds like the whisper of voices on distant floes. I often thought on such nights of the people of Lok's Land and what had become of them.

Only the ringed seals, who chew their own air holes in the ice, live so far north in the winter, and they are wary and small. At first the Germans tried to hunt for themselves, shooting whenever a seal would appear, but this only drove the seals back into the sea, whether wounded or not, before we could secure them. The Germans then took to following Hans and I at a distance so that they could seize any seals that we caught before we could take our own share.

But the white men wouldn't eat the guts of the seals—not at first—so I would collect them in a bag and take them back to our house. Punny was no longer playful but listless, and sat in the dark of the sleeping bench. Every few minutes throughout the day she would sigh and say in English, "I am so hungry. Oh, I am so hungry." And when you are hungry the cold soaks through your clothing, your legs grow heavy and your thoughts distracted, until you are no longer able to hunt. When you feel the cold stealing up on you like that it is time for desperate measures. So I began to count heads.

For friends we had only Tyson, and Jackson the black steward and Herron the Englishman. By now the Germans wouldn't speak to anyone in English, or smile or help or share. Poor Tyson could do nothing with them, as he had put all his energy into saving general stores on the night of the storm and had brought nothing off the ship for himself, not even a gun or a coat. For the same reason, he was confined to the hut from December to February, having no warm clothes to save him from the cold.

By now Meyer had fallen from favor and a man called Kruger was the leader of the German faction. He was the worst of the lot, a loudmouthed bully and a liar who still carried fat on his bones when the rest of us were starving. Much good would his fat have done him if things had got any worse. I would have eaten him first.

Tyson now lived all the time with Taqulittuq and Punny and I, because without proper clothes he needed the warmth of our lamp to keep himself alive. He sat on the sleeping bench all day, dressed in the scraps of canvas and wool that Taqulittuq had sewn into a jacket. He stared at the lamp, or hummed to himself, or played string games with Punny. Sometimes he would write in his diary and read back his own words aloud. He often lamented that he hadn't brought any books from the ship apart from his journals and a maritime almanac; this was his greatest privation, to sit confined to the snowhouse with nothing to look at but whatever it was that he saw in the flame of the lamp. It seemed to me likely that he would kill himself, so I didn't tell him about Hall's pistol, which was hidden in Taqulittuq's bag along with some other things of Hall's she had rescued from the ship.

We were all in the house one day in February when Kruger arrived with three other Germans. They stood outside and shouted to us to come out. We looked at one another, afraid, because we didn't want to have to crawl out of the low entrance in front of them, unable to raise our hands to defend ourselves. I'd left my own rifle and shotgun outside to preserve them from the condensation, so when Tyson went out first I took Hall's pistol from Taqulittuq's bag, hid it inside my parka and followed him outside.

The men crowded around Tyson, jostling him, and Kruger shouted at him that he knew that we had more food hidden away and that we should hand it over. I moved around behind the men, and as they seldom paid me any notice except when they stole food from me they didn't see me put my hand under my parka. Taqulittuq put Punny behind her own body and went over to the other side of the snowhouse where our shotgun leaned. I saw how the sailors followed the woman and child with their eyes.

Two of them moved toward Punny and Taqulittuq, not fast but deliberately, like wolves closing in on an exhausted musk-ox. Kruger swore and put a hand on Tyson's chest and pushed him away with all his force, so that Tyson fell back against the wall of the snowhouse. Then Kruger took out his pistol.

I also took out my pistol and cocked it, and at the sound the Germans turned and looked at me. While they were distracted Taqulittuq picked up my shotgun and drew back both hammers, though she knew very well that I kept it unloaded because I was worried about Tyson. She waved the barrels at the Germans who had approached her and our little daughter and they did not move any closer to them after that. Yet the other one, the one nearest to me, had raised his rifle to point it at me, and Kruger still had his gun aimed at Tyson. It would have gone badly for all of us if Tyson hadn't got to his feet and started to speak.

Tyson told them that without Hans and I they would all surely die, because all winter long the white men hadn't caught even one seal between them. And he asked them why they thought the Eskimos would stay to feed them if they harmed our women and children?

Now a terrible rage came over Kruger and he shouted at Tyson again, bawling and spitting, and I believe he would have shot him then, just as Hall had shot Pat, because he felt his leadership slipping away from him. And indeed the other Germans spoke to one another in their own language and when they talked to Kruger again they didn't sound friendly. The one who had been pointing his rifle at me turned it toward Kruger. Now with three guns pointing at him, Kruger had no choice but to walk away.

They didn't bother us again after that. Just to be sure, though, I gave Hall's pistol to Tyson: he had seen what I had seen in the men's eyes. I knew now too that he wouldn't use the gun against himself. And I was glad to be rid of it: a pistol is only good for hunting, murder, or suicide, and this was one that had murdered before.

Spring came, and we were now in more southerly waters. One morning I went out and the floe was rocking from side to side and waves broke only yards from our tents. We packed everything we could into the whale boat and made for a larger floe to the west. Then this too split and we had to move again. Always, the currents and the set of the ice drew us westward onto smaller and smaller floes, away from salvation in Greenland. We were weak from the hunger and damp, and had no choice but to take whatever passage seemed the smoothest: the whale boat was greatly overloaded and wallowed in all but the smallest of seas, with freezing water slopping over the gunwales while everyone bailed to keep it afloat. So we moved ever westward, until one day we saw the tips of white peaks in the west and knew we were near Baffin Island.

We now had to face another great worry: during our winter-long drift we had come so far south we must soon pass out of Baffin Bay into the wide southern ocean, where the last ice would melt and there would be no hope of landfall.

Captain Tyson and I therefore resolved that on the next calm day we should risk everything on the boat. We would load only the oars and spars and a couple of guns, food enough for a day or two, and make for the land to the west.

Yet Tyson was still worried that he might steer the overloaded boat into the fogs and tide races at the mouth of Hudson Strait. If he knew what course to steer, he said, he could make northwest for Frobisher Bay or southwest to the fishing grounds off Labrador. In either place we would surely meet a ship. But he didn't know our latitude: if only he had a sextant and compass he could make a good guess.

After parting with him I went to the sealskin tent that we then had for a shelter. Hidden in Taqulittuq's sewing bag were a sextant

and a compass, the very ones that Hall had with him when he
had first come to Cumberland Sound. She also had the wooden
box that Hall had got from Mr. Grinnell. Taqulittuq had wanted
to keep these things a secret. But now we would soon have to
discard them anyway. Better to let Tyson have them if they could
do us some good.

Taqulittuq was away from the tent so I took the sextant and
compass and brought them to Tyson, who had climbed a pressure
ridge to look at a cape to the west. He was very pleased to see the
instruments.

I watched him work with the sextant and write in his book,
and then he took up the compass and aimed it at the Cape to our
west, and he wrote again. Together we went back to the tent, and
there he consulted his almanac and did his calculations.

The land we saw to the west of us was called Lok's Land, he said. If
we landed there we would surely meet the whalers that came every
year to Cumberland Sound. Then he went to tell all the others.

When he was gone I took the compass and the sextant and I
fetched Hall's pistol from its hiding place in Tyson's bedding. I also
took the little wooden box from Taqulittuq's bag and I went out
again. While I had been inside the tent a fog had rolled over our
floe and I could no longer see the others, though I heard them
calling to one another, preparing to launch the boat for the last
time. But I didn't join them. Instead, I followed the sound of the
wavelets until I was at the edge of the water and there I stared into
the fog until I saw shapes in it.

When a woman gives birth, or a man commits a murder, they
must immediately get rid of everything they owned before that
time, their clothes and their tools and their weapons, and start again
with new things. Otherwise their old life will come after them.

I threw Hall's pistol into the sea, and reflected further.

Taqulittuq hadn't been able to discard her clothes when Butterfly died in America. Hall had told her to keep her old furs to

wear in the circus, since we couldn't get others to replace them. Similarly, when Little King William had died on the march we should have camped at the place of his death and waited until Taqulittuq had finished mourning and could dress herself in new clothes. But Hall had been in a hurry and had pressed us onward. And we had believed that he could protect us.

I threw the sextant after the pistol. It had been with Hall to Lok's Land. And so had I. I searched my memory. What did I have in my possession that had been with me when I went to that place?

I stood up and hurled my rifle into the fog. When I heard the splash I sat down again.

Here now in my hand was the compass. Without getting up I dropped it into the sea. It sank with a plink, drawing its canvas lanyard down after it. Without a compass, we would have to steer south by the sun, toward Labrador, where we might find a ship in coastal waters; we couldn't attempt to reach Lok's Land.

Only the little wooden box was left to me. I stood up, ready to join the others at the boat, and I was on the point of throwing the box after the other things when it came to me that I still didn't know what was inside it. It was quite a nice box, made of pale shiny wood, and from its weight it must have contained something of value. But it was locked. It didn't matter. I should still get rid of it. But as I extended my arm to throw it a terrible curiosity seized hold of me. I tried to wrench the box open, and when this didn't work I put it on the ice and stamped on it. But it was very well built, and my soft kamiks didn't protect my feet from its sharp edges.

The box sat there on the ice, only inches from the edge. A tap of my foot would have pushed in in the sea. But now I had to know what was inside it. I had to know, even though knowing couldn't do me any good. What use is any thing that can't keep you warm or help you to win food? But I've never been sensible. I'd gone with Hall to Lok's Land.

Voices were calling. There was the scrape of the boat's timbers being dragged across the ice. I heard Punny shout my name. Then I remembered that my knife was back in the tent, and that with its steel blade I could easily open the box.

I went into the tent and there was Taqulittuq. She was on her knees, rooting through her possessions, and I knew at once what she was looking for.

She didn't turn to me at first, so desperately was she searching, and I had to call her name twice before she saw what I held. Her face contorted, as if she were screaming. And yet she made no sound. Instead, she scrambled toward me, still on her knees, and started to strike me with her fists about the shoulders and head. I cowered before her and didn't resist when she grabbed the box from me. The only sounds had been the slap of her fists and the blood in my ears, and Taqulittuq's sobbing breath. I let her take the box from me and she put it inside her parka and went back outside again, leaving me alone.

I was still there when Captain Tyson came to look for me. I didn't want to talk to him, because I would have to tell him what I had done with the compass and the sextant. But before I could speak he told me that he didn't like the look of the fog, and that we wouldn't launch the boat until the weather had cleared. So my luck had changed again. The fog stayed with us for another four . days, as thick as a blanket, as we drifted on southward. On the fifth day, as the waves were washing over the floe and we had given up waiting for the fog to clear and were preparing to launch ourselves into the unknown, we heard a ship's bell ringing close by. Hans got into his kayak and paddled off into the fog, and that is how we were rescued after two hundred days on the sea ice, just off the coast of Labrador.

Polaris had grounded on the Greenland shore just after we last saw her. The rest of the crew—Captain Budington, Dr. Bessels, and all—had been rescued by the people of Etah, who fed them through the winter. In the spring they made boats and rowed south. A whaler brought them to Scotland. They were back in America before we were ourselves.

When we returned to America Mr. Tyson made accusations against Captain Budington and Dr. Bessels. The navy held an inquiry in Washington at which I and Taqulittuq both had to speak. In the end the Secretary of the Navy couldn't decide who was telling the truth. The doctors couldn't say for sure whether Hall had died of a stroke, as Dr. Bessels said, or of poison, as Hall believed himself. Although there was a lot of talk about drunkenness and mutiny, nobody was punished.

Punny was a very kind and clever girl, and she attended the school at Groton with all the little white children of that place. For her, unlike her parents, Groton was a home, the only one she ever knew. The teacher said she was the quickest child in her class and would have made a great scholar, but she was very weak after her six months on the ice and she got sick and died. She had lived for nine years.

By then we had become quite famous because of what had happened to the *Polaris*, and several men from the newspapers attended Punny's funeral. Mr. Grinnell didn't come himself, but he would have been pleased to learn that the name on Punny's stone was Silvia Grinnell Ebierbing.

Taqulittuq had learned to behave more like the American ladies who sometimes came to visit her in our house, and who I am sure were a comfort to her after Punny was gone. She was often alone after that, because I had started going to sea again, and even when ashore I would often go drinking in Boston or New London. I remember how very polite Taqulittuq was as she stood by the grave and listened to the priest say prayers for Punny. Taqulittuq herself made almost no sound.

I wanted to return to the north, but Taqulittuq wouldn't leave Punny and Butterfly alone in a strange country. She was quiet from that day on, and she said very little in the letters that she sent to my ships, which my sailor friends would read to me. I would mail her money whenever I could. I was just back from the sea when she died, a year after Punny. She was still quite a young woman, and might yet have had more children.

Taqulittuq was gone, and Punny was gone, and I couldn't stay in America without them. After her funeral I had to clean out the cottage because they said I could no longer stay there. I had to dispose of Punny's clothes and school books and the doll that she had grown too old to play with. I put it on her grave, as we had done with the toys of our Little Butterfly. I knew someone would steal it, but what can you do? Maybe some other little girl would have it.

Looking through Taqulittuq's things I learned that for her last year she had kept her own journal, just as Hall did. I couldn't read the words, but Mrs. Budington said they were mostly just shopping lists and accounts of what Taqulittuq had been doing on some particular day or other when she was alone in the house after Punny died. But sometimes she made little drawings—birds and seals and bears and suchlike, and other things that we had in the north. The last thing she drew, just before she died, was a map of an island. I could tell from the lightness of the pencil that she had been weak when she made it. There were no names on it. Mrs. Budington asked me if I recognized it. I told her I did not.

Also among Taqulittuq's things was the little wooden box she'd taken from me on the ice floe. It was still locked. Mrs. Budington wanted to open it but I distracted her with some other business and then I hid it in my bag. I didn't have a key for it, but if I ever decided to see what was in it I could find a way to look inside.

I said good-bye to the Budingtons and went back to New York, where I lived for a while in a lodging house close by the

Brooklyn Navy Yard. It was run by a church, and although they were cheerful and kind they made us sing songs and were strict about alcohol. When I came back in the evenings I had to make sure they didn't know I was drunk. It was easier for me than for my white friends, of course: nobody minded if I couldn't speak.

The lodgings were warm and clean, and it was the first time in my life that I ever had a room to myself. But it was very small, and the only thing I could see when I looked out the window was the brick wall of a neighboring building. There was nothing to do or to look at in that room. When I lay on the bed I had nothing to anchor my thoughts in the present. I saw only my future and past, over which I was powerless. I understood then why Tyson had lusted for other people's words as he sat in the dark on the ice floe.

When my money was gone it was time to ship out again. I knew I would never come back to the United States so I went over to Manhattan to say good-bye to Mr. Grinnell and his family. They were away, but the servants were pleased to see me and let me share their meal. They read me a letter that had been sent to me care of Mr. Grinnell. An American soldier named Schwatka wanted a guide to go with him to King William Island. He was looking for Franklin's books and all that sort of thing. I agreed to guide him.

Like Hall, Schwatka found only buttons and bones on King William Island—I could have told him as much before we left New York, but it wasn't my place to do so, and anyway I wanted to come here myself, because of the map in Taqulittuq's journal.

When Schwatka gave up and went home I exchanged my pay for ammunition and I stayed behind. You look in your book and you read about Schwatka, and you say that I must have come here more than twenty years ago, but I've lost count of years. Here on King William Island it's always foggy in summer. In winter there is no sun for weeks on end and the land and the sea freeze under the snow until you don't know which is which. I sit in my snowhouse with my blubber lamp and sew my own clothes and listen to the wind until I hear voices. I never feel lonely. Sometimes, when the weather clears, I go outside and I see people watching from a distance, but we leave each other be. Who they are I don't know. The Netsilik people only come here in summer, and then I move away to hide from them. I only showed myself to you because I saw your ship frozen in this bay and thought Schwatka had returned. But you say he died twelve years ago. It doesn't seem any time at all since I last saw Taqulittuq or Punny yet they are dead for more than twenty years.

This spring I became sick and for days I couldn't move my hand. When I talked to myself I couldn't understand the words. I lay in my tent for a while, eating dried-out blubber and scraps of old sealskin until I got better. But I knew that the illness would recur and that it was time to open my wooden box. I expected I'd have to break it open, but when I tried to pick it with a fish bone the lock turned right away. There was only that old clock inside it, and a name scratched inside the box. You say that the name belongs to some friend of Franklin who was lost a long time ago, and who am I to argue? I am a stupid man, who spent his life surrounded by signs that he wouldn't learn to read. The only word I can write is "Joe," which I signed for my pay in the navy, and even that is not my real name.

That is my statement. You may believe it or not as you wish. I will sign it, since you ask, so that you can account for the clock, but I don't care what you do with it, or with the statement, now that it's out of my hands. I'm no longer an explorer. But when I was, I was a great one. The white men came to these regions and looked for all sorts of things that they dreamed of, but they found only the ice and the islands and places so cold and dark that even the Inuit don't hunt there. Taqulittuq and I also dared the unknown, but we discovered Orkney and Hull and New York and London.

Signed: Joseph Ebierbing

His mark: Joe

Transcribed and witnessed this second day of February 1903 at "Gjoa Haven," King William Island:

R.E. Amundsen

PART FOUR

The Oates Coast

69°30'S 159°0'E

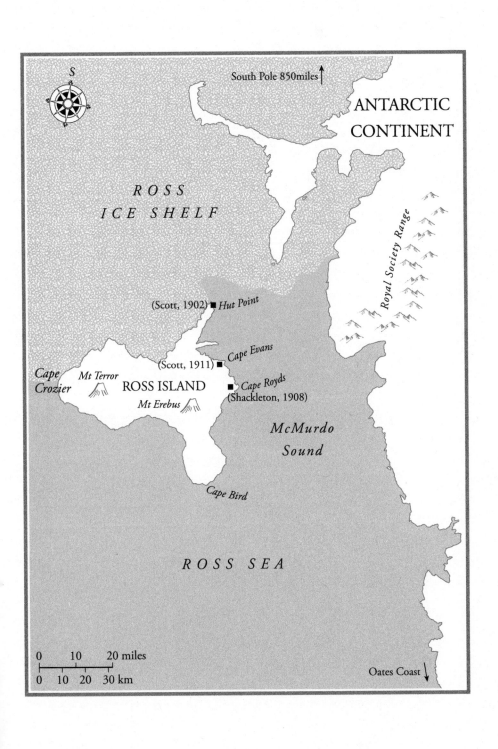

S

South Pole 850miles ↑

ANTARCTIC
CONTINENT

ROSS
ICE SHELF

Royal Society Range

(Scott, 1902) ■ *Hut Point*

Cape Evans

(Scott, 1911) ■

Cape
Crozier

Mt Terror

ROSS ISLAND

■ *Cape Royds*
(Shackleton, 1908)

Mt Erebus

McMurdo
Sound

Cape Bird

ROSS SEA

0   10   20 miles

0   10   20   30 km

Oates Coast ↓

Inuvik, Northwest Territories

When Fay woke up it was twilight outside. She had slept through the morning and now it was noon. She put shoes on her bare feet, wrapped herself in her coat, and went out onto the porch. It was very quiet outside and very cold. The sky was a dark yet vivid blue turning silver in the south. Spruces hunched under their burdens of snow, so quiet and still that she had the sudden notion that they were playing dead on her, frozen in place by the sound of her door. If I make another sound, will they run from me like deer? She stamped her foot on the planks of the porch. Nothing happened for a moment and then, on the other side of the clearing, a spruce bow dipped slowly, shed its snow, and snapped up again. There was the hiss of the falling snow, then the dull thump as it landed, then silence. Only a lingering puff of white dust showed that she hadn't imagined it. A coincidence, she thought, and then somewhere farther off, in among the trees, she heard the sound repeated.

She had slept at last and now she felt alive again. That weird business with Nelson-Nilsson felt as if it were behind her. She didn't want to think about it. She could do all that later, when she was back in the south. Now that she had visited the Distant Early Warning Line, now that she had ticked that box for her mother, she might as well enjoy her last hours in Inuvik. She would be a proper tourist and look around the town. In case she had to leave in a hurry—she was meant to check out today, and still didn't know when the next plane would fly—she packed all her things and left her bag inside the door.

When she came out again Ringnes was splitting logs beside the boiler room. She could see from the steam coiling slowly out of his mouth that the work didn't trouble him; she had to breathe in little gasps to protect her lungs from the razor-blade air.

"Do you know," she said, "if the airport is open yet?"

"Not yet. Probably later today. Tomorrow for sure."

"Then do you think I could use your phone to call a taxi? I want to go into town."

"He quit, did he?"

"Yes . . . He had to drive south. For his interview."

Ringnes lifted the ax. "That's funny. Because the passes are still closed. But if you wait in the office for a couple of minutes I'll run you into town myself. I have to go see about a plane ticket. I'm hoping to fly out tomorrow myself."

"Where are you going?"

He brought the ax down again, neatly splitting a section of wood. "Norway. Home. I could be gone until spring."

"That's a long break. Is it business or pleasure?"

"Neither." He placed another log on the stump he used as a chopping block. "My mother's not well. I have to go and look after her."

Ringnes had an old Ford truck with an upholstered bench that ran the width of the cab. It was a higher ride than Nilsson's SUV. Driving into town, the trees swept past Fay's window like the ranks of an army passed in review. She was very hungry. She would eat a big lunch and drink one or two glasses of wine.

Ringnes drove in silence.

"I wonder," she said, "if you could drop me at the Mackenzie Hotel. I want to see if they have a room for tonight."

Instead of just dropping her off in the parking lot he turned into a space and switched off the engine.

"I should have told you before," he said. "You're good to stay tonight as well, if you want. But you'll have to check out tomorrow morning. We can't hold the room for you after that."

"So your engineers are finally going to make it."

"They'll fly in from Whitehorse in the morning. I'll be leaving around then, I hope, but my assistant can look after them. And you too, if you need help."

"What time do you need me to check out?"

"That's the other thing I need to tell you. There's a problem with your credit card."

"Is there?" She had put money into her Visa account before she left England so she could use it as a roving ATM card.

"I couldn't put your number through the night you checked in, but I remembered to try again this morning. It came up declined. So I called the company. They said that your card had been canceled."

"Canceled? Why would it be canceled?" She felt herself blush, even though she'd done nothing wrong. And then she remembered. "It must be because of unusual activity. Because I'm suddenly using my card in a foreign country, they think someone might have stolen it. They did this to me before once, when I went over to France. I'll ring them and confirm that it's me. Then they'll reactivate it."

"That's not it. I called them myself when it came up declined—I kind of went to bat for you." For the first time, it occurred to Fay to wonder if he lived alone. "They said the card was canceled, outright. You can't just reactivate it. You have to go into your bank if you want to get it reissued. Even then it would take time."

"Canceled outright?"

"Yep . . ." He put both hands on the wheel. "The thing is, your bank thinks that you're dead."

She turned away from him and took in the car park. For the first time she noticed the *inuksuk* that stood by the entrance. It was a crude human figure made from flat slabs of limestone fitted together to suggest arms and legs and a trunk and a head. The Inuit used to construct them as landmarks, she had read, or to help them herd caribou into their killing grounds. Or maybe, perhaps, they built them so as not to feel lonely, maybe even just for fun; it's not like you could build a proper snowman up here—the snow would be much too cold and dry for that. It would just blow away on you. Not like back in Greenwich Park, herself and her mother, rolling balls of wet, sticky snow into big creaking boulders.

Fay and her mother used to have accounts at the same bank. After her mother's final stroke, two months before, Fay had filled in a lot of forms to close her mother's accounts and transfer what money there was to her own. It was supposed to be paying for this trip, her first real escape after twenty-five years of nursing her crippled mother. Perhaps she'd put down the wrong number somewhere. Or perhaps the bank had mixed them up.

"It doesn't matter. I still have some cash. I'll pay you in dollars and sort the card out later."

He looked uncomfortable. "Don't worry about that. You keep your cash for now. Without a card, you're going to need it."

"I can pay you," she insisted. "To be perfectly honest, I'm not really dead."

"I'm pleased to hear it."

"I'm not a fraud, either."

"I don't doubt it."

She reached for the door handle. "I'll sort out the card. I won't leave you out of pocket."

He started the engine. Now he seemed, if anything, a little embarrassed. "I know you won't. The fact is, that room you're in is paid for anyway. The engineering firm put a retainer on every chalet in the place. So whether you pay me or not, I'm still looked after. You're not even on the register."

She thought about that and decided to be amused. "So what you're saying is that I'm not really here."

She climbed down from the cab, and paused in the half-opened door.

"Yep. But enjoy the rest of your stay."

It was Friday afternoon in Inuvik, Friday night in London. Fay's bank would not reopen until Monday. She must wait until then to come back from the dead.

She went into the restaurant of the Mackenzie Hotel and ordered a steak and a glass of wine, then noticed the prices on the menu. While she was waiting for the food she counted her dollars—fifteen hundred and change. Everything here cost a fortune. She needed to go somewhere cheaper to sort herself out.

The restaurant was empty apart from herself and two middle-aged couples who sat at opposite ends of the room murmuring over their lunch. She could have eaten in the hotel's busy sports bar, which was loud with voices and the build-up to some hockey game. But the Canadian money felt strange in her fingers. Her cards didn't work, and her English mobile phone wouldn't connect to any network up here. She was alone in the world and wanted to enjoy it. The food, when it came, was delicious. She drank another glass of wine and decided to walk down the main street: it was her last chance to explore. There was no wind today (or was it tonight?) so the frost wouldn't bite her. The town was very small—a handful of streets in a bend of the river—and she already had her bearings. If she got too cold, in her thin London winter clothes, she could always duck into the Eskimo Inn and warm herself a while. There was also the little café where she'd eaten breakfast with Nelson. Or she could walk until her hands and face went numb and then take a taxi back to the chalet, unpack her bags and get some more sleep. It was entirely up to her.

There was a haze in the air that made haloes around the street lamps. Cars and trucks rumbled past, their tires sucking hollow on the packed snow in the street. She saw headlights flare and fade in windshields, dim faces behind them. Two kids were kissing in the alley between the Eskimo Inn and the government building. The lights of the cars, ebbing and flowing, threw romantic shadows from the banks of dirty snow. There was music too, across the street somewhere. It came from the Mad Trapper Pub, directly opposite.

If she wanted any cigarettes she would have to buy her own. Perhaps, she thought, I can get some in that bar. There was a perfectly good convenience store just down the street but she decided to ignore it. She would just have a quick look inside the pub.

She crossed the road, was about to climb the steps to the door of the pub, when she saw Nelson coming toward her down the street. Fay thought: I could dodge up the stairs to the bar to avoid him. But she guessed that he too would be going up those steps. And he must have seen her already, so she couldn't just turn and walk the other way. There was nothing else for it: she went past the steps and continued toward him. Better to meet him out here in the street.

When Nelson saw her he slowed. She thought for a moment that he wouldn't stop. When he did, it was at a safe distance. He looks worried, she thought. And then: Is *he* frightened of *me*?

"Hello," she said.

"Hi."

That should have been it, for the second or third time. They should have stepped politely around each other and continued on their way. But they stood there, face to face, not knowing what to say.

"I'm on my way to see the police," he said in the end. "To tell them about Bert."

How many parts of that statement were lies? Even Fay knew, after only two days in the town, that the police station was back the other way, across from the Mackenzie Hotel. She knew where he'd been going.

The music rose and fell as the bar door opened and closed. A cigarette appeared on the pub's darkened porch.

"You should do that. Straighten things out before they get any worse."

He stepped aside. He can see that I don't believe in him. But he doesn't care: he doesn't believe in me either. What a good understanding we have.

A voice called out from the darkness above. "Hey, Nelson? That you down there?"

He looked up into the shadow. "Mike?"

"You coming in here?"

Nelson glanced at Fay. "I guess."

"You found Bert yet? I asked a couple of people, but they haven't seen him either."

"No. No sign of him."

"Really? That's too bad . . . Well, come on up and have a beer and we'll talk it over. You should probably go tell the cops."

"I'll be up in a minute. I'm just saying good-bye to someone."

A cigarette meteored past them and hit the ice in a shower of sparks. The door opened and closed and they were alone again.

Fay looked at the cigarette butt. It lay there six feet away, still lit, but unable to melt the ice and put itself out. The ice is so cold, she thought, that it won't let it die yet.

"Well," said Nelson, "good-bye."

He offered her his hand. She ignored it. "That man up there. Mike. You know him well?"

"Sort of . . . I met him in the bar my first night in town. He's a local guy. He thought I looked like Bert."

"He knows your brother too."

"Mike is into history books. He said Bert and him used to talk about the old days."

"So he knows you, and he knows your brother?"

"Yeah."

"Maybe we should go in for a drink."

Nelson stopped inside the door and studied the scene that had once again been set for him. He smelled beer and whiskey, saw soft lights, dark wood, the gleaming taps and bottles. He could make sense of his life, if he wished, as a regression of bars. After a while you no longer went to the places where the young people went. You no longer talked to the kind of women who you knew deserved better. You looked for the sort of places where you recognized your friends, including the ones you'd never met before, and you avoided the pool table to keep out of fights. He no longer expected anything from any given night other than what he had experienced a thousand times before. If you were lucky, you got what you paid for.

But this place still had something about it. It was the only pub in the whole western Arctic, the last proper bar in the world. Cold and dark waited just outside its walls yet here they all were, men and women, drinking defiance at the end of the road. The people who came here were, for the most part, almost as transient as he was, and no longer young. But to Nelson, in here, they didn't seem done yet: they still seemed pleased to have made it this far.

Mike sat alone in the back where it was quiet. He wore his muskrat hat with the earflaps pulled up at right angles to his head. This made him look startled, though his black eyes watched them calmly as they came across the floor. Nelson wondered again how old Mike was: anywhere between forty and seventy, he would have guessed. With some of these locals it was difficult to tell.

The house band was a four-piece—three men in jeans and checked shirts and a huge lead guitarist with long hair and a kaftan. They played a boogie-woogie instrumental and people started to dance.

By leaning close and shouting Fay could still get Mike to hear her.

"So what did you and Bert talk about?"

He was watching the band, one leg crossed over the other, his foot tapping the air. "Mostly about recent history—my own life, and my dad's, and all the other Inuvialuit. And about what I'm doing now."

"What's that?"

"I'm a bear monitor. I fly out with the decontamination crews and drive around the sites on a quad bike. If I see a bear I light some firecrackers. If that doesn't scare it off I might have to shoot it."

"Sites?"

"Radar sites. The ones they don't need anymore, way out on the tundra. They're full of PCBs and asbestos and diesel oil and all sorts of crud. The government has to clean them up to protect the environment."

There it is, she thought. *Click click click*, like the meshing of gears. But she asked the question anyway. "What radar sites?"

"Distant Early Warning. The type of radar they use now has a much longer range, so they don't need so many ground stations to join the line together. So now they're dismantling the stations they don't need anymore. My dad helped to build the DEW Line back in the fifties. Now I'm taking it down again."

First the clock. Then her grandfather's name. Now the Distant Early Warning. What other threads of her life had Bert Nilsson been holding?

"My grandfather was up here in the fifties. He also helped to set up the DEW Line. Don't you think that's a coincidence?"

"Not really. If you were up here in the fifties, then chances are you had something do with the DEW Line. It was the only game in town."

"How so?"

"The DEW Line changed everything up here. It was the first time Ottawa really gave a damn about the Arctic. Before that they just left it to the fur traders and missionaries."

"But back in the fifties they were scared of the Russians?"

He laughed. "The Russians? Who cares about them? It was the Americans they were worried about. First they built the Alaska Highway across our territory in World War II, because of the Japs in the Aleutian Islands. Then at the end of the war they sent planes to photograph the Canadian Arctic, hoping to find new islands that they could claim for themselves. After that they starting pushing for the DEW Line to be built on our soil to watch for Russian bombers. At that point Ottawa finally woke up and realized that the Americans had more of a presence up here than Canada did. And that the people who actually lived here didn't give a damn if we were American or Canadian. So Ottawa made sure we got jobs building the DEW Line and started paying for health and welfare and education. Meantime the price of furs had gone to hell, so people moved off the land and started living in settlements for the schools and health and welfare. That was that. Welcome to Canada."

"The police were up here though, weren't they? Before the DEW Line?"

"Yeah. They were here. Mounties, missionaries, and the Hudson Bay Company. Three different ways to get fucked."

"Not a patriot, then."

He drew himself up in his chair and saluted. "*Au contraire*. Sworn to defend the realm. Canadian Rangers. Spare-time reservist. I get twelve days' pay a year, a World War II Lee-Enfield rifle and two hundred rounds of free ammo. All I have to do is watch for strange activity when I'm out on the land."

"Ever see any?"

"All the time." He was watching a young woman approach them through the crowd. "Never any Russians though."

★ ★ ★

When Nelson came back from a trip to the bar a young woman had joined Fay and Mike. She looked to be somewhere in her thirties and had jet-black hair tied back in a ponytail. To Nelson, the tooth she was missing made her seem even prettier.

"You look like your brother," she told him.

Her name was Rose. She was pleasantly drunk. When she talked she'd reach across the table and put her hand on his forearm. She wanted him to know what a nice guy his brother was. She hadn't known that Bert was missing, though he hadn't been in touch lately. She really hoped he'd be okay. "He could have just taken a plane somewhere. Sometimes he had to go away."

"Did you know him well?"

She laughed. "Well enough."

Fay sat with her arms folded on the table staring at old photos on the wall. Fay's last glass of beer was still almost full, so Nelson gave Rose the fresh beer he'd just bought. Rose smiled and touched his arm.

"You're just like your brother," she said. "Did I already tell you that?"

Sometimes, when Rose leaned closer, her hair brushed his face. She wore a nice perfume. Her kid was staying with her mother tonight. She didn't often get out anymore.

"Bert was in a real good mood last time I saw him. He was just back from London, England. He said he'd found something he'd been looking for for years. So we had a celebration."

The band had started playing again. Nelson had to shout. "Did Bert tell you what he'd found?"

"He did more than that. He left it in my apartment. I brought it here tonight in case I ran into him."

She fished in her bag and took out a book. The cover had photographs of old-time explorers with wooden skis and canvas tents and huskies and tobacco pipes. *Men of Ice*, said the title. *Leif*

Mills. Short biographies of two different polar explorers: Cecil Meares and Alister Forbes Mackay.

And what, thought Nelson, am I meant to do with this? He turned it over in his hands.

"Keep it safe," she said. "Don't go leaving it behind."

"Like Bert did?"

She punched his shoulder. "It was safe at my place! . . . That book meant a lot to him. He said he found it at some rare book store in England. It's the only book ever written about these two explorer guys he was interested in."

"Yeah?" He looked at the back but the words were too small for him. "Is it valuable?"

"It was to him. He told me it tied his stuff together."

"Tied what together?"

"He never really said. You're his brother. I thought you'd know what he was doing." She was watching the stage again. The band had struck up a new tune. This has to be their last set, he thought. They won't play on much longer.

"He must have said something."

"He said something about oats," said Rose, standing up. She took Nelson's hand and pulled him to his feet. "And about some guy called Cecil. That's a name you remember. Come on. We're dancing."

Ross Island, Antarctica, 1911

Blossom, Michael, Nobby, Punch. Blücher, Bones, Davy, Guts. James Pigg, Jehu, Hackenschmidt, Jones. Snatcher, Snippets, Uncle Bill. Weary Willie. Victor. Michael. Chinaman.

They did not belong here, but here they all would die, whatever that sentimental oaf Scott chose to tell himself. They would be worked to death in the snow and then shot and butchered and fed to Meares's dogs, and it would be he, Oates, who would have to do the killing while Scott stood by and wrung his precious hands.

The ponies were patient white ghosts in the dark of their stalls, their eyes gleaming in the glow from the stove. Outside, the wind off Mount Erebus sighed in the eaves of the little lean-to stable. A pony shifted its weight, snorted, and Oates caught the comforting smell of fresh-baked horse shit; for a moment it eclipsed the reek from the seal-blubber stove. From next door in the hut, through four layers of plank insulated with seaweed, he could hear the growl of talk and the plink of the player-piano. It was almost dinnertime: they'd all be in there now, yarning and scheming and pursuing half-humorous feuds—officers against ratings, gentlemen versus scientists, English against Australians, with Crean no doubt working his usual Irish mischief, singing "The Girl I Left Behind Me" deliberately off-key, or tricking Keohane into one of his famous Fenian outbursts.

Oates, who was an officer, a gentleman, English, would stay where he was in the stable, thawing out another block of the compressed fodder he'd paid for himself and smuggled aboard against Scott's direct orders. He would keep his own company until he heard the scraping of chairs around the long table.

Christ, he was sick of this. He had come here for real adventure, a famous journey, and had never felt more trapped in his life.

He had put it to Scott on the Ice Barrier, a hundred and forty miles south at the One Ton Depot: take the weakest ponies as far onward as we can, at least another thirty miles toward the pole, then put them out of their misery and cache them for their meat. It would only be a cruelty to try and bring the poor things back to Ross Island, half starved, up to their bellies in snow, the sweat freezing hard on their summer coats. Give them a last feed of mash, Oates had said (because he too could be sentimental), then when they're not looking, my revolver. They'll be fresh meat for the dogs in the next sledging season and for the men coming back from the pole.

Scott had ignored his horse expert, as Scott so often ignored the advice of his men. I'm afraid you'll regret it, sir, Oates had told him. And Scott, his lips aquiver, his eyes dull with the foreshadowing of his own failure and death, had bawled Oates out of it, effing and blinding as if he, Captain Lawrence Edward Grace Oates of the Inniskilling Dragoons, was one of Scott's common seamen. The ponies had suffered enough, Scott said. He'd have no further cruelty to animals for the sake of a few more days' march.

Scott knew nothing about horses and, if what Teddy Evans said was true, not as much as he should about battleships. But when it came to poetry, he knew all about that. He'd be at the head of the table already, jawing with Wilson about Tennyson and Ruskin, and he, Oates, would have no choice, being the army's sole representative on this naval expedition, but to sit at Scott's elbow and listen to his rot. And Scott, who for all his damned sensitivity was too bound up with himself to notice that Oates frankly despised him, would tease Oates for his silence, while Wilson, who saw everything, would smile like a saint with a spike up his arse and beatifically say nothing . . .

Davy and Jones had died before they even reached Ross Island, victims of the entirely predictable Southern Ocean storm that almost sank the overloaded *Terra Nova*. They had hauled the two dead ponies up through the forecastle skylight and consigned them to their namesake. It was as if Davy and Jones had been shipped expressly as offerings to the sea. If so, it had worked: the storm had stopped blowing.

Blücher and Blossom had collapsed on the Ice Barrier on the way back from the depot-laying trip last February, just as Oates had predicted. They died halfway back from One Ton Depot, where their corpses would be no use to man nor dog. Weary Willie had dragged himself on for another few marches before dying in sight of Mount Terror.

Guts had disappeared through a crack in the sea ice. Punch had died next, too numb to drag himself out of the water after missing his jump over an open lead; Oates, who had sent his revolver ahead, had to finish him off with an icepick. Then Uncle Bill got stuck in another crack and Bowers, whose pony he was, who loved the old thing dearly, insisted on swinging the icepick himself. That was no kind of job for poor Bowers. The skuas had wheeled around him like a blizzard, shrieking for their share. Nobby, Scott's own pony, was the only one saved from the debacle on the floes.

Of the eight ponies they had set out with to lay food depots for next season only two got back to Ross Island. None of the dead ones had been depoted anywhere useful. And when they finally got back to base at Cape Evans they found that Hackenschmidt, who had been left in reserve, had died in his stable after a short and mysterious illness. It was as if he'd foreseen what was coming and decided to have none of it.

Oates opened his notebook. He had already lost half of his ponies. There were only ten left.

Michael: lame near hind; ringbone; aged.

Bones: name speaks for itself; severe tapeworm infection.

James Pigg: sand crack near hind; aged.

Jehu: aged; debility, worn out.

Snatcher: half bald from lice.

Snippets: bad wind-sucker; doubtful back tendons off fore legs; lame off fore; pigeon toes.

Victor: narrow chest; knock-knees; bad eyes; aged; wind-sucker.

Michael: lame near hind bone; ringbone; aged.

Chinaman: ringworm just above coronet on near fore; the oldest of them all, which was quite a distinction.

Nobby: aged; spavin near hind, goes with stiff hocks; best of the lot of them. Which was why Scott had claimed him for himself.

The Mongolian horse traders must be laughing still. But it was Oates's own fault: he should have gone to Manchuria to select the ponies himself. Instead, he had allowed Scott to pass the job to Meares, who was going there anyway to buy the expedition's dogs.

The warmth from the stove made it hard to think clearly. He'd been outside in the cold air for most of the day, exercising his ponies. If I'm not careful, he thought, as his chin sank to his chest, I might drift off. He let his eyes flutter shut, pleasantly aware that he wasn't quite asleep yet, lulled by the comforting sounds of fed and restful ponies. Now he was sinking deeper.

And here they were again. He and his father, sitting in the lobby of the Bela Vista hotel in Funchal, waiting for Englebright to once again shoot himself. Englebright had shot himself before, the first time that Oates and his father had stayed in Madeira, when Oates had been only seven. It was on that same trip, he thought, that his father had died of typhoid fever. But had it been that trip, or the next one? Because he was sixteen now, and there was Father still alive, sitting across from him in a cane chair, his legs crossed, a newspaper folded in his lap, and when Englebright—aloof, ever-silent, said to be Swedish, or perhaps from Alaska—walked past them, taking the stairs that led to his death, William Oates smiled sadly at his son and shook his head. And Second Lieutenant Oates—now only days short of his twentieth birthday, wearing the khaki field-dress of the Second Anglo-Boer War, smiled back at his father. He would have to be especially nice to the old man today: there was something not quite right with him. Then he heard the shot he'd been waiting for in the hotel room upstairs. Presently, Oates knew, Englebright would once again be carried past them through the lobby, blood drooling from his temple. His father had gone back to his newspaper.

The stable door heaved open, jerking him awake. A man ducked inside and pulled the door shut. Oates's father was dead again. This intruder had killed him. The lower part of his woolen helmet was a mask of solid ice, but Oates recognized Cecil Meares from the quilted Cossack jacket that he wore around the camp.

Oates roused himself, tamping fresh tobacco in his pipe, as Meares stamped the snow from his boots and peeled off his balaclava, taking care lest the wool had frozen to his whiskers.

"I've been doing some thinking, Dearie," Oates said.

Meares, beating his arms around his body to warm himself, sat beside Oates on an upturned mash tub. He held his hands out to the stove. "Is that wise, Soldier? Doesn't it make your head hurt?"

"I've put it in my diary: it works out like this. Nineteen Mongol ponies. Cost: five pound each, not including transport halfway around the planet; actual worth here: fuck all. Three mechanical sledges. Cost: one thousand pound each; actual worth here: square root of fuck all. Your thirty-two Siberian sledge dogs. Cost: one pound ten a head; actual worth here: priceless."

Meares had peeled off one glove and was rubbing a patch of frostbite on his chin. "It's down to twenty-seven dogs now. The others seem to have eaten poor Vaska. When I dug them out of their drift this was all that I could find of her." He showed Oates a piece of bloody lampwick harness.

Oates lit his pipe, then threw another piece of blubber into the melting pan. It dwindled into a pool of hot oil, which drip-fed the ignition coil.

They sat for a while gazing into the fire. Silence was one of the things they admired in each other. Next door, voices were raised in argument, drowning out the pianola. The wind fussed outside in the snow.

Meares took his pipe from an inner pocket and polished its bowl. "If it stays fine," he said, "I shall take a run with the dogs down to Hut Point tomorrow. The sea ice has set in hard."

Hut Point again, thought Oates. Why is Meares always scheming to go back to that squalid hole?

"I thought," went on Meares, "you might join me. I need someone to drive a second team."

Oates was pleased at Meares's invitation, but he was practiced at hiding it: he had learned to buy horses in Ireland, at Smithfield and Ballinasloe. He tapped his pipe against the stove. "I expect the Owner wants someone to clean up the old hut a bit. He was moaning again last night about the state Shackleton's lot left it in the year before last."

Meares smiled. "As it happens, the Owner doesn't know I'm going there. As far as he's concerned, I'm giving the dogs a training run to the Ice Barrier. We should be there and back in the same day."

Oates stretched his bad leg out in front of him. A Boer bullet had left it two inches shorter than its neighbor. "Why not take Dmitri? I've had nothing to do with your mangy bow-wows."

"You'll like my dogs. They pull like an express train. Make a change from your sorry old nags." Meares rose to go. The chairs were scraping loudly in the main hut. Meares turned at the door. "Dmitri's a lovely fellow, but he's Russian. I need an Englishman tomorrow. One who has his own revolver."

"My revolver?"

"Oh yes." Meares gave him a wink. "One really ought to carry a pistol when driving dogs you don't know. Before they get used to you, they're just as likely to eat you. You just never know."

Oates considered that he lived in shrunken times. His hero was Napoleon, but he was sure that for himself there would never be an Austerlitz, nor even a frozen retreat. He would have to settle for the minor skirmish in the Klein Karoo that had shattered his leg, a silly affair diminished even further by the talk, which he scotched himself, that he ought to get a Victoria Cross for it.

Recovered enough to sit on a horse, he had spent the last months of the war with Rimington's Guides in the Orange Free State. He had hunted down starving farmers whose courage he rather admired, abducted their families, rustled their cattle, and set fire to their homes. His greatest triumph was to intercept a Boer wagon that was found to be loaded with baby chairs. For that, he remarked at the time, he would gladly have taken a medal.

Oates watched, bemused, the emerging mechanics of a new kind of war. By day, observation balloons were towed above the British columns, tethered to ox wagons. By night, search-lights flashed Morse on the clouds high above their camps, shar-ing news of the enemy's movements, of the names of his men, of the hills and the caves where his children were hiding. Armored trains steamed back and forth along Kitchener's new railways, their searchlights probing the dark.

One morning, leading his troop out on patrol, Oates came across a strange sight on the edge of their laager. A Benz motor car, shielded with boilerplate and mounting a Maxim gun, had broken down on the track. Its flimsy wheel spokes had buckled

under the weight of its armor. The driver said it had come from
the Rhodes mine workshop in Kimberley, one of Labram's last
ideas before that Long Tom shell killed him. Oates flicked his
reins to make his horse circle around the stranded armored car.
The next one, he thought, will work better than this. So much
for horse cavalry.

Soon after that he was back in a troopship, bound once again
for Madeira and the Curragh. In Ireland he would win every
steeplechase that a gentleman could enter. At the races in Punch-
estown, plunging over hedges with the Kildangan hunt, chasing
jackals in India, he never quite managed to break his own neck.

When war broke out between Russia and Japan in 1904 he
volunteered to go as a military observer. Even a secondhand war
would be better than none. But the Horse Guards refused him
leave of absence.

Cecil Meares had gone to that war. But as far as Oates could
tell, Meares had been some kind of private observer, neither
journalist nor military attaché. He had witnessed the fall of Port
Arthur, seen drowned Russian sailors in the Tsushima Strait.
Once, sitting together by the stove in the stables, Oates had asked
Meares point-blank what had sent him to the Far East in the first
place. Meares had raised his eyebrows and said, "I was trading in
furs." And Oates, who had seen that same bland look before, from
Castle men in Dublin, district commissioners in India, political
officers in Cairo, knew he should leave it at that.

It was Meares who had finally broken that silence. Reaching
into his Cossack jacket he took out a journal and—carefully, so
as not to open the pages to Oates's view—removed a paper from
it. Unfolding it, he showed it to Oates. It was, Oates saw, an old-
fashioned map of the Pacific coast of North America. Much of
the interior was blank, and the word "Oregon" appeared where
Oates would have expected to see "British Columbia." Meares
pointed to it.

"There," he said. "See that?"

Oates saw a small squiggle on the coast of Vancouver Island. "What of it?"

"That's Meares Island. It's named for my ancestor, John Meares. Have you ever heard of him?"

"I can't say I have, Dearie."

"He was born in Dublin in the eighteenth century and got a commission in the navy. Later, he began smuggling sea otter pelts into Macau from Alaska. To do that, he had to play the East India Company against the South Sea Company, the English against the Spanish, the Russians against the Cantonese, and the local redskins against the Yankees. He almost caused a war between England and Spain. It was thanks to his shenanigans that the Admiralty sent George Vancouver to chart that coast and claim it for the crown. And also, to look for the Northwest Passage, which my ancestor had sworn was somewhere thereabouts. So if it wasn't for John Meares, British Columbia would now be Russian Columbia. Or Yankee Columbia. Yet the man was practically a pirate."

"You seem to admire him."

"Oh yes: like me, he was trading in furs." Meares tapped the tiny island again, then folded the map, stowing it back in his journal. "Someday I shall go and live in those parts. According to family legend, he buried his treasure there."

The sun had set the week before and wouldn't rise until September. But its fossilized light, seeping up from the northern horizon, backlit the cone of Erebus where it smoked above the camp. To the west, across the ice of McMurdo Sound, this rumor of light touched the Royal Society Range, raising its peaks from the dead. There was a pink tint too on the ice to the northwest. Beyond that, Oates fancied he could see a water sky: perhaps the Ross Sea wasn't yet wholly frozen.

It was the sky above that shocked him. The sea ice, the western mountains, the island where he stood, were shades of black and gray and pastel, like a half-remembered dream. But the abyss above him blazed with life and business. Far above, a band of nacreous cloud caught the last of the year's civil twilight, a gauzy patch of iridescent pinks and mauves. The stars burned so fiercely that it seemed to Oates if he held his breath he would hear them. They shone so hard that he wanted to duck.

Meares and Dmitri were attaching the dogs to the sledges, a job that seemed to require a great deal of violence and swearing in Russian: the only language, Meares said, that his dogs understood. Oates watched until he saw how it was done, then grabbed a dog by the scruff of its neck and toggled its harness to a lamp-wick trace.

"Good," said Meares. "We'll make a dog man of you yet." He nodded at the fan of traces, half a dozen of them, which attached six straining dogs to the hoop of Oates's sledge. As the dogs heaved and whined, eager to be off, Dmitri turned the sledge on its side and anchored it with an ice hook.

Oates considered his sledge. No reins, no bits, no bridles, just half a dozen vicious Samoyeds sizing him up with their evil yellow eyes, panting slowly and licking their lips.

Meares handed him a whip. "It's very simple," he told Oates. "Your dogs will want to follow me on my sled. If you want them to go faster, crack the whip. If you want to stop, turn the sledge on its side. Try not to break your neck."

"How do I make them turn?"

"You don't. That's lesson two. For today you just sit tight on the sledge and your dogs will follow mine."

"Right . . . So what do you really need me for?"

Meares stepped up to his own sledge, hopped onto the end of it and pulled out the anchor. "Ballast," he said, then shouted in Russian.

He shot off across the crusted snow. Oates's dogs, yammering to follow, jerked so hard against their traces that they dislodged the anchor holding the sledge. Still not settled on the back, Oates was thrown backward onto the snow. Dmitri, hovering wisely a little to the front, jumped into the sledge and bawled at the dogs until they came to a stop thirty yards off. Oates heard ironic cheers from Wind Vane Hill; Cherry-Garrard had witnessed his defeat.

By the time he was underway again Meares was already a dot on the sea ice, veiled by the snow plume kicked up by his dogs. The landfast ice had settled in hard for the winter. Rounding Cape Evans to seaward, they encountered only a few small pressure ridges off its western tip, folds of buckled ice holding drifts of deep snow. Apart from that, the ice on the sound appeared smooth and unbroken, its flaws hidden by powder blown off the Plateau.

Oates, who was still some distance behind Meares, felt alone for the first time since the ship had left South Africa. His dogs paid him no attention. They were bent to their task, loping along, tongues lolling, their frozen breath jabbing the air. The sledge-runners sang like a bass violin. He could understand now why, as Meares had told him, the dogs loved their work.

Having weathered Cape Evans they steered a course across South Bay, threading the channel between Inaccessible Island and Tent Island, sheer black pyramids streaked with white ice. Little and Great Razorback islands passed to their left, with Turks Head rearing above them. Across the sound, the peaks of the Royal Society Range gleamed in the starlight. Oates felt he could reach across and run his finger down their edge.

His dogs, warming to their task, made ground on Meares, now a hundred yards ahead. Oates wondered why he couldn't feel the wind on his face. Then he realized his mistake, and slipped his hands from his wolfskin mittens to massage the blood back into his cheeks. Pulling his scarf up over his face, he watched Glacier Tongue spool past on the left, then he stretched flat on his back to stare up at the stars.

It had taken Oates and his ponies a day to reach Hut Point the last time he had gone there, during the autumn depot-laying expedition. He had considered that good going. Now, only a little over two hours after leaving base at Cape Evans, he was outside the disused *Discovery* hut at Hut Point.

The entrance was packed with hard névé snow compacted by the winter storms. He and Meares took turns attacking it with their shovels, shedding first their windproofs, then their jerseys, until they both stood in their woolen undershirts steaming in the cold. At last the tiny front door, sheltered by wide overhanging eaves, appeared at the end of their snow tunnel. They levered it open, replaced their jerseys, and crawled inside.

Snow lay thick on the south-facing skylights, admitting only a faint blue glow. A paraffin candle, once lit, conjured tinned food and biscuits, bits of old harness hanging from rafters, all furred with silver crystals, the petrified breath of the last men to leave.

"Let's take a rest," suggested Meares. "Have a smoke and a bite to eat. Then we can do our business and go."

What business? thought Oates. But he settled himself on a packing case and busied himself with his pipe.

They smoked in silence for a while, listening to the tethered dogs bickering outside. When Oates sat with Meares, or with Atkinson, in the hut at Cape Evans, Griff Taylor would make bets with his fellow Australians on which would be first to break his silence. Often the bets went unwon.

The hut was fragrant with pipe smoke when Meares finally spoke. "Will you go back to your regiment when the ship calls here next summer? Or do you still hope to be in the party that will go to the pole?"

Oates thought about the close confinement, the winter routine, the prospect of another season of drudgery commanded by yet another stuffy idiot whose rank exceeded his manners—it turned out that in this regard the navy was scarcely any better than the cavalry. And worse than that, even more dispiriting, because it was so unfamiliar, was his growing fear of failure: if the ponies proved a crock next season, as Oates was all but sure they would, Scott would put the blame on him. He dreaded the looks he would get in the mess room on the Curragh, the first meeting with his mother at their country place in Gestingthorpe.

"In principle, I'm only here for the ponies . . . Once their job is done at the foot of the glacier, I should return here in time for the ship . . . But if Scott does decide to name me in the polar party I'll have to see it through . . . That's hardly likely though: Wilson knows I've got a bad leg thanks to that Boer bullet . . . Then again, Scott's always so keen on paying compliments to me as the only soldier on this jaunt . . . The devil of it is, the Inniskillings didn't want me to come here in the first place. My particular chum, old Terrot, begged me not to go. He'd heard that Scott was a bit of a bungler."

Meares's pipe flared several times in quick succession, semaphoring his stifled laughter.

"I shall be going back with the ship next autumn," he said. "I shan't stay for the second winter."

Now that was a surprise. "You don't think Scott will want you and your dogs to go to the pole with him?"

Meares shook his head. "I don't. He doesn't believe in dogs, against all science and reason . . . But either way, I shall go back with the ship when it calls next summer. I'll have no choice. The ship will be bringing bad news for me."

"How do you know that?"

"I've already arranged for it."

Oates was inwardly delighted. This was a man who saw other horizons. "I see."

Meares tapped his pipe out, emptying the embers into a fruit tin on the floor. "There wouldn't be much point in me sticking around here for another winter. I shall have business in Europe: there's going to be a war. Dmitri can handle the dogs, if Scott still wants to use them. In any case, Wilson and Cherry are learning to manage them too."

"Dmitri can't handle the dogs half as well as you do," said Oates. "However did you learn to beat a Siberian at his own game?"

It was a direct question, almost unthinkable. Meares stood up and crossed the room. His boots drummed loudly on the bare wooden floor.

"I had plenty of opportunity to learn," he said. "Once, I sledged nearly two thousand miles from Okhotsk to Cape Chelyuskin, then the same back again. I don't expect you'll have heard of it, but Cape Chelyuskin is the most northerly point on the mainland of Asia, about as close to the North Pole as we are to the South Pole here. Not to boast, but I doubt if any other Englishman ever made that journey overland. Not many Russians either. I was a different man when I got back from that trip."

"Did you buy many furs when you were up there?"

"Not on that occasion. Things got a bit fraught and I couldn't stay long. I shall have to go back someday. Perhaps next time you can come along."

Oates worked hard to hide his pleasure. "I'm surprised the Russians let you go there at all. I hear they don't care much for foreigners wandering about in Siberia. Particularly Englishmen."

"I expect I forgot to ask their permission. Cape Chelyuskin is an interesting spot. If the Russians could find a reliable anchorage in that area they could switch their warships back and forth between the Pacific and the Atlantic without anyone being the wiser. Which would double their potential naval power in both theaters."

Oates knew of the Battle of Tsushima Strait, in which the Russian Baltic Fleet, having steamed very publicly halfway around the planet, was destroyed in one day by the waiting Japanese. Meares had witnessed it. Ponting, the expedition's photographer, had been there too, for *Harper's Weekly*.

Oates spat into the fruit tin. "Ponting says that the Russians took you prisoner during the war of '04. They thought you were a spy. The Japanese too. He said you were rather knocked up when he met you."

"That was all a misunderstanding. The Russians were rather upset, what with just having lost two fleets one after the other. And the Japs were only being prudent. I'm on much better terms with both of them now."

"I heard that too. Wilfred Bruce said that you shipped your dogs to Vladivostok on a Russian destroyer. He couldn't believe his eyes as he stood on the dock and saw you waving from the bridge."

"It was a stroke of good fortune. I happened to know the skipper. He said they were coming my way."

Oates sucked on his pipe, found it expired. He tapped it out and stood. "I brought the revolver, by the way."

Meares had gone into a corner of the hut. He was testing the frost-silvered floorboards. "Good man."

Oates followed him over. "The dogs seemed alright to me. I didn't have to shoot so much as one."

"Oh yes," said Meares. He was tapping a board with the toe of his boot. "They were angels. They're fine when they get running."

"I had a mad idea you were worried about Amundsen."

"Amundsen? No. He's hundreds of miles away. And besides, he's a friend of ours anyway. The Norwegians are keen on having allies in London to back them against the Swedes. Amundsen has helped us out before. . . . But of course, you never quite know."

Oates watched Meares kneel on the floor, gently pulling at the board. He lowered his head, peering at it, then grunted in satisfaction.

"This is it," he said. "Could you kindly pass me that ice ax? The one on the wall over there?"

Perhaps, thought Oates, I ought not to be involved in this. He didn't believe in a god, but he worshipped reserve, and it occurred to him now that reserve and secrecy were not the same thing at all. A secret was a form of compulsion, like marriage, or employment, and once he committed himself to Meares he could never decently repudiate him. If he went along with this, no ship could take him all the way back to hunting and yachting and mannerly boredom. Perhaps, he thought, I should go outside and see how the dogs are.

He went over to the far corner of the hut and collected the ice ax, which hung by its thong from a nail.

"Thanks, Soldier. Now would you mind fetching the candle as well?"

Oates stood over Meares, holding the light. Their breaths came together in one silver cloud. Meares inserted the point of the ax into the crack of the floor and rocked it gently back and forth, widening the gap without straining the plank. When the space was broad enough, he slipped both hands in on either side of the plank, close to where it was nailed to the joist. Then he hauled smartly upward. The plank came away in one piece in his hands.

Meares set it to one side, its protruding nails downward. Beneath the joists was a layer of felt insulation rimed with ice.

"Hold the candle a bit lower, please."

There was a hole in the felt, or rather a flap had been cut in it, three sides of a rectangle, and the felt then replaced. Meares reached down and pulled the flap upward. Beneath it, a wooden tea chest was sunk in the snow that filled the space beneath the hut.

Meares sat back on his heels and smiled at Oates.

"It's still here," he said.

"What is?"

"The thing I was sent to collect. I couldn't risk digging it up when we all stayed here together last autumn. Too many people around."

"You were sent? Scott told me he signed Ponting up to do the photography. He said it was Ponting who brought you in."

Meares stood up, easing his knees. "That's what Scott was meant to think. As for Ponting, this is probably my last job with him. He wants to go into the moving pictures when this trip is over. I'm going to need someone else."

Oates pointed at the tea chest. "What's in it?"

"I'll show you."

The tea chest was held by the ice, but by chipping carefully with the ax Meares freed two sides, then levered it clear. He set it between them and pried the top open, taking care not to tear the lead strips that sealed its plywood seams. Inside, the chest was padded with barley straw. From it protruded the neck of a bottle.

"Good old Mawson!" said Meares. He pulled out the bottle and showed it to Oates: Mackinlay's Rare Old Highland Whisky. Meares set it reverently down on the floorboards, then rummaged again in the straw. When his hand came out again it held an old hardwood case about eight inches square and six inches deep. A white-silvered clock face showed through its glass lid.

"It's a marine chronometer," Oates said doubtfully.

It seemed to Oates unexceptional: their own expedition had been issued with several chronometers by the Greenwich Observatory.

This whole jaunt is a joke. Meares has been teasing me, not testing me. And I'll be the first to laugh if it's the price of a swallow of whiskey on a dry expedition. "To whom do we owe the pleasure?"

"The chronometer?" said Meares. "It was lent to Douglas Mawson—the Australian geologist who was here two years back with Shackleton's lot."

"I meant the whiskey."

Ignoring him, Meares held up the clock for Oates's inspection. "This, Soldier, has been all the way to the south magnetic pole. It went there with Mawson and David and Mackay two years ago. They'd a terrible time of it. It's a miracle they made it back."

"It looks ancient. Couldn't Greenwich give Mawson a newer one?"

"Greenwich knew nothing about it. Mawson got this one from somebody else."

"From who?"

Meares stowed the chronometer inside his Cossack jacket. "From the people who sent me."

He reached into the straw and pulled out a leather-bound surveyor's journal almost as long as the tea chest was square. He flicked through it. Oates saw pages of maps and columns of figures—degrees and minutes and seconds. Meares closed the journal again and laid it on the floor. "Good."

He reached farther into the box and took out a bag tied shut with a drawcord. It seemed quite heavy. "Ah," said Meares, again pleased. He untied the drawstring, looked inside, and tied it shut again.

"What fresh delight is this?"

Meares shook the bag. It rattled. "Rocks. Mawson fossicked them in the mountains on his way to the magnetic south. But when he got back here he thought someone was trying to steal his things, so he hid them under the hut. I daresay he'd gone a bit mad after his terrible journey. Mackay and David certainly had. Before Mawson came back to his senses, Shackleton returned from eighty-eight south and whisked them all home."

"They must be very valuable if you've come all this way to get them. Or is it the maps that they wanted? Or the clock?" Oates still didn't know who *they* were.

Meares busied himself with the tea chest, replacing its lid. "I wouldn't know, Soldier. I was only told to fetch the contents of the box. Except for the whiskey. I was told I could keep that. Let's put the floor back the way it was. Then we can have a drink, and I'll tell you a little about Room 38."

Ross Ice Shelf, 1912

March 16th
On the Ice Barrier

Dearie,

For privacy's sake I'm folding this note into my diary, which I shall give to Birdie Bowers to pass on to my mother. I can trust him not to open it. Mother will find some way to get it to you—she already knows from my letters what great friends we are.

I need hardly say how sorry I am about this. As I feared all along, the decision to include me in the polar party was made by Scott at the last minute. It was a compliment to the army. And so a half-crippled cavalry man was honor-bound to walk to the South Pole and back. Or most of the way back, anyway. The wound from that Boer bullet has reopened because of the scurvy. My leg weeps constantly, my feet are gangrenous, and I can no longer keep up with the others. They are very good about waiting for me, but I know from their eyes what they think.

I wish I could describe this place to you as well as I should like. A haze hides the mountains to our west, so that we might as well be back on the plateau. Before us there is nothing but a level plain of sastrugi covering the Ice Barrier, some of them like ripples on the sea, others bent back on themselves like four-foot waves that froze while breaking. The sun never sets but only circles us constantly, staring at us through the canvas when we try to sleep at night. I should not say "night," for it only makes me long for one. Even the blizzards don't relieve us from the glare.

Tell old Jane Atkinson I send him my love, and Cherry of course. I hope that Birdie will make it back to join you all in the Tenements, though if he does it will be a fine-run thing. He and Wilson and Scott aren't much stronger than I am, though at least they can still walk.

Please consider my revolver a permanent gift. I can't think why you wanted to borrow it for your homeward journey: what anyone would want with your rocks and maps and chronometer I cannot imagine. Working for Room 38 must be very romantic. I should have enjoyed the fur trade, I think—all those wonderful secrets to keep.

Tomorrow is Saint Patrick's Day, and also my birthday. I recollect that you yourself were born in Kilkenny. When Saint Patrick's Day next comes around again, pour a whisky for him and another for me, and remember our toast in the Tenements: Down with science, sentiment, and the fair sex!

L.E.G. Oates

PART FIVE

Meares Island

49°10′N 125°50′W

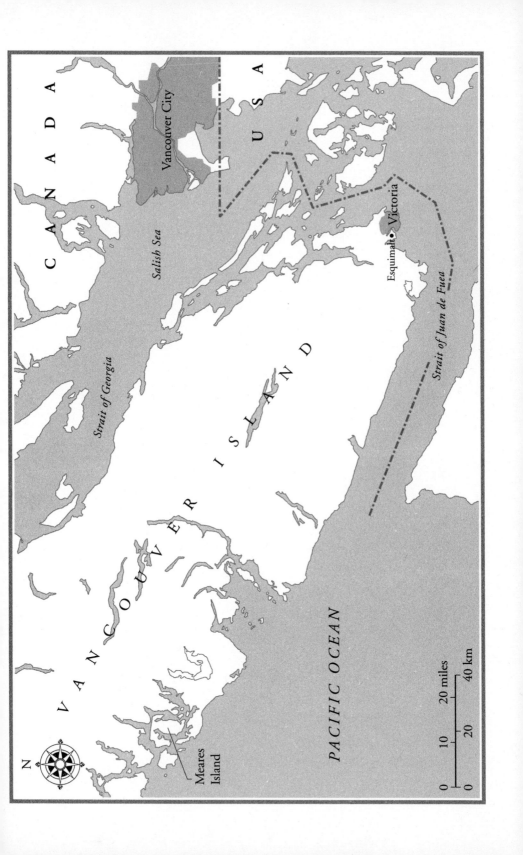

Inuvik, Northwest Territories

The curtains were closed and the light that oozed through them, the sodium glare from the parking-lot floodlights, leached all the color from the ceiling and walls. It fell across the carpet, turning scattered clothing into islands of a sea. The ribbed back of a chair threw a grid-shaped shadow. To Fay, lying on her side, the room looked cold and distant, but the air was warm against her bare shoulder.

By day Bert's carpet was beige, she remembered. Or rather, it was beige in the light of the bulb in the ceiling. She had never seen the apartment in daylight, and there wouldn't be any daylight today. But she couldn't sleep, and she had a bad headache and the rasp of cigarettes in her throat. She was still a little drunk, she knew; her headache would get worse.

She felt his breathing change. He turned on his side, put an arm around her, and pulled her back against him.

I should have sneaked away earlier.

She cleared her throat painfully. She needed to speak before he did, to set a hard, jolly tone before he could embarrass them.

"Do you think Mike got off with that girl Rose?"

His voice was muffled by her shoulder. "I doubt it. She's his niece."

Fay listened to the sounds of a new day outside the apartment. Engines coughed in the parking lot. Footsteps crunched in new snow. A door crashed open in the corridor, in the limbo outside the apartment, and a man and woman came through it, muttering together in slow tired voices, feet dragging on the carpet. They passed through the swing doors and ceased to exist. The light in the window didn't change.

"We should get up," she said finally. "I have to check out of my room today. It's booked for someone else."

"Oh . . . Where will you go?"

She didn't answer him. Lying as they did she couldn't see his face. And she thought: What else is there outside this room? But she had called him a loser, called him a liar, and then she got drunk and danced with him, and after that, this. It made it hard for her to look at herself, much less at him, and in fact she hadn't turned to face him in all the time she had lain there since she'd woken.

I really ought to look at him, to give the poor bastard his due.

She eased herself onto her back. The bed was so small that her left buttock lay half over his right hip. His right arm was still underneath her. It was uncomfortable for both of them, but she had no right to expect him to move. She turned her head and looked at him. His face was only inches from hers. They had kissed in the taxi. She remembered the taste.

"I'm sorry," she said. "I made a mistake." She saw the hurt on his face and added quickly: "I mean, about your brother, and all the rest of it."

His face relaxed, and she hardened her heart again. You don't understand, she wanted to tell him. We really shouldn't have done this. I really do have to go.

"No one could blame you," he said. "You found your grandfather's name on my brother's desk. That's a long-shot coincidence."

You don't know the half of it, mate. You don't know the part about my grandfather's clock. You don't even know that I'm dead.

Maybe I should trust him. Maybe I should tell him everything. God knows he has things of his own to be scared of: including me, if he has any sense.

The door into the sitting room was open. Without moving her head she could see the dark shapes of the books and folders piled on the desk, the rectangular screen of the laptop. What else was lying in wait for her there?

You're almost broke. He has an apartment. He has a desk full of questions and answers. He has the Internet and central heating. But if you tell him any more of your secrets he'll probably get scared and kick you right out of here.

"It's probably just chance." She was glad she didn't have to look at him. "Like Mike said: your brother and my grandfather both worked in the Arctic. They were both Canadians. They both had something to do with mapmaking . . . And if you look at the maps of the Arctic, and Antarctic too, you'll see the same people's names repeated over and over again. And most of those people were connected to one another. Maybe stories converge at the poles. Like the lines on the map." He said nothing. If I don't know what I'm bullshitting about, how should he? "What I'm saying is, it doesn't matter. Stranger things happen . . . Anyway, I have to leave town now. I don't have anywhere to stay."

She waited. He retrieved his right arm from beneath her and turned on his back, shielding his eyes with the back of his hand. Now that both his shoulders were on the mattress she was pushed half over the edge of the bed. She ought to turn onto her side, either facing him or facing away. Instead, she drew the comforter up to her chin. The cold air welled up under it where she overhung the bed.

"You know," he said, still shielding his eyes, "you could always stay here. Until you fly out."

She became so still that it hurt. She shouldn't do this to him. But she had no money and nowhere to go.

There was a little strand of cobweb on the ceiling, near the cord of the unlit bulb. She could only see it when it moved in the current from the heating vent. She fixed her eyes on it, as if it could anchor her.

"No obligations," he said. "It's just somewhere to stay if you need it."

Does he really mean that? "I thought you had to tell the police about your brother."

"I can wait until you're gone. Another day won't make any difference."

"What will you do after that?"

"I have that job interview down in Whitehorse."

She was grateful for his lie. It was something she could forgive him for, and she needed the trade: she'd be needing some forgiveness for herself.

"You could look through some more of Bert's stuff."

"Yeah?" She was careful not to sound too interested.

"Only if you want to . . . I guess you're probably right about him. It's probably just a coincidence. And Bert was crazy anyway."

"He could still turn up here."

"He'd have some explaining to do."

She yawned quite deliberately, to give herself a cue. "That book," she said casually, "the one that girl gave you last night. Was that Bert's?"

He had to think about that. "Book? . . . He left it at her place last time he stayed there. It was about two old explorer guys. Apparently Bert said it was very important to whatever he was doing."

"Maybe I'll take a look at it. While we have time . . . You still want to know what your brother was doing, right?"

"I guess. Why not . . . Though what does it matter now?"

I could tell him, she thought. I could tell him how much it matters to me, Hugh Morgan's granddaughter. But she'd had that chance already, and she'd already let it pass.

Victoria, British Columbia, 1919

When Hughie Morgan turned twelve his foster parents gave him a bicycle. It was a full-frame black CCM touring bike, one of the last to be built in the Vancouver workshop. Although bought secondhand it was as good as new; the first owner, a soldier returned from the North Russia Intervention, had brought the "Spanish Lady" back from Murmansk: overcome by the 'flu, he fainted right outside the bicycle store and never rode it once.

Hughie's birthday fell on a Sunday that year so he had to wait another day for his first proper go on the bicycle. The saddle was set much too high for him; even after Jim Morgan took a wrench to it Hughie could barely reach the pedals with his toes. He was still a small boy, slow to grow, a little stout maybe, and prone to asthma in the mild Vancouver Island winters. But Annie and Jim hoped he would grow into his gift.

The next day—it being the school holidays—Annie Morgan made him sandwiches and a flask of tea and sent him off on his first lonely cycling trip. Jim and Annie stood together in the door of their little clapboard house in Fairfield and waved to him gamely as he wobbled off down the road. When he was gone they turned to each other and tried to smile. Their claim to the child had always felt tenuous, and as Hugh vanished around the corner they understood that they were teaching themselves to say goodbye. They didn't see him crash into a brewer's dray, remount, and cycle off again, while the driver waved his whip and yelled curse words at his back. The scrapes and bruises didn't bother him. The bicycle was made of strong steel tubes with heavy chrome wheel rims: it could also take a bashing. He was gliding alone through the air.

His road took him south and west out of town to the naval port at Esquimalt. There he halted by the harbor and searched for the vessels of the Royal Navy's Pacific Squadron. There was only one, an elderly destroyer alongside the coaling quay. A keen reader of boys' newspapers, Hughie could see at a glance that this wasn't much of a warship: unfashionably spindly, almost Gothic in its lines, it had only two funnels—not enough for it to be a modern steam-turbine job—and its puny forward deck gun had no turret to encase it. Good enough for the eastern Pacific, Hughie thought scornfully. Real adventures happened elsewhere, far beyond the sheltered waters of the Strait of Juan de Fuca.

A team of sailors worked with shovels on the quay beside the old destroyer, their denims black with dust. A crane rose and dipped from a stokehold amidships. Hughie had been standing there for a minute or two, maybe more, staring at the sea beyond the Royal Roads, when he noticed that the sailors were going the wrong way about their work. They were moving the coal from the ship to the quay. And then he understood: it's all up with that old tub over there. She's being decommissioned. She'll be broken up for scrap, or towed out to sea and used for target practice. And with that his mood reversed, and he felt an aching need to say good-bye to the rusty old destroyer. He didn't know her name, and he would never see her again. The naval docks were closed to civilians (quite properly, he thought: there might still be Hun fifth columnists bent on rekindling the war) so had to say good-bye to her from here. If he could only know and say her name. But the ship was too far away for him to read the letters on her rail. He watched for a little while longer, then remounted his bike and rode on.

For the rest of his life Hughie Morgan would believe that this unremarkable little day trip had been his great turning point, his first leap into the unknown. He was only half right about this: his first great journey had in fact been made several years earlier, just after he'd learned to walk, when the incarnation of all warmth and love in the universe, sad gray eyes and a shabby red coat, had sent him toddling down the path of the Methodist mission in Victoria. Having achieved his task, he had proudly turned around to look for her approval, only to find she was gone. But he had long since lost hold of that memory: that doomed old destroyer was only the first in a series of messengers that came in disguise and never quite got through to him.

The bicycle was secondhand but it wasn't free. After the war came the slump, when Jim Morgan could no longer count on full-time work in the gardens of Vancouver Island. Nothing was said, but young Hugh understood and he needed no encouragement. The Canadian Pacific Telegraph office was looking for part-time messenger boys, own bicycle required. Hughie was still a bit young for the job, but Jim knew the chief clerk from chapel. With Hughie's agreement he had a word.

Hughie's new uniform consisted of a peaked officer's cap with a Canadian Pacific hat band, twill trousers, and a blue brass-buttoned jacket with pockets for notebooks and pencils and change. Leather gaiters sat over the tops of his boots, protecting his trousers from the bicycle chain. The trousers themselves were cut wide at the thigh and narrow below the knee, cavalry-fashion, and during his first weeks on the job he would often manage to catch sight of himself in the plate-glass front of the telegraph office. It might have been the cut of the uniform, or maybe some distortion in the set of the glass, but in that window he looked fitter and thinner. And very soon he really did: the war was over, but the Great Influenza had taken up the slack, and for his first few months on the job there was plenty of somber telegram traffic, both civilian and military, to keep him in the saddle for most of each shift.

Eventually the last men straggled home from the loose ends of war in Russia and Mesopotamia. The influenza burned itself out. Money was still short, and businesses were folding. But the office still had to keep several boys on standby in their bare wooden cubby at the back of the counter. At first, Hughie tried to pass the time with his reading—true adventures, mostly, and popular science magazines and tales of exploration—but the other boys were rowdy and refused to let him be. They were older than him, and most of them bigger, and he had to put up with their teasing and pranks. And by the time he was sixteen, and too senior to mess with, he had found something better to do at work than read books: his boss Sandy Rees, who had taken a liking to him, was teaching him Morse.

Hugh's sessions at the key came in the slack times, when the telegraph clerks went outside to smoke. At first Hughie was confined to the bush wires, the lines to sub-offices on Vancouver Island. Slowly at first, and then with increasing fluency, he learned to pound the brass, sending and receiving between Victoria and its outstations at Esquimalt and Nanaimo and points farther north. Soon he could easily do thirty-five words per minute, racing against his rivals in the bush offices. Each sender had their own accent or "fist," and he learned them all by ear.

Officially, Hughie was still a mere messenger, though he spent less and less time on his bike. One day the provincial manager came on the line from Vancouver to ask the name of the clerk in Victoria with the beautiful clear fist. Two days later Hughie was offered a full-time job as a telegraph clerk first-class, skipping the training grade. He went home and told Jim and Annie Morgan, knowing that they could use the extra cash. But they asked him to say no: he was, they pointed out, doing very well at school, and might even win the scholarship that would get him into college. And besides—though they didn't say it, though they all understood—if Hughie signed up full-time the company would send him away from them, to one of the tiny two-person bush stations that were spreading across the forests and the prairies. He himself wouldn't have minded: Victoria felt small. But he was a dutiful son, and he obeyed his parents.

Rees said he understood and congratulated him on his ambition. But Hughie thought he detected disappointment, maybe even resentment, in his boss. And his suspicions increased the next day when—on a raw mid-February afternoon—Rees yanked him off the Morse key and—despite the presence in the office of two other idle messengers—sent him on his bike to the Angela Hotel.

Old Captain Rant, who owned and ran the Angela Hotel, was a fanatical gardener who would allow nothing to spoil the perfection of his grounds—not even the temporary intrusion of a delivery bike. Hugh propped a pedal on the curb outside the gate, then looked around for suspicious characters: thefts were not unknown, even here on wealthy Burdett Avenue. But there was no one on the street, just a distant automobile hissing through puddles. A cold wind from the mainland tossed the crowns of the trees, showering him with drops.

The Angela was one of the oldest and largest buildings in this old and wealthy neighborhood, solid red brick with tall Gothic windows and a spike-roofed tower in the front. The main door was in the base of the tower, under a new porte cochere with brick and steel pillars, a nod to the rise of the automobile. Hugh paused in its shelter to shake the rain from his cape. Then—as telegraph boys were privileged to enter by the front, so that guests could observe their arrival—he pushed the door and went inside.

The lobby was warm and brightly lit. There was a fire in the hearth, and winter flowers stood in jars around the walls. A man and a woman, evidently guests, sat behind newspapers in cane chairs by the fire. Hugh smelled pipe-smoke and pine.

He waited dutifully in the doorway, stamping his wet boots. When neither guest reacted he started toward the office—the Angela was a residential hotel, catering to long-term guests and the more sedate class of tourist, and Captain Rant saw no need for a vulgar desk out front. Hugh heard the rustle of a newspaper.

"I wonder, young fellow, if that telegram is for me?"

The man by the fire had lowered his newspaper. His upper-class British accent was exaggerated by the briar stem clamped in his teeth: it clipped his vowels and tapped up his consonants. He looked to be in his forties and his cloudy blue eyes had a touch of a squint to them, as if he'd spent too much time looking into the sun. The hair was thin on top and his mustache was convention-ally trim, but his face was a little too lean and unnaturally dark, tanned by something other than weather. The woman read on, still invisible.

Hugh looked at the name on the envelope. "Are you Colonel Meares?"

"Lieutenant-Colonel Meares." There was a turn to his lips, as if his name contained a private joke.

Meares folded his newspaper, then stood up to receive his envelope. He opened it and read the telegram, then reached into his pocket and fished out a coin. "Here," he said. "There's no reply."

Hugh looked at the half-dollar in his hand. "We're paid by the company, sir. We're not supposed to take tips."

The colonel sat down. He curled his lip again. "Well, I usually give them."

Hugh wanted to say: Look, of course we take tips, whatever the company says; but this is too much. The colonel forestalled him.

"I'll give you the same again," he said, "if you'll do something for me. I'm expecting another telegram this evening. It's rather important. If it comes through, I'd like it brought to me as quickly as ever you can. And you give it to me in person, not the hotel staff. But it's only one particular telegram. There may be others but they're not urgent. They can wait for the regular rounds."

Hugh puzzled it over, still fingering the coin. This was unusual. "If there's more than one message," he asked, "how will I know which one is the urgent one?"

Colonel Meares, who had already picked up his paper, studied him over the top of it. "You'll know," said Meares, "from the name on it. If it says 'Commander Meares' instead of 'Colonel Meares,' it's the one that I need."

The woman lowered her newspaper. She was maybe fifteen years younger than her husband, her dark hair daringly worn in a bob. She looked at Hugh with droll brown eyes, then turned to her husband. "You aren't much bothered about 'Mr. Meares' today either, are you, dear? We can set him aside too."

Meares nodded gravely. "That's right. Just the Commander. He's the only man for me today. If Commander Meares gets a message, please bring it directly to me and no one else. If I have to go out I'll leave word where you can find me. Any other telegrams you can leave with the staff."

Mrs. Meares smiled at Hugh. "It's Valentine's Day," she said, as if that explained it. And then she winked at him.

Hugh beat his retreat. He was sure he was blushing. Are they messing with me or with each other? What's this funny business with the name and the ranks?

Later that evening, just as the office was about to close for the night, a telegram arrived for the Angela Hotel. The clerk pinged the bell and Hughie, who was the last boy on the late shift, reached in through the hatch and took the message from its rack.

There it was on the envelope: "Commander C.H. Meares RN."

He could hear the late clerk moving about in the office, putting his coat on, getting ready to lock up. He called out to Hughie. "Say, Morgan—that last message is logged in at ten-oh-two. You want me to say you'd just left for the night, so someone else can deliver it in the morning? That rain's trying to turn into snow."

Hughie looked at the name on the envelope and thought of the half-dollar in his trouser pocket. He didn't care a whole lot about the wet and the cold; he rather enjoyed them: they made him feel unaccountably joyful. But nor did he like to do tricks for money. And he didn't like fishy business, or being laughed at by rich people.

"I dunno," he said slowly. What was so important about this telegram? Once sealed by the clerk, it could only be opened by the recipient. Then he had an idea. "Did the message seem urgent to you?"

There was a rustle on the other side of the partition as the clerk consulted the wet-tissue copy of the message he had typed. "Nah. It's just a greeting. Four words: 'Happy birthday Meares. Carpendale.'" Hughie heard the rustle again. "It's from Nome, in Alaska."

There had to be more to this message than that. But if Hughie left it until morning someone else would deliver it. He wouldn't get the half-dollar. And he would never know any more.

"I'll take it up there now."

The wind was in his face on the stretch to the hotel, lashing him with sleet and the last dead leaves to have clung through the winter. It numbed his face and pinched his hands.

Meares and his wife were in the lobby with a crowd of merrymakers, dressed for a ball. They laughed and talked in loud foreign voices. The men wore ribbons and medals and the women gleamed with jewels. Every hand held a glass of champagne. Even the women were smoking. Hugh, who liked to think he was a man of the world now, ignored this loose behavior and, sidling up to Meares, who was listening to an old man tell an old man's story, slipped him the message. Now, he thought, I'll see some reaction. I'll learn something from this. But Meares, not even looking at Hugh, merely glanced at the name on the envelope, smiled to himself, and put it unopened into his pocket. His hand came out with another coin that he held poised between his fingers, keeping Hughie waiting until the old man was done. Then he turned and spoke quietly.

"Good work. Come see me tomorrow. I need a smart chap to run a few errands."

Hugh didn't take the coin. "I have school tomorrow. I only work part-time. Do you want to send a reply, sir? The office is closed so it won't go until morning."

"No. No reply. It's not urgent." That little smile again. He knows he's confusing me.

A band struck up in the ballroom, some old Irish tune. The door was flanked by tables covered in red roses. That's right: it's Valentine's Day. Meares glanced toward the sound of the music. His wife, who looked even prettier by night, was standing at the ballroom door, smiling across at them. Jesus, thought Hugh. Did she just wink at me again?

"Then come and see me the next time you're free. I asked Captain Rant to find me a bright young man from the telegraph office, and he talked to someone there who recommended you. Mr. Morgan—a nice piratical name. And Mrs. Meares likes the look of you. She said you seemed clever. Although that might just be your glasses. It's all the same to me though. I can always find some other lad to help."

Hugh took the coin. It was another half-dollar. "I can drop by tomorrow evening, sir. I get off school at four."

The following morning Hugh left home earlier than usual and stopped by the office on his way to school. Sandy Rees usually came in first thing to get ahead with his paperwork. Hugh found his boss in his little office, a plywood cubby in a corner of the telegraph room.

"It doesn't add up," Hugh told him. "One minute this man is an army colonel, the next a commander in the navy. I'm not even sure if he's really English. His accent isn't quite right. Too many R's. Maybe he's a fraudster taking advantage of Captain Rant— run up a big bill and then flit to the States."

Rees sat back in his swivel chair and made rapid turns right and left, as if surveying both sides of the problem. A sergeant in the Signals Corps, he had lost an eye in the war and always seemed to be aiming at something. "I think Captain Rant knows who this Meares fellow is," he said finally. "It was Captain Rant who asked me to send my best boy over to do a few jobs for him." Having settled the matter to his own satisfaction he stopped swiveling his chair. "Don't worry about it. You're allowed to run errands in your own time."

Hugh picked up his satchel and turned to leave. A bell pinged in the telegraph office. They heard the scrape of a chair and the scuffle of feet and then the duty clerk called to the boys in the messenger room.

"Angela Hotel. Some air-force guy. Wing Commander Meares."

Sandy Rees got up from his chair and reached for his coat. "I'll take that," he called. "I'm passing that way in the van." Taking Hughie by the elbow he steered him onto the street. "While I'm there," he said, "I'll have a word with Captain Rant."

Hugh was distracted for the rest of the day; he was even told off for not paying attention in physics, his favorite subject. After school he went straight to the office. Rees was back at his desk. He brought Hugh in and sat him down.

"I talked to Captain Rant." He kept his voice down. "It's on the level. He says you should do whatever you can for Colonel Meares. He says you should be honored to work for him."

"I don't understand."

"Meares was a lieutenant-colonel in the army. He was wounded at Ypres. Then he transferred to the Royal Navy Air Service. And when that merged with the Royal Flying Corps he ended up in the RAF. So he's got three different ranks from three different services, plus a whole bunch of medals as well."

"Oh . . . But why doesn't he just stick to using one title?"

"It's none of my business. As far as I'm concerned he can do whatever he likes. Do you know who he is?"

"A man with three pensions?"

"Don't be disrespectful, Hughie. He's Cecil Meares. The polar explorer. He went to the South Pole with Scott."

Oh, thought Hugh, deeply impressed. But no. No, he didn't go to the pole. Cecil Meares: the dog expert. He only went as far as the top of the Beardmore Glacier, then he was sent back to Ross Island with the last of the dogs. The men who went to the South Pole never came back at all. Scott. Oates. Wilson. Taff Evans. Birdie Bowers. Like many another boy in the Empire, Hugh knew the story of the *Terra Nova* better than he knew himself. It was the grandest thing that had ever happened—along, of course, with Vimy and the Somme.

Hughie was not in his uniform that evening so he had to go around the back of the hotel. The weather had changed in the night, as it often did in Victoria, and winter had turned into something like spring. The late afternoon sun, almost warm, shone through the jacarandas that grew around the boundary, picking out the winter blooms on Captain Rant's magnolias. Guests sat in twos and threes around wrought iron tables, grimly taking tea in the brisk evening air: this was Victoria, the Canadian riviera, where—the guidebooks all said it—you could dine outside the whole year around.

Meares lounged on his own at the corner of the terrace. Like the other guests he wore expensive tweeds. Unlike them, he had wrapped himself in a plaid blanket, and instead of tea or coffee he had a glass with something hot in it steaming at his elbow.

"Come on," he said. "Let's take a turn in the grounds."

Captain Rant was a champion of exotic alpine plants. Beyond the croquet lawn his garden was planted with rhododendrons and ferns and bamboo, screening a web of graveled paths.

Meares walked a couple of paces ahead, hands clasped behind his back and head bowed to the ground as if in contemplation. When he looked up again he was grinning in a way that Hugh would have described, had he been writing an essay for class, as "savage."

"So, young man: I hear you've been asking about me."

Hugh almost broke step but made himself continue. It was his turn to study the gravel. Couldn't Rees have kept his name out of it?

"I hear," went on Meares, "that you've been voicing concerns about my bona fides." Hugh listened to their feet crunching slowly on the pathway. He was aware of the upper windows of the hotel staring down at him. As if this wasn't bad enough.

"I beg your pardon, sir. It's just I wasn't sure about your rank. We're told to get these things right."

Their boots crunched on together. It's funny, thought Hugh, how when you walk with someone else you end up in cadence, if not always in step.

"You thought," said Meares, "that I might be some kind of confidence man. I expect that one hears of a lot of such people in these parts lately."

"Yes, sir."

"Anyone can have a war record these days. Coming up from California or down from Alaska. This whole coast is teeming with impostors, from what I read in the papers. Do you read the papers, Mr. Morgan?"

"Yes, sir."

"Good lad. I thought you might. You come recommended."

"Thank you, sir."

"You were quite right to ask about me." He heard Meares's steps slow and stop. He had no choice but to turn and look at him. Meares was still smiling, but more kindly now. "There's nothing wrong with a little snooping. It's just better not to get caught."

"Sorry, sir."

"Come on." Meares touched his elbow and they resumed their stroll. They reached the far corner of the garden and turned back toward the house.

"Mrs. Meares and I have just been staying in Santa Barbara, which as you may know is in California. It's full of the most dreadful hucksters and crooks and moving-picture people. We like it very much, and we're going to spend our winters there. But the summers are hot, so we're going to keep a second home here in Victoria. You follow me?"

"Yes, sir."

"Good lad. I shall have business to conduct with my various interests abroad, so from time to time I may need someone to run messages for me, particularly telegrams. I'll need my own fellow on standby to bring messages down to the office, see they're expedited, then wait for the reply. That sort of thing. That's not too irregular, is it, if you do it outside of your official hours?"

"I don't think so, sir. Not really . . . Especially not if it's being done for someone who was with Scott in the Antarctic."

Meares stopped again. "So you know about that? . . . It hasn't been in the papers here, has it?"

"I don't think so, sir. My boss Mr. Rees told me. He must have heard from Captain Rant."

"Oh . . . well, it's not exactly a secret anyway." An elderly couple came past on their evening constitutional. Meares and Hugh moved aside and touched the brims of their caps. When they were gone Meares continued: "Do you have any questions?"

Money. Hours. Terms. Hugh wondered about these. But they had completed their circuit of the garden and reached the stone steps that climbed back to the terrace. "Any questions," Meares had said to him. He might never say those words again.

"Did you know Captain Oates, sir?"

Meares, who had paused with one foot on the steps, shook out his shoulders, the stance of a man getting ready to bat. His face became blandly polite. "I did."

He's tired of that subject, thought Hugh. Of course he is. That was all years ago. There's been a war since then. But he would press him anyway.

"He must have been the most amazing fellow, sir." "Fellow": who talks like that in goddam Canada?

"Of course. Wonderful man." Meares took another step.

"What a thing that was, sir. To walk out of the tent like that and leave so much unsaid. 'I'm just going outside and may be some time.'"

Meares nodded thoughtfully. "Yes. Very stirring last words . . . Of course, we get those words from Scott's diary, not from Oates himself."

"There isn't any doubt, is there?" Hugh feared his moorings were coming loose. He had no choice but to give them a tug and see if they still held. "About what happened in the end, I mean. To Oates and Scott and the others?"

Meares, seeing his distress, looked unhappy in turn. "Of course not . . . I wasn't there myself when Atkinson's party went out and found the poor fellows in the tent—I'd gone back with the ship the autumn before. But I've no doubt that Scott's account was true . . . It's just I've always had one or two private doubts about whether those famous last words were strictly . . . verbatim."

"That a man going to his death would have said so little?"

"Having known poor old Oates, I'm surprised he said even that much."

★ ★ ★

Once or twice a week, when he was not working for the Canadian Pacific, Hugh would nevertheless put on his uniform and wait on Meares at the Angela Hotel.

For this Meares paid Hugh a dollar a shift, so much that it made Hugh uneasy. His own foster dad earned only a little more for hours of skilled pruning and planting. Perhaps, he told himself, I'm meant to see these big tips as a sort of retainer. Maybe I'm supposed to earn them by some service yet to come.

Sometimes, having just received a message or a letter, Meares would write a reply that Hugh would take down to the office. As a mere messenger, Hugh could have learned very little about his patron's private business: only if a customer chose to dictate a telegram—which Meares never did, preferring to scribble a note and place it in the envelope—would a bicycle boy know its contents. But Hugh was still allowed to take a turn on the Morse key in the office, and it became understood that when Hugh brought in Meares's telegrams he would send them himself. Hugh was sure that Meares wouldn't mind him assuming this function. After all, someone had to send and receive Colonel Meares's telegrams. Someone had to read them. Why not his own man when he happened to be there?

In this way Hugh built a picture of the hero's life and interests. They were startlingly dull. Like many wealthy Britishers who moved to Vancouver Island, Colonel Meares had been bitten by the mania for gardening. Much of his correspondence concerned queries and orders about exotic flowers: one, a Himalayan blue poppy, he presented to Captain Rant as a gift for the Angela's garden—there was a piece about it in the British Colonist.

Some of these messages made no sense to Hugh, who knew about gardens from helping old Jim. Why was Meares checking the availability of irises from Nome in Alaska—checking with the same man, Mr. Clarendon Carpendale, who had sent

Meares that birthday greeting the first night Hugh had met him?
Surely nobody was growing or selling flowers north of the Bering Strait? And why did Colonel Meares feel the need, one rainy
night just before closing time, to send him rushing down to the
telegraph office with an urgent message to a government circuit in London, notifying the recipient about the recent arrival
in Japan of irises from Blackburn? The reply came seconds later,
suggesting that someone at the other end had been waiting for
Meares's message. But Hugh, who decoded it himself, could see
no sign of urgency in the reply: "Do nothing for now."

Meares had waited for that reply in the hotel lobby, uncharac-
teristically anxious. He ripped open the envelope and then, with
the message half extracted, he stopped and looked at Hugh.

"What time does your office close? In case I need to send a
reply."

Hugh, who was sweaty from the bike ride, tired after a long
day of school and study, spoke before he could think.

"It's already closed, sir. But it's alright. They want you to do
nothing."

Meares looked at him a moment longer, then he took out the
message, read it and put it back in the envelope. His expression
did not change. He was still smiling, or almost smiling. He put
the envelope in one pocket and then, still smiling at Hugh, took
out a coin. Hugh saw it in his fingers—the usual half-dollar, held
loosely not between index and thumb but between the index
and middle fingers. As he watched, Meares began to run the
coin back and forth between his fingers without using his thumb,
manipulating it from index to middle to third to pinky and back
again in a smooth, wavelike motion. It was the kind of trick thim-
bleriggers performed at the carnival. When Hugh took his eyes
from the coin Meares was no longer smiling.

"Have you been opening my messages, young man?"

"I haven't."

Meares took a step closer. "You've read this one."

"Yes." What the hell had he been he thinking? He had been spying on this man! On his telegrams. Even the police weren't supposed to do that . . . Still he said nothing, hoping to find a way out.

Meares looked around the lobby. They were alone apart from a servant watering the flowers arranged around the walls. "I think you ought to explain yourself. I'm giving you a last chance to get out of this."

"I didn't open it," insisted Hugh. He saw the anger in Meares's expression, and added quickly, "I read it in the office. At the Morse key. It was me who took your message off the wire."

Meares transferred the coin to his left hand. He was equally adept with that. "*You* took it down? You were operating the telegraph? A messenger boy?"

"I learned Morse at the office, sir. I've been doing it for years."

Meares's posture had relaxed a little. "Really? And they allow that at Canadian Pacific? Is that not irregular?"

"It's unofficial. But it's common enough. That way they can train up people for free, I guess. I got so good that they offered me a full-time telegraph job. But I turned them down. My parents want me to finish high school."

Meares put the half-dollar back in his pocket. "Can you work the whole thing by yourself? The circuits and the Vibroplex?"

How does he know about stuff like that? But Hugh no longer dared to wonder about Colonel Meares's affairs. He decided to sound eager; eager was a cousin of innocent. "Oh sure. I even know the Phillips code, although no one in Canada uses it. I learned it from a book, just in case I ever work with foreign reporters or suchlike. I know the Q-codes as well, for shipping and aircraft."

"That's very enterprising of you."

"I'm even building my own wireless at home, sir. It's a short-wave receiver and transmitter. I saw the plans in *Popular Science*. I got a lot of the parts for it at the navy dump in Esquimalt. They throw out a lot of stuff that they should really repair. The rest of it I'm buying mail-order."

"Really?" Meares took him to the door. To Hugh's surprise, he followed him out front. It was a mild night, with a fog that wanted to be drizzle. Moisture dripped from the porte cochere onto the gravel. "What will you do with this wireless of yours?"

It was funny, thought Hugh, but he hadn't even thought of that until asked. The challenge was to get it working. If he had any plan at all, it was really just to listen and wait.

"I'll make friends with people," he lied brightly. "You can use shortwave to talk to people all over the world. You listen for their signals, and then you send them a message asking them to acknowledge. Then you write it in a log. Or if it's a commercial station—a voice broadcaster—and you work out which one it is, you send them a letter saying when and where and how well you received them, and they might send you a QSL card to say thanks. People collect the cards. It's like collecting postage stamps, only more modern." Jesus, he thought. You're laying it on a bit thick. He's trying not to laugh at you.

Meares took a dollar bill from his pocket and handed it to Hugh. "I'm not sure when I'll need you again. I'll send word if I do."

Hugh only heard the "if." Still, he thought, as he got on his bicycle, I shouldn't feel bad if it turns out it's over. I don't think I'm in trouble. And I've come out ahead. He could feel the dollar bill in his trouser pocket, the pleasant discomfort of it scraping his thigh through the thin cotton lining. But as he cycled home, wrapped in the thickening drizzle, he couldn't help feeling that something big, something that was moving, had just left him behind.

Spring arrived and the Meareses prepared to move on for a spell. A note arrived at the office from the Angela Hotel: starting the following week telegrams for Meares and his wife should be re-addressed to the new Olympic Hotel in Seattle.

The Meareses were to leave on a Saturday. Hugh, working the late shift on Friday, wondered if Meares would send for him one last time, if Meares would want to say good-bye. As the shift dragged on, and there was no summons from the Angela, he told himself that he was glad. What did he care anyway? He'd already been well paid.

It was a quiet night, like most nights in Victoria, and there was only one other boy in the messenger room. Twenty minutes before closing time they heard the muted dah–dits of the reso-nator inside the telegraph room, and then the chatter of a type-writer. The telegraph clerk raised his voice.

"Angela Hotel . . . Mr. Meares . . . *Mister* Meares, eh? That's the first time he's been a Mister, far as I know. I guess the war is finally over, fellas. He's your guy, Hugh. You want to take it over there?"

I don't care, Hugh thought. It's none of my business. "Hamish can take it, if he wants. It's on his way home. Meares tips pretty well."

That's it, thought Hugh. I chose not to go. That makes me the winner.

Now that he was alone, Hugh took out a book of short stories, a well-worn favorite by Jack London. He was deep in the Klond-ike gold fields when the front door opened to admit Sandy Rees, come to close up for the night. He whistled as he came through the counter, some old marching tune from his army days.

"Alright, boys?" Sandy called to the inner office. "Anyone home?"

"I guess," said the clerk. "Might as well not be."

"And in there?"

Hugh tore himself away from the bleak battle of wills between the evil half-breed Black Leclère and his hellhound Bâtard. "Just me, Mr. Rees. Hamish has taken a late message up to the Angela. He'll go on home from there."

"Right . . ." Jingling of keys. "You might as well go home now, Donald. If anything else comes in the next few minutes I'll handle it myself."

Hugh heard the clerk's chair scrape on the floorboards. "Thanks, Mr. Rees. I don't mind if I do."

Hugh went back to his book. The vicious mongrel Bâtard was sauntering toward his bound and helpless master, who teetered on a box with a noose around his neck. And though Hugh had already read this story two or three times, he felt his breath stop. As Rees's swivel chair creaked, Hugh heard Black Leclère's boots scramble on the slowly tipping plywood.

The boots danced into thin air. A phone rang in Rees's office. Hugh jumped at the sound.

"Yes . . . ?" Rees was quiet for a while. "Yes, of course." Then the click of the mouthpiece back on the receiver. There was silence for a few moments more, then Rees raised his voice again.

"Hughie? Can you come in here and sit at the key? I have to go out for a minute."

Hugh looked at the wristwatch he'd bought with Meares's money. It was five minutes to ten.

Putting his book under his arm, he passed behind the counter into the telegraph room. Only the nearest position was lit. He had his own custom-set Morse key, a Vibroplex "bug" that he'd salvaged from the navy dump and kept in his pigeonhole. Plugging it into the socket, he pulled the swing-arm resonator up to his left ear, wound the ribbon on the typewriter, checked that the circuits were closed and the "flash" bulbs unlit, and opened his book again.

But he couldn't concentrate on reading. What was wrong with him tonight? He loved this office very much: it put him almost on the edge of the center of things. He never minded staying beyond his shifts. But tonight he just wanted to be out of here. He wouldn't go home when Rees relieved him (and where was Sandy

Rees? It was already five after ten): he would cycle through the backstreets of Victoria, away from the brightly lit district around the Empress Hotel. Or maybe he wouldn't cycle; maybe tonight he would walk. Bicycles and melancholy didn't really mix . . .

He raised his eyes from his book and shook his head to clear it. Now he was looking at the spike.

The spike was a vertical steel prong set in a round wooden base. It sat on the bench a foot from his right hand. On it was impaled a thick wad of tissue papers. Whenever a message came in, the clerk would use an all-capitals Underwood to type it directly onto the telegram form. The purple ribbon of the typewriter used a water-based ink, so that a copy of the form could be made simply by pressing wet tissue against it. These copies were then impaled on the spike.

The uppermost of those tissues must be the last message that came here. The one for "Mr. Meares."

Hugh looked at the spike, then at his watch again. Ten after ten, and Rees still wasn't back. The office should be locked by now.

That message was none of his business. He didn't even work for Meares anymore. He had less right than ever to snoop.

When he flattened the tissue on the desktop the ink was still a little damp. It came off on his fingers.

The message had been sent from Nome, Alaska, relayed by Vancouver: "Enjoy Seattle. Carpendale."

Stupidly, he turned it over to look at the back of it, as if that could show him any more meaning. Then he heard the front door open and footsteps in the lobby. Rees was back, and about time too. He put the tissue back on the spike, remembering to impale it through the original hole, then gathered his book and stood up.

"I'd be grateful if you'd stay," said Meares. "I need to send a telegram."

He was standing in the door that led from the counter. His trench coat was silvered by drops of fine rain. Hugh, flustered by this unexpected visit, fumbled his book and let it drop to the floor. Had Meares seen him reading the tissue? What if he noticed the ink on his fingers? If he did, would he even know what it was? Hugh was pretty sure that somehow he would.

"We're closed, sir," he managed. "I'm just waiting for my boss. He's supposed to come back and lock up."

Meares reached into his coat pocket and took out a large bunch of keys. Hugh recognized Rees's key fob—the crest of the Signals Corps.

"He says you can lock up afterward. I'll make sure the keys get back to him. I have a car outside."

Hugh wouldn't bother pointing out that this wasn't supposed to happen. Neither would he ask where Rees was, or why Rees wasn't there to help Meares himself. It was understood that Hugh would go along with anything that was asked of him. Any objections would have to be practical. "But this station is closed, sir. Everything from here to the outside world goes through Vancouver or Seattle. If we try and send anything after hours they'll want to know why we're still operating."

"We won't be sending anything out through Vancouver or Seattle." Meares came and stood beside him, on his right, so as not to interfere with the resonator at Hugh's left ear. "I want to send a message on a local wire, inside Vancouver Island. You know how to raise the navy signals at Esquimalt."

It was a statement, not a question. There'll be nobody there, thought Hugh. But it wasn't worth saying aloud. Meares, he was sure, would know what he was doing. "What's the message?" He picked up a pad. Meares pushed the pad away.

"No writing. Just get them on the line, then I'll dictate. And you don't need to give them your sine. They'll already know where it's coming from."

He did as he was told. Moments later, the "flash" light came on for the bush wire to Esquimalt harbor, just down the coast, followed by the naval station's letters, tapping in the resonator.

Meares straightened abruptly and walked in a quick circle behind Hugh's back, as if he were shaking off a sudden cramp.

"Good . . . Send this: 'Carpendale just arrived Nome from Siberia' . . ."

Hugh tapped away at his sideswiper key, the dahs of the button, dits of the paddle. He kept to a slow twenty-five words per minute; the navy people weren't always as quick as commercial operators like himself.

". . . 'Says offered Blackburn Iris blueprint by Vladivostok freelancer' . . ."

Blackburn Iris, thought Hugh. That explained it. He still read the boys' papers: the Blackburn Iris was the RAF's newest seaplane.

". . . 'Freelancer said English source William Forbes Sempill. He Jap agent. Advise arrest. Dearie.'"

Dearie. Now Meares was going by a different name entirely, as if it were some kind of code. But what a thin code it was: Meares had even used someone's name "in the clear"—a term Hugh had learned from his Baden-Powell cipher book.

"Now," said Meares, "you're not going to ask me a whole lot of questions, are you, Mr. Morgan?"

"No, sir."

"Good. Let me ask you one: do you fancy a cigarette while we wait?"

"We're not allowed to smoke back here, sir. The ash and grease can clog the relays. Wait for what, sir?"

"For a reply, of course."

"From Esquimalt, sir?"

Meares took out a cigarette case. "Yes. Leave the line open."

Hugh thought about that. It would be almost impossible for anyone outside the island to have eavesdropped on Meares's last message, sent as it was after hours on a bush line. And in Esquimalt, a Royal Navy station, they would presumably have codebooks and long-distance wireless. The conversation, whatever it meant, would have moved from Alaska to Seattle to Victoria, then by separate means to Esquimalt, thence again—he had to assume—by coded wireless to London, and now they were waiting for a return. Only one person sat at the center of the exchange. Only one person could follow it all. Two, if you counted himself.

He took a cigarette from Meares, although it was forbidden and he never smoked.

Meares eased himself into the chair to Hugh's right. "We'll need something to use as an ashtray." His eyes scanned the bench, then spotted Hugh's book.

"Ah. Jack London . . ." He nodded at the book. "Very interesting fellow. Dead these eight years."

"You've read him, sir? I've read all his books."

Meares shook aside some litter in the waste bin, making a clear space where he could flick his ash. He lit two cigarettes.

"Read him? No. I'm not a great one for fiction. I never have time. But I met him once. When we were both young fellows knocking about."

This was something, Hugh decided, that he could be openly keen about. It was also an excuse to put down the cigarette he'd been holding just short of his lips. "Were you a stampeder too?"

Meares blew a smoke ring at the ceiling. "The Klondike Gold Rush? No. I was still in India back then, trying to grow tea . . . But I met Jack London a few years later . . . It's a story from a war that you've never even heard of."

"I know about the Boer War," protested Hugh. "My mother's brother was in it. Imperial Yeomanry. Were you in that too, sir?"

Meares put his feet up on the bench, a desecration that could scarcely be believed. "I was in the Transvaal Scottish Horse. Promoted all the way up to lance-corporal." He pulled a face. "Not an honorific I've been known to use lately, is it, Mr. Morgan? Lance-Corporal Meares, care of the Angela Hotel."

"No, sir."

"I'll save that one for a real emergency ... But that's not where I met Jack London. That happened a couple of years after South Africa, back in '04." He took a silver flask from his pocket and showed it to Hugh. "He told me the most wonderful story ... We could be here a little while yet. Unless you suggest otherwise, I propose to drink alone."

The Korea–Manchuria border, 1904

From *The Ghost of the Yalu River* by Jack London (1876–
1916): memoir, unfinished at the time of his death.

The ghost first appeared on the night of the battle, that
immortal world-shaking engagement in which Kuroki
defeated Zasulich and crossed the Yalu stream.

A Japanese foot patrol, scouting the Russian rout into
Manchuria, spotted a dark figure in the gloaming, creeping
down a steep hillside toward the Japanese lines. The Japanese corporal, a veteran of '94, knew well this land and the
virtues of patience, so he drew his men into the shadows and
waited in silence. At times their quarry disappeared, merg-
ing back into the mountain, but then a dim shaft of moonlight would find a pale face as it turned to the sky. This was
a white man, like the fleeing Russian soldiers, but coming
the opposite way.

So silently did he glide down that rocky slope that the
corporal, when questioned later, confessed that he had been
seized by a sudden horror: the stranger drew nearer and yet
nearer to the place where the ambush lay, and yet even six
feet away, almost within arm's reach, near enough to have
made the sod tremble beneath the corporal's feet, the Japanese could hear or feel nothing but the sigh of the wind in

the grass and the stones. He had thought to take this man a prisoner, but now all resolution left him, and—like one who lashes out vainly in a dream—he thrust his bayonet at the specter, just to see if it was there. And there it was, resistance, yes—the bayonet broke through a quilted Cossack jacket, a man grunted in surprise and pain, yet when the bayonet had been turned and retracted the victim was still standing, shouting in some unknown and barbarous tongue.

Another thrust might have done for the *gaijin*, the corporal said later, though with the air of one unconvinced, but the white man, wriggling clear, next called out in Mandarin, which sobered the Japanese and made him think again. Who but a spy would be traveling as this man, by night, toward the Japanese positions? What white man but a spy would speak a Chinese dialect? The patrol seized and bound its prisoner and brought him back inside their lines.

The wise old corporal, having already attempted to bayonet his prisoner once, had no wish to molest him any further. He may indeed have been a little frightened of him. But the corporal's lieutenant, taking delivery of the prisoner, thought it his duty to question him in the field, and repaid the bound man for his silence with several blows of his fists.

At regimental headquarters, the intelligence officer grew resentful at what he perceived as a willful refusal to understand his questions. By the time the prisoner reached General Kuriki's compound he could only just stand.

Here his escorting captain met a reverse: there was no one present who would relieve him of his prisoner. All of the general's intelligence men were engaged in the study of captured maps and documents and the interrogation of high-ranking prisoners. Had he interviewed the infiltrator himself? And had he got anything from him? No? Well, so much for that. We are fighting this war by European rules, on General Kuriki's orders. In Europe spies are not beheaded. In Europe spies are hanged or shot.

And so the prisoner, battered and shivering, scarcely able to keep on his feet, was shoved back against the nearest sturdy wall, that of an old Korean farmhouse that housed the general's foreign press corps. He slumped there, half dazed, blinking blood from his eyes, while the soldiers of his escort, only three in number, formed up five yards away, their rifles leveled, while their officer stood to one side, one hand holding a lantern, the other a sword poised in the air. The prisoner shook his head and blinked again, trying to understand the meaning of this tableau, and then a word barked out and the sword swished down and three rifles spoke as one.

There was nothing the writer could do to prevent it. He had turned the corner, lost in thought, hands deep in his pockets to ward off the bleak mountain wind, and he discovered the scene in its moment of enactment: the lantern's gleam on the blade of a sword; the wind fidgeting with the neckcloths of the firing squad; the face of the condemned man, ghastly pale. It is a white man! the writer thought, some poor Russian prisoner! But as he threw himself forward, a cry on his lips, the sword descended, the rifles crashed, blinding him with their muzzle flashes, and the Japanese officer, perhaps stunned by the sound so close at hand, or shaken by the enormity of this terrible thing he had attempted and achieved, dropped the lantern to the ground, where it spilled and gave birth to a pool of pale flame. All else was plunged into darkness. I am too late, despaired the writer. I have failed another of my own race. With a howl of rage he threw himself at the Japanese captain.

"You brute! One ought not to shoot a dog so, much less a captured foe!"

He seized hold of the little officer and shook him like a rag. Then a rifle butt swung in the darkness. His head burst into stars and he was lying on the cold stones with his legs sprawled across the dead man. He tried to speak but he could not. Other boots crunched on the stones around him, voices shouted in outraged Japanese. And then he felt something even more ghastly than his mortal predicament: beneath his own body a hideous spasm, the dead man's legs jerking in their last grim convulsions! He scrambled away from that macabre motion, unwittingly avoiding the thrust of a bayonet, and jumped to his feet, dizzy from pain and from horror. Bayonets glinted and a rifle bolt clacked. But he knew a little Japanese, the coarse dockyard patois he had picked up as a seaman in the bars of Yokohama. He must summon it now.

"Stop! I am an American journalist!"

There was a moment of silence, the scrape of a boot, the hiss of the wind on the hilltop. Then someone coughed, a painful cough followed by retching, and a voice spoke in English.

"I notice that you sling the bat, old man. I'd be very grateful if you would ask these fellows not to shoot at me again. Please tell them I'm British. Tell them I've come to see our military attaché."

"And the luck of it was," Meares told Hughie, passing him the flask, "it turned out we really did have an attaché at Kuriki's headquarters, though I'd just been chancing my arm: I'd actually come looking for Ponting. Even better, the attaché was someone I knew: Sir Ian Hamilton. I'd been with him at Rooival when we finished off the poor Boers."

It was past ten thirty. Hugh had pulled the shutters down in the front office, but one of them was broken and would not close all the way, so they switched off the lights and made do with the glow from the telegraph dials.

Hugh's head swam from his first nip of whiskey. He found it made him bold. "But what were you doing there in the first place?"

A match flared. Meares's face danced in its mystery. When he shook the match out it was replaced by the point of a cigarette.

"I was on my way home."

"Home from where?"

"Siberia. Cape Chelyuskin. Quite a trip it was too. Very hard."

"Tougher than Antarctica?"

"Antarctica was a doddle in comparison. For a start, there were no Russians at the South Pole trying to stop me getting about. And when I worked for Scott I already knew how to handle my dogs. When I went to Cape Chelyuskin I had to learn as I went along. It nearly killed me—when that trip was over I felt like I'd come back from the dead."

"Why did you go to Siberia in the first place?"

A precise nasal exhalation of two funnels of smoke. "I was trading in furs."

"And then Jack London saved your life."

"You might say that . . . I also owe a lot to a shakily held lantern, and to the fact that soldiers usually shoot high in the dark . . . But London was very kind to me. He stayed with me while the officer sent for General Hamilton, just in case the Japs got it in their heads to finish the job. And after Hamilton had vouched for me London took me down to the army hospital and stayed with me all night. I couldn't sleep from the pain of that bayonet glancing my rib. We talked until morning. My God, the life that man had led! I thought I'd knocked about a bit, but he had me beaten all up."

"Did you ever meet him again?"

"No . . . Next morning he was dragged from my bedside by a very polite Jap sergeant who was supposed to be his minder. The whole flock of correspondents was being herded on across the river and he had to go with them, though he was sick of being paraded about like a buckshee trooper. After talking to me he was all for jacking in his commission, or whatever it is that war reporters have, and crossing to the other side to write about the Russians."

"Maybe he decided the losers make a better story."

Meares stirred in his chair like a man jerking out of a doze. "Yes! Yes, that's rather good. The losers make a better story . . . They do, don't they? . . . That explains a lot . . ." Hugh heard the flask's stopper being unscrewed, caught a fresh whiff of Meares's whiskey. A hand touched his shoulder and the flask appeared in the dim light of the dials. Hugh took another nip and passed it back.

Meares continued: "So yes, London wanted to go over to the Russian side. I think he hoped he could join me there. But I'd decided to go elsewhere. I needed to get to Alaska."

The whiskey made Hugh's head swim in a way he decided he liked. "But you said you were on your way south when the Japanese caught you. You said you were going home."

"I thought I was. But something that London told me made me change my plans."

They had given the foreigner his own little corner of the field hospital, screened by a paper partition from the rest of the long canvas ward. His bed was of western design, as was the chair provided to the writer, who—wrapped in a striped army blanket to keep off the night air—poured brandy into two pewter mugs. Having passed one to the patient, he then raised the glass of the paraffin lamp and used the flame to light two cigarettes.

"So, you have come here all the way from Siberia," the writer began. "How I envy you your journey . . . I have been told that Siberia is very like our own American north country. Its forests, climate, animals—the bears and wolves and caribou—its mountains and trees, resemble so closely the wilds of Alaska and the Yukon. Yet Siberia is west of our own lands, and makes easterners of us: it turns us around, like reflections in a mirror. And how easily we forget—we who hunted seals amongst the Aleutians, or who climbed the White Pass and rafted down Lake Laberge to the Klondike—that the czars once owned those lands before us, and were it not for a few audacious Hudson Bay traders and for the prescience of Secretary William H. Seward, those lands would have been lost to us, their gold and their secrets promised to another race."

The man in the bed stirred but did not speak. Yet the lantern found an answer in the shadows of his eyes.

The writer continued: "And yet traces of this older dispensation leap out at those who look for them: a double-sparred cross above an Aleutian harbor; a rusted Muscovite flintlock in the hands of a Tagish trapper; the names of Shelikof Strait and the Kotzebue Sound . . ."

The man on the cot coughed and turned on his side, wincing at the pain of it. "I'd trouble you for some more of that brandy, if you please. The Japanese gave me a pretty good beating."

The writer tipped some more brandy into the patient's mug. He sank carefully back on his pillows, grunting in thanks or in pain. The writer sipped, then went on.

"I heard a strange story once about just such a relic of the old Russian dispensation, and although I have heard many tall stories around the campfire, and told a few myself, this was the oddest tale I have ever been told and yet believed to be true."

"Please do go on. I wasn't planning on sleeping. That bayonet gash is playing hell with my rib."

"I'll bet it is . . . Anyway, the man who told me this story was a Russian himself, one of a few who still haunted the Yukon River when I arrived in '97. We called him Ivan, of course, and what his real name was we neither knew nor cared, as we scarcely knew or cared about our own names back then; we took the names that others gave us: a man was Red, or Tiny, or Lefty, or Dutch, or had won some nomadic fame in Jo'burg or Deadwood or Kalgoorlie, which served him better than any Christian name that his mother had once wished for him."

"Your own name is rather a good one for a writer. Jack London. Is it the name you were born with yourself?"

The writer laughed. "That would depend on who you ask . . . But I was talking of Ivan and his uncanny story, a story so strange that scarcely a day goes by even yet, years later, that I don't hear its echo . . . Ivan was born on the Russian frontier. His father and mother had fled a farm west of the Urals, escaping serfhood and the persecution of the church, which was then rooting out certain ancient beliefs anathematized by the Muscovite patriarchs. But after a boyhood of idyllic freedom, trapping and hunting in forests unknown to the Cossacks, young Ivan heard rumors of a new railway, still far to the west: the railway that thirty years later—" the writer tipped his mug to his listener—"now speeds the czar's army to Port Arthur to contend with our present kind hosts."

"Much good will their railway do them."

"Ivan thought the same. Although barely lettered, he understood that railways bring with them policemen, and tax collectors, and monopolists of furs. So he said farewell to his parents and set off east to preserve his freedom, just as men of our nations escape to the west. He hunted on the Amur, fished for crabs out of Vladivostok, lived among the Chukchis of the East Cape. Then, still driven eastward, though he could not say why, he crossed the Bering Strait and took to prospecting for gold. For what else does a white man do in Alaska?"

"There are those," said the man on the cot, "who trade in furs."

The writer ignored him: he was still picking his way to the start of his story, and had, in the manner of his trade, set himself a roundabout path.

"Ivan was known along the Yukon valley long before the stampede to the Klondike creek. He was at the Forty-mile River in '86, at Circle City in '93, and at a dozen wildcat strikes and false bonanzas in between. Fair of hair yet swart of skin, he had the heavy, stoical features of a natural aristocrat. Such was his quiet authority, his unforced superiority, that one detected in his veins the blood not of the servile Slavs but of a proud Germanic race, one of those pioneering bands who crossed the Volga in Great Catherine's time, or an offshoot of an even more ancient penetration—those stern Norse warriors who founded and then scorned the Muscovite principalities, and who went on to guard the kings of Byzantium. When he spoke, which was seldom enough, others leaned forward to listen."

"I find that Russians generally don't talk a lot. Not even in Russian."

I had better, thought the writer, speed things up. A plainer style is now coming into fashion. And he may fall asleep before I'm done.

"Well, anyway, that was Ivan. August of '96 found him at Forty Mile City. He had come in from prospecting a distant creek, intending to tap Jack McQuesten for credit to blow off some steam and lay in a winter outfit. But he was in Bill McPhee's saloon on that very same night when Lying George Carmack threw onto the counter a Winchester shell full of soft Klondike flake. The next morning Forty Mile was a ghost town, its stoves and its candles still burning, and Ivan was at the head of a fleet of canoes on the Yukon, battling two hundred miles upstream to stake their new claims on the Klondike.

"By the following year, when two tons of pure gold steamed across the bar into Seattle's harbor, Ivan had made a vast fortune. And that fall, just as the Yukon froze again, isolating the boom town of Dawson for its second winter of existence, the first trickle of outsiders rafted down the stream. They brought with them rumors of an even greater swarm of tenderfeet detained in the southern mountains and waiting for the spring. They told how Soapy Smith's army of bunco men, killers, and lawyers had seized Skagway and Dyea on the American side, preying on stampeders as they tried to cross the passes. They said that Ottawa had decreed a new telegraph line to Dawson City, and that a cable car was being rigged to speed stampeders over Chilkoot Pass. Worst of all, as far as Ivan was concerned, there was already talk of building a railway. So by the fall of '97, long before the main body of stampeders even reached Dawson City, Ivan had decided it was time to move on."

"I expect he was broke."

The writer was taken aback: the man on the cot, it seemed, knew something about the ways of prospectors. "You're right. He was. He'd spent every poke he dug from the ground on women and whiskey and faro, just as he did every time he struck rich. He lost his claim on the turn of a card in Belinda Mulroney's saloon, and was secretly glad to be rid of it.

"And so, free once more, Ivan borrowed a grubstake, turned his back on the squalling infant city, and entered the darkness beyond. While others who had struck it rich were taking their profit and heading south, Ivan went the other way, turning his face north and east, the same path he had followed all through his days. His plan—if you can call it that—was to head north to the valleys of the Peel and the Porcupine, find his way thence across the eastern mountains, then pan the untouched rivers running to the Arctic Sea."

The man on the cot coughed, then raised his mug for a refill. "You're very kind," he said. "Please do go on. I expect we're getting to the strange part you mentioned."

The writer silently cursed himself. It was hard, hard it was, to break the habit of a lifetime. But a new century stretched ahead of him, a taciturn, unadorned age in which a man might no longer grow wealthy by charging by the word.

"I'm just getting to that: Ivan followed the ancient fur trail north through the Tombstones, along the Porcupine River, then up the Bell 'til he reached Summit Lake—that heart-shaped mirror of the continental divide, which feeds its still waters to two different seas. From there, he followed Two Oceans Creek to the head of the Rat River. And it was there, amid the tumbled rocks and willow thickets of that treacherous stream, that he received the first great shock of his journey."

"Ah. Good."

"For there, where he had thought to find only desolation, was a strange sight indeed—a shanty town had sprung up by the frozen rapids of the Rat, a filthy hodgepodge of cabins and wigwams and huts, some little better than holes in the snow. And those who dwelled there were not mere Indians or half-breeds, but white men like himself. Aye, and white women too! Halting at a distance, he heard the shouts of angry voices, the scream of a woman. He smelled the ordure that fouled the snow of the campsite, and he saw the boats upturned by the frozen rapids, where the first sudden thaw would seize them and shatter them.

"The yelp of his dogs brought swaddled figures in twos and threes from the smoky shelters. When he reached the bottom of the draw there were four dozen people all waiting in silence, staring at him as if at a ghost. Then one of them, a little taller than the others, with a face burned black by frost and by sun, stepped forward and held out a hand. 'Welcome to Destruction Ceety, mah frien'. Mah name is Lefèbvre. Tell us, Ah beg you: 'ave you jus' come from dee Klondak? Are dere any claims yet for dee takeeng?"

"Now Ivan understood the nature of their madness. These lost, benighted souls were the remnant of an army of stampeders who had sought to reach the Klondike not by taking the coastal routes, but by passing through the Arctic itself!

"Oh it was a long way, to be sure, the merchants of Edmonton had soothed them, waving the fanciful maps they gave free with their overpriced outfits. It was a long way, to be sure, they said, but it was the quickest and most convenient—see: apart from a few trifling portages at the southern end of the route, and over the continental divide in the north, the path to the Yukon is downriver all the way—you need only sit in your boat and watch the banks of the Mackenzie drift past you; at night you feast on fresh moose and bear shot without even rising from your thwart. What better and more commodious route was there for men who must—who absolutely must—be sure of reaching the Klondike before winter?

"Ah yes. The winter. Those who took this long northern road were not, for the most part, men who thought themselves soft. They were men—and a few women too, for there is good business to be done in a gold rush by certain kinds of lady, and not all of them whores—who came for the most part from Canada or the northern states of America. They knew the bite of winter in the pine woods and the cut of a January wind. But they did not know the winters of the Northland, nor had they ever viewed the valley of the Rat, a friendly squiggle on their deceitful maps, a mere shortcut between the kindly Mackenzie and the easy Yukon River. And it was their fate to meet both the Rat and the winter at the same time and place—a place that they cursed as 'Destruction City.'"

"Rough spot," remarked the man on the cot. "What was so bad about it?"

It had been the writer's intention to gloss over the specifics. Things often seem worse if you leave them to the imagination. Let your audience or reader do the work for you. "Nothing, really . . . It's just that winter comes early up there—it's beyond the Arctic Circle. And the Rat River is no picnic, I'm told, although I didn't go that way myself. There are a lot of shallows and cataracts, apparently. And most of these poor fools had bought heavy boats built for rivers and lakes, not canoes or scows fit for portaging or towing. They had the devil's own job trying to handline them upstream through the shoals and rapids—the banks were often so broken or overgrown that they had to drag them from the creek bed itself, up to their waists in ice water from the mountains. By the time they reached the rapids of the middle Rat, where most of the boats were damaged, it was too late to go any farther or to turn back that year. They had to settle in for winter."

"One would think they might have foreseen all that," said the man on the bed. "One would also think that reasonable people might have guessed that all the claims on the

Klondike would have been staked already by the miners who lived on the Yukon."

"Reason had nothing to do with it. I do not know who first termed it 'the Stampede,' but they named it well. We stampeders did not give it half a thought; we just lowered our heads and charged. Only the merchants and barmen got rich, as merchants and barmen will. Some of the wiser harlots did well from it too."

"One can only hope that the ladies didn't waste their hard-earned wealth by taking handsome husbands."

"Alas, most of them did just that . . . Anyway, by the time Ivan found them the people of Destruction City were in a bad way. They had flour and bacon enough, and sugar and beans and the rest of it, but they had not the skill or strength to hunt for themselves, and so they had no fresh meat to preserve them from scurvy.

"Their leader was a scowling brute named Lefèbvre, a Red River half-caste who had fought for Riel in the north-west Rebellion. Though he knew how to live on the land, and had saved his followers many times over, he had lately fallen through the ice of a creek and lost half a foot to the frostbite. Until the stump healed he could no longer stalk those caribou and moose that still lingered in the woods. And he told Ivan, having drawn him aside from the rest, that it was useless to send out *cheechakos*—the tenderfeet—to hunt: a deaf moose would hear them a mile away.

"Their party had included one other proven hunter, a wandering Texan named Timothy Brown, but he had gone out alone a week before and not been seen since. Meanwhile the situation had grown desperate; there were clear signs of scurvy in the camp: the blackened gums, loosened teeth, the listless temper, stinking breath, old wounds that reopened and bled afresh.

"But Lefèbvre could see that Ivan was a sourdough, a true man of the north: would he consent, the half-caste begged him, to hunt for them for wages, until they had enough fresh meat cached to eke out their store-bought rations? He would not ask for himself, but his woman was with him, and their little girl now cried all day and complained of aching joints . . ."

The man on the cot nodded impatiently. "Ivan didn't care about money but he couldn't say no. What happened next?"

"Well, as you guess, he agreed to hunt for them."

"Nice people, the Russians, if you get on the good side of them. They'd give you the coat off their backs. That's how I got mine." It hung on a hook at the foot of the bed, a quilted khaki cotton jacket. Tufts of kapok protruded from the bayonet gash under one arm. This is a man, thought the writer, who lives only by inches.

"The next day he set off alone down the valley of the Rat. It is a difficult country, with steep gullies and screes and thickets of willow and alder, and often he had to retrace his steps or climb a steep ridge to find better going, but he had woven himself a good pair of snowshoes and he knew how to use them.

"He was following a nameless creek—nameless to him, at any rate—through a shallow portion of its valley, here almost a mile across, circular in shape and surrounded by bare wind-swept ridges. The sheltered floor of this valley was thickly wooded with birches—just such a place where a few caribou might linger, having failed to keep up with their migrating herd. So he uncased his rifle and entered the trees."

"I have a feeling," said the man on the cot, "that we're getting to brass tacks."

Of course we are, thought the writer. I'm slowing the pace of the narrative to set out a scene. I wouldn't do that if something important weren't about to happen.

"The wood was utterly silent. No breath of wind stirred the crowns of the trees. It was deathly cold, and the snow-laden branches were as hard and unyielding as porcelain. The only sound that Ivan could hear was his own bated breath and the hiss of his snowshoes.

"Onward he crept, stopping every few feet to cock his head and listen, to sniff the air and to read 'the great white book of the forest,' as the snow was known in the land of his boyhood. It showed him tracks of smaller beasts and birds—of squirrel and ptarmigan and fox and porcupine—but no sign of moose or caribou. And as he penetrated deeper into that silent forest, into the trees that seemed to watch and to judge him, he began to wonder why the deer would shun such a sanctuary, what it was that had scared them away. And as soon as he had that doubt he just as soon had an answer, one that stopped him in his tracks: somewhere close at hand, not ten or twenty yards ahead, he heard a sound like a man's stifled cough."

The man on the cot held up a hand. "Before you go any further, please: another cigarette? I want to get settled."

"By all means. This is where it gets good . . . So: he heard a cough. And that is not a sound that a man wants to hear in a place such as that. Could it be another hunter, like himself, or an Indian checking his trapline? It could. But in the wild places, when one is alone, one summons one's own demons, and not all of them take human form . . . So he waited in silence for a long time, and when his patience was exhausted, as the cold crept into his bones, he started forward again, stopping every two feet to watch and to listen. So he came at last to the edge of a clearing, which he observed from behind the last trees.

"There was a cabin in the clearing. A wooden cabin, made of split logs. Yet it was not a cabin of the sort built in this country—a crude foursquare shanty or roofed-over burrow—but a true wooden house, a Russian *izba* such as he had known in his Siberian youth, with a porch and carved shutters. And there above the gable end, at the pitch of the roof, where a Siberian would have carved his *okhlupen*, the friendly spirit that protects his household, was mounted a wooden cross—a Russian cross, with a short crossbeam on top, a longer one beneath it, and some way beneath this another short beam, slanted up to the right, to show where Jesus had smiled on the repentant thief who hung from his own cross beside him. On the other gable was a windvane, its rusted arrow pointing south.

"Ivan understood the little house at once. It was a hermitage or mission: he had seen them before, deep in the woods, far beyond the reach of the jealous Moscow patriarchs. And though he had devised his own wordless faith in his wanderings through the great northern forest, still he fumbled a hand from his mitt and made the sign of the cross with two fingers."

"An Old Believer. The woods are still full of them east of the Urals."

"Quite. The house was decades old, he could tell that at a glance, but lately some effort had been made to repair it. The walls had been chinked with new clay, and fresh sod replaced the shingles missing from the roof. In the middle of the roof, offset from the ridgepole, was a new metal stovepipe. From it emerged a trickle of smoke."

"Somebody's home, then."

"The creek, beneath its sheath of ice and snow, ran along one side of the clearing, leaving an open space before the house. As he peered through the branches Ivan saw two rectangular shapes on the ground—two six-foot-long mounds of round stones from the riverbed. Such are the graves one finds in the north country, where the soil, frozen like rock only two feet below the sod, does not allow any deeper excavation.

"Now Ivan received another surprise—he could see two wooden grave markers lying flat in the clearing—each of them a Russian cross. There was something about those snow-covered graves—their heavy silence, the inhuman neglect of those tumbled-down crosses—that unnerved Ivan. But he had formed an idea of who might be lodged in that cabin. Lefèbvre had told him that his missing hunter, Brown, had set out in this direction before he disappeared: might he not have been injured while hunting, and taken refuge in this cabin until he recovered? So Ivan crossed the clearing and banged on the door.

"There was silence at first, so prolonged that he felt embarrassed, as if he were intruding. Perhaps, then, there was nobody home? But he had heard a cough and seen smoke from the chimney; he knocked again, and this time there was a sound within like the scuffle of rats in a ceiling, whispers like the hissing of snakes. The door swung open, and a gust of warm air belched into his face, bringing with it the stink of unwashed humanity and the smell of a freshly cooked stew . . ."

"Was it this Brown chap?"

"No. It wasn't Brown. It was two other men from the States, a pair of stray stampeders from a different crew. Their names were Cuthfert and Weatherbee, and—"

"No, I meant, was it poor Brown in that stew you just mentioned? In this kind of story some poor bugger always ends up in the pot."

"If you'll only let me finish, you'll find that this is not a story of any kind you have heard before . . . And no, it wasn't Brown in the pot—Lefèbvre found Brown the following spring, frozen in the snow. He'd gone through some ice and not been able to build a fire quickly enough to keep himself from freezing . . .

"Their names, as I said, were Cuthfert and Weatherbee. Cuthfert had been a man of wealth and cultivation, Weatherbee a commercial clerk, a crude, pretentious fellow. The only thing that had united them at first was their intended destination, the Klondike stream. Yet though they immediately despised each other when fate threw them together in Edmonton, the trail had since taught them—with its backbreaking labor, the heaving of oars and portaging of cargo, the chopping of logs and the hunting of meat—that they had another thing in common: a vicious strain of idleness, a crafty yet resolute determination never to do their fair share of anything. This alienated them from the rest of their company and forced them to make common cause.

"The pair had stumbled across this forgotten cabin the previous fall, while pretending to scout ahead of the others as they handlined their boats waist-deep up the Rat. Sensing an easy way out of this ordeal, the two shirkers decided to claim their share of the communal stores and pass the winter in the comfort of the house, the existence of which they kept from the others. And the rest of their party, who were determined to press on to the Klondike that winter, were very glad to be rid of them."

"How would Ivan have known all this? Surely Cuthfert and Weatherbee didn't tell him such discreditable things about themselves?"

Why does he not just let me tell my story? Would it really matter if I were just making it up? "Their fellow travelers told Ivan this. And I was there when they did so. By the time I reached Dawson myself, in the thaw of '98, it was too late to stake a claim of my own. So I took a paid job on Bonanza

Creek, working one of Big Alex McDonald's fractions. Ivan joined us there for a few weeks, after this adventure that I speak of, as he worked to raise a grubstake before he moved on again. He told us his story one night in our cabin, after some rotgut had loosened his tongue. And among those present were a half-breed voyageur called Jacques Baptiste and a tough little scrap of Yankee gristle named Sloper. They had been the leaders of Cuthfert and Weatherbee's party, and remembered them all too well. Jacques Baptiste said he had never met two such lazy scoundrels, and yet vain and proud as Lucifer."

"Ah. Please carry on."

"The cabin was smeared with ordure and rotting scraps of food and soot and ashes from the stove. Their bedrolls teemed with vermin. Unwashed pewter dishes lay in a basin of foul greasy slops, now frozen solid, showing that it was long since either man had drilled through the creek ice to draw water for washing. Ivan would have turned and fled, but the door was held for him by a pair of staring red eyes in a red, ragged beard. At the back of the cabin another filthy wretch stood over a stove, stirring a pot with the blade of a bread knife. They shrank from the light that seeped through the door, like creatures exposed by the turn of a rock."

"Now, you did say that this Brown chap was not in that cooking pot?"

"I did, yes . . . Ivan had seen cabin fever before. He had known men who had been 'bushed'—maddened by the silence and darkness, by the malign, stalking cold of the great northern winter and by agonizing solitude, or worse even than solitude, by the constant confinement with another of one's kind, one whose presence becomes unbearable, whose every whisper and breath, every eccentric habit or careless movement, kindles flames of searing hatred, of homicidal

rage . . . Ivan had seen this before. But there are in the Northland laws of hospitality: he could no more turn away from
breaking bread in their company than they could refuse him
the warmth of their shelter. And so he leaned his rifle on the
porch and stepped into that vile shambles."

"It will soon be morning. Your keepers will come looking
for you."

"Very well. I'll get on with it . . . Ivan was offered an old
crate to sit on while the man at the door—Cuthfert—sat on
another and acted as host. The second man stayed beyond
the pine table in the middle of the house, but he reached
across to shake hands, muttering his name, Weatherbee, and,
as an afterthought, his city of origin in the United States.
Then he went back to his work at the stove, stirring the pot
as he listened to the talk, smiling as if at some private joke.

"As Ivan's eyes grew accustomed to the murk inside the
house he saw that the gums of both men were quite black
and that most of their teeth were already missing. Weatherbee's feet were bandaged in rags, but Ivan could tell that
some of the toes were no longer present. The pair were
deathly pale—the pure, milky white pallor of men who
have lost their battle of wills with the winter, who no longer
dared to go outside, even in the twilight, to chop wood or
draw water or hunt for fresh meat. They were both in the
late stages of scurvy. Unless they were rescued they would
not see the spring."

"I've never seen it myself, but I'm told that the scurvy is a
bastard when it gets a hold."

"It is . . . So presently Weatherbee passed them both mugs
of coffee. Ivan looked at it suspiciously; it had a greasy sheen
on it, the look of the slops in the frozen tin basin, but as the
two of them stared at him he had to take a sip. Not only was
the coffee foul with grease and lumps of rotten matter, but it

was so thick with sugar that the mere taste of it made Ivan's head swim: he had to force it down past his own rising gorge.

"Seeing his distress, Cuthfert asked him if he did not like the coffee, and Ivan could only say that the drink was very sweet. At that Cuthfert looked at Weatherbee, and a cold expression came over his face, and he asked him very quietly from which of their two private hoards of sugar the guest's portion had been taken. Weatherbee made no reply except to bare his black gums and the stumps of his few remaining teeth. From the reeking tomb of his mouth there issued an intermittent creaking hiss, an eldritch sound like a lizard's death rattle: Weatherbee was laughing at Cuthfert.

"Ivan saw a terrible stillness come over Cuthfert's features, the blank, ugly set to his eyes as he gazed back at Weather-bee. Off to one side, in the shadows, Ivan saw a flicker of movement like a rat creeping along the wall, and when he peered closer he made out a hand—Cuthfert's hand, inching toward a curious old ax that leaned near his chair: a hook-nosed Finnish ax with a bearded collar, such as Ivan had known in his youth. Watching the hand steal toward it, Ivan understood how dire relations now were between his hosts, and so he spoke in a loud, jolly voice.

"If their sugar was in short supply, he said, they ought to come back with him to Destruction City. There was sugar there aplenty, and soon there would also be fresh meat: he would find caribou enough to get them all through the winter. But—he lowered his voice now, and looked at them meaningfully—in their present condition, and without fur-ther help, he feared that when spring came they could go neither forward nor back, but must be locked away forever in their secret prison.

"As he looked from one to the other he saw how their eyes remained locked in a mutual loathing as cold and as final

as the land into which they had blundered. Then Weatherbee snickered again, and Cuthfert showed the broken tombstones that flapped from his gums, and both men told him
that they had no wish to go on from here, nor to turn back
in the spring, but would stay where they were. 'Because,' said
Cuthfert, 'not all the treasures of this land are hidden in the
Klondike creek.'

"Now Ivan guessed it: it was the lust for gold that held
them here, dying; they must have thought there was color
in that frozen creek and—too lazy and weak to grub through
the winter, thawing and digging and piling up pay dirt for
sluicing in the spring—they would squat here until the
land thawed and—contrary to the code of the prospecting
brotherhood—keep their good luck to themselves.

"But then Ivan had another thought, and even as it crossed
his mind he felt ashamed of himself, as if he had been cor-
rupted just by sitting in this fetid air. Spring would not come
for Cuthfert and Weatherbee. If there really was gold here,
he need only leave them alone with it until they murdered
each other, or let the scurvy soften their bones and their wills
until they could do no more than lie on their beds, the stove
untended, watching the frost flowers creep up the walls ... Yes,
Ivan could go back to Destruction City, honor his pledge to
hunt for its people, take what money they paid him, and then
return alone to this place in the spring with his pan and his
shovel ... He must be sure to get here before the thaw, when
the corpses would rot and make this house unlivable ..."

"He really opened up to you, this Ivan chap. He seems
very chatty for a Russki."

"Look: if I embellish a little, it's just to fill in the sort of
details that are implicit from the general context, stuff you
could pretty much work out for yourself if you thought it
through."

"Fair enough."

"All this went through Ivan's mind in an instant. But he put his dark thought aside and remonstrated with his hosts. Better to come back with him to Destruction City while they still had the strength to follow the trail he would break for them.

"And at that a curious look came over Cuthfert's face, an expression at once fearful and cunning. No one was going anywhere, he said. And now, as their guest was here, perhaps he would join them in their meal."

"Now remember, old chap: you can't go back on your word about who's in that stew."

The writer refreshed their mugs from his bottle. "Poor Ivan would rather have eaten his own foot than anything that came out of Weatherbee's pot, but there was no possible excuse: he could hardly claim, having come from the forest in forty degrees of frost, that he wasn't hungry: he was famished. So he sat there in dread while Weatherbee scraped the filth from three pewter plates, smacking his lips with the wet, dismal sound of a fish's dying spasms in the bottom of a boat."

"I say! That's rather good."

"Thanks. While Weatherbee doled out the stew, Cuthfert went to the stove, took out a tin, and set it on the table. It was a loaf of fresh bread, piping hot, with an odor so pleasant that it almost made up for the stink of the hovel. Cuthfert divided the bread into three equal chunks that he set on the table, leaving the tin to one side. The bread did not repulse Ivan, so he bit off a chunk to settle his stomach. When it came, the stew too proved surprisingly wholesome: after only a moment's hesitation Ivan was able to swallow a spoonful, then a second and a third. Cuthfert sat opposite, while Weatherbee overturned a bucket for a seat and placed it by Ivan's side. The two of them watched their guest eat, grinning at his appetite. Only when he heard the scrape of their spoons on their plates, the sound of their gums sucking and mashing on the meat in the stew, did he dare to look up from his meal. It was then that he noticed the pages in the bread tin.

"To keep the loaf from sticking, Cuthfert had lined the baking tin with leaves from some unwanted book. As Ivan stared at the pages he found himself, for the second time that day, making the sign of the cross with two fingers. He saw before him, still clearly legible despite the scorching of the paper, the Cyrillic letters of his half-forgotten childhood. And though he could not read Greek, he recognized at once the columns and rubrics of an Orthodox Bible.

"Now Ivan was not, as I said, a religious man, in the sense that men of the south are religious. Yet still it seemed to him blasphemous to rip up a Bible. Surely his hosts knew what those pages were: one did not need to be able to read a book to see the cross upon its cover. His Russian blood stirred in him now. Letting his spoon fall to his plate he wondered, as if in passing, where they had found those curious pages that lined the baking tin.

"A strange look passed between his hosts, and then Cuthfert gagged down a piece of imperfectly chewed gristle. 'I guess there's no harm you seeing it. Who are you going to tell?—Weatherbee: show him the stuff.'

"Weatherbee took an old flour bag from a jumble of crates at the end of the house and carried it back to the table. It made a soft but firm thud when he set it down. Something metal clinked inside it.

"'Go on,' said Cuthfert. 'Look.'

"Ivan loosened the knot that tied the sack and tipped the contents onto the table. There were books, at least a dozen of them, leather-bound volumes with stiff linen pages coated with wax to preserve them—journals or logs of some kind, filled with handwritten letters and figures and sketches for maps. Ivan spread them out in front of him, but he could not read Roman letters, and the maps were of islands and seas that he did not know. He raised the sack again, tipped it higher above the table, and as the rest of its contents slid out, Ivan became aware that Weatherbee was close behind him, peering over his shoulder."

The man on the cot stirred, as if about to sit up, then sank back onto his pillow. The writer could see the glint of his eyes in the lamplight.

"Ivan next saw a holy icon, a Virgin and Infant, inscribed and painted on a wrought silver cross. He picked it up and held it in his hands, turning it over, stupefied by its unexpected beauty, its call to the very depths of his soul. He had not seen such a thing since he'd crossed the straits from the East Cape. Yet how had it come here, far beyond the bounds of Russian Alaska? And how had its beauty survived the rust and decay of the long Arctic winters? He set it down, and considered the other objects on the table.

"The second thing was also familiar to him in its form and function: a revolving pistol. Although very old, it was also untarnished by time. He was about to pick it up when Cuthfert reached over and slid it away from him. 'It's loaded,' he said. 'Better be careful.'

"The third object on the table was a puzzle to Ivan. It was a hollow metal tube, about a foot or so long, made from pewter or tin and sealed at both ends with soldered metal caps. There was a mark stamped on its side, an arrowhead symbol formed by three thin triangles that joined at their tips."

The man on the cot rose up on one elbow, wincing at the pain in his side. "A message tube," he said. "The Royal Navy used to issue them to ships in the old days. They'd put them in stone cairns, to leave word where they were going. The stamp is the broad arrow of the Board of Ordnance."

"You're quite right. But how did you know that? Ivan had no idea what it was. I had to work it out for myself later, from his description. It's not the kind of thing you see every day."

"Oh, I'm quite keen on that sort of thing. Exploration and science and that." He pushed himself upright, grimacing, until his back leaned against the wall of the tent and his feet swung over the side of the cot.

The writer went on: "So. The thing in his hands was a message tube. And although Ivan could not open it, much less read its contents, he understood it was a wonder from another age. He put it down and then he looked at the antique revolver, which sat out of reach between Cuthfert's hands. Untarnished, still loaded? Then he thought of the ax in the corner, the good Finnish-forged trade ax, the indispensable tool—knife, weapon, spade, hewer of firewood—without which no Siberian would go into the forest . . . Where had it gone? Why was that ax no longer in the corner?

"As the hairs rose on Ivan's neck, he had time to wonder whether it was the horror of his predicament that made his nape crawl, or the poisoned breath of the wizened ghoul who, Ivan knew without looking, stood close behind him and hefted the ax."

In another cubicle, somewhere close at hand, a voice babbled feverishly in Japanese. The man on the cot leaned forward to hear the writer better, swinging his feet in the air. "Oh boy, as they say in California."

"Oh boy indeed . . . You've been to California? Where? San Francisco? That's my hometown, you know."

"I passed through two years ago, on my way to Japan . . . But do please go on."

"Alright . . . So Ivan felt his skin crawl, and understood his deadly peril. Across the table from him, Cuthfert showed his fangs again, nodding at him as if humoring a child, but his hand stole toward the pistol on the table. No one was going anywhere, Cuthfert had joked with Weatherbee . . . Their lair was to remain a secret . . .

"Ivan threw himself forward and sideways, crashing into the table with all of his weight. The ax plucked harmlessly at the back of his jacket as he rolled across the floor.

"The table slammed into Cuthfert, who yelped and fell backward, spilling the pistol. It spun across the room and landed on a cot.

"Ivan rolled away as the ax swung again, embedding itself in the floor by his head. He heard Weatherbee hiss in the shadows, but his attention was all for Cuthfert, who skittered on his hands and knees toward the pistol on the bed.

"Ivan was upon him just as Cuthfert's fingers closed on the butt of the gun. As the two of them wrestled for the weapon, Ivan could hear behind him the slow, measured shuffle of Weatherbee's steps, his rotten stumps wrapped in their pustulant foot-cloths, closing the range on his unprotected back.

"Ivan had very little time, but he had the advantage of health and vigor: Cuthfert was little more than a wraith. With a heave, Ivan jerked the pistol free from Cuthfert's hand; as it came away, the trigger guard, twisting on Cuthfert's finger, tore it from the knuckle as a wire cuts through cheese."

"Ouch," said the man on the bed.

"Cuthfert howled, the startled gurgle of a mewling infant. Yet Ivan, sprawled across Cuthfert, heard only the shuffle of feet in the shadows behind him, their cessation, then the creak of floorboards as weight shifted from one foot to the other, as shoulders wound up to swing an ax.

"Despairing, Ivan seized Cuthfert by the shirtfront and rolled over on his back, bringing the howling man across him. The ax glinted as it swung, and Ivan felt the dull thud as it sank into Cuthfert's back. He heard Cuthfert stop howling and felt his limbs go limp.

"The shade that was Weatherbee withdrew the ax from Cuthfert's body with a wet, sucking noise and a scrape of steel on bone.

"The ax swung up again, spraying blood across the ceiling.

"The cabin flared white and vanished, the air filling with the choking, sulfurous smoke of a black-powder discharge. Ivan rolled away, releasing Cuthfert's inert carcass, and fell off the end of the cot. He cowered by the wall, blinded by the muzzle flash and deafened by the shot, pistol raised blindly to menace the void.

"How long did he crouch there? Slowly, the gift of sight, of life, returned to him; the stars in his eyes faded and died, and he could see again dimly in the twilight from the shutters. There were two men on the bed, and neither one was moving.

"Ivan got to his feet and went closer, pistol at the ready. Weatherbee had staggered forward and fallen into the arms of Cuthfert, who lay on his back on the bed. A dark patch on Weatherbee's shirt showed that the first lucky shot had drilled through his heart. His face rested on Cuthfert's shoulder like an infant seeking comfort from its mother.

"Cuthfert lay face up, his unblinking eyes staring up at the ceiling. A log in the stove shifted, throwing a few sparks through its half-open door. They expired on the tin fireguard; all was still once more. And Ivan, alone there in that place of madness and horror, remembered another iron law of the Northland: as the last man standing, it was his job to bury the dead. His sense of justice revolted at this prospect:

what duty did he owe these creatures who had schemed to deceive and to kill him? What humanity did he share with these things that were so much less than men?

"But a law is a law. Ivan would do his duty, though he knew that had he defaulted no other man living would know of the lapse or judge him harshly for it. He would have to work quickly, to lay the corpses out before their limbs stiffened . . . He would also have to make a fire in the clearing, to thaw out some ground for yet another shallow grave. What terrible, backbreaking work, and this time with no pay dirt to sift at the end of it. If he could only walk away . . . But no. He seized hold of Weatherbee's shoulder and started to drag his corpse away from Cuthfert.

"'Leave him,' whispered Cuthfert. 'It is right that we should lie together in death. With all my soul I loathed him. He was the fittest companion that I ever had.'

"Ivan let go of Weatherbee and sprang away from the cot. Cuthfert's eyes moved in his head, following him into the shadows.

"'That creek is full of gold. It's yours now, I guess.'

"Ivan said nothing. Was this thing on the cot still alive or was he hearing from a specter?

"'There are some nuggets on the windowsill, in that old tobacco tin. You should take them for assay.'

"And what, thought Ivan, does it want in return? He had heard tales in his youth of lost houses in the forest, strange figures in the trees, of Baba Yaga and bartered souls. It was better, he knew, neither to listen nor speak when the devil wants to bargain. The house was growing cold; he walked over to the stove, opened the door, and picked up a log.

"'Please don't feed the fire,' murmured Cuthfert. 'I want to lie here in peace and watch the frost climb the walls. Take what you want and leave us as we are.'"

"The message tube," said the man on the cot, sitting forward. The writer was surprised by his listener's eagerness. "Did Ivan take that? And the journals and maps? What happened to them?"

"He put them," said the writer, 'back where they had come from, into two airtight metal cases he found in the corner, marked with that same broad arrow stamp. He put the ancient pistol in his pocket and pried the ax from Weatherbee's dead hand. Cuthfert's eyes flickered as Ivan moved back and forth, passing through his field of dying vision, but he never spoke again. The fire in the stove was already no more than a glow and the beautiful frost flowers bloomed on the walls.

"His preparations completed, Ivan went to the windowsill and picked up the tobacco tin. He shook it, looked inside, then put it back where he had found it. The black joke was complete: they had ruined themselves—ruined themselves utterly—for an ounce of fool's gold.

"Ivan took the other things outside and closed the door behind him. Nothing now would ever make him go back inside: a man would only be given one warning. He crossed the clearing. Now that he stood over them, he could see that the two graves had been disturbed. Two narrow depressions in the snow, set close beside each other, showed where respectful hands had made the original excavations, shallow rectangles clawed into frozen soil. But the rocks that had been piled over the two graves had lately been displaced, pushed to one side, making it look from a distance, under the trampled snow of the clearing, as if the two graves were farther apart than they were.

"There was a shovel by the porch. Two feet down, its blade struck wood under the snow. Reaching down, Ivan pulled the lid from a coffin. Then he dropped the shovel and started back.

"The subsoil of this Arctic region, which does not thaw even in summer, had preserved the eyes that now gazed up at Ivan. They looked as if they were still capable of sight. The face was that of a man of about fifty or sixty, of Tartar or Mongol appearance, with black hair attached to the scalp and a scrap of black beard on his cheeks. Only the frost-blackened skin, drawn tight across wide cheekbones, spoke of the many long years he had lain in the darkness, his lips shrunken back to show stained, yellow teeth. The upper body was hidden by a deerskin coat made by some northern tribe unknown to Ivan: around his neck the sleeper wore a strange amulet, a necklace of whalebone, carved in the likeness of a screaming human face. There was such terror in that image that Ivan, never a fanciful man, almost lost his nerve and fled. But he mastered himself, and continued to gaze. A pistol's lanyard still circled the dead man's neck but the ends had been cut and the pistol was missing. As was the man's lower body, from the waist down. A loop of frozen intestine, severed by an ax cut, protruded from under the caribou coat.

"Ivan had underestimated Cuthfert and Weatherbee. Their scheme was not as doomed as he had imagined. They had stumbled across a way to beat the scurvy. They had found a supply of meat—fresh meat, more or less, after it was thawed and stewed. And—in his own person—they had found a way to augment their supply . . ."

"I told you there'd be some poor bugger in that pot! You misled me!"

"I did not mislead you! You asked if it was that Brown fellow, the Texan who'd gone missing from Destruction City. It wasn't him. You misled yourself."

"Well, anyway. The second grave, please."

"So. The second grave proved harder to open than the first: groundwater had seeped into it and frozen hard, and the lid of the coffin was welded shut by the ice. But he found a slim crack between coffin and plank and slid the ax blade into it, and after a little jimmying he had pried off the lid.

"The second corpse had not yet been scavenged. It was that of a white man, dressed in the plain woolen cassock of a Russian cleric. He had a full white beard and a broad, Russian face, much lined by the years. His eyes were closed as if in sleep, his hands folded on his breast. In them he clasped the remains of a book, a Bible, most of which had been ripped away."

The man on the bed nodded quickly, hurrying the narrative on. "A missionary or mystic hermit. Or a pious envoy of the old Russian–American Company. But what was he doing so far east of Alaska?"

"I don't know," said the writer impatiently. He was caught in the grip of his own story. "The first grave was longer than the priest's grave. At one end a little wall of stones separated the grave itself from a smaller excavation, also flooded, in which two square depressions chipped in the ice showed where the two tin boxes had once been buried. Covered over with the rocks, this little compartment would have looked from above like part of the grave. When in fact it was, Ivan realized, really a cache, a hiding place."

The man on the cot nodded quickly. "Very good. So what happened next?"

"Ivan did the right thing. He put the things back in the boxes—the message tube and journals. He kept the pistol for the dead men's sake: a gravedigger must have his tip, or the dead will have no luck on the other side . . . Ivan would also have liked to keep the ax, but you can't take a man's last ax: it must be buried with him.

"After saying a silent prayer he laid the icon and the loose pages of the Bible on the dead priest's breast. Then he closed both coffins and replaced the stones. When he was finished he turned and looked at that silent, ghastly house. Though he had felt no breath of wind the weathervane had moved to a little north of east, the way he had wandered all through his days. It was past noon, and the weathervane cast a long shadow on the snow, a fraction east of north. Thirty years before, Ivan had kissed his mother good-bye on the porch of their warm little *izba*. Each step he had taken since, a little north of east, or a little east of north, had brought him to this place, to this silent house in a desolate clearing so like the one he had left. He knew now that his journey was over. He would turn and go back. Facing east and north for the last time, he gazed into the watchful trees that crowded around the clearing: what, after all, were they hiding? What was beyond them? He re-erected the two fallen crosses, shouldered his pack, and went back to Destruction City, where he did not tell the others about what had befallen him. He did not want anyone to find that hidden place again."

"The crosses," said the man on the cot. "Did he say if there was anything written on them?"

"He did. There were names on them. But he couldn't read them. They were both written in Roman letters, not in Cyrillic."

"That's rather odd . . . So whoever buried them there, and cached the valuables, wasn't Russian . . . Did he say anything about finding any instruments?"

"Instruments?"

"Navigational instruments. Mapmaking tools—sextants or compasses or chronometers or the like."

And where, wondered the writer, might these questions lead? But there was something about the man on the bed, some quality of imperviousness, that prevented him asking. This fellow is somehow special, he realized: I don't want to scare him off. "No. Nothing like that. Just the maps and the tube and the journals. And the icon, the pistol, and the ax."

"I see . . ." The man on the bed tipped his mug up, draining it, then fixed the writer with a straight look. "And your story is true?"

The writer laughed at the directness of the challenge. "Is it true? Who can say? But it's true that Ivan told us all that— well, almost all of it—that night in the cabin on Bonanza Creek. And those were the last words I ever heard him speak. The next day he took his pay and bought a Tagish canoe and set off alone down the river. Some say he crossed back to Siberia. He was never seen in the Yukon again."

"So there's no way to find him now. No way to confirm his story or get directions to that cabin?"

"No . . . There's no proof at all . . . But he did show us the gun."

"What?"

"He showed us the gun. The pistol he took from the cabin. The one he used to kill Weatherbee. As I said, he brought it away as his gravedigger's tip. He showed it to us that night in the bunkhouse. It was very old—a cap-and-ball black powder Colt five-shooter. It's a wonder it would still fire. Yet it would have been worth a fortune when it was new—revolvers were a wonder when they first came on the market. And this one was clearly a valued possession—its owner's initials were engraved on the receiver."

"Really . . . I don't suppose you remember what these initials were?"

"Oh yes. I took a note of them for my short story. 'F.R.M.C.'"

"F.R.M.C. . . . F.R.M.C. . . ." The patient lay back on the bed, moving his lips silently. He's memorizing the initials, thought the writer. He won't write them down while I'm watching.

The man on the bed sat bolt upright again, struck by some private revelation. "F.R.M.C.!" Then he remembered the writer, and what he'd just said. "Your short story? What story is that?"

"I write fiction, you know. It's my main living. I only dabble in journalism; the *San Francisco Examiner* made me an offer so generous I couldn't say no."

"And you think this silly old yarn would make a good story?"

"Don't you?"

"Well ..." The patient was rubbing his eyes and his face, as if trying to massage some thought into them. "Well ... Don't you think it's a bit far-fetched? All these Russians and corpses and cannibals and suchlike? It would strain credulity."

"That surely doesn't matter if it's true."

"But people won't *think* that it's true. Not only will they think you're making it up, they'll think you're overdoing it. It's a new century, you know; that sort of Gothic, sort of supernatural thing, is going out of style. Everything is very plain and modern now."

"I happen to know that most readers love the Gothic and supernatural stuff."

The patient rubbed his face some more, then stopped and smiled at the writer. "It's just that if you hone that story down there's a better story hidden inside it. More in tune with the twentieth century."

"Like what?" And why, thought the writer, would I take his advice on how to write stories? He doesn't seem the literary type.

"Well ... Well ... How about this: what if you take out Ivan and the cannibalism and the maps and all that? What if you just have Cuthfert and Weatherbee alone in the cabin, slowly going mad from isolation and mutual loathing, until finally they crack up and kill each other?"

"Where would that get me?"

"It would make it a much starker story. Much more modern. That way, it's about how silence and isolation find the cracks in a character, the points of weakness, the things that truly define a man, far more than his strengths do, and how they use those weaknesses to tear him apart. It's about how we rely on a very thin layer of civilization to hold us together. That sort of thing."

The writer thought about that, sighed, then poured them both another brandy. "You know," he said, "I think you might be on to something. If Ivan hadn't stumbled into the scene, Cuthfert and Weatherbee would have killed each other anyway. As far as their story is concerned, the Russian is just another detail too many."

The man on the bed nodded vigorously. "So cut him out. He gets in the way . . . But you could still have the lonely unexplained graves outside the mysterious old cabin. I like that part, so long as they're not dug up. And the weather-vane emblem is good, though to be honest I don't know what it means. Not that I ever do . . ."

"The next morning the Japanese dragged London off with the rest of their tame correspondents. Two days after that I set out for Alaska." Meares was talking to himself by now: Hugh, drunk on three swallows of whiskey, had lost the thread of the story and was trying not to nod off. "I went back through the Russian lines and found a ship to the East Cape. From there I crossed the Bering Strait and went up the Yukon River and then across the divide. I searched up and down the Rat River but I never found that cabin. If it weren't for one or two details I'd swear that London had made it all up . . ."

The alarm sounded on the telegraph board, jerking Hugh back to full wakefulness. It was Esquimalt again. Meares pulled an old envelope out of his pocket and placed it on the table beside Hugh's typewriter. "Write it here," he said. "I don't want any impressions left on your ribbon."

Hugh transcribed the Morse into a penciled message then offered it to Meares.

"I can't see in the dark without glasses. Read it aloud."

"'Your accusation absurd. Stop. William Forbes Sempill is courtier Etonian peer Highlander. Stop. Desist.'"

Meares tipped his head back and closed his eyes. He became very still. Watching him, Hugh had a notion he might have stopped breathing. "Do you want to send a reply?"

Meares opened his eyes again. "No. No reply. There's nothing to say . . ." He stood up, patting his pockets to make sure he still had his flask and his cigarette case. He looked tired. "I'll slip out the side door while you lock the office. I'll be waiting in the car. It's parked on the corner."

"I still have my bicycle."

"Your blessed bicycle . . . where would we be without it? I can put it in the back."

Part Six

The Amundsen Gulf

70°30′N 122°30′W

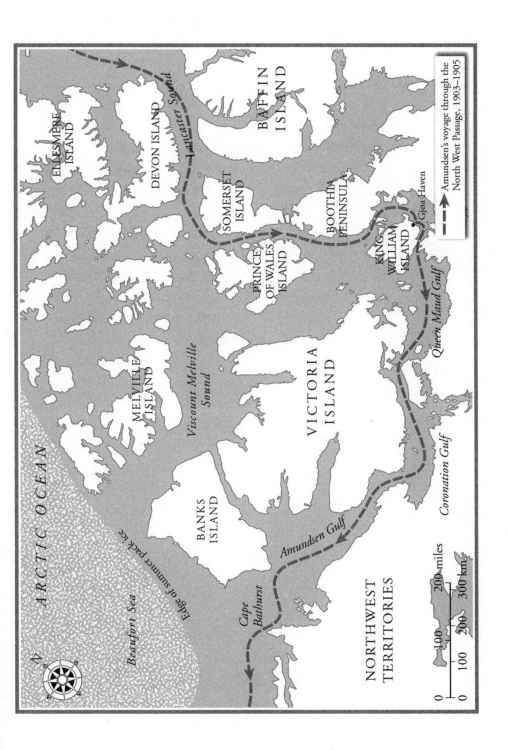

ARCTIC OCEAN

ELLESMERE ISLAND

DEVON ISLAND

Lancaster Sound

BAFFIN ISLAND

SOMERSET ISLAND

PRINCE OF WALES ISLAND

BOOTHIA PENINSULA

Gjoa Haven

KING WILLIAM ISLAND

MELVILLE ISLAND

Viscount Melville Sound

VICTORIA ISLAND

Queen Maud Gulf

BANKS ISLAND

Coronation Gulf

Edge of summer pack ice

Amundsen Gulf

Beaufort Sea

Cape Batburst

NORTHWEST TERRITORIES

N

Amundsen's voyage through the North West Passage, 1903–1905

0   100   200 miles
0   100   200   300 km

Inuvik, Northwest Territories

The last time Nelson had seen Bert was at their mother's funeral in Grande Prairie, Alberta, three years before. The previous time was at their father's funeral, also in Grande Prairie, a year before that. The time before that Nelson couldn't remember.

Their parents both ended up in the same nursing home— their father was crippled by arthritis, among other things, while their mother was mad. They were kept on separate wings because Charlotte Nilsson no longer spoke to her husband, whom she believed had helped to abduct her from her true family, the Romanovs of Russia. He had stolen a princess from history, and her history from her.

Bert paid the bills, but he lived in Ontario most of the time and seldom visited. Nelson only saw his parents in the seniors' home once, when he was driving up the Alaska Highway and couldn't think of an excuse not to stop by. He went to see his mother first but she wouldn't talk to him, or accept the box of her favorite licorice that he'd bought at a specialty store in Edmonton. "I don't like licorice," she said, and smiled at him sourly, as if she'd just made a crushing point.

"Well, hold on to it anyway," he said. "Next time Bert comes by you can give it to him. He loves licorice."

"Who's Bert?" She made the smile again. But he knew damn well she was mad, not demented.

His father had been delighted to see him, at least at first. But the longer Nelson stayed, the quieter his father became. He wants to escape, thought Nelson. When he saw me at first he thought—or couldn't help hoping—that I'd come here to spring him. And for a few lovely moments he let his mind run with that notion: just him and his old dad, sticking together, muddling along, happy together at last, until they came to whatever end fate had in store for them. He saw it as a road movie. But the happy moment passed. His dad was too old and too sick to live in a car with him. So they talked for a while longer, about anything other than what was glaringly obvious, the chasm between them, between the two of them and Charlotte, between the two of them and Charlotte and Bert. Then Nelson told his father some lie about the job he was going to up in Dease Lake. His father nodded politely, knowing that his son only ever lied out of kindness, and the two of them then said good-bye. They both guessed correctly that they wouldn't meet again.

Their mother wouldn't come to her husband's funeral. A year later, she was buried by his side.

Nelson remembered being happy as a boy. Their house had been small but warm in the winters. He remembered, when he could have been no older than four or five, how a Chinook wind had thawed their front yard just after he and Bert built a really good snow fort. To cheer them up their mother drew a smiley face in the steam on the window. She used to sing to us. He remembered his grandfather buying them ice cream, his parents holding hands.

From that to this. All he knew for sure was that Bert had grown silent and his mother distant. His grandfather died and his father was very sad about it. Little gaps appeared in the family and were widened by time. He started getting into trouble at school. Teachers said he was bright, but he couldn't do his homework. He would look at it until his head and chest hurt and then he'd have to push it away. To make up for this failure he would stick up for Bert, who wouldn't stick up for himself, and that led to other problems. After a while, with all the tears and the threats and the shouting, you had to decide for yourself that you were basically on your own. You had to put your head down and charge at life, fists flailing. And when you finally calmed down enough to pause and look around you, you had proven yourself right: you really were alone.

When his father died he left the money from the sale of the house to Charlotte. When she died a year later it turned out she had already given most of it away, writing check after check to charities she found in the dayroom's old magazines. Bert and Nelson would have only six thousand dollars to split between them. But it would take a while for the estate to be probated, so Bert gave Nelson his half in cash right after the funeral. Nelson hadn't asked for it, Bert just did it off his own bat. He couldn't tell Bert how grateful he was. All he could say was: Let's go for a drink.

It was one of the very few times they had ever gone to a bar together. Nelson suggested a favorite old dive, to see if they still remembered him there, to see if by some miracle he was still banned. But the head barman was just a kid and there was no one there he knew.

They sat at the bar and ordered beer. The place was quiet. After he served them, the barman went back to restocking shelves with glasses and bottles. The only waitress sat reading a book by the service counter. Nelson watched Bert pour his beer in a glass then sip it like he thought it might hurt him. He's still frightened, thought Nelson, and felt his chest flood with pity. He's lived with that all his life, wherever it comes from. And yet when you think of all the things he's done . . . Well, Nelson had lost track of that a long time ago, but he remembered that his brother had once passed a winter at Alert, the most northerly inhabited place on the planet, had spent several seasons in Antarctica, had done fieldwork alone in the barrens of Keewatin ... Nelson could never have done that. He had never been afraid of anything much, but he knew early on that he would never show any practical guts.

"Two whiskies," he said. When they came he drank his in one go while Bert watched him sadly. Bert's face was lined now. His hair was thin on top. It had once been brown with licks of red but the brown was all gone so it was now red and gray. But his beard was still red: Nelson was glad he had shaved his own beard the year before: when they were younger, they looked too much alike.

"So," said Nelson. "How's Ottawa?"

"I'm leaving it. I'm going to live full-time in the north."

"New assignment, huh?"

"I'm switching jobs. I'm going to teach geography in a high school in Inuvik."

Nelson didn't know where Inuvik was. "Teach high school? Aren't you a little over-qualified?"

"They get a lot of over-qualified people up there—teachers and civil servants who move up from the south before retirement. It's up in the Arctic, so you get special tax breaks plus northern pay rates. It bumps up your final pension."

"But that's not why you're doing it."

"No."

At that point Nelson could have asked Bert why he was doing it. He did want to know. There would, he was sure, be an interesting answer. But he had just noticed again the weight of three thousand dollars counted in hundreds in his inside jacket pocket.

Bert hadn't asked him any questions. He hadn't asked where Nelson was living. He hadn't asked what he did with his time, where he got his money. Bert had gone to the bank and taken out three thousand dollars of his own cash to pay off Nelson's half of the will and he had done it without asking. He hadn't asked how little Lizzie was, which meant he knew that Donna had kicked him out for good, that Nelson had lost them. Donna must have called him. Or Bert had called her.

Bert hadn't drunk his shot yet, had hardly touched his beer. Fuck him.

"Two more whiskies," Nelson said to the barman. He didn't look at Bert. "Drink up. I'm buying."

Nelson made breakfast of scrambled eggs and toast. He would have added bacon but the bacon was all gone. Fay ate at the desk in front of the computer. She turned her swivel chair so he couldn't see her face as she read from her book. From time to time she put down her fork to check something on the Internet. When the book was face down he could see the cover: it was the book that Rose had given him the night before: *Men of Ice*, by Leif Mills.

He leaned back on the couch and shut his eyes. He might have dozed for a bit, but not for long. When he opened his eyes again a strand of her hair, still a bit wet from the shower, had escaped from behind her left ear. Her nape, which was pretty much all that he could see of her, showed two long wedges of fine dark hair. He had a shockingly clear recollection of the feel of her neck, those soft hairs under his fingers.

Why was she still here? Not for his sake of course. He could see how she felt about him, about last night, from the way she hid her nose in his brother's weird papers. He told himself that he'd expected nothing more. He had offered to let her stay for her sake, not for his. It was obvious that he would sleep on the couch.

Maybe I should ask her if there's anything in that book about her magic granddad. But he didn't want to mock her. Part of him really did want her to stay.

He watched her read for a while longer then he got up and went to the window. She stirred when he moved but did not turn around.

The hospital looked like a cruise ship on a sea of dirty ice. It hadn't snowed any more in the night. The sky was clear and pale as shoal water. Out on the highway cars came and went, occluded by their own headlights. Were the passes open yet or was that local traffic?

"Do you want to drive out to the airport? To see if there are any flights today? Or if the highway is open?"

She didn't seem to hear him so he said it again. Dragging her eyes from the book, she stared at him for several moments before she replied. "What?"

"I said, we could go to the airport to see if it's open."

"Oh . . ." He saw her glance at the desk again. "I looked that up on the Internet. It's still closed. So is the highway."

"Well, how about just going into town for a drive? I feel kind of cooped up."

"Of course. Go ahead."

He hadn't expected that. "You don't want to come? What will you do here?"

"I suppose I'll just read a bit more. Some of this stuff is quite interesting."

He went over to the door, put on Bert's old coat. He could, he supposed, buy some more smokes. He could also use a little time by himself.

She had already opened the book again, was lost in its pages. He felt a sudden stab of anger.

"That book must be pretty good. What's in it?"

He saw, with some satisfaction, how painful it was for her to return to the room. "This book . . . ? It's just two short biographies of British explorers. They went to Antarctica on different expeditions. They didn't even know each other. One was called Alister Mackay. The other one was Cecil Meares."

"Meares? There's a folder with that name on it. I was looking at it yesterday. Didn't make a lot of sense."

She turned a page without looking up. "Really . . . ?"

"You sure you don't want to come for a ride around town? Get some fresh air and some lunch?"

"I'm fine for now, thanks."

So that's it, he thought. She says I can go now. She's the type who reads, I'm the type who eats. He walked over to the desk and grabbed a random folder. "I'll take this with me. It's good to have something to read when you eat."

"Okay." She still didn't turn around.

Halfway down the corridor he realized that he'd left the keys to the apartment on the table inside the door. He stopped, was about to go back and get them. Perhaps she'll have gone out by the time I come back. But he didn't want to have to knock on the door and get her to open it, not right then, before he'd had a chance to have a smoke and a drive. He was afraid of what he might say.

Fay heard his footsteps slow when he was halfway down the hall. They stopped. She put down the book she was reading and waited. He stood there for a few seconds and then went on down the corridor.

Please, she thought. It's not my fault. But I haven't got time to be nice to you. This chance, the chance to find out who Hugh Morgan was, might never come again.

She had lied about the airport and the highway being closed. Or at least, half lied: she had made a point of not checking the Internet that morning. If they had reopened she didn't want to know.

She sifted through the unread papers until she found the file marked "Cecil Meares." Then she made herself more coffee and began to read.

When she closed the file again most of her coffee was still in the mug, only now it was cold. Her head swam.

The Meares folder contained only one document—a short story perhaps, or maybe a fragment of a novel, or a memoir. It bore the name of the writer Jack London who, she knew from her own general knowledge, had written a lot of stuff about dogs and the Arctic. But there was no mention of any such memoir or novel by Jack London in the bibliographies she'd found on the net. Was it fake? Or was it real but unpublished? . . . Unlike much of the material in Bert Nilsson's collection, this document wasn't handwritten. It was a copy of a typescript. Maybe Bert had taken a chance on having this one photocopied. Maybe because it was too long to write out by hand. Or perhaps because it looked pretty harmless: how could a literary work be a secret?

The answer, she guessed, must lie in the identity of the patient, the unnamed man in the hospital bed at whom the story was addressed. She knew from the book that the explorer Cecil Meares had, like the man in the bed, been some kind of presence at the Russo-Japanese war of 1904. He'd been arrested by both sides and treated as a spy . . . That might explain why Bert had put this story in a file with Meares's name on it.

What linked this British explorer to a beaten-down Irish sea captain, to an idealistic young Frenchman, to her elusive grandfather and his revenant clock? Or to that old Inuit hunter, Eskimo Joe, whose weird statement she had read that morning?

All of them were lost. They disappeared in the ice. No one saw what became of them.

Was that it?

But Meares had died in bed of cirrhosis of the liver. It said so in that book. There was no mystery about his death. It was his life that was largely a blank space.

She picked up the next folder. She'd been looking forward to getting to this one since she'd read the last line of the "Eskimo Joe" file.

"Roald Engelbregt Gravning Amundsen: from Room 38."

She already knew quite a bit about this man. In 1912, Amundsen had won the race to the South Pole. He'd beaten Scott's British expedition, which included Cecil Meares and the famous Captain Oates, another man who had walked off alone into the snow.

Bert's papers included a note to Cecil Meares that was supposedly copied from Oates's diary. She read it again now, then tried to check it on the Internet. According to the web, Oates's diary had been found in the tent with the bodies of Scott, Wilson, and Bowers. It was then passed unread to his mother. Years later, when a would-be biographer asked to see it, Mrs. Caroline Oates, a devout and austere upper-class widow, denied that the diary had ever existed. But Bert had somehow found a piece of that diary, referring to a gun and a chronometer and a Room 38.

She had a vision of clockwork, of wheels within wheels, the hint of bigger wheels lurking behind them. She could see how a few of them fitted together but she didn't know how they were meant to turn. The spring was still hidden from her in the source of Bert's secret papers, the place or thing known as "Room 38." And she still had no idea where or what that might be.

Cape Chelyuskin, Siberia, 1919

Just before Amundsen left London he was called to an interview with Admiral William Sims, commander of US naval forces in Europe. They met not at Sims's office, where Amundsen's presence would surely be noted, but the admiral's rooms at the Carlton Hotel: a world-famous explorer would be quite unremarkable there.

Amundsen couldn't think why Sims wanted to see him. It was July of 1918 and the Germans were again advancing on Paris across the line of the Marne, just as they had done four years before. Scores of U-boats roamed the oceans, attacking ships of all nations. The war was in a very fine balance; surely an admiral had better things to do.

Meares was waiting in the bar of the Carlton when Amundsen came down again. He wore the blue tunic of the new Royal Air Force; it was the third uniform that Amundsen had seen him in since 1914. Two pink gins sat on the counter.

"I've brought you those instruments you wanted to borrow," Meares told him. "For a man who says he doesn't believe in luck you're very fond of your charms . . . Anyway. What did Sims want you for?"

"He wanted to tell me that there shouldn't be any submarines in the Barents Sea when the *Maud* is passing through. He says the U-boats assigned to the Arctic station are all sunk or out of service or else en route to Heligoland to refuel and rearm."

"I was going to tell you that—he got it from our code-breakers in Room 40 at the Admiralty. That's just secondhand gossip. What does he want in return?"

"He wants to know about the ice conditions in the Barents Sea and the Kara Sea, and reports on the weather. He wants any information I can give on the political situation at any Russian ports we visit—whether they're held by the Reds or the Whites, if there's food for soldiers or coal for ships or forage for horses. He wants to know about dock facilities, local sympathies, all that sort of thing. I'd guess that they're going to send troops to fight the Bolsheviks."

"They are. As if we didn't have enough wars already . . . He's asking a lot in return for so little. How does he expect you to send all this stuff?"

"By wireless. There's a set aboard the *Maud*."

Meares put his drink down. "Sims wants you to send secret information by wireless? From up there?"

"He's given me a codebook. He says it's unbreakable. But it only works one way. I can only use it to send, not receive."

"And have you agreed?"

"I couldn't think of a way to say no. The Americans have been helping to fund my expedition on the quiet. Now I know why."

Meares finished his gin, signaled for two more. "You take my advice and have nothing to do with it. The *Maud* is a neutral Norwegian ship on a scientific voyage to the north pole. The U-boats won't respect that but everyone else will. Even the Reds. But you'll be boarded and searched every time you make port. If you're caught with codebooks, or maybe even just a transmitter, you'll be in big trouble. A ship and its crew could just disappear on that coast. I know. I've been there."

"So what should I do? I can't afford to snub Sims."

Meares took out a cigarette, considering the problem. "Here's what you do. You wait until the *Maud* is a day or so out of Norway.

Then you disable your transmitter—I'll have someone show you how to make it look like an accident. After that you don't need the codebooks anymore. So you put them in a sack with a couple of bits of ballast and chuck them into the sea. Just don't let the others see you doing it."

"Without a wireless I can't do anything for Sims. Or you for that matter."

"Yes, you can." Meares took a page out of his pocket and showed it to Amundsen. "There's a White Russian wireless station still in operation at Khabarovo, on the Yugorsky Strait. Farther on, there's another wireless station on Dickson Island. And if you get anywhere near the Bering Strait, you can send messages through a friend of ours who trades in furs at the East Cape. His name is Clarendon Carpendale—an Australian chap I met in South Africa. He can send messages through the telegraph at Nome in Alaska." Meares tapped the paper he'd put on the counter. "One of these innocent phrases—'happy birthday,' 'hope you are well,' and so on—dropped into an ordinary telegram, would speak volumes to me. You just have to memorize them and what they refer to." He pulled a droll face. "And of course I'll be sure to keep Sims informed of your progress."

Amundsen frowned at the page but didn't pick it up. He wouldn't be able to read it anyway: he'd needed glasses since his boyhood but was too vain to let anyone know. For this childish conceit, he thought, I will have to commit myself now without even knowing what they want from me. I shall have to leap into the unknown.

"Alright," he said. "For old times' sake." It was, he told himself, the kind of thing that explorers did. And he was in a hurry to finish with Meares and be on his way: it was his last night in London, and Kiss waited for him in a room at the Cecil Hotel.

Amundsen hadn't brought a wireless when he went to Antarctica eight years before. It probably wouldn't have worked anyway, back before the war, that far from any base station. And what was the point of it anyway? "Dot dot dash hello stop we reached the south pole stop we'll see you in a month or two stop or if the ice is too thick for the ship to collect us we'll see you next year stop." Instead, he had brought the news himself, sneaking ashore at Hobart disguised as a common sailor, his men sworn to silence until he'd set the stage.

Even Scott, who had access to the most advanced wireless gear in the Royal Navy's inventory, who could rely on British relay stations in New Zealand and the Falkland Islands, even he must have understood the principle. When Scott went south that last time he didn't bring a radio either. What if he had? What if Scott's people had started signaling from Ross Island as soon as he failed to come back before winter, telling the world that Scott and his polar party were certainly dead? Where was the dramatic tension in that? Instead, the British public had to endure a third winter of silence and then, when the survivors returned by ship, learn everything at once—the collapsed tent only ten miles short of the One Ton Depot, the stoical diaries, the beaten, dying faces in the photos from the pole. Oates walking shoeless and alone into a blizzard. "For God's sake look after our people."

It seemed to Amundsen that if Scott had survived, having come a brave second, he'd have gone back to the Admiralty and they'd have given him another dreadnought. He'd have spent the war with the Grand Fleet in Scapa Flow, slowly swinging around his anchor chain. He'd have died of old age, knighted and forgotten. Not now though, not now. Scott was more alive than he was. The news of his death, which broke a whole year after Amundsen returned from his conquest, had stolen all the glory that he'd thought was in the bag.

Wireless and telegraphy would bleed you to death if you let them. How could a man hide from them? How could he disappear and reappear again, still the author of his own story? On

the evening the *Maud* left the Varangerfjord, with the unlit Vardø
lighthouse still a white dot astern, he had left the others on deck
and slipped into the wireless office. A few minutes later, when the
others smelled smoke, he was already asleep in his cabin.

At Khabarovo there was a trading store, a militia post, a shed that
housed the wireless station, and not much else. Nenets herds-
men in bright beaded clothing sat patiently outside the trading
store, hoping it might somehow reopen, while their reindeer
steamed and snorted in the sharp August air. Paul Knutsen, who
had been this way before and knew a few words of Russian,
struggled to talk with the nomadic Nenets, who spoke little
Russian themselves. It seemed a warning had come the day
before: the Reds were drawing near, were maybe a day away.
The White soldiers had left by boat in the night and the traders
had gone with them.

So much, thought Amundsen, for sending messages to London. "Then the Russians are all gone?"

Knutsen listened, then translated. "No. There's still one."

He was a blond kid, skinny, about twenty years of age, with
heavy brows and a strong dimpled chin. He sat alone in the wireless office wrapped in a blanket, staring placidly over the half-
door. He got to his feet when Amundsen appeared.

"You are Captain Amundsen." He spoke excellent Norwegian,
though with a Russian accent. "I am Gennady Olonkin, telegra-
phist second-class. I will send your dispatches. And there's a message for you from London."

He went over to a cabinet and opened a drawer. Amundsen had expected none of this. "How do you speak such good
Norwegian?"

"My mother is from Vardø. She married an Archangel sea captain." Olonkin took out an envelope and handed it to Amundsen.
"Here it is . . . May I please ask, Captain, if you need any more

hands on your ship? I'm good with engines and I can operate wireless and Morse."

Amundsen, fumbling with the envelope, gave him an offhand answer. "I don't need a wireless operator. Our transmitter is broken. And I like to keep a tight crew. There are already nine of us."

Olonkin nodded, apparently untroubled by the rejection. "Then would you please take me as far as Dickson Island, then let me off?"

Amundsen, who had extracted the message from its envelope, now understood. The Bolsheviks might arrive at any moment.

"Well . . ." he said doubtfully, unfolding the message, "I suppose I could take you to Dickson . . ." He looked down at the message. It consisted of four words in English: "Hire this man. Dearie."

The ship's transmitter was ruined—the Norwegians all agreed it would never work again—but the shortwave receiver was still in operation. Olonkin, when not on duty as second stoker in the engine room, spent most of his time in the wireless office. He would sit up half the night, puzzling over urgent bursts of Morse, over fragments of strange speech and music, over a bored voice that came on late at night to read long lists of numbers in English, bookended by a few tinny bars of some old folk tune, one that Amundsen half remembered from quayside farewells in Seattle and Hobart.

Olonkin was so good at repairs that he could probably have fixed the transmitter itself, if Amundsen had let him. But when Amundsen had first showed him around the ship Olonkin peered into the carbonized guts of the transmitter, poked at the fuse that had started the fire, then turned and looked at Amundsen. Amundsen had stared evenly back. The young Russian said nothing and left.

After that, Amundsen relied on him completely. He needed someone he could trust. In mid-September *Maud* rounded Cape

Chelyuskin and went into winter harbor twelve miles to the south. But its crew wouldn't spend the dark months doing nothing. There would be magnetic observations, specimen collection, hunting for fresh food, meteorological work. Amundsen himself would be doing some mapping—anchorages, natural harbors, potential landing beaches, that sort of thing—and he needed an assistant who wouldn't ask questions. Olonkin never asked questions: he seldom spoke at all.

In February, when the sun showed itself again, Olonkin and Amundsen went sledging whenever the weather permitted. They would leave the *Maud* early in the morning, when the stars blazed overhead and the snow crust groaned like the deck of a steel ship. Amundsen, who had broken his arm twice in the winter—once in a fall on the ice, the second time when attacked by a bear—couldn't do much to help with the sledge. Instead, he skied ahead to give the dogs something to follow. When Amundsen spied their last positional marker, a red flag on a tall bamboo pole, they would tether the dogs and throw up a snow-wall, pitch their tent, melt pemmican and chocolate in the dish of their Nansen stove. Then, as the sun crawled over the Byrranga Mountains, leeching the life from the southernmost stars, they would go to work with theodolite and plane table, triangulating the Cape's bays and islands. At noon Amundsen would take a control sight on the sun while Olonkin stood by with the ancient chronometer he'd borrowed from Meares, noting their local time relative to Greenwich and thus their exact longitude. He was the only man Amundsen trusted with the lucky old clock. When the twilight deepened it was time to go home.

Sometimes the wind would rise in the night and blow drift snow across the stars, or the great stillness would descend with its minus-fifty temperatures. Then Amundsen would stay in his magnetic observatory, the snowhouse he'd built on the shore of the bay where *Maud* lay sheltered in the ice. Here, the delicate instruments wouldn't be disturbed by the ship's ferrous metals. It was a private place for him to work on his maps and his measurements, warmed by the patent vapor lamp that hissed on a bench by the door.

One windless night, above the hiss of the pressurized kerosene and the tick of his clockwork self-registering instruments, he heard a sound in the snow outside.

Amundsen turned on the crate that he used as a seat and stared at the door, straining his ears. He was sure he heard footsteps, someone pacing around the snow-walls then stopping at the door. He waited. Nothing. Then nothing again.

He could no longer stand it; he went to the door and pushed it open. The lamp threw a square of yellow light on the snow. There was nothing there.

He walked around the hut, the lamp raised in his hand, just to be sure that nothing hid behind it. On the second circuit he saw footprints. He halted, held his breath. Then he realized that the footprints were his own. He cut short his work and went back to the ship.

The next day was clear, so he and Olonkin trekked the dozen miles to Cape Chelyuskin. They were getting very close to the end of their mapping. Alone in the tent, Amundsen warmed up their lunchtime stew. Outside, he heard a boot scuff in the snow. Olonkin, he thought. What if it was him last night?

On the way back to the ship a haze spread across the sky from south to north until the stars were hidden and the evening turned gray. They followed their own tracks homeward, the men in silence, the dogs subdued. The wind grew stronger and it began to snow, the tiny dry flakes of the high Arctic, drizzling steady and fast. Amundsen, dropping behind to adjust a ski binding, found himself alone in a pale spinning void. Yet he could hear the dog-team somewhere close ahead, panting and whimpering, as if it were receding from him in a large and empty room.

Descending a shallow streambed, he had to stop every few feet in case the accumulation of speed, imperceptible in the white-out, sent him spinning from the tracks and into the unknown. At the bottom of this draw he came across another track beside the sledge trail: huge, oval prints like a man wearing snowshoes. He stopped and studied them. The sun and the frost, he knew, could do strange things to prints in a snowfield. These must be bear tracks, and they must be quite old, given the state of their decomposition. But it was odd how they paralleled the sled-tracks for several hundred yards before they diverged at a shallow angle, vanishing into the curtain of falling snow. He hooked his mittened thumb into the lanyard that looped around his neck, felt the comforting weight of the pistol on the end of it. He'd noticed no such tracks on their outward journey.

Next day it was still snowing. Despite warnings from Wisting about whiteouts and bears, Amundsen skied across to his observatory. But this time he brought the revolver, hidden from the others inside his parka. He also brought a patent Ever Ready lamp. Crossing his skis in the snow ten yards from the observatory, he hung the pistol and the flashlight by their lanyards from the crux. That's not too close, he told himself. The metal shouldn't affect the magnetics. Or not so much that he should care. He had to be pragmatic. Some aspects of this voyage were more important than others.

Inside the hut the vapor lamp sang to him. He took off his parka and mittens and worked in his silk gloves. The ink, warmed by the lamp, flowed easily from his pen.

This time there was no doubt about it. There was somebody outside. Two steps, then three, feet squeaking in the new-fallen snow. A bear, he knew, wouldn't make so much noise. A fox would be silent.

He stole to the door and opened it a crack. It was pitch black outside, the overcast hiding the stars. Snowflakes flitted like moths through the thin bar of light from the crack in the door. He could barely make out the black cross of his skis. Did his pistol still hang from them?

His heart pounded. A foot crunched. Then another. The stranger made his way slowly along the side of the hut toward the door.

Amundsen threw the door open and hurled himself toward his skis. He could see them through the whirling snowflakes. I have the advantage, he told himself. I'll be first to the gun. But his feet were strangely heavy, or perhaps the snow was deeper than it had been when he'd come from the ship. He felt his head and shoulders draw away from his feet. He felt oddly bemused. He was falling.

The skis clattered around him as he sprawled in the snow. His hand found the flashlight but the gun wasn't there. Turning onto his back, he felt the shock of fresh snow invading his clothes. The observatory, its door flung wide, dazzled with light.

His enemy could be anywhere outside the cone of its illumination. He could be coming at him from the darkness. He might even have the gun.

Amundsen switched on his torch but the batteries, left out in the cold, had died. He rose to his knees, holding the torch like a weapon, and heard his breath moan in his ears. It felt as if his heart would tear itself in two.

Nothing. Snowflakes brushed across his cheeks and his ears. He was desperately cold, so cold that his frozen knees made him gasp with pain when he got to his feet again. He looked to where the ship must lie in the ice, snug in its snow-banks and awnings, but the falling snow had closed around its shadow, hiding the lantern that hung from a yard.

I have to go back into the observatory. If I don't, I'll die. That's where my coat is. That's where there's warmth.

But the observatory frightened him. The vapor lamp, set just inside the door, shone like the light of some demonic shrine, throwing everything beyond it into quivering darkness. There was someone moving about in there, at the far end, where he'd set up his instruments. He could see it, a pale, slender figure with no meaning here.

No one, not even his many enemies, had ever suggested that Amundsen lacked courage. But it took an effort of will that left him trembling and sick before he could drag himself back to the door. There was nobody there, of course. If there'd been any tracks they were drifted with snow. Fastening his skis in the darkness, he felt something hard brush his gloved fingers. His pistol lay in the snow where it had fallen.

He stayed on the ship the next day. The following morning was clear again. The deep new snow, not yet compressed by wind and time, made for heavy going to their destination—Cape Chelyuskin itself. Olonkin had to join him in front of the sledge to break trail for the dogs, tramping down the snow with their skis, sometimes their whole bodies, puffing and heaving. The temperature had dropped again, back to minus thirty, and the dogs strained at their traces as the sledge runners snagged in the dry sandy snow. By the time they found their last map marker, on a low rise above the sea ice, it was almost local noon; just in time to take a control fix on the sun.

The day was bright and almost windless. Once the sun fix was taken, Olonkin set up the tent to make lunch. Amundsen, who could do little to help because of his stiff arm, skied inland a short way to keep warm. Here the land sloped gently down to the sea; the tent and the sledge, the fluttering flag, the intermingled tracks of dogs and men, formed a tiny patch of detail against white-and-gray strata of land and sea and sky. A mountain of bruised cumulus hid the seaward horizon.

By the time they'd finished their work that day the early stars burned in the north. The sun's last rays brushed low across the snowfield, and just over there, a couple of hundred yards from where they'd placed their last marker, Amundsen noticed a strange discoloration, a patch of dark gray that showed through the snow.

It's nothing, thought Amundsen. He tried to focus on the strange object but tears had frozen in his eyes. He decided he'd have to inspect it up close. But he had only gone half the distance when he turned to Olonkin, who had finished packing up the tent, and shouted for him to come too.

Olonkin did most of the digging, using their only spade. Amundsen, hampered by his injury, would scrape and heave until his one good arm was trembling, then take a break and watch.

A little stone cairn had been hidden by the snowfield, all but a few inches that showed at the top. It was three feet tall and almost as broad, made of flat gray stones fitted together in the shape of a barrel-chested man. A large, flat stone on top vaguely suggested a head. Two stubby stone arms protruded at the sides: it was facing inland, or else out to sea; without eyes or a face there was no way of telling.

The evening was getting dark, and very cold, and they worked as quickly as they could without breaking a sweat. It took an hour to clear away the snow down to the base of the cairn, where sedges appeared in the lumps of crumbled ice. They paused, ate some chocolate, and then, working silently together, they broke open the cairn, throwing its stones on the snow banked around them.

A message cylinder was hidden in a chamber built into the rocks. It was made of weathered pewter, a foot long and two inches wide, soldered shut at either end. Turning it over in his hands, Amundsen saw the broad arrow sign stamped in the metal. Board of Ordnance. The last time he had seen that symbol had been in a ruined hut on Beechey Island, on rescue stores left half a century before in case Franklin's men should ever come back.

Amundsen stowed the tube inside his clothing as Olonkin watched. It was so cold now that they no longer shivered. They would have to put up the tent again and stay here for the night.

The moon rose above the barren snowfield, ringed by a silver halo from which moon dogs shone like eyes. Turning inland, Amundsen saw something that looked out of place. Off to the south, where the sloping snowfield curved against the stars, several dark figures stood on the skyline. Behind them, an aurora trembled in the haze. It reminded Amundsen of his visit to Flanders during the war, of the light from distant shellfire flickering against the low clouds. The figures didn't move, but he was sure that they were watching him.

Olonkin came out of the tent. If I say nothing, thought Amundsen, if I just stand here and stare at them, he'll follow my gaze, and if he sees what I see he's bound to say something, and if he sees nothing he'll say nothing, and there won't be anything there.

"Are you alright, governor?"

There was nothing there but the moon and the aurora.

The dogs settled in their snow burrows. Amundsen, pushing his feet inch by inch into his frozen reindeer bag, took comfort in their sighs and whines. If there was anything out there, any bear or thieving fox, the dogs would alert him. He watched the side of the tent, only inches from his face, ripple from the stirrings of the wind. When he heard Olonkin snoring he went to sleep himself.

The next morning the distant mountains were sharp against a pink-and-silver sky. Olonkin loaded the sledge while Amundsen skied up the hillside. He made a broad sweep above their camp, half a mile out, where he judged the skyline had showed itself to him the night before. But there was no sign of disturbance, no prints of man or bear. Turning at the top, he looked over the frozen ocean.

The sun, breaking low over the mountains, threw a pink flush on the sea ice, picking out the frozen turmoil of the currents around the Cape. Far off to his left, half lost in the haze, he could see a group of little islands, white pillows on the sea. Turning due north, a bank of fog or low cloud sat on the sea ice. The wind must be blowing out there, clear of the lee of the continent. It seemed to him that the cloud hid streaks of sharper white, of deeper shadows, a half-glimpse of jagged black peaks with snow-filled cols and tumbling glaciers. He stared until the mountains began to change shape in the mist and the clouds closed in around them.

When they reached the ship it was already suppertime. Despite his exertions Amundsen couldn't sleep. It was as if the two-day absence had given him new energy. Lying in his silk-lined cabin, staring at Kiss's portrait on the bulkhead over his bunk, he thought about his magnetic observatory. It was in that little snowhouse, where no man would disturb him, that he could open the message tube and learn the answers or riddles that it contained.

The others slept in their cabins as he dressed and crept outside. Amundsen paused at the top of the gangway and saw Jacob the watchdog sitting on the snow bank that sheltered the hull. The dog stared south toward the mountains, his cocked ears twitching as he strained to hear. Noticing Amundsen, he thumped his tail once then went back to his vigil. It must be wolves, thought Amundsen, far away in the mountains, howling at the moon. He must long to join them, though he knows that they'd rip him to shreds.

He stopped at the foot of the gangway to pat the head of the unheeding dog. Holding his breath, he listened to the night. But he could hear nothing, just the hiss of his own ears. Then far out to sea, beyond the Cape itself, he heard a low groaning noise, then a great shuddering convulsion, the sound of ice floes working in the tide. Jacob ignored it, his ears spread to the south. I wonder if he'll follow me. But the dog stayed where he was.

The lamps of the self-registering needles burned like eyes at the far end of the observatory. Their warmth was enough to keep the clockwork instruments from freezing, but Amundsen pumped his pressure lamp to give heat and light for his work. Now that he was here, away from the warmth and comfort of his cabin, he began at once to feel sleepy. I've made a mistake, he thought. I'm too tired for this. But the message tube called to him.

He took it out and hefted it in his silk glove-liner. He felt unaccountably nervous. His heart beat in his ears. The ticking of the clockwork forced him to admit it: his pulse was not quite sound.

Stupid. There was nothing to it. He listened to the night outside the snow-hut, but he could hear no sound apart from the tick of clockwork and the hiss of pressurized kerosene. The light of that lamp is quite beautiful, he thought. Mesmerized, he stared at it until black spots were burned in his retinas, then he roused himself and looked away.

The message tube was still there before him, lying on the crate where he must have set it down. His two hands, forgotten, lay on either side of it, palms upward, fingers curled.

I should get on with this.

He turned the cylinder over. Which end was for opening? It didn't seem to matter, so he chose the end indicated by the arrow; it would look more respectful to his friends back in England when he handed it over.

The solder was badly weathered by the cold: brittle, almost crystalline. Amundsen took out his knife and inserted the point in the gap. Very carefully, he wiggled the knife into the narrow space, loosening the solder, until he could work a little more of the blade inside. The solder crumbled and fell away. Slowly, he worked his way around the cylinder until the solder was gone. Now only friction held the cap to the tube. He seized both ends of the cylinder and pulled. The cap came away with almost no effort.

There was a paper inside, as he'd expected, rolled up and molded into the curve of the tube. I'll have to be very careful, he thought. After so many years the paper could be stuck to the metal. It could tear into pieces or turn to dust. He gave the tube a hopeful shake. The paper slid out and fell on the crate.

He sat and stared at it. It can't be this easy, he thought.

Using his knife as a paperweight, he pressed the lower end of the rolled-up page onto the packing case, then gently unbent the rest of it, just as far as was necessary for him to inspect it. His fingers were numb, which was strange: the temperature in the snow-hut was well above freezing.

The page was the yellow-red color of ancient ivory. Letters marched back and forth across its surface, nonsense, beyond his understanding. Amundsen felt an irrational anger. Then he remembered his spectacles, the ones he kept hidden in his jacket.

He put them on, polishing them with the end of the silk scarf that Kiss Bennett had given him. Now he recognized the page in his hands.

It was a commonplace form that used to be issued to Royal Navy ship decades before. Blank lines were provided at the top of the form for the name and position of the ship, followed by another three lines for general notes, and then a space for the commanding officer's signature. Underneath, a printed message in English, French, Spanish, Dutch, Danish, and German politely requested anyone who found the paper to send it to the Admiralty or the nearest British consul.

These forms were intended to be thrown overboard in bottles to help trace ocean currents, or deposited in cairns on remote capes or anchorages to leave word of the ship's movements: such was long-range communication in the years before wireless.

Amundsen had seen such a form once before, in the Admiralty in London, on his return from the Northwest Passage expedition. Meares had shown it to him when he brought in the things he'd recovered from King William Island.

The form that Meares showed him was a famous Arctic relic— the only note ever found from the Franklin Expedition. Dated 1848, it was recovered years later by Leopold McClintock, who had sailed his little search vessel through the Bellot Strait. The note said that *Erebus* and *Terror* were abandoned in the ice and that the survivors were trekking south. It had been left in a cairn at Point Victory, on King William Island. Signed: Captain F.R.M. Crozier.

And now Amundsen saw Crozier's signature again. No ship's name, no date, just the Irishman's name at the top of the page, faded and blurred, written in what looked like charcoal.

F.R.M. Crozier, Captain, RN, requested the finder to forward this message to the Admiralty, London, with a note of the time and the place at which it was found.

No date had been written on the form itself. But there *was* a position, a map reference. He squinted at it, moving his lips. Sixty-eight degrees, seventeen minutes, thirty seconds north; a hundred and thirty-five degrees, twenty-two minutes, ten seconds west . . .

But that was nowhere near here. That was somewhere in northern Canada, not far south of Herschel Island, where the *Gjøa* had wintered after sailing the Northwest Passage. Somewhere in the Richardson Mountains, Amundsen would have guessed.

What did it mean? What message was to be forwarded?

He could, he noticed, no longer feel his hands very well. It was difficult to tell, in the yellow light from the lamp, but his fingertips looked an odd shade of blue. He turned up the kerosene lamp to pump out more heat. Then he turned the page over so he could look at the other side, the side that was normally blank. There were symbols written on it: not letters or words, just clumps of numbers, of code, running a third of the way down the page. Amundsen was sure that Crozier had written them too.

Crozier was here, he thought. Here, thousands of miles from King William Island, on the opposite side of the Arctic Ocean.

But then again, how did he know that Crozier had himself left this cylinder at the Cape? Someone else might have done it. The answer was surely in the code on the back of the form, perhaps in the map reference. But it made no sense to him.

I shouldn't have opened the tube. It wasn't for me. I ought to reseal it and pass it to Room 38, its rightful recipients. Presumably they can decode it. His head was throbbing. It hurt him to think.

He rolled up the page and tried to put it back inside the tube. But his fingers weren't working for him. They no longer felt cold, but when he looked at them he saw they were blue to the knuckles.

It's just the light, he told himself.

Then he heard the noise again, a footstep, crunching in loose snow. Just the one, and then only his own breathing and the hiss of the lamp.

He wasn't afraid this time. It was only a pity that he had such a headache that it made it hard to think. He lifted himself off the stool just an inch, so he could shift the crate from under him without scraping the duckboards. Now he was standing. His revolver was snug in his hand.

The wind gusted outside. Amundsen listened to the sound of dead snowflakes, no longer unique, worn by their long drift into one common dust, and he heard the ghost that was moving among them. It stood by the door, just beyond the thin plywood. Would it wait for him there, or would he see the door shift and then slowly swing open?

"Olonkin," he said loudly, because he thought it was best to err on the safe side. He waited three seconds, then fired through the door.

The sound of the shot, trapped in the narrow snow-hut, hammered his eardrums, flashed pain in his eyes. The cordite smoke was sickening. Yet he felt himself swept up on a red surge of triumph. I've got you, you bastard. I've got you, I bet. He fired another shot through the door, lower this time, then charged it with his shoulder.

The whole door gave before him, ripping out the wooden pegs that held its frame to the snow-walls. Amundsen sprawled across it. He fired again, blindly, as he staggered to his feet.

Light blazed from the lamp in the observatory. He wheeled about, waving his revolver. His heart was beating crazily, as if he had sprinted through deep snow. Stars danced in his eyes but he couldn't see the sky.

He had to find his enemy, the one who was trying to steal the tube. Whoever, whatever, it was, they hadn't come from the ship, or at least not directly: he could make out only one trail in that direction, the tracks of his own skis. He staggered around the snowhouse, feeling himself sink to the knees with each step. But when he looked down he saw his stockinged feet gliding over frost-hardened snow. When had he taken his boots off? The pistol had lost all the heat from the firing. Cold metal burned his bare hand.

The land loomed above him, the raised beach at the back of the strand. The Arctic night seemed very dark. But he was sure he could see a faint track on the snow, the prints of feet, without skis or snowshoes, moving along the beach to the north. He turned and followed them as best he could, but his legs were very heavy and he found it hard to breathe. Something tripped him and he fell on his face in the snow.

The snow molded itself to his cheek like a pillow. He closed his eyes to rest a minute, to recover his breath and to slow his heart, or at least to find a rhythm for it. He sighed deeply, his lungs craving air and his mouth filled with powdery ice.

No matter how tired you are, you don't fall asleep in the snow.

He spat out the snow and rose on his knees, still gasping for air. His pistol hung from its lanyard around his neck. His bare fingers found the strength to grasp it.

He saw now what had tripped him. He was kneeling in a ring of stones—round, head-sized beach rocks worn smooth by summer tides, their upper halves protruding from the snow. It was a tent-ring, a circle of heavy stones used by natives to hold down their skin shelters. Such rings were to be found on all the coasts of the American Arctic, on Greenland, even on those islands far to the north where no natives had lived for centuries. Yet surely no Eskimo had ever crossed to central Siberia. And this tent-ring was smaller than the Eskimo rings, less than two meters across, like the circles he'd found once on King William Island, on the icebound coast near the magnetic north where his Eskimo guides were too frightened to go.

His own snow angel, imprinted by his fall, was neatly contained in this circle of stones. How long had the ring been here? How were its stones showing over the snow?

They must have built it since that last storm.

A pale, thin figure emerged from the mist that swirled around the tent circle. The pistol was fiendishly heavy and he had to use both hands to raise it. He aimed and tried to fire, but the hammer wouldn't draw back for him. He couldn't work out if it was the mechanism that had frozen or his fingers or both.

Then he saw who it was and let the gun fall from his hands. He should have known her before, when he'd glimpsed her in the shadows at the end of the observatory.

It was Marie, his landlady from Antwerp. He remembered her pale body, no longer quite young, grinding against him, her youthful lodger, in his cold little bedroom under the stairs. He remembered the final scene of renunciation, then later, the burning smell from the zinc buckets, the blue veins on her thigh.

She smiled at him sadly, holding her arms out, her skin mottled blue. She must be very cold, he thought. Dressed only in her chemise like that last time I saw her, lying on her kitchen floor.

He understood, anew, again, as he had so many times before, why the joy he felt at seeing her was always troubled, though at first he could never think why: he would surely wake up and she would be dead again, before he could explain to her, before he found a way to make it right. But this time she didn't move away or fade out of reach. She stepped into the circle, lifting her bare legs clear of the stones, still smiling sadly, and he watched the muscles move in her thigh, and when she reached out to him he pulled her down onto the snow.

Amundsen lay on the bunk in his cabin moving in and out of morphine dreams. His hands and feet were bandaged. Kiss's portrait stared down at him from the cabin wall, from the silk furnishings she'd arranged for him herself. It was somehow for her, he recalled, that he had set up this voyage. It had been something to do with proving himself—though when he thought back, surely he had proven himself already, many times over?

He had wanted Kiss to make her home with him, abandon her family. For there to be warmth there must also be desolation. But looking at her portrait he was no longer sure that he wanted her. He needed to prove himself again.

"Carbon monoxide," said Wisting, standing by his bunk. "From your pressure lamp. There was a problem with the burner. And of course the observatory has to be airtight so there was no place for the gas to go. You've been slowly poisoning yourself all winter, every time you went in there. The medical books say that the effect builds over time. It could be months before you're completely recovered. Tell me: did you have any strange sensations or experiences before you broke down?"

Had there really been a tent circle? Clearly there had not. He could ask Olonkin, who was the first to come in search of him, alerted by the shots. But he couldn't bring himself to ask him, even though he was sure he knew the answer. There was a more urgent matter between them. After Wisting had gone he called in Olonkin.

"The metal tube. I left it in the observatory. Did you find it there?"

Olonkin nodded. He put the breakfast tray down by Amundsen's bunk. There was condensed milk and buttered bread. It was all that his stomach could manage.

"What did you find?"

"The tube. It was opened. There was an old paper beside it."

Amundsen levered himself up on his elbow. The effort made him gasp. He glared at the kid by his bed.

"Did you look at the paper?"

"Yes. I couldn't read it."

Amundsen fell back on his pillow. "Who has the tube now? Wisting or Hansen or Sverdrup?"

"They don't know about it." Olonkin reached into his jacket and fetched out the tube. He handed it to Amundsen. He snatched it away and brought it close to his eyes, then looked at Olonkin.

"It's sealed."

"I soldered it shut with the paper inside it."

"Who the hell told you to do that?"

"You did. When I found you in the snow. After I stopped you from shooting yourself."

He wasn't much use for the rest of that spring. Harald Sverdrup took over the magnetic work and Amundsen would walk the deck, slowly regaining his lungs and his legs, watching parties of hunters and specimen collectors set out across the ice.

In June, when the sun never set, brown patches appeared in the snow on the mainland. Flocks of brent geese arrived from the south. Later, the rivers and streams broke free of the winter, hurling huge blocks of ice far up their banks with the boom of artillery. The sea ice too was shifting, with tide cracks appearing near *Maud*'s winter harbor. In a month, maybe two, she might escape from this place and push on to the east. Amundsen allowed his plans to stir again.

The tube would have to be sent back to Room 38 for decoding. He couldn't understand its message and he didn't want to be responsible for it, not here, on this coast where ships vanished. More than that, he didn't want to look inside it again, even though he couldn't be sure of its contents: he was sure he had seen Crozier's name, and some ciphers, and a map reference for some place in Canada, but these told him nothing. The riddles he'd been set on King William Island—on another icebound boat in another winter harbor fifteen years before—had been left unanswered, had in fact only multiplied. And he wasn't yet ready to see this as a blessing.

The transmitter was broken so he was entitled to send some mail back to Norway. He would dispatch a couple of his men with a sledge to the Russian weather station on Dickson Island, five hundred miles to the west. From there they could make their way back to Norway by boat. Paul Knutsen would lead them; he'd been along that coast before with Otto Sverdrup's expedition. Peter Tessem would also go; all winter long Tessem had whined about headaches, as if he were the only one who suffered in the dark. The *Maud* would be well rid of him; she had other such winters ahead. To bulk out the mailbag, and to give extra justification to his decision to send off two precious crewmen, he would include the scientific records of the expedition up to now. In amongst them would be tucked a separate package for Kiss containing the message tube and instructions for forwarding it. And he would also send back the chronometer that Meares had lent to him, the one he himself had brought back from King William Island. He felt it would no longer work for him: his luck had finally changed. He wouldn't be fit for sledging this year. The expedition had already failed.

In September the ice broke out to sea. Amundsen climbed into the crow's nest, with Olonkin pushing him up from beneath, and watched the cracks reach ever closer to the ship. Tessem and

Knutsen helped the rest of the crew to dismantle the observatory, restow the stores that had wintered on the ice, and prepare the ship for sailing.

On the evening of September 12, with the nearest lead of open water still a mile from the *Maud*, Amundsen touched off the fifty sticks of dynamite that his crew had drilled into the ice. Fifty charges went off at once, fifty geysers of crystal and smoke. The tide tore the floe along its line of smoking perforations, clearing the way to escape. *Maud*, making half-revolutions on her semi-diesel engine, became a living ship again. The men on deck cheered and waved their caps. There were more cheers from the shore, across the soupy bay ice. Turning in the crow's nest, Amundsen saw Tessem and Knutsen wave from the beach then turn and disappear up the mouth of a gully, marching back toward their camp.

A path had opened to the east, a long lead shining in the moonlight. Amundsen turned to look north toward the loom of Cape Chelyuskin. It was a rare Arctic night, clear, with no hint of haze or fog, and from the crow's nest he could see a band of white cloud sitting on the horizon, stark in the moonlight. But it was more than cloud, he was sure of it this time. Lifting his binoculars, he steadied his elbows on the rim of the crow's nest. He was right: there was land beyond the clouds, black mountains streaked with eternal snow. He adjusted the focus and saw that this unknown island, or continent, floated just over the horizon, supported on a silver haze. It was a mirage, he knew that well. But a mirage might once have had substance, might be the echo of some remote event or object—refracted, reflected, enlarged, or inverted, a story distorted by ice and by light. The old sailors had a name for this phantom: they called it "Cape Flyaway."

He looked down to the deck. Helmer Hansen was in the fore-peak behind the canvas weather shield, spotting for sunken growlers that his skipper might have missed. Tønnesson and Rønne bustled about, securing bits of running gear, while Wisting stood at the helm. They can't see my mirage from the deck, thought Amundsen. It's beyond the curve of their world down there. Every now and then Wisting glanced from Hansen to Amundsen, waiting for instructions to con *Maud* through the ice. But the open crack grew wider with the tide, a quicksilver line pointing due east. The way north was closed. Amundsen couldn't change course to steer for Cape Flyaway.

He knew now that the ice would beat him back from his attempt to cross the polar basin. The boat would be herded east along the coast until it finally reached Alaska, where he would quietly abandon her and her crew. He was running out of time: he needed something faster and blunter than boats and dogs—airplanes, perhaps, or even dirigibles. Then he could feel again the weightlessness of starting life from scratch.

He thought of the evening when the *Fram* had dropped anchor off Funchal, Madeira. That was nine years before, the last time in his life when he'd been unknown and free. He had slipped quietly ashore in his seagoing clothes, bringing with him the texts for a series of telegrams informing the world that the *Fram* would not be sailing to the Arctic as he had told his sponsors, including the King himself. Instead, he would be stealing a march on the British in the race to the South Pole.

He remembered how he had stopped in the door of the telegraph office, annihilated by choice. I haven't sent anything yet: I can still go north to honor or south to glory. I'm both those men at once. I cancel myself out. It was a warm autumn evening in Madeira, the sun gleaming on the harbor and the breeze soft in the trees. He could stay here forever, dissolved in this air. But some tiny flaw in the fabric of the universe, some original sin in space and time, determined that he was doomed to exist, to be one thing or another. So he sent his telegrams to Scott, to Nansen, to his sponsors, to the King of Norway. Afterward he walked up the hill to the Bela Vista hotel and checked in as he was, with only the clothes that he stood in. Then—feeling unaccountably tired and low—he climbed the stairs that would take him to his room. Seated in cane chairs in the lobby, an Englishman and his teenage son silently watched him go past.

He shivered at the thought of them. Why had they reappeared to him here, nine years later, in another life? He turned his binoculars to the north, searching for any leads in that direction. But the sea ice held firm. It shepherded them eastward for the rest of September, then closed in for another year. After only twelve days of freedom the *Maud* was again forced into winter quarters, six hundred miles short of the Bering Strait. Tessem and Knutsen were never seen alive again.

Inuvik, Northwest Territories

Fay had known that Roald Amundsen was Norwegian, and that he'd beaten Captain Scott in the race to the South Pole. That was it. She hadn't known, until just now, when she'd read it online, that Amundsen had led the first expedition to reach the North Pole too.

But then, Amundsen hadn't known it either. After the failed attempt to reach the North Pole by ship in the *Maud*, Amundsen had taken to aircraft instead. First ski-planes, then flying boats, and finally—his last desperate attempt—a semi-rigid airship he'd bought from Mussolini. When he finally saw the North Pole in 1926, circling three hundred feet above the sea ice in the *Norge*, Amundsen still believed, like the rest of the world, that Commander Robert Peary of the US Navy had already been there, having crossed the ice from Greenland. But Peary had falsified his journals. So had another US naval officer, the aviator Richard Byrd, who claimed to have overflown the pole in his airplane three days before Amundsen took flight in his airship.

So the *Norge* had been first after all. Taking off from Spitsbergen, the Italian-built airship had flown direct across the North Pole to Alaska—the first ever visit by mankind to the "Zone of Maximum Inaccessibility," a huge unexplored area between Greenland, Siberia, and Alaska.

It took three and a half days to fly two thousand nautical miles over an expanse of the planet that no one, not even the Inuit, had witnessed before. There was room enough in that unknown region for an island the size of a continent, or for the fabled open polar sea, or even for a hole in the earth's crust giving access to the interior. Who would claim it and give it a name?

It turned out that there was nothing there but ancient sea ice. Amundsen, who had dreamed all his life of claiming new lands for his new country, had been dreaming of something that did not exist. This was his last expedition, and he spent it sitting on a chair and staring out of a plastic window. Another first for Amundsen, thought Fay, turning away from the computer screen: that's how we all do our exploring now.

She too had just drawn a blank, sitting on her chair and staring at her plastic window. None of the search engines or online encyclopedias could give her any clue as to why this cardboard file marked "Roald Engelbregt Amundsen" contained only one short US newspaper clipping. A clipping in which Amundsen wasn't even mentioned.

Billings County Pioneer, March 20, 1941
QUEEN BESS OF THE ARCTIC

MRS. BESS CROSS of Deering, Alaska, has been paying her every-fifth-year visit to the States. Sounds prosaic, but to her sourdough friends in and out of Alaska, and to the fashionable feminine apparel dealers in New York, it is an event eagerly awaited.

To every sourdough—miner, trapper and those in other lines—to every Eskimo, in fact, to all Alaska, Bess Cross is known as "Queen of the Arctic." She went to Alaska as a bride of 16. Her first husband, Mr. Samuel Magids, operated a trading post and she assisted him. When he died, Bess carried on, and expanded. Today she has a large string of such posts all over the Alaskan wilds, and especially along the shores of the Arctic Ocean.

In Alaska, Bess wears a fur parka, walrus-hide boots, sealskin trousers as a matter of necessity, not from choice. She is definitely feminine, and about once every five years she comes to the States, always traveling by plane. She goes to New York and indulges in a regular orgy of clothes buying. She selects the daintiest, most luxurious of feminine apparel; lives in a fine suite at the Waldorf; entertains lavishly for a period of from two to three weeks, and then flies back to her string of Alaskan trading posts, to the white men and Eskimos who love and respect her, and to whom she is always "Queen Bess of the Arctic."

Fay had wasted two hours online trying to work out the relevance of this ancient puff piece. Nothing. Whatever Bess Cross had meant to Bert Nilsson, to Fay she was just another loose gear.

PART SEVEN

Hjalmar Johansen Seamount

82°57′N 3°40′W

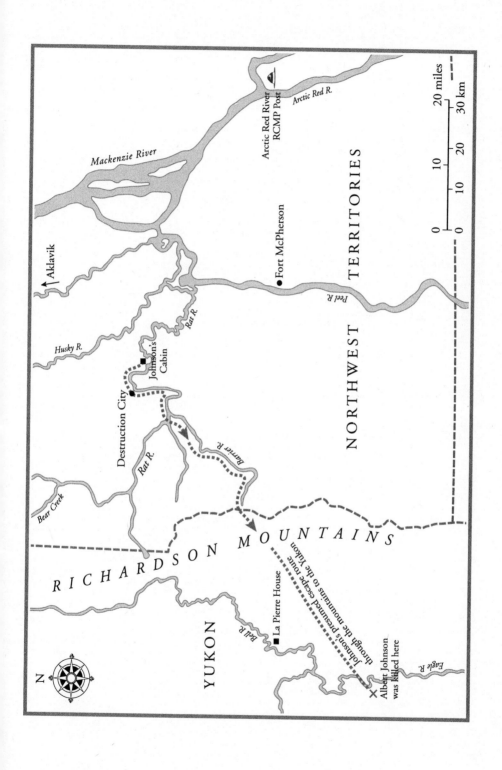

Mackenzie River

Arctic Red River
RCMP Post

Arctic Red R.

←Aklavik

Fort McPherson

NORTHWEST TERRITORIES

Peel R.

Husky R.

Johnson's
Cabin

Rat R.

Destruction City

Rat R.

Barrier R.

Bear Creek

RICHARDSON MOUNTAINS

Bell R.

La Pierre House

YUKON

Johnson's presumed escape route
through the mountains to the Yukon

Eagle R.

Albert Johnson
was killed here
×

N

0   10   20 miles
0   10   20   30 km

New York City, 1928

The news was brought to Bess with her morning coffee, in a copy of the *New York Times*.

Kings Bay, Spitsbergen, June 19, 1928.—There has been no news here tonight of Roald Amundsen and René Guilbaud, who left Tromsø, Norway, yesterday in a French seaplane to aid in the search for General Umberto Nobile and his crew of the dirigible *Italia*.

She waited until the maid had left her hotel room, then put on her gown and went to the window. Far below, trucks and cars snarled down Fifth Avenue. They shivered in the hot fug of June.

She tied up her black hair, straightened her shoulders.

He had disappeared before, five times, in his ships *Gjøa*, *Fram*, and *Maud*, in his Dornier seaplane, in his airship the *Norge*. He had always reappeared. Coming back from the dead was his calling in life.

He'd been missing for three weeks that time before last, three years before, when his plane was trapped in the ice north of Spitsbergen. Three weeks: twenty-one days. Twenty-one or bust. Shall I hit or shall I stick? What a bind she was in, what a perfect predicament. Bess dearly loved poker, was said to be the boldest player between the Yukon and Point Barrow—the best dog-driver too, natives excepted. But she didn't care for blackjack. She could always read faces, but she couldn't count cards.

She looked around her hotel room. Her bags were packed, all but one, over there in the corner. If she had to she could move pretty quickly. When she'd left Seattle for New York, only five days before, she hadn't been sure that her husband wouldn't follow her. Her room at the Waldorf was booked to one "Engelbregt Gravning," Amundsen's alias. The steamer for Oslo would sail in three days, and perhaps she'd be on it. But she knew very well that Sam Magids might change his mind and set out to retrieve her. She would have to sit tight in the Waldorf with only the money that her husband had given her, the chance contents of his wallet, numbly presented to her in their hallway in Seattle, her bags already waiting on the stoop outside. Most of that money had been spent by now on trains and on boat tickets.

Should she go back to Sam, or was it too late?

Twelve days later, when her ship berthed in Oslo, Mrs. Samuel Magids was met at the gangway by a telegram from Amundsen's brother.

```
Regret inform RA still missing. Kindly proceed
Victoria Hotel Oslo. Await instructions from
attorney H. Gade. Discretion advised. Do not come
Uranienborg. Do not speak journalists.
```

She tipped the messenger half a dollar; it was almost the last one she had. Behind her, the sheer metal slab of the *Hellig Olav* obstructed her view of the fjord. In front was the customs shed, the formalities she had yet to undergo. Between the ship and the shed she was nowhere, perfectly poised.

What should she do now? She drew herself up to her full height, which wasn't very tall, and counted her dwindling options.

Amundsen's brother Gustav was shunting her off into a siding after only two weeks without news of him; the Amundsen family was sticking on fourteen. But Bess, having nothing left to lose, decided to hit. Instead of wiring her husband for the fare back to New York, which she knew that he would send her, she threw in her last chip. She checked into the Victoria Hotel. If she was going to have her heart broken she would do it on Amundsen's dime. For three years he had begged her to join him in Norway, to leave her husband and her friends, the dizzying freedom of her life in Alaska, and as soon as she had wired him that she was on her way at last he had fled into the north again, a glorified passenger in a self-serving race to save General Nobile, a man he could not stand. Bess had paid—paid everything she had—to see Amundsen's hand, but not for one moment had she guessed that he was bluffing. Perhaps, it occurred to her now, he hadn't known that himself.

It was Gade the lawyer who came to see Bess first, the morning after her arrival. He telephoned in advance and arranged to meet her in the hotel lobby. It was ten o'clock and businessmen sat in twos and threes at the tables by the window, washed by the cool gray glare of an overcast morning. From time to time the men would glance at Bess, as was normal.

She waited on a high-backed chair and read the *Times* of London.

Amundsen's continued absence was buried deep inside the paper, a couple of paragraphs in the wider story of the search for the airship *Italia*, which had crashed during a flight over the pole. The reporter contrasted the intermittent wireless calls from General Nobile, adrift with several survivors on the pack ice north of Spitsbergen, to the silence from Amundsen, whose missing plane was also equipped with a radio.

The *Times* reporter observed that the esteemed Norwegian explorer, conqueror of the Northwest Passage, magnetic north, the South Pole, the Northeast Passage, the North Pole, and the Arctic Basin, was known for his peculiar "ill luck" with wireless telegraphy. Had not his wireless-equipped airship the *Norge*—like its sister the *Italia* designed and piloted by the Italian aeronaut Nobile—vanished off the face of the earth two years before, just as it entered the most significant phase of its flight, the crossing from Spitsbergen to Alaska of the icebound Arctic Basin, never before observed by human eyes? And had this artful silence not left the whole world holding its breath until the *Norge* reappeared, conveniently close to an Alaskan telegraph station, whence exclusive articles sped to newspapers favored by virtue of their generosity to Captain Amundsen? Did history not suggest that the astute Norwegian would yet again emerge from the northern mists with another tale of adventure to tell to any agency willing to pay for it?

The waspish tone did not surprise Bess. She knew that Amundsen had fallen out with the British, even with those—the factions of Shackleton and Mawson—who had supported him against the ghost of Scott. He had likewise taken against the Germans, who had once provided him with his training in magnetics, with Teutonic admiration, and with aircraft and funds. And he had then gone to war with the Italians, whom he felt had tried to usurp his command of the *Norge* expedition.

Until now, Bess had accepted these rifts as the price of achievement; in her own life, a journey that had started in Winnipeg thirty years before, passed on through Seattle, the Kotzebue Sound, New York, London, the North Slope, and—this week—Oslo, she had always observed that the farther you went the fewer people kept up with you. You left places and people behind you. But until now no one had ever left her.

Gade was Norwegian but he wore a checked American suit and had acquired informal manners in Chicago and at Harvard. He pulled up a chair and ordered them both coffee, though Bess didn't want any. Then he looked about the lobby. He's watching out for journalists, thought Bess. But they would all be up in Tromsø, or Hammerfest, or Spitsbergen, competing to file from the most northerly dateline. She had learned the ways of newspapers since she'd fallen in with Amundsen.

"Is there any definite news?"

Gade looked around to see if anyone might hear him, then pursed his lips and stared down at his coffee.

"I'm afraid not."

"Then is there anything you can tell me that hasn't been in the newspapers?"

Gade seemed to be searching for a formula. He looked away from her again, toward the windows and the light.

"We feel . . . I believe . . . that the newspapers are too optimistic about the chances for Roald's survival."

So he will be "Roald" now. How very un-Norwegian. Of course, Gade had been his friend since they were at school together. And of course Gade was, like herself, almost an American. But *Roald*. Even she called him Amundsen.

"I see."

He paused, choosing his words. "Much of the optimism about Roald and his men is based on the fact that Nobile and his people have survived on the ice for over a month now. And of course, Roald's experience of the pack is second to no man alive. Excepting Nansen, I suppose."

Nansen, thought Bess. After all he has done, Amundsen still can't get out from under Nansen, that frozen old man in his ridiculous tower.

Gade was still talking. "But what the foreign newspapers don't seem to appreciate, and what the Norwegian ones don't care to print, is that Roald is unlikely to have made it as far as the ice. It's much more likely that his aircraft went down in the open sea before it even reached Bear Island."

Having nothing better to do that morning, she idly clutched at some straws.

"It's a seaplane. They might have landed on the water and made it ashore somewhere."

"It's very unlikely. We've already searched Bear Island and checked the coast of Spitsbergen. And you have to understand, their Latham was designed for lakes and sheltered inlets. It was light in construction. It wouldn't have survived for long on the open ocean. It couldn't land safely in anything but a flat calm."

She decided she would sip her coffee after all. "The *Daily Telegraph* has an interesting story. It says that one of Amundsen's French pilots once broke a wing-float landing on the sea. He rigged an empty petrol tank in its place and flew off again."

"The Frenchman was only on the sea for an hour. Anyway, Roald and his men don't have enough food or water to last them this long. They were to pick up their emergency provisions at Ny-Ålesund."

Gade looked at her beseechingly. And she knew—she knew—she'd known it already. Why was she doing this to him, to herself? She banged her spoon against the side of her coffee cup, enjoying her moment of petulance.

Embarrassed, Gade took out his cigarette case. "Do you mind?"

"Not at all. I'll have one too, please." He looked pained: perhaps it wasn't yet done for ladies to smoke publicly in Oslo. But she stared at him until he passed a cigarette and then waited for him to light it for her. One of the young businessmen, glancing across, saw that she was smoking and nudged his companions; they all turned to stare. All this went on behind Gade's back. I'll bet he's wondering why I'm smiling, thought Bess.

Gade studied the point of his cigarette. "We were wondering what your intentions are should Amundsen fail to return."

It's possible, she decided, that Gade might mean well by me. He'd always been friendly before, at Chicago, in the Waldorf, at

Amundsen's Norwegian estate at Uranienborg. She hadn't felt that Gade was a fake. But she also knew he was Amundsen's man and Amundsen was gone now. What would Amundsen's brother, Gustav, want from her? It was a pretty sure bet that he wanted her gone. She was still married to someone else, after all, and Amundsen was a national hero. And there'd be an estate to divide, perhaps quite a large one.

"I shall stay here until there is word of Amundsen. I'm his fiancée, you know, Mr. Gade. We have an engagement."

There it was, her only card, face up on the table. And a moment before she hadn't intended to play it at all. If Amundsen is gone for good, she'd told herself. I'll slip away from here, move on again. She still had her nerve and her looks. There were plenty of places she hadn't yet been. But it had suddenly seemed to her that she needed something to take with her—a bankroll, a grubstake—so she wouldn't have to wire Sam and ask him to pay her to stay away. Or ask him to forgive her.

She wouldn't yet admit her real motive, which was that she couldn't let Amundsen go without clawing something back from him. He'd already taken enough from her: she was thirty years old now, but he was fifty-five.

So they sat there, Bess and Gade, in the lobby of the Victoria Hotel, contemplating the thing that lay between them. I'll learn everything about him from how he plays this one, she thought. The engagement was a secret one, a bluff that he can call if he wants to play the heel. What kind of man is he? She knew that Herman Gade was a businessman, a lawyer, a former mayor of Lake Forest, Illinois, and lately a diplomat, Norway's envoy to Brazil. The signs weren't good.

Gade ground his cigarette into the ashtray. "An engagement with Roald," he said. "Who else have you told about that?"

"Only my husband." Never had she needed her poker face more.

He nodded slowly. "That's just as well."

Here it comes, she thought. I'll be easily got rid of. A few secret words between a dead man and a foreigner, a runaway wife, not even divorced yet. It means so little now.

Suddenly she couldn't bear the lowness of it all. "I don't give a damn about such matters. I'm not here to enforce any arrangement. I don't act for money. My husband always gave me everything I wanted. He and his brother are two of the richest men in Alaska. But I'll stay here until this is over. Amundsen sent for me and I came."

Heads had turned. Was I speaking so loud? Gade's face was twisted, as if in pain.

"You misunderstand me," he said. "Your status isn't in question, and certainly not your behavior. Roald had already taken steps before he went north. There's a considerable settlement. I have the papers at my office, witnessed and signed."

Then perhaps Gade's a good man after all, she thought, surprised, sinking back in her chair. Legal papers, like inconvenient playing cards, can be made to disappear.

"I don't want to talk about these things," she said. "Not while there's any chance he's still alive."

In the newspapers Amundsen *was* still alive, trekking across the pack ice or manfully steering a raft. While aircraft from all over Europe circled Nobile's camp on the pack ice, dropping supplies on the buckled floe, it was expected that Amundsen would soon appear on skis to win the glory and vengeance of saving his old rival. That was his sort of entrance. On the sea, in the air, on the ice, there was no one to match the bold Captain Amundsen.

These flights of romance were a torment to Bess. When she tried to sleep she saw the sun flash on varnished wings, heard the wind keen in stay-wires, smelled the fumes from a manifold, just as she had six done years before, skylarking in *Kristine*, his new Curtiss ski-plane.

Was it for that that I loved him? Until then he'd only been an adventure, the only one she had ever been almost ashamed of. Because his fame was behind it: he was otherwise too old, much too old for her. But up in the air he'd turned into a kid again, a comical big-nosed boy who laughed as he buzzed a herd of caribou, scattered them into the lake and the muskeg, then zoomed upward, skimming the snow-streaked slope above her husband's trading post at Deering, then down again, only feet above the huts and storerooms, the Eskimo kids gleefully diving for cover, and out over the ice-choked sound, climbing northward, slowly northward, across the Arctic Circle and toward the gleaming Brooks Range. It was there, beyond those mountains, that he still saw a young man's horizon, that infinitely fine, eternally impending line between everything and nothing.

One night in her half-sleep she saw his plane seized by one of those torrents of the upper air that the Japanese had lately discovered. She saw him blown far from Spitsbergen, held up by mirages and magnets and ionic emanations. He was flying above an ice-free northern ocean having found some secret geography—a new island or continent, an Anián Strait or opening in the globe—in strange vapors that welled from the magnetic pole. She slept for a few minutes and heard his voice above the slipstream, arguing with his French pilots about which country would claim the discovery.

Morning came, and with it more newspapers. *Krasin*, the famous Soviet icebreaker, had been diverted from a mission to far-off Cape Chelyuskin and was plowing toward the marooned Italians. It seemed to Bess, who had little use for sentimentality, that this gray tortoise would win where the planes had failed so romantically. And then, with no visible men left to rescue, the world would stop pretending that Amundsen was still alive. It would be time for her to act again. Where would she go?

The sun shone in through the curtains as they twitched in the mild summer air. Through the half-open sash the traffic noise soothed her; she loved cities as much as she loved wilderness, and mountain and forest hemmed Oslo on three sides. She closed her eyes, sank back in her armchair, and flew to a ridge above the city. There she stood among the spruces that had followed her all through her life, from Winnipeg to Oslo. She thought she could smell them, even here, in her armchair, from which she looked down at the tiny boats whose wakes creased the fjord like wrinkles on silk. She slept without dreaming and didn't wake until noon.

Gade called again that afternoon. He wanted to take her for a walk around Oslo, a tour of a city that still hardly knew itself as a capital, which many still called "Christiania." She'd driven around the town a few months before, at Christmas, in a motor car with Amundsen, but he hadn't wanted to be seen in public with her and had hurried her on to Uranienborg. She accepted Gade's invitation; she felt that the chance would not come again.

They visited the Storting, the harbor, the Akershus, and the new underground railway to the National Theater; it had only opened days before and was still an object of fascination for country visitors, who rode its carriages in stiff Sunday clothes. For once Gade had little to say for himself beyond a few muttered dates and descriptions. Bess wondered why he'd suggested this tour when his mind seemed to be on other things. Then he led her down a little side street, almost an alley, near the East Station, and stopped in front of a cheap-looking guesthouse.

"That," he said, pointing with his chin, "is where Johansen was staying when he did away with himself."

"Johansen?"

"Hjalmar Johansen. He went to Antarctica with Roald in the *Fram*."

"I don't think I remember him."

Gade was still looking at the guesthouse. A heavy old woman, well dressed, but with the mean fleshy face of a debt-collector, came out and glared at him. Bess saw him hold her gaze for a few seconds then coolly turn away. Does he know her?

"You've heard of him alright," Gade told Bess as he led her away. "He went to the Antarctic with Amundsen, but he was already famous in his own right by then. He'd been with Nansen years before when the two of them left their ship in the pack and tried to walk across the sea ice to the North Pole."

And she did know that story. It had thrilled her as a child in Manitoba, translating the frozen Red River into the Arctic ice sheet, stands of snow-bent birches into the islands of Franz Josef Land. But the name of Nansen's companion hadn't stayed with her. That's what happens to the other men of history. She'd heard the name spoken once at a lecture in Winnipeg. She had heard it as "Johnson."

Gade touched her elbow, steered her westward onto Karl Johans gate.

"Johansen was an expert skier and a very promising army officer. But after the ordeal with Nansen he couldn't cope with normal life. People said he was like a changeling, as if the real Johansen had been lost on the ice. He'd spent months dragging a sled and a canoe across the sea ice, then a whole winter in a snow cave on some godforsaken island with starving bears clawing at the door. And if that doesn't sound bleak enough, he was alone the whole time with Fridtjof bloody Nansen. When he got back he drank away his commission. His wife and children left him. Then he begged Nansen to help him, for old times' sake. So Nansen got him a job with Roald."

The royal palace frowned at them down its dark avenue. At the junction with Frederiks gate they turned left, then right onto Ibsen gate, skirting the royal park. They wouldn't be visiting the palace today.

"Roald had heard that Johansen wasn't the man he used to be—everyone knows everyone else here, of course. But he took him on as a favor for Nansen, who then had the power of yea or nay over Norwegian exploration.

"What Nansen didn't know was that Roald wasn't going north, as he'd told everybody, but to the South Pole instead. Peary had just announced that he'd been to the North Pole, and Roald never saw any point in being second. But all of the money that Roald had raised was for a northern expedition, which was supposed to be scientific, all the usual guff about measuring ocean currents and water temperature, all sorts of thing that Roald really didn't give a damn about: they were just cover for his real aim, which was to search for new lands and be first to the North Pole.

"Now Peary said that the North Pole was taken. But the South Pole was still there to be won. So Roald decided to go there instead. But he wouldn't tell anyone about his change of plan until he got to Madeira. Under the circumstances, Roald felt it wise to grant Nansen the favor he'd asked for, advance damage limitation before the fuss began. So he hired Johansen."

Bess had first seen Amundsen six years before. He had stood at the rail of the SS *Victoria* as it sailed to Nome from Esquimalt. She had already known he was on board: everyone did; it was in all the newspapers. He had watched Vancouver Island slip past in the dusk, black pines with red trunks that glowed pink in the sunset. She had passed him three times on the rain-slick deck before she could find anything to say to him. She had never approached a man before. But he'd seemed to her more than a man. He would never have addressed her himself, she was sure. He was above that sort of calculation.

"Was Johansen no good, then?"

"That depends who you ask. When they got to Antarctica he accused Roald of endangering lives; they set out for the pole too early in the year and were driven back by a blizzard. One man got left behind and would have died if it wasn't for Johansen, who brought him in single-handed. So Johansen was right to complain. But that didn't matter to Roald. Right or wrong, he had to be the boss."

Gade will soon have me thinking of him as Roald, she thought. She couldn't bear that.

"You're saying that Amundsen mistreated him," she said shortly.

They were approaching Solli plass and the National Library. It was a warm day for Oslo, and students were walking arm in arm, talking and laughing, turning their faces, like flowers, always to the sun.

"Not as Roald saw it . . . He spoke to the others in ones and twos behind Johansen's back, and when he was ready he called a meeting and told Johansen that because of his insubordination he wouldn't be going to the pole with the main party. He'd have to stay behind at their base."

A thin strip of grass appeared on their right, with a handful of benches shaded by beech trees. Gade steered her toward this forlorn little park. A tram clanged to a halt right in front of them, forcing Gade to stop and wait for it to move again.

"As soon as they got back to Tasmania he kicked Johansen off the ship. Johansen drank what pay he'd been given and had to wire Roald's people in Norway to beg for a third-class fare home. They paid it just to keep a lid on things.

"*Fram* made a slow passage homeward, milking the triumph, so Johansen actually arrived back in Norway before his old ship. He was in a terrible state, begging for money again. Roald's lawyer put the strong arm on the Oslo papers, warning them not to have anything to do with Johansen or they'd be cut off from the hero explorer when he got back."

"So Johansen wouldn't tell his own side of the story?" No wonder, she thought, that Amundsen had taken to the air. Up there he was absolved of all responsibility. Except, perhaps, the obligation to land.

The tram had moved on but still they stood facing each other.

"That's right. Though Johansen never did try to make any trouble. He was quite the good soldier, for all of his problems. And the polar triumphs meant such a lot to Norway back then. We'd only just got our freedom from Sweden and we needed to show we deserved it. To us, Nansen and Amundsen were winning generals. They gave us a name in the world. Without them, we'd have had to make do with the likes of Munch and Ibsen." He seemed to find this privately amusing.

Taking her elbow, he steered her across the tram tracks, under the trees.

"Just over there," he said, "about a mile past the palace, is the big park of St. Hanshaugen. That's where the crew of the *Fram* were put on a stage for the crowd to cheer. All except Roald, who was already too grand for that sort of thing. Johansen wasn't invited but he turned up anyway and watched it from the crowd. He was very drunk, of course.

"Then someone recognized him and he was shoved toward the stage with everyone cheering him, because he'd been one of the two biggest heroes in Norway not long before. Very few people knew about the row in Antarctica.

"He was halfway up the steps when Roald's lawyer jumped in front of him and told him to clear off, right there where everyone could see and hear them. To make matters worse, the lawyer was a brother of Nansen, whose life had been saved by Johansen many times over."

Gade pointed to a wooden bench under a dusty-looking beech tree. A young couple sat on it, murmuring softly, about to hold hands.

"And now Hjalmar Johansen is forgotten in Norway. Otherwise those kids over there wouldn't be courting on the bench where he shot himself." Gade pulled a face. "The police searched his hotel room after they found him. All he had left in the world was his shaving kit. When they turned his body over he was smiling."

Ten days went by. The Russian icebreaker rescued Nobile. The foreign air crews packed up and left. The journalists drifted south, their stories written, and for a day or two they crowded the Victoria, eating and drinking and talking too loudly. Bess, who had become quite free in her ways, walking in the streets and hills each day, kept to her room again. She didn't think that they knew enough to look for her, but she wasn't yet ready to give up the game. Then the journalists were gone and it was time for her to leave too. It was still barely August but there was a smell of the fall in the hills above town.

She found a lawyer on the Akersgata and took him to Gade's private office near the harbor. There, against Gade's strong advice, she signed a notarized document waiving any claim she had on Amundsen's estate. She asked only for enough money to set her on her way. The family should arrange it. She'd never trouble them again.

"You understand," Gade had told her, "that I can't act for you in this, or for the family either. With Roald gone I no longer have any part in the family's decisions. And I have to return to my embassy in Brazil this week. From now on you'll have to deal with Gustav Amundsen yourself."

"I only want traveling money. Amundsen had plenty of cash put aside. Tell them that if they don't give me some I'll have to stay here in Oslo. They hardly want that, do they?" Bess was quite ruthless about money when money meant freedom.

"I'll talk to him before I leave. But until Amundsen's will is sorted out—and it's bound to be disputed by his creditors—let me lend you some cash. You can pay me back when Gustav pays you."

Bess refused. She had her principles. And she knew that she wouldn't get a penny from Gustav after she left Norway.

That evening Gustav Amundsen phoned her from the lobby, proposing to come to her room. She remembered the slow way that he had looked at her the previous Christmas when she visited Uranienborg. She declined his suggestion. Also, the lobby was, for her, a more promising field of engagement. Her awkward presence in smart hotel lobbies was the currency in which she would trade.

Gustav Amundsen resembled his brother, except he was older, bearded, fleshier about the torso and face. Bess took him for a drinker. He had, she knew from Gade, wasted an army commission, ran businesses that failed. There had, she guessed, been disgraces. She would dispose of him easily; many such men turned up in Alaska, but they seldom lasted there for long.

They sat together in the corner of the lobby beside a tall vase of peacock feathers. Now Gustav would barely look at her. He was watching the doors. It was quite dark outside and the lights of automobiles flared on the windows. The lobby was quiet; most of the guests would now be at dinner. If I have chosen the ground, she thought, then he has picked his hour.

"I have no ready money that's not tied up in the will," he told her. "But I can still help you. My brother left some valuables in storage. They appear on no official inventory of his estate, so the creditors won't look for them. Furs mostly, and some jewels, which he collected on his travels. If you took them to London or Paris you might easily sell them. They're worth thousands of dollars."

"I don't deal in furs," she told him, though in point of fact she had done little else for the past fourteen years. "Kindly sell them yourself and give me the proceeds. There are plenty of dealers in Oslo."

Gustav watched a young woman crossing the floor. She was a tall Norwegian girl, fair-haired and quite beautiful, but she seemed lost and self-conscious in expensive New York clothes. The girl sat all alone on a sofa across from them and awkwardly crossed her legs. Anywhere else, thought Bess, I would say she was a prostitute. Gustav couldn't take his eyes from her.

"It's not that simple," he said, reluctantly sparing Bess some attention. "The person who's minding the goods for my brother won't give them to me. She's being unreasonable. She says she'll only give them to you, in person."

"She?"

"I've already discussed it with her. She'll meet you at the Høsbjør Tourist Hotel tomorrow evening. It's near Hamar, a couple of hours out of the city on the main line to Trondheim. If you go up on the train she'll have a motor truck ready to bring you back to the city again. With the furs."

She considered him in profile. From the side he resembled Amundsen quite closely. He was still staring at the girl across the lobby. She's almost a child, she thought. About as young as I was when I first met Amundsen.

Gustav had given Bess a name: "Mrs. Christine Bennett." An Englishwoman, from the sound of it, or American, yet living in Trondheim. Whoever she was, Amundsen had trusted her above his own family. There'll be some sorrow in this business, Bess thought, as she took the train north from Oslo to Hamar. I'll just have to meet it head-on. Forests and lakes scrolled past her second-class window, moving smoothly into her past. But I'll be back this way tomorrow, she told herself. And she would be free by then, a different person. She felt a dizzying surge of impatience. It ought to be tomorrow already. Why should she have to do this? Was it to rob her of freedom that Amundsen had sent for her? Is that what possession had meant to him? Was that why he'd flown away in the end?

The Høsbjør Tourist Hotel belonged to the same company as the Victoria Hotel in Oslo; it had been arranged for a car to meet

Bess at Hamar station. The car took her up a side road through several miles of fields and woods to a high hillside, almost a mountain, from which the hotel looked over the sweep of Lake Mjøsa. The Høsbjør was a quaintly muddled building, with asymmetric wings of two and three stories joined by a tower with a little round turret. The lobby surprised her—marble and pine, and bright flowers. It was busy with foreign tourists who had come there for the air. She had expected much less of Gustav Amundsen, with his greasy eyes and his second-class train ticket; this was the sort of hotel where she and Amundsen used to stay when not in the wild. It was one of the things that had brought them together, the taste for hardship laced with luxury. In the Waldorf Hotel, at the Olympic in Seattle, they had stolen their comfort together. There had always been someone else to pay the bill.

A room was ready for her in the side of the tower that faced on the lake. It must, judging by the view from the window, be one of the best rooms in the hotel, and she wondered how she'd come by it, given Gustav Amundsen's stinginess with rail fare.

She sat by the window to wait. Presently, she saw the hotel car depart again, winding out of sight down the driveway through the birch trees. She was still watching an hour later when it returned. It stopped out front in a huddle of porters but the woman who got out had only one bag. Bess couldn't see the face beneath a flat woolen cap. She was tall, Bess thought, dressed simply in London-cut tweeds, and though she looked slim she moved with some years on her. Then the woman stopped on the gravel below and looked up at Bess's window. Bess, meeting her eyes, knew now who had paid for her room. A few minutes later there was a knock on the door.

Mrs. Bennett was still in her traveling clothes. She had emerald green eyes and dark blond hair. Bess gave her the chair

by the window then sat on the end of the bed; the arrangement reflecting the gap in their ages: Mrs. Bennett must be in
her forties. But the self-conscious way in which she crossed her
legs reminded Bess of the young girl in the Victoria the night
before. She's Norwegian, Bess guessed, not really English. She
probably isn't used to this sort of arrangement. I'll have to be
nice to her.

"It's very good of you to arrange to meet me here," Bess
began. "What a charming place this is. Did you come down from
Trondheim?"

Her guest stifled a yawn. "It's my understanding that the
arrangement was yours. I was told I ought to meet you here.
I almost didn't come." She had a very proper, English way of
speaking. Bess could hear no trace of Norwegian. The yawn sup-
pressed, Mrs. Bennett went on: "I have the things you want at the
station in Hamar. But first we have to talk."

"By all means," said Bess. Her guest's tone was brisk, not much
short of insulting. For Bess this made things easier.

"The furs," said Mrs. Bennett, "and the jewelry—what do you
propose to do with them?"

"I'll sell the furs. Probably the jewelry too, unless there's something I'd like to remember him by."

"How sentimental you are."

Bess sat forward on the bed, resting her elbows on her knees,
her fingers joined primly in front of her lips. "Mrs. Bennett," she
said, "is this a negotiation?"

"It's an interview. If you're successful, you can leave with the
things that Amundsen gave me. I don't want them anymore. But
don't try and bargain with me. You may think you have something to sell but you don't."

"Sell?" The woman's face, Bess saw, was dangerously pale.
Without dropping her gaze, Bess mentally rehearsed the layout

of the room. She had learned in Alaska, when the miners started drinking, that it was useful to know the best way to the door.

Mrs. Bennett uncrossed her ankles, sat forward. "My husband has always known about Amundsen and me. We long ago made our arrangements." She spoke in a low, tight voice. "And if you think you can go to the newspapers, think again. I doubt if they'd publish details of a dead hero's private life, and if they did I wouldn't much care. I'd rather that than give in to blackmail."

That's it, thought Bess, her face impassive. She *is* Norwegian; not Christine Bennett, but Kristine. *Kristine*: painted on the side of his Curtiss Oriole as it banked and rolled over Kotzebue Sound.

"I assure you, Mrs. Bennett, I never thought I'd any sort of hold over you. Before yesterday, I'd never even heard of you."

"And yet," said Mrs. Bennett, "you've summoned me here with menaces. I only came because I wanted to see who you were. Who, and what. So I can decide whether to give you Amundsen's things. Or take them back to Trondheim and throw them in the fjord."

Gustav Amundsen. He must have thought that this would be a cheap solution. "I summoned no one," Bess said. "I was also told I should come here."

Mrs. Bennett stared back at her, then yawned again. "I'm sorry," she said, from behind her hand. "I've been having difficulty sleeping."

Bess shrugged. She supposed that Mrs. Bennett could see from her eyes how things were with herself.

Mrs. Bennett smiled. It seemed to Bess that she smiled apologetically. "I expect his brother is behind this," said Mrs. Bennett. "You don't seem like a blackmailer."

"Gustav told me you were keeping things for Amundsen that Amundsen wanted me to have. He told me I'd have to meet you here to collect them. He didn't tell me who you were."

"I expect he didn't."

"I'm not some adventuress, you know. I've already signed away my interest in Amundsen's will. He'd left me his estate at Uranienborg."

Mrs. Bennett held her smile for a few moments. Not apologetic, Bess realized, but pitying. Then Mrs. Bennett surprised her. She put her head back and laughed.

"Uranienborg? He left you the estate, did he? Now that is quite amusing." She shook her head. "I remember when Uranienborg was supposed to be for *me*."

"Kristine. That was the name of one of his planes in Alaska. Where I first met him."

Mrs. Bennett nodded absently. She sank back in her chair. She seemed to be losing interest.

"His second plane," went on Bess, "he called Elizabeth. That's my name."

Mrs. Bennett shook her head. "Elizabeth is my second name. They were both named after me."

"Then I guess he lied to one of us."

"Or more likely both."

Mrs. Bennett had turned in her chair so she could see out the window. The evening light left half her face in shadow, giving her a tragic aspect. Yet Bess, watching from the foot of the bed, saw her smile once or twice at whatever she was seeing. Bess allowed her upper body to sink back on the bed until she was half lying, her feet still on the floor. There was a plaster rosette in the center of the ceiling from which depended a pretty stained-glass lightshade. The bulb was unlit and the shadows gathered in the corners of the room. Amundsen was in the corners of the room.

And then it came to her: he had really been here! Kristine Bennett had chosen this hotel and paid for it herself. She had been here with Amundsen. Perhaps this very room. Bess let her eyes widen for a moment, childishly: she knew Kristine couldn't see her. This very bed. How had it been between them? Perhaps he'd been much younger then. Bess had been surprised at Amundsen's strength, the hardness of his muscles. She had traced the scars on his back and buttocks, made by an ice bear at Cape Chelyuskin. He had wanted so badly to be young still, and had often almost managed it. But when she first met him he already had the thin lips of an old man. She had never cared much for his kisses. That was one of her secrets from him. It angered her sometimes that he never seemed to guess.

"Do you know if there were others?"

There was a pause, as if Kristine were thinking. It's better not to look at each other, thought Bess, pulling the ceiling in and out of focus. We can be honest this way.

"I know of one for certain," said Kristine. "Another Norwegian woman. He had her after the Northwest Passage. Then there was me. I was the South Pole. And Gade once told me about another one, much earlier, after Amundsen was accepted as a mate for the *Belgica* expedition. She was his landlady in Antwerp, where he studied navigation. She wanted to elope with him. When he refused, so he could go with the *Belgica* to Antarctica, she killed herself with carbon monoxide. Her name was Marie. That's all Gade knew."

"My God . . . Was she married?"

"We were all married, my dear. I still am."

Bess searched her voice for any hint of an insult. She couldn't find one. She stretched her arms sleepily over her head and waited for Kristine to speak again.

"Three years ago," went on Kristine, "after he escaped from the pack ice in his Dornier, I finally gave in to him. I wired and told him I'd leave my husband in England and spend the rest of my life with him. Then he suddenly lost interest in me. After thirteen years."

"I met him six years ago. Three years ago he started begging me to leave Sam. He was suddenly so serious."

"Well then."

What was I to him? thought Bess. She knew she was beautiful and what that was worth to men, particularly older ones. But she was never one to sell herself. She'd married Sam Magids for love. Or so it had seemed at the time. He was still a young man then, back in Winnipeg, the same age she was now. And he'd been fizzing with dreams. He was going to go north and make his fortune in places from Jack London stories and Robert Service poems. And oh, how he'd needed her.

And now it seemed quite possible that Amundsen, whom she had made herself fall in love with, hadn't needed her at all. Kristine had been the South Pole. What had he done before he treated himself to Bess Magids? What had Amundsen won, or done, or learned or lost, at Cape Chelyuskin?

Why, when I telegraphed last month to say that I was coming, did he abandon his retirement and start begging for a plane to go searching for Nobile?

I would have been his last woman. That would have been the death of him. Instead, he's up there in the north and always will be. Where will I go now?

"I hope you understand," she told the ceiling, "why I need to take those furs. It's a practical matter. I can't go back to my husband after this. It wouldn't be fair to him."

"Oh, I understand. I do feel sorry for you." Bess heard her shift her weight in the chair. "There's something else too," said Kiss Bennett. "A package."

Bess squinted into the light from the window. Kristine was a black shape against the sunset. "A package for me?"

Kiss gave a short laugh. "Hardly for you, if it's in my keeping. He wasn't that bad . . . He sent it to me with a note asking me to forward it to someone in England. An old friend of his called

Meares. He said I should deliver it by hand next time I was in London. But I want no part of it. It's your job now. You were holding the chair when the music stopped."

It seemed to Bess that Kristine was going all-in with this bid. "He asked you to do it," she countered. "He sent the package to *you*."

"He also gave me the furs and the jewels that are now at Hamar station. The stuff that *you* want me to give to you."

She has the advantage, Bess thought. She can see my face and I can't see hers because of the light from the window.

"I suppose that's fair . . . Do you know what's in the package?"

"It was sealed. The note said not to open it. But I opened it anyway—why should I trust him? There's a closed metal tube and an old wooden-cased clock."

"Where did Amundsen send this package from?"

"From Siberia. He was wintering in the *Maud* at a place called Cape Chelyuskin. He sent letters home with two of his men."

Bess sat up and stared at her. "But that was nine years ago! Those two men disappeared."

The shape in the window seemed very still. "I know."

I don't need to hide my confusion, thought Bess. It would seem very strange if I did. "The Russians found one of the bodies a couple of years ago. Tessem. He was within sight of the weather station they'd been trying to reach. His head was bashed in. The other one was never found at all. Why didn't Amundsen say anything when this package showed up again? It would have been a sensation in the press."

Kristine shifted in her chair, abruptly, as if relieving a cramp. "Amundsen never knew. I only received the package two days ago. Someone left it at my house in Trondheim."

Bess lowered herself back onto the bed. The ceiling was dark but the last of the evening was reflected in the lampshade. Kristine was a heavy, heavy silence between herself and the fading light. She must be very frightened, thought Bess. No wonder that she came to meet me. The shadows overflowed the corners and met in the middle of the room.

"I'll deliver the package," Bess told the shadows. "I'd have done it anyway, if you'd asked me. You didn't have to try to bribe me."

"Bribe you? I thought I was blackmailing you. I was hoping to do some blackmailing on my own account. There's such a lot of it about."

Bess's eyes, adjusting to the light, softened the glow behind Kristine. She could see her face again. "Do you go back to Trondheim tonight? Must you go to the station soon?"

"There'll be no more trains tonight. I've taken a room here."

"That's good, I suppose. I'm sure we're both tired."

Kristine stretched her arms and legs convulsively then rose to her feet. "Yes."

"And I'm very hungry," said Bess. "Perhaps you would be so kind as to buy me a meal."

A few days later Bess Magids left Norway for the last time. She traveled to Paris and then, after a brief stop in London, to New York, which she reached at the end of August. Anyone watching her might have said she was full of some urgent new business.

On her arrival in New York she received a telegram from Gustav Amundsen informing her that a boat fishing off Tromsø had netted a wing-float from Amundsen's plane. What remained of the search was promptly called off.

Bess took a train north to Toronto and then west to Vancouver. From there she crossed the Salish Sea to Victoria.

Six weeks later, also near Tromsø, another boat picked up a petrol tank from the missing aircraft. Someone had attempted to turn it into a makeshift float, hoping to repair the ditched airplane or perhaps to build a raft. The French airmen, Bess knew, were young and full of life and scheming. So was Dietrichson, Amundsen's Norwegian deputy. They would have fought until the end. She wondered if Amundsen had fought alongside them. She did not think that he had. She saw him as he was last photographed at Tromsø, hunched glumly in the nose of his doomed seaplane, already drifting off into the north. She swore that she would never play poker again.

Inuvik, Northwest Territories

The swing door in the corridor opened and shut. Fay recognized the shuffle of his snow boots. They stopped outside the door. There was a jingle of change. Fay could see his keys on the little table by the door, but she waited until he gave up looking for them and knocked.

"Fay? I forgot my keys."

She was already back in her chair as he kicked off his snow boots.

"You learn anything new?" he asked.

"Not really."

He laid down the folder he was carrying to take off his parka, then he picked it up again and went to look out the window. "Right . . . Do you want to go to the airport and see if we can get you on a plane?"

There was something offhand about his manner that made her uneasy. I should cut my losses and go, she thought. But she wasn't done yet. "The planes are still grounded. I checked the web a few minutes ago."

"Oh . . ." Nelson took out his cigarettes and lit one for himself. It was the first time she'd seen him smoking in the flat. Up until now he'd kept it pure for his brother. "Well, that is kind of strange."

"What do you mean?"

"I mean I've just been to the airport. The planes have been coming and going all day. The highway's open too."

She turned back to the computer, ostentatiously checking the Internet. "That's not what it said on the transport department's website . . . Here it is . . . Oh. You're right. The airport and highway *are* open. They must have been slow updating their site."

She folded her arms, her back still turned to him, and waited. It was a while before he spoke. "I'm not as dumb as you think I am."

Yes, you are. Yes, you *are*. She hated herself for being caught out. "I don't know what you mean."

"You're way too interested in my brother's business. You're looking for something and you think I don't know it. If you weren't you wouldn't be here."

"Yes, I would."

"Don't bullshit me. That's why you came back here last night."

"That's not true." Or at least, it wasn't last night.

He took the landline phone from the coffee table. "I'm calling you a taxi. It'll take you to the airport or wherever you want to go."

"I don't have anywhere to go."

"Then that makes two of us. But you're the one who has to leave."

The worst thing was, she thought, this wasn't even necessary. She could have told him everything before now and he probably wouldn't have believed her anyway. She could tell him now and it wouldn't do her any good. But it mightn't do any harm either.

"You're right. There's a couple of things that I didn't tell you."

"No! Really?"

"If you don't want to hear them, just call me a taxi."

She watched him thinking it over. In a second, she thought, we could both be done with this.

"Okay, then. Why not?"

"Alright . . . My grandfather, the one who was in the Canadian air force, who's mentioned in Bert's papers . . . He went missing up at Tuktoyaktuk. Back in the late fifties. He had something to do with the DEW Line."

"So you went to Tuktoyaktuk looking for clues."

"No. I went there for my mum's sake. She was born in Canada and always wanted to go back. But she was sick for a long time. I had to mind her. And then she died. So I came instead."

"Okay . . . Is that all of it?"

"No . . . You know how my grandfather's name is in your brother's papers? He helped to retrieve those secret files about that French lieutenant, Bellot?"

"So you say. I don't know who your grandfather was."

"I do. Sort of. And that's definitely him. Well, there's another connection between him and Bert. Even weirder than the first one. You remember that newspaper article in Bert's Crozier file, the one about the mystery chronometer? The one that was issued to Franklin's lost ships, then turned up again a few years ago?"

"Sure."

"My grandfather used to own that clock. After he disappeared my granny kept it on her mantelpiece in Ireland. I have a photograph of it in my flat . . . Well, in storage. I gave up our old flat before I left London."

"Your grandfather had Franklin's lost clock?"

"Yes. My great-uncles must have sold it after my granny died. That's probably how it got back to Greenwich."

"Okay."

She was surprised how calmly he was taking this. "Don't you think that's really weird? All these connections?"

He surprised her again. "Weird is a matter of context. Right now weird seems pretty normal. What else have you got?"

"Nothing. That's it . . . Oh, wait. There's one other thing. My bank thinks that I'm dead. There's been some kind of mix-up

between me and my mum. They've cut off my credit card. I'm
broke until I can prove that I'm alive."

She was finished. She straightened her back and put her hands
in her lap and waited, like a schoolgirl who's just delivered a
report. He said nothing. And she had the time to think, as she'd
always done when she was on the carpet at school, about what
she would do when this ordeal was over. She would get a taxi
to the chalet, pick up her bag, then head to the airport. If she
couldn't get a plane right away she would camp at the airport
until she did. Once she reached Whitehorse or Edmonton she
would sort things out and decide what came next. She could go
back to London. Or she could stay in Canada if she wanted—she
was a citizen, thanks to her mother's birth. She could be a Canadian, for Alice's sake.

Finally he spoke. "For someone who wasn't looking for clues
you sure found a few."

"Too many."

"Sitting there, tapping away on Bert's computer, looking for
answers online."

"What else could I do? And surely you want answers too?"

"I thought I did . . . But for Bert there's probably only one
answer really. Maybe it's better not to know."

"Do you want me to stop looking?"

He thought about that for a while. "No. That's alright . . . But
maybe you're going the wrong way about it."

"What do you mean?"

"We have all these notes and letters and stuff, but we don't
know what they're meant to add up to. Bert must have kept all
that in his head. Or on his computer where we can't get to it. So
it's like we're trying to put together a jigsaw puzzle without being
able to look at the picture on the box."

"Okay. But where do we find that picture?"

"Maybe we should switch off the computer and go ask around."

"I asked you what your brother was doing. You didn't know. We asked Mike. He didn't know. Neither did Rose. Who else can we ask? We don't even know where he gets this stuff from."

"Do you remember that cop we met up in Tuktoyaktuk?"

"Sergeant Peake? You want to ask *him*?"

"No . . . not yet, anyway. Though he seemed kind of knowing. But remember he mentioned that he'd sent me, meaning Bert, to go and talk to some old Eskimo guy in the hospital? Maybe Bert did go and see that guy. Maybe *he* can tell us what Bert was asking about."

"I'd forgotten about that."

"The old guy's name is Moses Isaac."

"You've a memory for names."

"Not really." He handed her the folder he was holding. "I just saw his police service record in this folder I was reading. This one marked 'Albert Johnson.'"

The seniors had their own dayroom in the hospital with newspapers and games and armchairs and TVs. The attendants wore ordinary clothes, which Nelson thought was a nice touch. He remembered the home where he'd last seen his father, the sterile white scrubs prefiguring the end. His father had lowered his voice whenever he saw an attendant, as if he were spooked by them.

The old folks here wore slacks and sweaters and bright woolen cardigans with maple-leaf pins. Wire-rim glasses hung on colored cotton cords. The program director, Eunice, was an Inuvialuit woman in her thirties. She looked at them doubtfully.

"So you're wanting to talk to Moses?"

"It's just for a chat," said Nelson. "Sergeant Peake suggested we come and see him. My name's Nilsson."

Eunice considered them both. "Oh, Moses likes to chat alright. But he's been pretty sick lately." She mulled it over. "I'll go and ask him. If it's okay with him I guess it's okay with me."

The old man waited for them on a straight-backed chair in a room furnished with several empty couches. He was alone. Voices murmured in another room across the hall, and Nelson guessed that Moses must have come out here to talk in private. He wore a maple-leaf baseball cap and held an orthopedic walking stick between the knees of pressed blue jeans. His hands, resting in his lap, were a mesh of old scars.

"You're not Mr. Nilsson," the old man said.

Nelson stopped in the door. "I'm his brother."

The old man stared up at him, his expression unchanging. His face was smooth apart from two deep lines from his nose to the corners of his mouth. The lips were pursed in what looked like half a smile.

"Then I guess you're a Mr. Nilsson after all." He waved one hand at a couch opposite him. "Where's the other one?"

"We're not sure where he is," said Fay, sitting. "That's why we've come to talk to you. We heard he'd been to see you."

Moses nodded slowly for a few moments and then, just when Nelson had decided that he hadn't understood, he spoke again. "Who are *you*, lady? Are you the police?"

"No. I'm just a friend of Mr. Nilsson."

"Which one?"

He *is* smiling, thought Nelson.

"This one. I haven't met the other one."

The old man nodded again. He moved both hands to the clasp of his stick.

"I used to be police myself, when I was a young fella." He had a gruff, slow way of talking, as if speaking fluently in a foreign language. "I was a special constable at Arctic Red River— Tsiigehtchic, they call it now. They wouldn't let me serve back home in Aklavik." He gave a single snort of laughter, like a large animal exhaling. "Nobody's going to respect you where you're born, not when you're only a kid." He looked at Nelson.

"If you're worried about your brother, have you talked to the police?"

Nelson understood the nodding now. It buys him time to do his thinking. He knows he's not as quick as he used to be but he wants to get there in the end.

"I talked to Sergeant Peake, the sergeant from Inuvik. He told me my brother had been to see you. I figured it might help if I knew about what."

Eunice appeared in the doorway. "You okay, Moses? Not too tired today?"

"It's fine, Eunice. Just more folks from the south come to ask about the old days. Same old stories. I could tell them in my sleep."

Eunice made up her mind and prepared to go. "I wish you *would* tell them in your sleep, Moses. That way you'd get the rest you need." She looked at the visitors. "He's getting over a bout of pneumonia, so please don't take too much out of him. He'll be ninety-two next birthday. I've got twenty bucks on it."

The old man smiled to himself.

When Eunice was gone Fay spoke again. "Is that what Mr. Nilsson wanted to talk about? Your time as a Mountie?"

Moses shook his head. Nelson saw his eyes drift toward a small TV set in the corner of the room, although the TV was off.

"I wasn't a Mountie." His eyes left the TV and moved to a window, a square white glare in the hospital wall. "I was a special constable. They hired us locally. We helped the white Mounties who came in from the south. They couldn't speak the languages or move on the land as good as we could. When I'd made enough dough to pay for my own outfit I quit the police and went hunting on Banks Island. That's where I spent most of my life. Hunting bear and Arctic fox out on Banks Island." He chuckled again. "I'd be out there still if I could."

His expression changed as he stared out the window, seeing his island again. Then he remembered his guests. "Your brother was asking me what everyone asks—all the writers and filmmakers and suchlike. He wanted to talk about Albert Johnson."

Fay had skimmed an online encyclopedia before she came over. But she would let the old man tell the story his way. "Albert Johnson?"

"Albert Johnson," he said again, as if the name was some kind of clinching argument. "He's a legend up here from back in the thirties. He was a drifter and loner who came from outside in the Great Depression. He tangled with the police and shot a couple of them for no known good reason, then fought off a whole bunch more in a gunfight at his cabin. After that he went on the run on foot in a real bad winter. It took the police and army six weeks to get him. They had dogs and sledges and local trackers and radios. They even brought in a plane. All he had was his rifle and snowshoes. They finally ran him down and shot him dead over in the Yukon. But they still don't know who he was."

"The Mad Trapper of Rat River," said Nelson. "That's what the papers called him. That's how the bar in town got its name."

The old man stirred again. "Up here, most people didn't call Albert Johnson a trapper. They called him a man who stole from other people's traps. Whether it's true or not, I don't know. But he never got himself a fur license—that's why the police went looking for him in the first place." He lifted the stick out from between his knees and laid it flat across his lap, as if cradling a rifle. "I knew men who were on the posse that got him, elders from Aklavik, who said that Johnson knew bush tricks even they didn't know. And he was just a white man, appeared out of nowhere all by himself." He bent his lips. "Few years ago, a TV company came and dug up his bones in Aklavik. They did a bunch of modern science tests hoping to find out who he really was. They couldn't match him to anyone. All they found out for sure is he wasn't from Canada. And that he wasn't a mountain man. He'd had big city dental work before he came up."

"Was there anything in particular about Albert Johnson that my brother wanted to know?"

Moses put his head back and closed his eyes. "I get a lot of people coming to see me about Albert Johnson. Your brother . . ." He opened his eyes again. "Your brother had a photograph he wanted to show me. A really old picture taken at a trading post in the Yukon, a few years before Johnson showed up here. It's supposed to be a picture of Johnson when he went by a different name—the only picture they've got of him from before he was shot dead."

"It was a new thing, this picture?"

"No. A writer showed it to me years before. He dug it out somewhere down in the Yukon. It's been in lots of books and stuff since then."

"And my brother knew that it was nothing new?"

"He knew. But he thought he knew something else about the photo. He thought he knew who the guy in it was."

"He knew who Albert Johnson really was?"

"He had another photograph, an older one, which he thought was the same guy when he was younger. He was wearing US Army uniform. He wanted to know if I thought it was the same man."

"And why did he think you in particular might know?"

The old man smiled, picked up his stick and set it back between his feet, adjusting it to the vertical like a sentry with his rifle.

Fort McPherson, Northwest Territories, July 1931

His sisters had made him a paddle to bring on his first long canoe trip. He dipped it in the water a few strokes at a time, aping the motions of his mother in the prow. The swarming blackflies had driven them from the slack water under the bank and his mother strained against the strong current midstream. From time to time, switching sides with her paddle, she would glance back at her son, sat up on their bundle of furs. His efforts with the paddle threw off her rhythm, dripped water on their cargo, but she never complained. This was how he would learn.

It was just past noon and the day was hot. The canoe came around a wooded bend and there at last was Fort McPherson, a few tin and shingle roofs on a ridge above the Peel. His mother, who had never been this far south before, rested her paddle, looking for a gap in the alders that grew on the riverbank under the ridge.

The sun smoked off the water, and as the canoe turned broadside to the current the child glimpsed a shape in the heat-haze. It might have been a waterbird holding its wings out to dry, or a sail boat with only its upper sails spread, but as his mother started paddling again the shape turned into a raft made of logs lashed with willows. On it stood a man with a long-handled paddle. He was a white man—his blond-brown hair showed this from two hundred yards away—but he was traveling light; the boy could see a burlap sack tied to his back but there was no gear on the raft, no pack or rifle, not even an ax.

The raft drew closer, drifting downstream from the south. Coming under the bluff, the man began to paddle it ashore. And the boy's mother, assuming that the stranger knew where he was going, shifted her own course to follow. A gash of bare sand appeared in the alders where several canoes were already beached. A dirt path led up through birch trees to the settlement above.

Their canoe, moving faster, overtook the raft, almost near enough for the paddles to touch. The boy's mother, who was suspicious of all men and white men most of all, gave the stranger a silent nod. He stared back at them without expression, blue eyes in a broad stubbled face that was burned red and brown. He wore a duck jacket and torn canvas pants. His boots, bleached by sun and water, were bound with the same willow twine that he'd used to lash the raft.

The boy heard his mother mutter a charm and then the canoe scraped on mud and she jumped into the shallows to drag it from the stream. He waited until the canoe was high and dry and then he followed her, feeling the sand crunch under his feet.

His mother took a couple of turns of rope around a birch that still clung to a mud bank scraped bare by the thaw. Thus the child, and he alone, witnessed the stranger's landfall. The raft, coasting up to the riverbank, bumped into the sand. The stranger, dropping his paddle in the water, simply stepped ashore and, without a backward glance, abandoned his craft to the river. It bobbed in place for a few moments like an unwanted dog then slowly slunk off with the current, bound for Aklavik and the Beaufort Sea.

The boy tried to help his mother haul the furs from the canoe, but the bundle weighed a hundred pounds or more and she shooed him away for fear the load might injure him.

He retreated sulkily and instead watched the stranger. The
white man stood on the shore with his back arched and his arms
outspread, as if stretching himself after sleep. Then he shook himself and started on his way. He had the slow, straight-backed walk
of a man in no hurry, but the boy could see the skin stretched
tight across his cheekbones, the prominent knobs of his wrists. He
decided that the white man must be rather hungry; hunger was
something the boy already knew.

His mother had succeeded in hauling the pelts onto her back,
hooking her thumbs under the sinews that bound them together.
She stood there, swaying under the weight, and the white man,
who had drawn abreast of them, paused for a moment, looking
down at the little dark woman in her best woolen trade clothes,
bowed by her load, who was staring back at him.

Looking from one adult to the other, the boy saw no emotion
on either face, just a bored kind of watchfulness, like the face his
father had worn when he waited for hours by a seal-hole in the
ice. Then the man turned his head and looked at him and the
boy moved close to his mother and took a hold of the hem of her
jacket. The stranger stretched himself again, as if his back were
hurting him, then disappeared into the trees.

When he was gone the boy's mother put the furs back into
the canoe and put her son on top of the furs and pushed off
into the river. She paddled upstream another two hundred yards
until she found another sandbank, green with sprouting willows,
where she dragged the canoe up to the edge of the forest and
covered it with driftwood. She shouldered the furs, and then she
remembered their rifle, and that it couldn't be left in their boat,
not in this place full of Loucheux and white men.

The boy would have to bring it for her; she could carry nothing more, and he waited for her to empty the rifle of the three
bullets that—along with the pelts and the rifle itself—were all
she had left of worth in this world. Yet this time she neglected to

unload the weapon; she merely handed it to her son and told him not to fiddle with it and to stay close beside her.

There was no trail here, and the rifle was too heavy for him, so that he had to pull it along by the barrel, its butt dragging in the mulch and undergrowth, over wind fall trees still wet from the morning, but he felt a surge of manly pride that his mother, slipping and scrambling behind him, dragging herself upward by branches and roots, had trusted him with a loaded gun.

This was the quiet time of the year at Fort McPherson, when the mission schools were closed and the people went out on the land fishing and hunting. The poles of their autumn shelters stood here and there along the low ridge. A white man in a black suit waved at the boy from a church with a square-pointed turret. A string of dogs dozed outside a split-log kennel, dulled by the sun, too sleepy to bark at the passing strangers. A few yards away, beyond the dreary gray mud of the felled zone, the spruces resumed their march into the north. To the west, across the river, the ground climbed in folds from the far bank, ridge after ridge darkly stubbled with forest, farther and higher and fainter, until they merged with a blue haze in which white summits floated. The boy had never seen the mountains so close before; they belonged to other people than his own and defined the edge of his world.

A couple of young men in store-bought clothes were passing the time outside the Hudson Bay store, sitting on the stoop and smoking rolled-up cigarettes. They fell silent when they saw the boy and his mother, then started talking again. And although neither the boy nor his mother knew Gwich'in it was clear that they were wondering what it was that brought a couple of Eskimos this far from the coast, and why they had no man with them.

Ignoring them, his mother set her pelts on the porch and then sat beside the bundle, her eyes closed, fanning herself and getting her breath back: she would need her self-possession for the bargaining ahead. The boy placed his back against the shingled wall and stood with one hand around the barrel of the rifle, its butt resting by his right foot, like the soldier he'd seen in a picture at the mission school, protecting the King in his palace in England. But the muzzle of the rifle stretched half a foot above his head and when the two young men began to laugh at him his mother reached over and touched his hair gently and then she took the rifle and laid it down beside her. From her pocket she took some dried meat bound in moss and she shared it out between them, sitting there in the sun. They washed it down with rainwater that they scooped with their hands from a butt by the wall, then they rinsed their hands clean and it was time to go inside.

The trading post was dark and cool and smelled of furs and new cloth and coffee and paraffin. Its walls were lined with wooden shelves stocked with tins and blankets and knives and all the blessings of southern civilization. Cooking pots and bolts of cloth and coils of rope and wire hung from nails driven into the rafters. Kegs of flour and sugar and oatmeal and chests of coffee and loose tea sat on the bare wooden floor. There was a rack of rifles and shotguns by the counter, secured by a steel bar that ran through their trigger guards. To the child it looked exactly like the Hudson Bay store in Aklavik, the one that he and his mother had left empty-handed before setting out on their long paddle south.

The trader, a rangy man with a black beard and black eyes, was in his shirtsleeves at the counter. He pretended to read his ledger while keeping an eye on someone in the corner. The boy recognized the stranger from the raft; he was examining a leg-hold trap, opening and closing it to try out its action. The man looked at them with no more apparent interest than he'd shown before, then went back to flexing the spring on the trap. But the trader closed his ledger with a snap and smiled at the boy and his mother; he seemed oddly pleased to see them.

"Hello there," he said, spreading his weight on his hands on the counter. "What can I do for you? Or would you like to look around first?"

He was not, thought the boy, like the trader in Aklavik.

His mother nodded wordlessly and turned away from the counter. She needed wire traces for her snares and a couple of new traps to replace the ones taken by wolverines; it had been her first winter trapping alone, and she'd had to learn the hard way how to anchor her leg-holds. But the stranger loitered in the corner where the traps were displayed, hung by their chains from hooks in the wall. So she went to the other side of the room and pretended to look at tins of fruit and vegetables and condensed milk, although she didn't need them, couldn't afford them, and wasn't in any case able to read.

"So," the trader said loudly, addressing the room, "two new customers in one day. It's not normally so busy here in summer." His voice sounded hollow in the big wooden room. The boy saw him glance at the man in the corner. But he too had his back turned, and he too kept his silence.

The trader persisted. "You've come up the river from Aklavik? What brings you down here?"

His mother, though mortified by the white man's attention, could not politely ignore it.

"I have pelts," she said defiantly.

"Oh," said the trader, and he raised his eyebrows and nodded his head, as if struck by the novelty of what she had said to him. He nodded a couple of times more, then looked at the man in the corner. "And yourself, sir," he ventured. "Where have you come from today?"

The man hung the trap back on its hook and turned and looked at the trader. His eyes moved on past the counter to the gun rack. He came across the room, skirting the dried goods piled up in the middle, and tried to pick up a single-barrel shotgun.

But the bar through the trigger guard held it in place, and when he tried to speak he could only rasp. He coughed, cleared his throat, then managed some words.

"Open this, please."

The trader made no move. He nodded at the weapon. "Nice piece, that. From the States. I've got it in sixteen-gauge too, if you prefer something lighter . . . You thinking to buy in cash, sir, or are you here to trade?"

The stranger ran a finger down the barrel of a squirrel rifle, then turned and looked at the boy and his mother. "Cash. You can serve these people first."

He had an odd way of speaking English, more up and down than the teachers in Aklavik. It sounded like the words hurt his throat.

"Okay," the trader said slowly. He turned to the boy's mother. "So, you have pelts." His tone was now brisk. "Why didn't you sell them to the Bay in Aklavik?"

"The price was not fair."

"The Bay sets the same price for pelts wherever you go. It goes by the grade. I don't control it." He tapped the ledger, claiming its support.

His mother was unswayed. "Some traders don't grade fair. My husband told me that. He said that he heard that McPherson was better."

The trader stared at her, mulling this over. Was it a compliment, or a suggestion of weakness on his part? He glanced at the listening stranger.

"Who is your husband? He an Eskimo too? Or did you marry up the river?"

"His name was Peter Isaac."

"Oh." Standing by his mother, his arms rigid at his side, the little boy felt proud of his famous lost father. "He was the one on that broken-off floe . . . ?"

The boy's mother said nothing. The trader tapped the ledger a couple more times, as if coming to a decision, then opened it again. "Take your pelts into the storeroom next door and we'll break them out and have a look at them. I promise you'll get a fair grade for them. You won't get a fairer." And he shrugged, almost helplessly, because they all knew that after Fort McPherson she had nowhere else to go.

The boy's mother left him by the counter and dragged her pelts into the storeroom, which occupied the back half of the post. The trader came out from behind the counter and slid out the bar that held the guns to the rack; it hadn't been locked.

"Help yourself. The rod's just to stop kids messing about when I'm in back in the storeroom. Nobody's going to steal 'em. Not up here."

The stranger picked up a lever-action rifle, racked the lever, and eased the spring. "Savage thirty-thirty," said the trader approvingly. "Feather-weight trigger. That one's a—"

"I'll take it." The stranger leaned his purchase against the counter and pointed at a .22 squirrel gun. "This one too. And the shotgun. In sixteen-gauge."

The trader was taken aback. This was no way to buy weapons. There were rituals, decencies. "There's no hurry. If you want, I'll give you a few shells and you can go out back and try them first."

"I'll take a hundred-fifty rounds for each of them." The stranger turned away, scanning the room. "Can you sell me a canoe?"

"We don't sell canoes here. But I think Abe Francis might have one for sale. He's camped a mile or two up the river. The Snowshoes boys, outside on the porch there, can take you to see him. But if you don't mind me saying, you seem to need a lot of stuff."

The boy could see his mother through the storeroom door. She had broken out her pelts and was on her knees, spreading them across the floor.

The man unslung the burlap sack he had tied to his back, rested it on the floor, and unknotted the twine that held its mouth shut. From inside it he took out an oilcloth bag folded over several times to make a watertight package. He had to get down on one knee to unwrap the oilcloth on the floor, and as he did so he exposed for an instant a neat wooden box, a spidery black gadget made of metal and glass and a dented old baking powder tin. Selecting the tin, he folded away the oilcloth and its other contents and put them back in the burlap sack. Then he unscrewed the lid of the tin, fishing carefully inside it, as if to make sure he didn't accidentally pull out any more of its contents than he chose to reveal. When his hand came away from the tin it was holding a fat roll of currency. He peeled off some Canadian notes and laid them on the counter.

"I'll need grub too. And an ax, matches, hammer, chisel, needles, and thread. A bolt of medium duck. A whip saw and a bow saw. A wood stove and a stovepipe and an elbow. A twelve-inch window glass and some nails. Wire and wax."

The trader looked at the money but made no effort to count it. "It sounds like you need a whole new outfit. You planning to spend the winter up here?"

"I lost my boat in some rapids. My outfit too. All except that sack."

"Ah . . ." The trader nodded wisely. "You were traveling alone?"

The stranger showed his teeth. They were straight and almost white. The trader turned away and began taking out boxes of bullets and counting them out on the counter.

"They never did find any gold this side of the mountains," he remarked, though seemingly absorbed in his task. "You should have stayed in the Yukon if it's gold you're after. You've come from the Yukon, right? Down the Peel?"

The stranger said nothing. He had taken some coffee beans from an open sack and was chewing one thoughtfully.

The trader went on: "If you want to trap, you'll need to go to the police post in Aklavik and get yourself a fur license. Inspector Eames will want to take a look at you anyway. He likes to be sure that any white men who come into the Arctic will be able for the winter."

The stranger's mouth twitched at the corners. "Sure. I'll see him when I pass through Aklavik."

The trader had stacked up the boxes of bullets and shotgun shells. He was admiring his handiwork. "Passing through . . . ? You sure you know where you're headed? There's not a lot downstream of Aklavik. That's pretty wild country."

"I heard there's an old trail there, back west into the mountains. Are there any white men trapping there?"

The trader blew into his cheeks. "You mean the old Rat River trail? The Indians used to use it to smuggle with the Russians in Alaska. Kept it secret from the Company for a hundred years."

"Are there any white men trapping there?"

"It's no place for a white man . . . You're going to want cleaning gear for your guns. I've got pull-throughs for all calibers and four-by-two lint and gun oil. You have to go easy with the oil in winter though, otherwise—"

"Why do you say it's no place for a white man?"

The boy saw the trader blink a few times. He didn't like being interrupted. Nor did he like the stranger's flat stare. Ducking under the counter, he fetched an empty biscuit box and began stacking the bullets inside it.

"Because," the trader said, "during the Klondike rush a bunch of stampeders thought they'd steal a march on all the others. Instead of going through the Alaska panhandle, they figured it'd be easier to come by boat through the north, from Edmonton over to Lake Athabasca and then across the Slave Lake and down the Mackenzie. They figured they'd handline their boats up the Rat River, then down to the Yukon on the other side. But they got stuck for the winter up there on the Rat." The last of the bullets were inside the biscuit box. The trader looked up at his customer. "You want a lid? I could find one out back."

The stranger shook his head. "The stampeders," he said.

"The stampeders? They called their camp Destruction City. Only a handful of them ever made it to Dawson, too late to stake any claims. The rest of them either turned back or starved or got lost in the woods. Every few years some Indian'll come in with a story about finding a cabin in the forest with one or two skeletons, and maybe the skeletons shot themselves, or maybe they shot each other, or maybe they just starved."

The stranger nodded, disposing of this line of conversation. "I'll take the pull-throughs, the lint, and the oil. Do you have anything for pains?"

"I've got Beecham's Pills. They're good for most things. Anything stronger you'd have to get from Dr. Urquhart in Aklavik . . ." The trader lowered his voice. "I've got whiskey and gin too, if that's good for what ails you. But it's only for white men. I have to keep it in the back."

The stranger grinned. "No whiskey. I'll take the pills now. And some bacon, some flour, some oil, and a pan. For the rest, I give you a list. I'll come back and get it when I've found a canoe."

The trader turned to the shelves behind him, a honeycomb of little compartments used to store his smaller, more valuable wares. Then he turned back, reluctantly struck by a thought. "You're hungry . . . ? You'd be welcome to join my wife and me for dinner. We eat at my house."

"No." The stranger turned and went back to the traps.

The trader blinked hard, as if he'd been slapped. But instead of getting angry, he stared at the stranger's back for a few moments. The boy saw him shake his head and look confused, and then he looked sad. He backed away, searching about him, until his eyes settled on a small wooden crate on the end of the counter. Reaching into it, he took out two small round objects wrapped in wax paper. He laid them on the counter beside the box of pills.

"Here," he said. "Something for you on the house. I've still got a few oranges, came down the river on the *Distributor*. I have to give them away before they go bad. There's no one around here to buy them."

"Put them with the other stuff." The stranger didn't look around. Then after a few moments: "Thanks."

The trader nodded to himself, somewhat propitiated. Then he noticed the child, standing silent by the door of the storeroom. He took a pencil and a block of paper from under the counter and set them down beside the bullets and the pills. "You make me that list. I have to go in back and take a look at that Eskimo squaw's pelts."

He was halfway through the door when a thought struck him. He turned and spoke to the stranger's back. "Hey, mister. I didn't get your name. Mine's Firth. William Firth. Born and raised in Fort McPherson. My father was an Orkney man, my mother was from here: Gwich'in Indian."

The stranger, who was turning a stovepipe elbow in his hands, didn't take the bait. The trader waited a moment and then tried again.

"Your name, mister. I need to ask it. Inspector Eames likes to know who's been buying our guns."

The stranger muttered something that the boy, still unused to white man's names, couldn't make out. Neither could the trader. "What's that you said?"

The man put down the pipe and turned his back so that now they could hardly see his face at all. He muttered again, only a little louder.

"Johnson?" said the trader. "Albert Johnson? Is that what you said?"

"Sure," said the stranger. From what the boy could see of his face, he might have been smiling. "That's right. Albert Johnson."

The trader paid his mother a fair price for her pelts. She could buy bullets for the rifle and shells for his big sister's shotgun and fish hooks and flour and sugar and beans and cloth for new dresses. They were good for another year, and his mother sang quietly as they stacked their purchases on a toboggan borrowed from the store. Together, they dragged it past the watching Snowshoes brothers and down the muddy trail to the beach. When they got to the beach his mother stacked their goods by the water and then she dragged the unloaded toboggan back up the trail to return it to the store, leaving the boy to watch over their purchases. She would come back to him by water, having fetched their canoe from its hiding place under the willows. Before she left, she shucked the three bullets from the rifle, put them in her pocket, and left the rifle with the boy. He was upset at first, but then he reflected that he could still mount a ceremonial guard, so he stood over the boxes and sacks with the rifle grounded as before, the butt beside his right foot, muzzle pointing skyward, and watched the water flies skimming the current, the ripples broadcast by the rising trout. A breeze had got up, enough to drive off the blackflies, and he began to feel drowsy. After a while he sat on the sacks with the rifle between his knees. He would sleep in the canoe. His mother wouldn't need help with the paddling; it was downstream all the way home.

A branch cracked on the edge of the beach and he opened his eyes and looked around. The Snowshoes brothers were coming toward him, followed by Albert Johnson. He had the Savage hung on one shoulder and his burlap sack over the other. The boy could hear the clink of cups and pans inside the bundle. Johnson was eating something he held in his free hand. The two Gwich'in boys walked stiffly, eyes wide, as if afraid to look behind them;

their faces reminded the child of his first day at school, when the teacher had caught two older boys speaking their own language and had marched them off to be thrashed.

He ported his unloaded rifle but the procession moved past him without taking notice. The two Gwich'in boys, still taking care not to look back at Johnson, pointed to their canoe. Johnson put his bundle into it and watched as the Indians launched the boat. They waded knee-deep out into the current then climbed in and waited for their passenger to join them, backing water with their paddles. Johnson turned and looked at the boy.

"Here," he said. And he handed the boy a soft round object wrapped in wax paper.

Inuvik, Northwest Territories

The old man was still talking about Banks Island. His mother had told him not to go out there. There was nothing on Banks Island, she said. She had been born there, in the old days. No trees, not even willows, she had said. But there were willows there now, a hundred years later. He'd seen their shoots two summers ago, in a riverbed north of Sachs Harbor, and then he got sick and had to come stay near his niece in Aklavik. The Barrens were getting much warmer. Where the willows grew, there would soon be alders, then spruces. A hunter had shot a strange-looking bear out there, a couple of years before, and the scientists did tests and said it was a cross between an ice bear and a grizzly. There were never grizzlies up there before.

"Was it him?"

The old man paused, drew a breath, then asked Nelson politely, "Was what who?"

"The man in the photograph that my brother showed you. Was it Albert Johnson?"

"You mean the photo from the Yukon or the one from the city?"

So he was keeping track of this after all. "The Yukon."

The old man nodded a few times, wrapping his hands around his stick.

"It's hard to say. It was a long time ago. The one in the Yukon I would say maybe. It could have been Albert Johnson."

"And the man in the other photograph? The guy in the American uniform?"

"I don't think it was him."

"You don't think it was the person who Mr. Nilsson thought it was?"

"That's not what I said. I said I don't think he was the man who called himself Albert Johnson—the man I saw in Fort McPherson."

"Did my brother say who he'd thought the Trapper really was? I mean, did he mention a name for the man with the uniform?"

"He didn't tell me anything. I asked him a couple of questions myself, but he didn't care to answer them straight." The half-smile again. "He kept his notions close to his chest. Like a policeman would."

"But when you couldn't confirm the identities, what did he say?"

"He asked me to look again, a few times. He seemed pretty pleased when I said the army guy wasn't Albert Johnson. Which seemed kind of odd to me. Most people who come to show me old photos want me to tell them it's Albert Johnson—they're still trying to prove who he really was. Your brother was the opposite. He wanted him to be someone else."

Edmonton, Alberta, 1932

CONFIDENTIAL REPORT OF CONSTABLE WILLIAM CARTER
RCMP ON THE PURSUIT OF THE FUGITIVE KNOWN AS ALBERT
JOHNSON, DECEMBER 1931 TO FEBRUARY 1932

On February 2nd, 1932, I was summoned to the office of Superintendent Acland, Officer Commanding G Division RCMP,
for a private interview. At this meeting I was ordered to prepare
myself to join a plane flying to Aklavik to assist Inspector Alexan-
der Eames of the Western Arctic subdivision in the hunt for the
criminal known as Albert Johnson, wanted for the murder and
attempted murder of two policemen. I was further ordered, in
secret, to keep a close watch on Inspector Eames and his conduct
of the manhunt, and to report back only to Officer Commanding
G Division in Edmonton.

It is therefore my duty to inform you that after Johnson was
killed, Inspector Eames went around separately to the men of the
posse, both natives and white men, and had them agree to a story
that differs from what actually happened in a number of important respects. I will set these out now.

Number one. Inspector Eames states that he first sent his constables to interview Johnson at his remote cabin on the Rat River
because the man had been trapping without a license. But no
animal pelts or traps were recovered from his body or from the

dynamited ruins of his cabin, which makes it seem unlikely to me that he was engaged in illegal trapping. Nor, contrary to Eames's report, is there any clear evidence that Johnson was robbing from other people's traps. I talked to a couple of the local special constables and they told me that Johnson had angered some of his Indian neighbors by rudely chasing them off when they came visiting, and that they therefore blamed him for mishaps that could have other causes, such as wolves and wolverines.

Number two. It seems to me that the treatment of Johnson was from the start strangely aggressive. I have been informed that when Constable King first knocked on Johnson's door on December 26th last he had orders from Eames to bring Johnson into Aklavik for questioning, instead of just having a word with him where he was. This might explain Johnson's refusal to come out of the cabin or reply to his visitors on that first occasion.

Number three. I cannot confirm Inspector Eames's statement that Johnson was solely to blame for the gunfight in which Constable King was wounded at the cabin after he returned with an arrest warrant five days later. I do not believe that Constable King would have been party to any deliberate provocation, but when you are very cold and tired and you have been forced to mush for four days at Christmastime in temperatures of minus forty just to sort out a trivial matter of a trapping license it would be easy for tempers to rise and mistakes to get made.

Number four. It is evident to me, having talked to the survivors, that the incident leading to the death of Constable Millen four weeks after Johnson went on the run did not happen as Inspector Eames describes it. When Constable Millen and his three companions snuck up on Johnson's camp on January 30th last they opened fire without warning on his tarpaulin shelter, which was all that they could see of it. The posse then fired off two hundred rounds without reply, shooting blind into Johnson's tarp. It is little wonder, in light of this, that Johnson chose to lie silent in the cover of a windfall tree and to shoot to kill when his attackers closed in on him. It is also not surprising that after his three battles with the police he never sought to surrender, and that he ran and fought to the bitter end.

Number five. While Inspector Eames portrays the fugitive as a ruthless and determined murderer, it seems to me that Johnson sought only to avoid contact with the law, and only fought when he was cornered, like an animal.

Inspector Eames has written in the papers that Johnson behaved like a professional gangster. But no southern gangster would have the bushcraft and the stamina that Johnson displayed when on the run. As any policeman knows, your average city criminal is a lazy and undisciplined fellow, fond of his comforts and usually home-loving, given to braggadocio and bullying but not at all suited to life out of doors.

Yet from his appearance in the north last July, Johnson showed himself to be remarkably at home in the Arctic bush, able to provide himself with food and shelter using little more than an ax, a drill, and the weapons he bought from the store in McPherson. Once the chase began, he surprised his pursuers with his extreme endurance and cunning in the snow. For a long time, he confounded the faster-moving posses by keeping to the hard packed snow on the ridgelines, by crossing rivers only where the wind had exposed glare ice, and by using caribou tracks to disguise the trail of his own snowshoes. He was skilled at looping around on his tracks to get behind his pursuers. He had a trick of putting his snowshoes on backward to send trackers in the wrong direction.

Particular cunning was shown in his practice of making long zigzag legs when he was crossing deeper snow and could not help leaving a trail. The zigzags allowed him to get a close look at his trackers without their being aware of it. It seems to me that it would have been a simple matter for a "ruthless killer" with these skills to lie in ambush amid the tangles of cottonwood and poplar and willow that fill the river valleys and pick off any number of his pursuers while they were still caught in the open. Yet he never once attempted to do so. Similarly, he made no attempt to prevent Constable McDowell dragging off the injured Constable King after the first gun battle, although he could have killed them both. Constable Millen was also dragged from the second gun battle without further injury or shooting, although sadly it turned out he was already dead.

Number six. The popular characterization of Johnson as some type of animal, endowed with subhuman strength and endurance by a brutish, insensitive upbringing, is contradicted by Dr. Urquhart's autopsy. This revealed the dead man to have had recent and expensive dental work, including gold bridges, such as you would only expect to find in a wealthy man from the biggest cities in the south.

Number seven. The strangest thing of all for me is that for most of the hunt "Johnson" seemed oddly unwilling to make good his escape. It would have been a simple matter after the shooting of King, or again after the failed assault on his cabin by Eames and his dozen men, for Johnson to make a beeline westward to Alaska, where he would have been safe from arrest.

Yet for five weeks after the gun battle with Inspector Eames at his cabin, Johnson seldom strayed more than thirty miles from his starting point. Time and again he veered up into the foothills of the mountains, even as far as the tundra that forms the eastern slopes, only to double back down draws and wooded canyons. It was as if he could not escape the pull of the Rat River. Or maybe there was still some unfinished business, something he was searching for and had not found yet, that prevented his escape.

Inuvik, Northwest Territories

The bulb in the desk lamp was too bright for its task and Fay's eyes looked sore and tired. She put down the book she'd been skimming, one she'd taken from the shelves in Bert Nilsson's bedroom.

"There really was a Constable William Carter, just like the one who wrote that report in Bert's file." Her voice was so tired that Nelson could barely hear her, though he was only six feet away, sitting on the couch. "He really was sent up to spy on Inspector Eames during the manhunt, like it says in that report. He really did suspect that the Mad Trapper story was not on the level. He really did accuse Inspector Eames of suppressing the truth."

"How do you know that?"

She handed him the book she'd been reading, one of several about the Mad Trapper that she'd found on the bookcase. It fell open on the page that Bert Nilsson must have looked at most, a black-and-white photograph of two men standing at the door of an old-fashioned ski-plane: Captain Wilfrid "Wop" May, legendary bush pilot and World War I ace, and his mechanic Jack Bowen. They were on their way north to help the hunt for Albert Johnson. The same photograph, magnified many times, was pinned to the corkboard over Bert's desk.

"Part of Carter's report has already been made public," said Fay. "A few years ago a TV company tried to find out who Johnson really was. Like Moses Isaac said. They'd identified a number of really good suspects—people who'd gone missing around that time in Canada or America and whose descriptions and behavior sounded like Johnson. Then they got DNA samples from surviving relatives so they could check if they were right. But the tests ruled them all out.

"One thing they did find was this secret report by Constable Carter. For some reason it hadn't been filed with the rest of the stuff relating to the case. But their researcher only found part of it . . . Your brother seems to have all the rest."

"Trust him . . . Is there anything important that hasn't been published already?"

She opened the folder and selected a page. "You could say that, yes."

Edmonton, Alberta, 1932

Finally, there is a curious inaccuracy in Inspector Eames's version of the gun battle on February 17th, which resulted in the death of Johnson and the wounding of Staff Sergeant Hersey of the Royal Canadian Corps of Signals. While the general particulars of the fight are accurate enough—I can vouch for this, having been there myself—it is not true, as Eames writes, that the first man to reach Johnson's body was Constable Sid May from the post at Old Crow. In fact, the first man to reach Johnson was an individual who has not been mentioned in the official report at all and whose true identity I must admit that I do not know.

This mystery man had flown up from the south with me on the chartered plane piloted by Captain Wilfrid May. I had been given the impression that he was a representative of the airline and did not question his presence. Wop May addressed him as Deary. There was also a younger man who accompanied him and who I took at first for a second mechanic.

I did not seek to question this gentleman on the way up as he was very reserved and I took it for granted that he must be what he seemed: an important passenger with an official role in the hunt—to fit the two extra passengers Captain May offloaded a drum of fuel at Fort McMurray and we still took off dangerously overweight.

Mr. Deary was a medium-size wiry fellow with an upper-class way of talking. He sat up front with Captain May on our series of flights down the Mackenzie valley. The younger man sat close behind them and helped with the maps.

It was hard to hear above the roar of the engine and the blast of the headwinds that we bucked for four days to Aklavik. But from what little I caught of their conversation Captain May appeared to have known this fellow in Europe when May was a flyer in the war—they talked about Von Richthofen, the famous Bloody Red Baron, who had been lining up to shoot down Wop May when he himself was hit and killed.

After we arrived at Aklavik I saw nothing of these men for some time, being myself most of the time on the trail with the posse. I quite forgot about them until the final day of the hunt when Johnson, wounded and pinned, was still holding off our posse from a scrape-hole in the ice of the Eagle River. I was then very much surprised to see the pair appear on the scene, both traveling on skis while driving their own dogsled.

At great peril to themselves they advanced through the hail of bullets toward the place where the fugitive lay, apparently crippled, out in the middle of the river. Seeing them approach, the fugitive raised one hand, as if in greeting or surrender, but then he was struck by another bullet, fired, I believe, by one of the men working along the banks above him. His hand fell to the snow, and he was not seen to move again.

Being in advance of Inspector Eames, I was only a short distance off when Deary turned Johnson over.

Meanwhile the younger man broke open Johnson's pack, as if in a hurry to search it before the rest of the posse could catch up. With my own eyes I saw him remove from the pack a small wooden case and two metal boxes and some other stuff wrapped in a sack.

As the younger man shoved these items onto their sled, I saw Deary lean over and whisper something in the man's ear. Then

he stepped back and put his hands in his pockets and stood looking down at the dying man.

It now became urgent for me to think of Sergeant Hersey of the
Corps of Signals, who had been wounded by Johnson in the first
exchange of fire and who lay bleeding in the snow nearby. I was also
distracted by the antics of one of the native trackers, an Eskimo from
Aklavik, who was smashing his rifle against an outcrop of rock, saying he could not hunt food with a gun that had killed a man.

With all the fuss over Hersey and the Eskimo, I only thought
of the unidentified pair again when I chanced to turn around and
saw them both disappearing up the river in the direction from
which Johnson had come.

I did not see either of them again. They did not return to
Lapierre House that night or the next, or to Aklavik in the days
that followed. I do not believe that they came back into the
Northwest Territories at any time in the following weeks.

I do not know where they got their dogs and sled from, nor
how they came to use skis in a land where snowshoes are the rule.
My guess would be that Captain May ferried them across the
mountains from Aklavik in the plane and set them down close to
our posse. But when I asked Captain May about them he denied
any knowledge of the pair.

He said that they had joined our plane at Fort McMurray,
Alberta, from where it set out, having come there on a flight from
British Columbia. They told him they were on government business and needed a ride to the north, and he had taken them at
their word. When I asked to see the passenger manifest so I could
check their names May said he had misplaced it—the kind of
oversight you get in "a war," he claimed. After that, he got angry
with my questions, saying he had told me all he knew and that I
was being impertinent.

When I tried to ask Inspector Eames about the two men he
said to me, "I thought you brought them," and then had nothing

more to say on the matter. I cannot escape the feeling that he was "covering" for them, which was particularly odd as I had gleaned from his manner, when he first saw them emerge from our plane at Aklavik, that he knew who they were and was not pleased to see them. It is curious in the extreme that he does not mention their interference with the body in his own official account, especially since the dead man was found to have nothing on his person that could identify him.

To me it beggars belief that two men were able to introduce themselves uninvited and unidentified into the middle of the biggest manhunt in our country's history, one which became a running news story all around the world, and had people in New York and San Francisco waiting by their radios for hourly news bulletins, and then to just disappear without trace, taking evidence with them.

I suspect strongly that to identify them would take you more than halfway toward discovering the true identity of "Albert Johnson." Something about the mournful way that Deary stood over him as the man lay dying in the snow, his smile freezing into a terrible grin, made me think that they knew each other from before.

PART EIGHT

Morgan Island

68°30′N 75°00′W

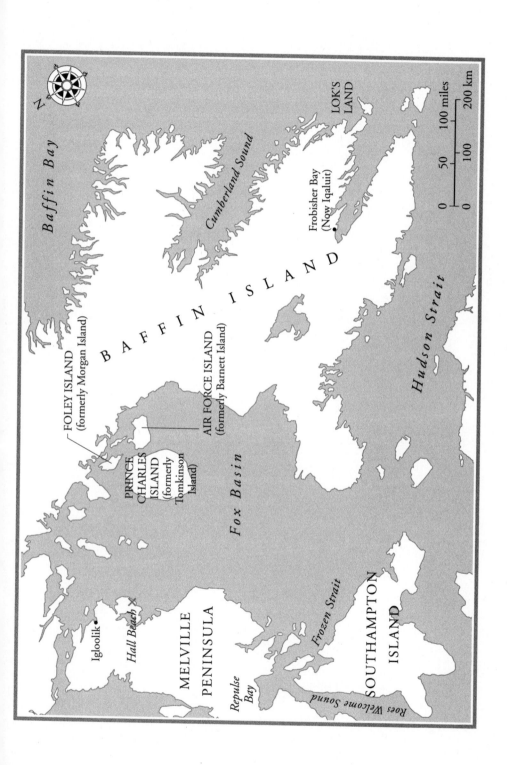

Inuvik, Northwest Territories

There was nothing left on the desk that they hadn't examined. Bert's computer sat dormant, waiting for fingers to bring it to life again. The computer could access most of science, art, and history, but the things that really mattered to Fay and Nelson, the files that Bert Nilsson had kept for himself, were locked behind his administrator password. The stuff in the folders, the things they had read, were just fragments, or footnotes, of some vision shimmering beyond their sight.

Fay turned away from the desk and sat on the couch. Nelson was in the kitchenette, making them coffee.

He came back into the room holding two mugs. Seeing her in his place on the couch he stopped inside the door.

"You're finished," he said.

"Yes."

"I guess that trip to the hospital didn't clear up too many questions for us."

"It makes my head hurt even worse."

"So much for playing detectives." He gave her the coffee and retreated to the desk, settling himself on the swivel chair. "What do you want to do now?"

"You should tell the police about your brother."

"Maybe they can figure it out."

"If there's anything to figure."

They sat in silence for a while. She's helpless right now, thought Nelson, but she won't ask for help. I could help her but I can't make that offer. When did getting drunk and sleeping with someone become such a chore?

"We should go to the chalet," he said, "and pick up your bags. You were supposed to check out today, right?"

"I'd forgotten about that . . . I should find another hotel if I can't get a plane."

But you don't have the money. He left the thought unsaid. They could work it out in the car, where you sat side by side and didn't have to look at each other. He didn't mind if she stayed there another night or two. She could have the bed; he was used to sleeping on couches.

On the desk a telephone rang.

They both turned and looked for it. It rang again, but they still couldn't see it. The apartment's cordless landline phone sat silent on the coffee table.

"It's Bert's cell phone," said Nelson. He swept aside a clutter of files and there it was, plugged in and charging, just as he'd found it when he arrived. It rang for a third time, vibrating on the desk.

"Have you heard it ring like that before?"

He thought of the night after he found Bert's maybe-suicide-note, when he'd got drunk and used the cordless phone to call Bert's cell phone. He had listened to it ringing on the desk until the call timed out and went to voice mail. Then he could hear Bert's voice again, saying "Hi, please leave a message."

"No."

"Answer it."

"It's password-protected. I already tried to get into it."

"But you can answer an incoming call without knowing the password, right?"

It rang again.

"Put it on speaker," she said.

Fay stared at the screen as he held the phone between them. "Hello?"

There was a pause and then a man spoke. "Mr. Nilsson?"

Fay nodded at him.

"Yes. Who's this?"

"Hello, Mr. Nilsson. My name is James and I'm calling from MasterCard lost and stolen cards." He had an odd accent— English, well-spoken. "There's been some unusual activity on your account that we need to check with you. But first, to establish your identity, may I ask you some security questions?"

Nelson began to feel uneasy. He had never defrauded the credit-card companies—or at least, not in any way out of the ordinary. But he knew people who had, and that it seldom ended well for them. Nelson looked at Fay and shook his head. She nodded emphatically.

"Okay. Go ahead."

"Your full name, please."

"Albert Henry Nilsson."

"Your birthday."

"January twenty-sixth."

"Your mother's maiden name."

"Armstrong."

"Right . . . Well, that's all in order, Mr. Nilsson. Now, because we've been seeing some unusual activity on your card, may I ask you in which town or city you are at the present time?"

Before he could answer, Fay took the phone from his hand. She killed the call and brought the screen up to her face.

"What?" Nelson could think of nothing else to say.

"Shit." She dropped the phone back on the desk. "It's gone back to lock-screen. Now I can't see the rest of the number."

"What the hell are you doing? It was only the credit-card company. Why did you hang up on them like that?"

"If that was the credit-card company, why did the caller ID show a number in England?"

"Did it?"

"Allow me to know. I'm from there. The country code is forty-four."

"Then who was it?"

"Someone who wanted you to tell them exactly where you are."

"Why would anyone care where I am?"

She lifted her eyes to the ceiling. "Because they think that you're Bert!"

He picked up the phone again. It had gone back to lock-screen and could tell him nothing more. Then he thought of a flaw in her argument.

"What if the strange credit-card activity is in England, and that's why they're calling from there?"

"Because you have his credit cards. Have *you* been using them?"

"No." Though it had crossed his mind.

"Then nobody's using them. They're making that up."

She went back to the couch, sat down, then stood up again. "This doesn't feel right. Who would be looking for your brother, apart from you? Who would be prepared to lie to try and find him?"

"I've no idea."

She walked over to the window, opened the curtain a crack and looked out into the snow. "This isn't right." She closed the curtain and turned to Nelson. "At least there's one bit of comfort. From the drift of their questions they don't know where we are."

The landline phone buzzed on the coffee table.

Nelson loaded his old Taurus and shifted Bert's Equinox into its rightful place in the garage. He took nothing from the apartment except for Bert's Antarctic parka. The rest of Bert's stuff was left for the cops or whoever else might come snooping after they'd gone.

Ringnes had left a note for Fay on the locked door of her cha-
let. He had gone to catch his flight. If his manager wasn't around
Fay would find her bags at reception, which he'd left unlocked.
"Don't worry about the money. Good luck with being dead."

On the highway Nelson missed the sign again, the one that
showed the airport turnoff. By the time he remembered to look
for it—if it had ever existed at all—they were on the right road
anyway. Second time lucky, he guessed. And now there was
someone else with him. She sat on his right, looking out at the
aspens bent under the snow. If he stopped the car now, if he pulled
a U-turn and went back to look for the airport, would it still be
there? Or would it have vanished, a Hy-Brasil or Shangri-la from
which he should never have taken her, stranding her here on the
wrong side of time. She wouldn't last long here. Whitehorse was
only a day away.

The road wound south in long bending coils through the forest of dwarf spruces. Every now and then a car or truck overtook
them and Fay would see patterns in the snow sucked up behind
it, ghostly shapes whipped high in the air, then slowly dissipating.
Ahead, bare mountain peaks glowed in the twilight. Beyond those
smooth passes, a few hours' drive from here, they would cross the
Arctic Circle and she would see the sun again. There, in a day or
two at the most, they would go their separate ways.

After Fort McPherson the road began a steady climb into
the mountains. The spruces shrank and gave way to bare tundra.
Funneled by the passes, the westerly wind spattered ice against
the windshield and buffeted the springs. Snowdrifts appeared
on the iced-over highway, creeping out from the rocks that had
sheltered their birth.

The road rose higher still into unobstructed uplands. Now the
wind tore at doors and windows, found gaps in perished rub-
ber seals. It seeped into the footwells and crept up around their
kidneys. Fay pulled her knees up to her chin, hoping to find a

layer of warmer air to thaw her feet. Sometimes, when the road curved back in a hairpin, she could see a dim panorama of the land they had just left, forests and valleys and snow-covered rivers forming and dissolving in gaps of the wind. So that was it. The true north. The place or idea that had haunted her mother, where her grandfather had disappeared. By leaving it now am I saying good-bye to them? She clutched her knees so hard that her thighs began to cramp.

"Can we stop for minute?" It was the first time either of them had spoken in a while.

"Sure. Why?"

"I want to get out."

He took his eyes from the road. "What? Here?"

"Up ahead, maybe. Wherever there's shelter . . . I want a cigarette."

"You can smoke in my car. I don't mind."

"I want to stretch my legs."

They stopped in the lee of an outcrop where the road carved through a rib of the mountain. Nelson watched her button her coat and put on her gloves. When she was ready she pushed her door but the wind held it shut. He put his hands on the wheel and looked through the windshield, his foot hovering just above the gas. A few feet ahead, just beyond their sheltering outcrop, the blizzard scorched the highway like a flame.

He lit two cigarettes, gave her one, zipped his own coat and put up the hood. "Slide over and get out on my side."

He had to hold the door with both hands to prevent it being wrenched away in the backwash of wind.

They hunkered together with their backs to the side of the car, looking down the mountain. Beyond the torrents of wind that roared down the passes the landscape was silent and still. As far as he could see, for hundreds of miles, there were no houses, no antennae, no sign of the road that had brought them here, just snow-covered rivers and rashes of trees. If they find Bert, what will they make me do with him? Will I have to go back there to bury him? Or should I bring him south to be with Mom and Dad in Grande Prairie? How would I pay for that? I guess he'll leave some money. Who would he leave it to but me?

What if he makes me rich for a while? What would I do with the money?

He thought of Lizzie, the kid he had tried to raise. He could send some money to BC to help her education. She would be going to college in ten years or so, if she was smart enough and not screwed up. He could send the money anonymously maybe, or make Donna swear to keep it secret from the kid. He didn't want to try and make Lizzie think of him. By now, if she remembered him at all, she would certainly know what he had found out a year before Donna threw him out, that the child he had loved wasn't his.

They got back in the car. It's funny, she thought, but I don't feel cold. A minute later she began to shiver violently. Her hands and feet burned as the blood flow returned to them.

They reached the head of the pass, a wind-torn saddle between lunar summits. A sign said "Welcome to the Yukon Territory." They had gone a little way down the other side of the divide, to a point where the road began to drop steeply, when they turned a bend and found a snowplow blocking their way, its beacon flashing in the gloom. Seeing them approach, the snowplow halted in the middle of the road. Unable to pass, Nelson stopped too. The door opened and the driver climbed down into the sheltered side of the plow, beckoning to Nelson.

The driver was a woman, elderly and small. She wore a set of old tan Carhartts and her muskrat hat was rammed down as far as it would go. Reaching for his shoulder, she pulled his head down to shout in his ear.

"What time did you pass McPherson?"

"I don't know . . . More than two hours ago, I guess."

"Yeah?" She seemed quietly angry. "It took you that long to get this far? You're driving pretty slow, aren't you?"

He turned and looked back at the Ford, where Fay was watching. "My friend is from England. I'm driving her down to the airport at Whitehorse. She's enjoying the view. She'll never come this way again."

The old woman peered up at him suspiciously. "Two hours? You sure about that?"

"Sure I'm sure. What's the problem? Was there an accident or something?"

"We closed the highway at McPherson two hours back because of the new storm." She looked across at Fay. "You're on vacation up here? In the winter?"

"She is. I'm not. She's going home."

"Okay." She was still watching Fay. "Okay. I'll believe you. You just missed the lights. But you're lucky you already made it over the pass. If not, I'd have sent you back to McPherson." She nodded back down the road she had come up. "Right this moment there's a long line of truckers waiting back at Eagle Plains, pissed as all hell cos I closed the gates until I could run the plow through. When they see you come down the road all alone they're going to be even madder. If anyone gives you trouble you can tell them that Laurie let you through. They know not to bitch at me."

"Thanks."

"The road shouldn't be too bad from here on. I've already cleared most of it. But if you hit the rhubarb or get stuck in a drift make sure you stay with your car. There'll be someone along presently."

"Okay."

"Better give me your names, in case you get stuck and we have to come look for you. And tell your girlfriend from me to enjoy her vacation."

The plow pulled over a couple of feet until there was just enough room for Nelson to pass.

"What did she want?"

"To send us back to Fort McPherson. The road's closed again. She thought we ran the boom."

"But she let us go anyway?"

"She thinks that we're sweethearts."

Just short of Eagle Plains, near the marker that showed where they crossed the Arctic Circle, two wolves came out of the trees. They stopped in the middle of the highway, staring at the approaching car, their breaths coiling around them. Then they turned, looked back toward the next bend in the road, and vanished again. A moment later a long line of trucks appeared around the bend, headlights shining in the night. The snowplow lady had reopened the road.

The Eagle Plains rest stop was built on a plateau where the highway turned south parallel to the mountains. It consisted of a hotel, a garage, and a transport depot standing in line along a siding off the highway. The buildings looked east across falling ground toward a line of low foothills. Beyond them the mountains rose pale in the night. To the south a black cloud was eating the stars.

Dawson City was a whole tank of gas away on the far side of the Ogilvies. If they wanted to drive on to Whitehorse that night they would have to reach Dawson before midnight, when the gas stations closed. There was little time to spare; Nelson took the car to the gas station while Fay ordered food in the hotel.

The dining room, recently abandoned by the stranded truckers, was littered with the wreckage of half-eaten meals. A picture window showed snow and black spruces. Every spare bit of wall was decorated with relics of the past—old photographs, wicker snowshoes, picks and shovels, antique leg-hold traps, trophy heads, a stuffed caribou. Having ordered two meals from the counter, Fay went over to look at the photos on the walls.

Time showed her its faces. A group of Norwegian sailors glared from the deck of a sloop wintering at Herschel Island. Two Indian boys and a whiskery storekeeper stood outside a store in Fort McPherson. Constable Edgar Millen of Arctic Red River, hatless, smiling, not yet killed in a gun battle with Albert Johnson, displayed the jug ears that would soon no longer be funny. Albert Johnson's frost-blackened face showed his teeth to the Aklavik inquest. He looked almost cheerful, winning his game of Guess Who. But she'd already given up on that one. A voice called from the counter; their food was ready.

Turning away from the wall, her eyes slipped across another photograph, one she thought she'd seen before. She took a couple of steps toward the lunch counter then stopped and went back.

It was the same photograph she'd seen in Bert Nilsson's apartment, pinned to the corkboard over the desk: a black-and-white photograph of Wilfrid "Wop" May, the famous bush pilot and war ace who'd helped to hunt down Albert Johnson. He was standing with his mechanic by the door of their ski-plane. Or rather, it was almost the same photograph as the one she'd seen in Bert's place. This one must have been taken just before that one, because there were two other men in the frame. The photograph in Bert's apartment, she recalled, had only two shadows where the men were now standing, shadows that Bert had circled several times.

These two extra men must have fled the frame after this photograph was taken: they already seemed to recoil from the camera. Fay leaned in closer to look.

The older of the two men, hatless, was almost bald, with a trimmed mustache and a thin, timeworn face. His eyes were sidling away from the camera lens as if to say, "Who, me? You don't want me." The younger man wore a leather hat pulled low over his forehead. His scarf, wrapped loosely around his neck, hid his mouth. He squinted at the camera as if saddened by it; his hand was frozen forever in a failed attempt to block the lens.

There was a caption under the photograph, reproduced from the long-forgotten true detective magazine from which it had been cut.

Bush pilot Wilfrid "Wop" May and party about to fly north to hunt for "The Mad Trapper of Rat River." This photograph was taken at Fort McMurray, Alberta, on February 3, 1932. Captain Wilfrid May (center left), Air North mechanic Jack Bowen (center right), and two unknown men who joined them from a flight from Vancouver. These were listed on the Vancouver manifest as a Mr. C. Meares and a Mr. H. Morgan.

There were footsteps behind her. She ignored them, still staring at the caption. She heard Nelson speak.

"You're not going to believe this," he said.

She thought, You want to bet?

"I'd just finished gassing up the car when the highway guy came over. He said the road is blocked again, but this time it's south of here. Three feet of snow just dumped in the Ogilvie Mountains between here and Dawson. It'll take at least a day to clear the drifts."

He waited for her to show some response. But she just turned away from him, back to some old picture on the wall.

He tried again. "The joke is, the road back north is open again."

Of course it is. She touched a finger to the glass that protected the photograph. She covered the young man's face until she could only see his eyes. She had seen them many times before on the wall of a flat in Lewisham.

"I want to go back north. I want to go to Aklavik."

"Why? We're already a quarter of the way to Whitehorse!"

She showed him the caption. "Because my grandfather went there."

He thought about what she had said to him two days before, about stories converging at the poles, like meridians. Or like the meshes of a net. They had both assumed she was humoring him.

"We can't drive to Aklavik without passing through Inuvik. There's an ice road from there across the delta. We'd have to stay in Bert's apartment again."

"Do we have any choice? If the road south is closed?"

He looked more closely at the photograph. So that was the famous Meares. And Fay's granddad had really existed.

"What did your grandfather *do* in the air force?"

"I honestly don't know."

Frobisher Bay, Baffin Island, 1948

It was a warm day for July, a little over twelve degrees centigrade. The mild air sucked water from Frobisher Bay, raising a fog that shut down operations. The Lancasters and Cansos of Number 9 Detachment, 413 Squadron Royal Canadian Air Force, drawn up in line on the Crystal Two apron, swam in and out of the mist like fish half glimpsed in the depths of a pond. The aircraft were all in good order, ready for the fog to lift, if it ever did. There was nothing for their Canadian crews to do but laze about the hangar and stare at the curtain of gray.

They heard the strange plane long before it came over. This was normal: final approach into Crystal Two airfield came directly up Frobisher Bay, so that the mountains of Hall Peninsula and Meta Incognita funneled the sound to the strip. They had plenty of time to drink their tea and wonder who this arrival might be; the US Air Force control tower expected no incoming traffic today. And how, the Canadians all wondered, did that poor bastard up there propose to put down on this godforsaken runway when you couldn't see the tower from the hangar, only thirty feet away?

The unknown plane passed unseen overhead. It was a big one, the idlers could tell that from the sound of four radial engines: probably a DC-4 freighter diverting from some other fogged-over strip. Good luck to it. It would have to try elsewhere today.

The plane banked and began to circle, avoiding the hills that rose on three sides. It orbited for an hour more, until it got boring, until the men on the ground had got so used to its droning, invisible presence that they scarcely noticed it anymore. And then, just when the strange plane was starting to get interesting again—how much fuel did it have left? The nearest alternative was the short gravel strip at Coral Harbor, five hundred miles away— the pilot must have sensed a gap in the weather, because he flew off to the southeast, turned back, straightened out, the roar of the engines booming off hillsides, and a few moments later, as if by magic, an American B-29 appeared on the apron, its propellers tearing spiral tunnels in the fog.

The mist closed in and everyone lost interest. The Americans ran this bleak airstrip, which they had built and paid for in the war. They could do what they liked with it. A beer delivery was the only good thing that could happen up here, and even then the wet canteen was off-limits for Canadians.

Nobody thought to wonder, at first, why the giant bomber didn't kill its engines on the American side of the apron. It was three years since the war had ended, and nothing interesting happened up here anymore. Most of the wartime buildings stood empty, the mist rolling in through broken windows and doors. Crystal Two barely counted as an airbase by now: the Americans used it mainly as a weather station, while the Canadian photographic detachment had come up in the spring to map Baffin Island: God willing, it would go back to Ontario in the fall, mission accomplished, never to return. Frobisher Bay was Canadian soil, but if you asked most of the 9 Detachment types, the Americans were welcome to it. If they'd only let us into their goddam canteen . . .

So nobody thought it strange when a stooped, slightly stout man in US Air Force Arctic gear walked in from the mist and asked for the skipper. It was only when he shook off his coat to reveal a blue battledress tunic that they took notice: what kind of Canadian wing commander appears unannounced in a total whiteout fog? Outside, the B-29 revved its engines, taxied back to the threshold, and hurtled blindly off into the void. It had only been on the ground for ten minutes. It hadn't even bothered to refuel.

How does a mid-ranking Canadian officer get an American strategic bomber to give him a ride to the end of the world?

Wing Commander Hugh Morgan chose a private room in an isolated Quonset hut where no one would bother him. When he woke the next morning he lay in his cot and listened to a loose sheet of metal banging in the wind. The sound told him that the weather had changed in the night and the fog must have lifted. There was a square of black felt tacked over the window, but the glare around its edge said that it was morning. The day had come and there was nothing else for it.

He packed his kit, hid his empty Mackinlay's bottle under the hut, and set off on foot through rows of abandoned billets, relics of that recent past when Frobisher Bay had been somewhere that mattered. The morning was cool and overcast, the Arctic sun glaring from everywhere at once. He felt gravel crunch beneath his soft flight boots, saw white foam on the wavelets that washed up the shore. There were children down there by the inlet—Inuit kids from the base's twin village, sitting on boulders and fishing for char. Across the head of the bay the northern slopes of the Meta Incognita clung to their last winter snow. He had been here before in the winter, during the war, when Crystal Two was a refueling stop for new war planes being ferried to Europe via Greenland and Iceland. Now the world had passed it by again. Apart from the Inuit, only a few American weathermen stayed here year-round. It was as it should be. The rusting trucks and jeeps, the empty oil drums, the disused barracks and collapsing tin shacks were strewn along the shoreline like the leavings of a tide.

The plane for today's operation stood on the apron in a clutter of fuel drums. It was a four-engine Lancaster, built to bomb Germany then modified for photo-survey work. Morgan should have gone straight to the operations room but the familiar outline drew his feet from their path.

He remembered a warm autumn evening by a cornfield in Lincolnshire, the idling motor of the truck that had brought them to dispersal. The boys of T-Tommy, smothered in their heavy flying kit, cracked jokes to cheer up their anxious WAAF driver. When the tower flashed the signal they gave her their unsmoked cigarettes, as if by a casual afterthought, then heaved themselves into the plane. He remembered their voices on the intercom, oddly bored, almost apologetic, as they advised the skipper about courses and searchlights and clusters of flak. He had climbed into the astrodome and watched, amazed, as the whole world turned to fire—the circus city blazing below, flak shells bursting Santa Claus red, bundles of fighter flares blazing like Christmas, lighting the sky for the night fighters and their streams of glittering death. Another Lancaster, flying just below them, had blossomed into flower, drifted gracefully down and away from them, bursting in a rain of golden sparks. He remembered all that, but he couldn't remember the names or the faces of the crew of T-Tommy, having only met them once, in the briefing room before the operation. The following morning, on their return from the Ruhr, a jeep was waiting at dispersal to drive him back to Bletchley. T-Tommy, he later learned, had gone out again the following night and that was the end of her.

He walked slowly around this other, living Lancaster, running a hand over its duralumin skin. The gun turrets had been gelded, patched with sheet metal like the front of a derelict house. Its wartime camouflage paint was now stripped to bare metal, gleaming dull silver in the overcast sun. Three new windows had been installed in the floor and sides for the trimetrogon survey cameras. There too, protruding ventrally, fore and aft of the new windows, were two T-shaped antennae: the aerials for the SHORAN distance-finding radar. When it became operational this would take precise triangulation readings from transmitters at known positions on the ground, allowing the cartographers to peg their mosaics of mapping photographs to established geodetic control points. Thus regions of the north where surveyors had never even set foot could be aligned to the European and American trigonometrical surveys. Soon there would only be one world to live in, one made of numbers not names.

Morgan passed slowly along the side of the aircraft. He stopped beneath the reared-up nose where the bomb-aimer's bubble stuck out like a chin. There was nothing painted there—no cartoons, no pin-up girls, no name, no sticks of little black bombs—not even the *Camera Bashers'* crest of the 22nd Photo Wing.

A few yards away, by the port inner engine, some airmen worked a hand-pump attached to a fuel drum. Morgan turned to their corporal. "Does this Lanc have a name?"

The corporal had been trying to ignore this unannounced inspection. "We're not allowed to paint nose art anymore, sir. Peacetime regulations."

"I know that. But what do you call her?"

"Just her number. Two-one-four. She's a war baby. She came off the Mississauga line in March '45 and went straight into mothballs. If it wasn't for this mapping job she'd have never flown at all."

Alice, decided Morgan. Her name is A for Alice, at least today.

The operations room was built inside the hangar, a long, plywood lean-to attached to one wall. Its windows looked over the apron on one side and the hangar floor on the other. Squadron Leader

Harbison, the detachment commander, was waiting there with
Barnett the pilot and Tomkinson the navigator. Over in the corner, behind a screen of charts and noticeboards, an airman fried
slices of spam on a hotplate. They all stood to attention when
Morgan came in. Harbison saluted. He must have kept his hat on
while he waited for me, thought Morgan, just so he could salute.
Up here, of all places. They have no idea who I am.

He returned the salute. "Please carry on. We're a long way
from Rockcliffe."

He took out the sealed envelope containing his orders—the
orders that he had typed himself the night before, at the new
American strip at Thule in northern Greenland—and handed
them to Harbison. "Today's job."

"Thank you, sir. Would you like some coffee and a spam sandwich while I read it? The Americans are supposed to cook for us
up here, but their chow line doesn't start until after takeoff."

"No, thanks." Morgan didn't think he could stomach food yet.

"You sure, sir? Our own boys will be eating anyway. There's
no galley on the Lanc. Not much heating either."

"Really . . . ? Well, thanks, then." The grease might dampen
down his hangover until he could get on the plane and take a hit
of oxygen. As Morgan ate he watched Harbison read the orders,
look at him, then pass the paper to Barnett and Tomkinson.

"I don't get it," said Tomkinson. "Why do we have to fly *there*?"

"It's a fill line," said Morgan. "One of your other detachments
screwed up a trimetrogon survey line on the Melville Peninsula
last fall. Between Hall Beach and Igloolik. Rockcliffe needs it
completed this season."

"Okay. But why not just fly direct to the fill line, sir? These
orders have us doing a huge dog-leg to reach the target area—
north over Baffin Island then due west across Foxe Basin."

I should have put something about that in the orders, thought
Morgan. I'm getting careless. He thought quickly. "Because they

want you to do an ice reconnaissance while you're up there. To see if the upper Foxe Basin has thawed yet."

"Why?" It was Tomkinson the pilot this time. "No one ever goes there, sir. Who is *they*?"

"That'll do," said Harbison. "You have your orders, boys. Go prep your machine."

"There's another thing," said Morgan. "I'll be riding along with you." He saw them exchange looks. "I need to do some calibration on the new SHORAN set. That's my job during the flight."

Barnett spoke up. "The SHORAN?"

"Yes."

"What are you going to calibrate it against, sir? It's not operational yet—we don't even have any ground stations set up. What will you listen to?"

"I'll be looking for any stray signals that might bleed onto the SHORAN frequencies. I've just come from seeing the Operation Polaris people at Thule. The Americans say they've noticed some problems with ghosting. Probably due to the ice in the air, or maybe the proximity to the magnetic pole."

None of these officers had trained yet on SHORAN, but they still had to know that he was talking bullshit. He might as well get to the point.

"That's my affair anyway. And if you look at the orders you'll notice that they aren't signed with my name. This is because my presence here is classified as secret. My name is not to appear on the flight manifest or in any of the logs. And I'll have to ask you to forget what I just told you."

Barnett twisted his mouth. "I don't think you've told us anything, sir."

Tomkinson took out a pipe and polished its bowl. "I flew for a bit with 101 Squadron in the war," he said conversationally. "They made us take an odd bod on operations. A Jewish guy. Half German. He had a box of tricks that he wasn't allowed to explain to anyone—even the skipper wasn't told what it did. Once we were over the continent he just sat with his back to us, listening to his headphones and twiddling his knobs. We never found out what he was up to." With his index finger he tamped tobacco in his pipe.

Morgan figured he'd better give them something. "He must have been an ABC operator: 'Airborne Cigar.' They picked men who spoke German and trained them at Ludford. The idea was to detect and jam the radio links between the German night fighters and their ground controllers."

"Really? . . . Well, it didn't work too well for this poor bastard. A fighter shell took half his head off." Tomkinson struck a match and lit his pipe. "Were you on ops, sir?"

There it was. They had given him the DSO and DFC, among other things, but it didn't do for him to wear the ribbons. "I was more of a boffin. Radio. Radar. Magnetics."

"Magnetics?" Barnett's tone was a little too solemn.

"Magnetic anomaly detection. Looking for submarines under the water. That sort of thing."

"I didn't know we could do that sort of thing. Must have been important." Tomkinson barely hid his sarcasm.

"It was." Which, Morgan thought, smiling apologetically, is why you didn't know about it.

Lough Neagh, Northern Ireland, 1942

To make a target for Morgan's secret test, the 422 Squadron fitters welded six empty fuel drums end to end. This dummy submarine was then smuggled from RAF Castle Archdale to Bannfoot on the back of a truck. Watched by a solemn Ulster farmer and his no less solemn dog, the 422 types rolled their hollow steel tube down the bank of the Bann where it entered Lough Neagh. As anticipated, the current carried it a little way into the lake before the inflowing water, seeping through the bungholes, dragged it to the bottom. Flight Lieutenant Morgan, watching from the blister of his circling flying boat, could still see its outline in the shallow lake. That was good: this test wasn't meant to be blind.

The PBY flying boat banked and flew north over the lake. To the west, the Sperrin Mountains were red with heather. To the east, the whins were a yellow flame on the ridge of the Antrim hills. As the plane climbed higher, preparing to turn, a gray line of distant ocean peeped over the checkerboard fields to the north.

It was a rare clear day in a gray Irish summer, and the sun funneled in through the observer's blister, soaking Morgan's tunic with his sweat. The sunlight overwhelmed the glowing green spikes on the cathode ray tube mounted in front of him, making them almost invisible. Morgan didn't yet know how or if this secret new magnetometer, "borrowed" from the unwitting Americans, actually worked. Now he couldn't even see its readout. He should have left the cathode tube where the British and Canadians had found it, mounted farther up the fuselage behind a blackout screen. But he needed to match its readout to his visual sightings of the dummy submarine. Otherwise how would he know what a submerged U-boat was meant to look like on the tube? And who would have bet on a clear day in Ireland?

This was a problem. What to do next? The aircraft decided for him. As it banked to the east, preparing to come around for a run on its target, the port engine sputtered, backfired, and died. The plane lurched sideways then straightened again, the starboard engine roaring to full revolutions.

"We've lost number-one engine," said the pilot in his earphones. "It's that fuel pump again. And number two's already running hot. She won't hold altitude with the weight of your gizmo. I'm going to have to put down near here for repairs. Do you prefer Aldergrove or Langford Lodge?"

Morgan figured the angles. Aldergrove would be bad—lots of RAF brass who would want to stick their oar in. Langford Lodge would be much, much worse: it was a depot for the US squadrons based in England, and Morgan didn't fancy having to explain to the Americans how one of their latest antisubmarine aircraft, fitted with a technology so secret that even their allies weren't supposed to know about it yet, came to be flying around Northern Ireland disguised in RAF markings. The Americans had written it off after its crew ditched their malfunctioning aircraft and took to their dinghies at the entrance to Lough Foyle.

"Neither," said Morgan. "We'll put down on the lake. The 422 types can help us moor until we get it fixed."

"There's quite a wind down there, Hughie. It may be only a lake, but it's still pretty choppy."

"We still have one engine. We'll be able to taxi."

The plane turned south and flew inland for a couple of miles, passing over the belt of rushy fields and bog and ash woods that fringed the lake to the south. To the east, a train puffed self-importantly up the Dublin–Belfast railway line. The plane turned again, nose into wind. Morgan saw the faces of the ground crew staring up from the riverbank. Now the PBY was over the lake again, gradually descending. The second engine, he noticed, was running slightly rough.

They were supposed to go sailing that day, but none of Elizabeth's church group knew anything about boats, and even their guides from Lurgan Sailing Club struggled to cope with the wind. It pinned their dinghies to the muddy shore of Kinnego Bay, flapped sails in their faces, drenched them with spray from the short urgent waves that beat on the hulls.

Elizabeth, who feared deep water and easily became seasick, was glad when the Reverend Emerson gave up on boating and skipped to the picnic. But now they faced another problem: any place that offered shelter from the wind—any lakeside hedge or tree or wall—had already been occupied by swarms of black lough flies. The flies didn't bite—having no mouth parts, living only one day in order to copulate—but whenever the wind fell away they smoked up from their hiding places, clouds of fractal desperation, frantic to mate before they died. They ruined the picnic—embedding themselves in the jam tarts and kicking sadly in the tea.

It was more than Elizabeth could stand: she had looked forward to this outing all summer, her one sure escape from her home in Banbridge, from her cold, watchful brothers and the care of her mother, bedridden since her first stroke . . . The day was fine enough—you wouldn't complain about a bit of wind like that if there was no rain on it—but she felt her old darkness descending. She needed to stay at least one step ahead of it. She slipped away from the others and into trees.

The Lough Neagh rescue boats were at Aldergrove and Langford Lodge: it would be most unwise to call for their help. But the wind, veering wildly from west to south, spun the helpless plane around on the wave tops. Crosscurrents of air and water raised a short choppy sea, vicious enough to threaten the wing-floats. They put on their Mae Wests and readied the dinghy, and then the engineer opened the nose hatch and paid out a sea anchor. It steadied the flying boat, holding its nose to the waves as it drifted downwind. Through his binoculars, Morgan saw the ground crew waving from the shore.

"The wind's carrying us away from them. If you can get them on the radio, tell them we'll be blown ashore somewhere on the southeast corner of the lake. They need to be there to drag this thing ashore or we'll be for the high jump."

Elizabeth's feet carried her northward along a path of imperfectly dried mud skirting a field that had been left for grazing. The headland was snowy with cow parsley. Primroses grew through a barbed-wire fence. Gusting over the long grass of the pasture, the wind made tortoiseshell patterns of silver and gray. She buttoned the red cotton coat she had bought with her savings for this special day. It was more of a town coat, she reflected, and this place, though not exactly wild, was a good deal less tame than what she was used to.

Water gleamed through the alders that screened off the lough to the north. She knew from a map at the sailing club that this was Oxford Island, which formed the western side of Kinnego Bay. On either side, ragged green fields sank into brown meadows that looked like they flooded. A few cattle lay under a hedgerow, out of the wind. There were no houses or farm buildings. Today, this place was just for her and the self-contained livestock. But why did they call it an island when you could walk here from the shore? Had no one ever tried to sail around it? The sky was pale and almost cloudless, the sun beat down from the sky. She ought to go back, to rejoin the picnic.

But her feet took her onward. It seemed to her that there were things here to discover.

"Paddle? Goddammit, Hughie. This fucking thing has a hundred-foot wingspan. You think you can row it against this wind?"

"We're going to pass only a few yards from that spit. If we can just get a line ashore there we can tow her in behind those trees and radio the men to tell them where we are."

"And where are we?"

"Here. See? This peninsula here."

"That's an Admiralty chart. It doesn't name land features."

"I'll figure something out."

"Okay. You want to get a line ashore? Let me tell you about flying boats, Hughie. Sometimes there's only one way to do it: you tie a line around your waist, you climb out on the wing and then you jump off and you swim."

The path narrowed as it entered the thin band of woodland. Under the trees it was cool and dark and the sun and wind had not reached the mud. Cattle passed this way often, coming to drink from the lake, and their feet made holes that brimmed with green water. Elizabeth felt the mud suck at her boots. The ferns, crowding in on her, tickled her face and left dew on her clothes. Then she came out the other side, onto the edge of the lough, where grass and wildflowers sloped down to a band of mud and rushes washed over by the waves.

And there it was, the miracle she had prayed for, an intrusion from a much wider world.

It bobbed and swayed on the waves, a great gray airplane with the body of a boat, so close she could have almost touched its wing. And standing on that wing, in line with the northern horizon, so that he seemed to be walking on the lough, was a sad-looking man stripped to his underwear. A rope was coiled around his arm and tied to his middle; he hugged himself and shivered, looking at the cold water. In a few moments, she saw, the wind would carry the plane past the spit and into the dead end of Kinnego Bay.

"Hello!" He was only a few yards from her, but he had to shout above the wind and the hiss of the waves on the mudflats. "Can you tell me what this place is called?"

He sounds American, she thought. But there was an RAF roundel on the side of the plane.

Elizabeth summoned her nerve. "It's Ulster," she called. "County Armagh."

A second man stuck his head out of the front of the plane. He was wearing a leather helmet and had Bakelite cups on his ears. "For Chrissakes, Hugh," he shouted. "You're wasting our chance. Get that line ashore!"

The man on the wing ignored him. He was looking at the girl in the red cotton coat. She had anxious gray eyes. From the way that she stood she might turn and vanish in an instant.

"I meant, specifically. What is this place called? The place where we are now?"

"It's called Oxford Island."

The man in the cockpit said a word that she had heard only once before, at the horse fair that took place on the fringe of the Armagh Agricultural Show. "It's a goddam island. Forget it, Hughie. The men don't have a boat. We'll have to take our chances on the mainland."

The man on the wing was still looking at her. The wind had turned his skin a pale shade of gray. His legs and chest were dark with hair, which surprised her: she didn't know that men could look like that. He was a little older than most of the foreign servicemen whom she saw about Banbridge, coming and going from pubs and from dances forbidden to her. She had never spoken to one of them before. They didn't come to her church group.

"It's not really an island," she heard herself shout. "I came here on foot. I don't know why they call it that."

He took a step toward her, so that he was balanced on the very tip of the wing. Then he hunkered down, as if that would make their shouted conversation more intimate.

"That looks like a raised shore that you're standing on. Maybe the level of the lake used to be higher. Maybe it really was an island when they named it that."

"Jesus Christ," shouted the pilot. "What does it matter? The line, Hughie. Ashore."

The man on the wing took the coil from his arm.

"Do you think, if I threw you this rope, could you give it a couple of turns around one of those trees? It would save me from having to swim."

Frobisher Bay, Baffin Island, July 1948

The weather reports were uncertain, the alternate runways remote and unreliable. So Barnett squeezed every drop of fuel possible into the wing tanks and the long-range auxiliary tank in what had once been the bomb bay.

The engines roared. Yellow-tipped propellers became yellow-edged discs and the earth pushed away from the undercarriage. Heavily laden with fuel, the plane barely cleared the high ground west of Frobisher Bay.

Morgan unbuckled his harness and stood in the navigator's astrodome behind the cockpit. He had no intention of doing any navigation, but he always got airsick when he couldn't see out. Thin overcast feathered above him, a soft gray ceiling shutting out the sky. Beneath the aircraft, the Great Plain of Koukdjuak stretched west and north, brown tundra bemazed with white lines and blotches, the rivers and ponds yet unfrozen by spring.

You could do what you liked with your cameras and radar, Morgan thought, but this was an impossible landscape. You could map it if you liked, at the government's required scale of one inch to a quarter million. But what was the point of trying to map chaos? Such a map would have no purpose or meaning. Who would ever want or need to look at it? From this altitude he could see two whole sheets of the government's new set of maps without even turning his head. But what names would you print on those sheets? He could think of just one: "Amadjuak Lake," the great ice-free triangle ahead and below where the Inuit went to fish and hunt caribou. You could do nothing for the rest of it, an impassable swamp of muskeg and ice. It made sense only in winter when covered with merciful snow.

The overcast cleared just south of the Arctic Circle. The plane was then over Nettilling Lake, a vast sheet of ice turned turquoise and green where the meltwater pooled on its surface. It was almost noon and the sun glared down from a brilliant blue sky. Far off to the east, the Penny Ice Cap shone white above Cumberland Sound. To the west, the Foxe Basin was clear of ice, a sheet of rolled silver. It was too much for Morgan. The light made his head hurt. He would have to abandon his place in the dome.

"Skipper, I'm going back for a spell. I need to do tests on the SHORAN."

Bent over his chart table, Tomkinson ignored Morgan as he crawled through the central compartment. The wireless operator, head drooping, might have been asleep: his position at the rear of the compartment, where the heating ducts entered from the engines, was the only warm place on a Lancaster. Taking care not to wake him, Morgan crawled into the tunnel that led aft over the bomb bay.

In wartime the rear compartment would have been occupied by the mid-upper gunner and the tail-gunner and the snaking metal trays that fed bullets to their guns. Now it was unmanned apart from the aerial photographer who—having nothing to do until they reached their survey line—sat wrapped in a blanket and reading a comic book, his back turned to Morgan. It was bitterly cold.

Morgan put his mouth close to the photographer's ear and shouted above the engines. "Go up front and warm yourself. We're still a couple of hours short of the fill line . . . Leave the blanket for me."

He watched the grateful photographer scramble across the wing spar into the central compartment. Then he picked up the blanket. Morgan had won a new US Air Force parka and flight pants in a poker game at Thule two nights before. But even the superior American kit would not warm him by itself. Keeping his headset on, though still unplugged, to give him some relief from the battering engines, he wrapped himself in the blanket and settled on the floor, knees bent, back resting against the curve of the fuselage. Then he pulled up his hood to block out the light. In a minute or two he was gone.

He was dazed by the noise, unsure where he was. The photographer bent over him, fumbling for his intercom cord. Morgan sat there, blinking stupidly, and watched as the photographer plugged him into the circuit.

"I've got him, skipper," a voice said in his ears. "He wasn't jacked in."

The sun blazed through the port trimetrogon window, set low in the side of the plane. We must have turned west while I was asleep, thought Morgan. We must be almost there.

"Pilot here—I think you'd better come up front, Wing Commander. There's something down there that you'll want to see."

There was no one in the central compartment. The wireless operator had moved forward into the cockpit, crouching behind the pilot and flight engineer. Tomkinson the navigator must have gone into the nose, thought Morgan. He probably saw it first.

He felt very tired despite his short sleep. He had done his part. He had brought them here, to the last place on earth. That ought to be the end of it. He plugged in his headset and keyed the mic.

"We should fly a couple of photo survey lines. Otherwise no one will believe us. Don't worry about fuel. I'll scrub the rest of the operation. We'll go home when we're done here."

* * *

The Lancaster climbed to survey altitude at twenty thousand feet and turned onto a south–north photographic line. Morgan, who had gone back to the astrodome, turned his face to the tail. He watched clouds being born in the track of the aircraft, four white lines, ruler-straight, across the empty blue sky. Prison stripes. A graticule descending on the unmapped lands below.

"You're absolutely sure?" Barnett was still pestering the navigator. "We're not too far north? That's not Rowley Island?"

"A hundred percent. I've taken a sun fix, radio fix, dead reckoning, everything. Besides, that island must be eighty miles by sixty. It's way too big to be Rowley Island. Or the Spicer Islands. Or anything else on the charts of Foxe Basin."

"Then how come it's not on the map?"

"Beats me . . . Drake and Goldsmith flew this way two years ago and they didn't see it."

"I guess there could have been sea fog that day, like that patch up ahead there."

"Whatever it is, it's bigger than Prince Edward Island . . . Looks like we've discovered our own province, boys."

"It's nothing but muskeg and ponds." This was a third voice, less elated. Maybe the flight engineer.

"Still," said Barnett, "real estate is real estate. How's it going back there, photographer? No one is going to believe us if you screw up this line."

"Fine, sir. All good."

Morgan was still watching contrails form in the vortices behind the engines, boiling away from the plane. Off in the distance, above the horizon, they softened and spread, turned gray and organic. Then they were no longer there anymore, sublimated back into the air.

"Navigator here. I can see two more new islands down there. One off the starboard beam. The other dead ahead."

"I do believe you're right, Tommo . . . Do you see them, Wing Commander?"

"Yes," said Morgan, still watching the contrails.

"They look pretty small."

"Only compared to the big one," said the navigator. "That one out to starboard must be twenty miles by ten . . . As if this country wasn't big enough already."

"Three brand-new islands. Not bad for one day's work."

They fell into silence. The aircraft droned onward, following its gyros to the geographical north. Morgan looked at the compass repeater mounted in the astrodome. It moved in leaps and jerks, randomly driven by vibrations of the airframe. To a magnetic compass everywhere up here was the same. He turned to the front and looked down.

Treeless brown tundra grouted with streams.

The new islands sat low in the water: other airmen might have overflown them in winter and mistaken them for landfast ice. Travelers by sea—Foxe, Parry, the whalers, Charles Hall— could have missed them in the fogs that smothered these waters in summer.

That is what the cartographers will tell themselves. They won't even notice that their job is done.

The aircraft cruised at twenty thousand feet. From here he could see about a hundred and seventy miles in any direction. A circle three hundred and forty miles across. The diameter of that circle was about five degrees of the earth's circumference. One seventy-fourth of the full way around. This was more of the world than he wanted to be able to see in one go.

What could he see, measured as an area? He was good at arithmetic: he did the rough sums in his head. By his reckoning, he was looking down at about half of one-thousandth of the planet. That sounded better, but not much. And if he went only a little higher he would see a lot more. The B-29 that had brought him to Frobisher Bay could go better than thirty thousand feet: you had to go high when your bombs were atomic. At that altitude the curve of the earth would be clear to eyes that looked for it. Soon people would go higher still, until the sky turned black and the stars shone without blinking and the shrunken globe twisted beneath them, visible in its entirety, naked, nothing to hide, a futility framed by a void.

But at twenty thousand feet the world hadn't yet lost all its mystery. To the west, slabs of drifting pack ice seemed to float above Foxe Basin, borne upward by the light. Beyond that, on the horizon, was the murky coast of the Melville Peninsula, where Charles Hall had wandered in search of Franklin's ghosts.

The plane now crossed the northern edge of the largest of the new islands, over a nameless new sound, clear of ice, which stretched between it and its two smaller neighbors. That white line below must be waves on a beach, waves breaking on land that, relieved of the weight of the ancient ice cap, the ice cap that lingered on those mountains far ahead, slowly re-emerged from under the water, rising an inch a year faster than the melting ice could raise the sea level around it. Someday that ice cap would return. From up here, if you could only watch for long enough, you would see how the planet was breathing.

The Inuit of Fury and Hecla Strait had told Francis Crozier that a strange and terrible people lived down there, the last survivors of a much older race. Maybe they were still there. If so, Morgan hoped that they, like himself, had the sense to keep hidden.

"Hey," said the navigator, "I've been thinking: what do you reckon they'll call these islands?"

"Now there's a question," said Barnett. "We saw them first. We should get to name them. We're the explorers, right?"

"Then I want the big one," said the navigator. "Tomkinson Island."

"I'm the skipper. I should get the big one!"

"I saw it first."

"Okay. *Noblesse oblige.* You can have the big one. I'll take the second one. I christen thee Barnett Island. God bless her and all who freeze on her."

"What about the third island? That little one? Who gets to name that?"

"Wing Commander? You're senior. Do you want your own island? Somewhere to take the wife and kids?"

Morgan remembered Meares Island, up the west coast from Victoria. It was uninhabited, so Meares had hired a boat to go and claim it in person. As a joke, he'd said. But Morgan's own name was a common one: there must be lots of Morgan Islands.

What about Elizabeth Island, then? There must be plenty of them too. He knew of one in particular: Elizabeth Island, two hundred miles southwest of Cape Horn, where Francis Drake had landed four centuries before on his voyage around the planet. Drake had collected wood and plants and water, killed penguins for food. He had claimed this new land for England and named it for his queen.

Elizabeth Island had been England's second-ever land claim in the New World, five years older than Virginia or Newfoundland. The only older claim was Frobisher Bay, where Morgan's plane had taken off that morning. Frobisher Bay had been lost for three hundred years before Charles Hall rediscovered it. Whereas Elizabeth Island, after Drake left it, had never been seen again at all. It had vanished in the storms of the great southern ocean, evading all attempts to relocate it. Maybe, thought Morgan, it's been hiding up here.

Elizabeth. You shouldn't get married during a war, when everything is about to be nothing and it seems almost stupid not to pretend that a stranger could be anything you want them to be. And you shouldn't bring a child into your delusions. Alice was not like either of her parents. She was fierce and hot. She didn't belong in a cold place like this. So not Alice Island either.

He keyed his microphone. "It doesn't matter what you call them. As discoverers, you only get to pick a temporary name. The government has a committee that will decide on the permanent one."

"That doesn't seem fair," said Tomkinson's voice. "Why would they change the old rules?"

To assert sovereignty and control. To stop the Americans—who we happen to know are running secret photographic flights over the Canadian high-Arctic—from claiming anything new that they might find up here. Which is also the real reason why Ottawa is now so keen on getting you lot to map the whole Arctic. But he couldn't tell them that. "There's a committee for everything now," he said.

"Well, I'm putting my goddam name on the map," said Tomkinson. "Where it belongs."

"Not me," said Barnett. "If it's only a provisional name, I'm calling mine 'Shitty Island.' I'd like to see them print that in the *Ottawa Citizen*."

"Go ahead," said Morgan. "Call them anything you like."

Maybe the next time someone came looking for these islands they too would be gone, like Frobisher Strait and Elizabeth Island. Or like Jan Mayen Island: how many different peoples had found and then lost that frozen volcano between Iceland and Spitsbergen? Irish monks, Viking explorers, the lost Inuit tribe of northeastern Greenland, who were encountered only once by Europeans and then never seen again . . . Henry Hudson, blown far off the course that would eventually take him to Hudson Bay and the Hudson River, was said to have seen Jan Mayen in eruption, but his name had not stuck. It took those most scientific of sailors, the whaling captains of Holland and England, to fix it to the map.

After that, it was thought, Jan Mayen Island would never have secrets again. But Gennady Olonkin had spent more time on Jan

Mayen than any person alive, and when Morgan had visited him
there, two summers before, he had a different opinion.

"They say that this island is dead," Olonkin had told him. "But
I don't believe them. I feel it moving under my boots."

Olonkin had waited for him on the black sand of the beach,
smoking a cardboard Russian cigarette and watching Morgan
paddle his dinghy ashore. In case of bears, Olonkin carried a rifle.
It had been a rare gentle day for Jan Mayen Island and the wavelets were vivid with emerald seaweed. Olonkin helped Morgan
to drag his dinghy up the beach and then waved to the Catalina
flying boat anchored on the glassy water just offshore.

"One hour," Olonkin had shouted to the RAF pilot. "I don't
need any more." When he spoke English he still sounded Russian,
not Norwegian. Yet it was almost thirty years since he'd signed up
with Amundsen.

He took Morgan to the cluster of deserted shacks and huts
that the homesick American signalers had called Atlantic City.
They sat on office chairs outside an old Quonset hut and looked
north to the Beerenberg, its crater hidden by the clouds. It had
once been the world's most northerly active volcano, the antipode
of Mount Erebus, but now it was deemed to be extinct.

Olonkin poured whiskey into two tin mugs. It had been years
since they'd last seen each other, back before the war. Morgan clinked
his mug against Olonkin's. "How long have you been alone here?"

"Five months. The Americans pulled out of this listening post
in February. Then Norway took it over. I'm Norway. The other
Norwegians are still on the other side of the island, running the
weather station. Eventually they'll move over here too. But I'm
not doing anything to hurry them. I like it here by myself."

"What do you do all alone here?"

"I listen."

Olonkin had taken him a little way up the bare lava slope
above the camp. A thirty-foot mast was braced by steel wires.

"Huff-duff," said Olonkin. "How we detected those Nazis on Greenland. The Americans stripped out the other antennae when they left. But they didn't take this one."

"They do tend to leave a lot of stuff behind."

Olonkin laid his rifle on the scree, opened his rucksack, and took out a curious gadget. It was a small Bakelite box in a home-made metal frame, soldered at the corners. At one end of the box a wire attached to what looked like a microphone taken from a telephone. The other end was wired to a bundle of batteries taped together like sticks of dynamite. Olonkin used some more tape to fix the microphone to the antenna, then plugged a headset into the Bakelite box. He offered the headphones to Morgan.

"Listen."

Inuvik, Northwest Territories

Someone had slid a letter under the door of Bert's apartment. It was waiting for them when they got back from Eagle Plains. On the back was a handwritten note: "Sorry Bert. I just found this in my mailbox. Mailman must have made a mistake. Hope it wasn't urgent—I just got back from a month in the south. Dougie in number 14."

It was long past midnight. Nelson's eyes were tired from the long drive back from Eagle Plains. He dumped their bags inside the door and handed the letter to Fay.

Ottawa, December 13

Sandrine Levieux
Toponymy Specialist
Canada Centre for Mapping and Earth Observation
Natural Resources Canada

Dear Bert,
It was such a pleasant surprise to receive your last email—we all thought you had retired for good when you moved up to Inuvik. I guess it's true what they say around here— old geodesists never die, they just refine themselves out of existence.

To answer your questions I had to dig pretty deep in the files of the Geographical Names Board. Please find enclosed copies of all the relevant documents and maps that I was able to find: pdf attachments would not have done them justice, hence the snail-mail reply.

From what I can see it is true, as you suggest, that Prince Charles Island, Air Force Island, and Foley Island up in Foxe Basin really were the last large land masses to be added to the map of our planet—Prince Charles Island is about half the size of Wales. The map stops here, so to speak. And so recently at that—1948!

The names of the three newly discovered islands were determined by the Geographical Names Board in accordance with protocol. The largest island was named for Prince Charles, the first son of then Princess Elizabeth, who was born that year. The second largest, Air Force Island, was given that name to recognize the work done by 413, 414, and 408 Squadrons RCAF, which mapped two million square miles of northern Canada after the war. The smallest of the three, Foley Island, was named after an officer of 413 Squadron who died in a plane crash a few months after its discovery.

It turns out you were onto something when you queried whether these were the first names given to these islands. According to a preliminary sketch map I found in the old annex, which was drawn by the air crew right after their discovery flight in July 1948, the two biggest islands were originally marked as Tomkinson Island and Barnett Island— the names of the navigator and pilot of Lancaster FM-214, which discovered them by accident.

The smallest island (now Foley Island) was marked as Morgan Island—why they called it that we have no idea. There was nobody of that name on the manifest of that flight or on the ration strength of 413 Squadron. It might have been some private joke between the men on the airplane. They're all dead now, so I guess we'll never know.

Next time you're back in Ottawa please drop by and see us.

Best wishes,
Sandrine

P.S. I thought I'd better not mention it in office email, but some guy who said he was from the Ministry of Defence in London has been asking about you on the phone. He wants to know why you still have a top-security clearance despite being retired. I said that I assumed that you had handed in all your passes when you left and that it was none of our business if you hadn't: you were seconded to us from National Defence, so he should take it up with them. I don't know what the exact problem is: the guy wouldn't even give his name. But if you're nosing around where you shouldn't, please take care. x S

"Morgan Island," said Nelson.

"It says in the letter that he wasn't on that plane."

"Seems to me he had a trick of not being places. He wasn't on the manifest of Wop May's plane when it flew up to hunt for Albert Johnson. Neither was Meares. They're not mentioned anywhere in the lists of men on the posse. But we know they were there . . . Did you ever try to see his service record?"

"Of course I did. But they said it was missing. Most of it."

"So what did the rest of it tell you?"

"It told me when he joined up. It mentioned some medals. And it told me where he was last seen alive."

Tuktoyaktuk, October 1957

The emergency room of the Distant Early Warning radar base was located at the furthest end of the module train, beyond the sleeping quarters and recreation area. No more than a repurposed bedroom, it contained a shortwave transceiver on which the crew could call for help in case of a fire or enemy attack that took out all their other systems. Now that the Tuktoyaktuk site was operational, along with the rest of the Distant Early Warning Line, people seldom went into that room anymore. So Group Captain Morgan made it his temporary home. The station chief—a civilian contractor, like most of the men on the base—thought of objecting but then decided against it. All he really knew about Morgan was that he had arrived completely unannounced, ferried in a small boat from Arctic Red River by a native special constable. He had a vague but impressive set of orders from the high command at NORAD. He was a friend of Colonel Milner, the US Air Force controller for that sector of the DEW Line. Most importantly of all, he had said that he wouldn't stay long. So Morgan was left alone in the emergency room to sit up late and drink whiskey and listen.

The shortwave was crowded now, thirty years after he first tuned in on his homemade radio. Moscow. BBC World Service. Voice of America. Peking. Prague. Tirana. CBC International. Pyongyang. RFI. Everywhere you tuned they jumped out and accosted you, lying and boasting and begging with menaces. The first snow fell outside, and as the daylight declined—and with it the atmosphere's ionization—the voices grew louder, clearer, increasingly inhuman. They seemed to want to silence each other, to oppose their amplitudes until they canceled each other out.

Well. If it came to that. Morgan could walk down the four-hundred-foot corridor that ran the full length of the module train—the twenty-four prefabricated huts joined on stilts above the tundra—until he reached the surveillance room at the far end. There, the duty radicians sat alone in the darkness, tracking their screens and attending the radios, observing the airliners on great circle routes, the supply flights coming up from the south, the transiting nuclear bombers, or perhaps even one of the occasional bogies, never explained by the military controllers, that might or might not be top secret new spy planes.

Apart from watching the radar, the radicians' other main job was to wait for a routine signal that would be relayed at least once a day along the Distant Early Warning Line—sixty-three radar sites, two hundred miles above the Arctic Circle, spanning four thousand miles from the Aleutians to Greenland. This routine signal ordered each station in turn to consult its codebook and then broadcast its own routine, bored announcement, coded to correspond only to that particular station and that precise minute in Zulu Time, the time set by Greenwich: a routine announcement to the B-52 bombers circling even farther north, over Lancaster Sound and Ellesmere Island, and which consisted of only two letters in NATO phonetics, two letters that instructed those nuclear bombers, at least once a day, not to peel out of their orbits, not to turn out across the polar basin toward their pre-set Russian targets, not to silence forever all radio chatter. Or at least, not yet.

Skyking, Skyking. This is Red Flush, this is Red Flush. Do not answer. Do not answer. Break, break. Silver Cup Charlie. Time is 190723 Zulu. Authentication is Whiskey Tango. Whiskey Tango.

"Go/no go." That's what they called it. That was what it was
meant to boil down to up here. Black or white. Living or dead.
And the switches were getting finer and finer. The Distant Early
Warning Line had only been operational for three months and
already they were preparing to swap some of the gear out, replacing glass tubes with these new things, transistors. On or off, said
the transistors. Who would miss us?

But when Morgan listened to the shortwave band, late at night,
alone in the Emergency Room, he still conceived of the universe
as he had done as a boy, not as on or off but as waves on distant
beaches. If any of it came from somewhere other than himself he
would never be alone, would never have truly been lonely. Any
signal at all, if it could only be confirmed—if it could only be
authenticated—would contain in itself the whole of creation.

He was fifty years old and not in good health and he had to
come to places like this to comprehend his baffled love for his
wife and his daughter, for his dead foster parents, for Meares, for
all the strangers he had glimpsed and then lost sight of in the war.
It was so cold outside, yet in here it was warm. And the people
here left him alone.

The first big snows of October had fallen and the low spit of
land on which the base stood turned from gray to white. The sea
itself hadn't frozen yet, but it would soon be white too, indistin-
guishable from land. The Distant Early Warning base would then
be the only landmark for dozens of miles in any direction, except
when it was swallowed by the blizzards and the fogs. You should
not go outside in these whiteout conditions: it would be easy to
wander out onto the tundra or the sea ice and freeze to death
there, or be taken by the bears that could scent you in the fog.

Whenever the weather was clear, in what little daylight was
left to him, Morgan would go outside and perform a slow tour
of the base's antennae, floundering through the fresh snow, sucking razor blades into his lungs. Sometimes he'd be interrupted by

the roar of supply planes from the south, or by the helicopters that flew crew and supplies along the DEW Line. Morgan had to stamp his feet and clap his mittened hands together and wait until the aircraft had killed their engines or flown away. Then he could listen again, using the homemade pickup gear that Olonkin had first shown him.

Each type of aerial had its own voice. The two giant antennae for the White Alice communication link, thirty-foot dishes of welded steel plates, made a low, hollow hum counterpointed by a whistle, like someone blowing across the mouth of a jug. When the wind dropped completely and the great cold descended, dropping to minus forty or lower, White Alice would click her tongue in disapproval, tsk, tsk, tsk, fainter and slower, until she too was cowed by the silence.

The VHF aerials were used to communicate with nearby aircraft, with those few people who went outside the module train in winter, and with the handful of workers still in the construction camp down by the airstrip. They were terrible gossips, buzzing and crackling and fizzing with mischief. Once Morgan was sure he heard voices in the static and, whipping off his headphones, pressed his ear against the cold steel. He paid for that with a large piece of skin. The voices, he discovered, had come from the cord that connected his earphones to the pickup on the aerial: it had become its own wireless set, receiving local interference.

The wooden telephone poles, which carried phone lines to the airstrip and construction camp and to the RCMP post in the nearby Inuvialuit settlement, groaned and tutted like old men and women enjoying their own slow decay.

Loudest of all was the big Doppler tower, an open steel gantry bisecting the sky for three hundred feet over the base. When he placed the pickup on its girders he heard moans and sighs, the creaking noise of feeding beluga whales, the sound of metal giants turning over in their sleep.

None of this made sense yet to Morgan. He wasn't sure that it ever would. When Olonkin claimed that his aerials talked to him, Morgan had argued against: it's only the wind in the stay wires, the warping of wood and contraction of steel. Loose rivets popping, the hum of imperfectly soldered connections. Cross-modulation. Ground loops. Capture errors. Meteor scatter—that effect caused by vaporized shooting stars, which allows radar beams and VHF signals to transcend, for a moment or two, the limits set for them by the curve of the world. There's noise in your headset and your wires and your microphones. There's noise in your ears and inside your head. What if you could correct for all that and you were left with only silence? Do you think you could stand it? That's why you think you hear words in the noise.

I hear words in Russian, Olonkin had insisted that day on Jan Mayen Island. Why would the voices speak only in Russian if they aren't talking to me? Who else on this fucking volcano speaks Russian?

Apophenia. Loneliness. The vertigo you get from living too many years. Who wouldn't want to turn and go back again, if only you could? But Morgan didn't say this to Olonkin. The Russia that Olonkin had fled as a boy no longer existed. Let it speak to him now however it could.

As for himself, Morgan didn't think that the universe would or could use words if it wanted to talk to us. He would listen for its message in the silences between, in the contraction of cold metal, the warping of wood, the wind singing in the stay wires. He would never be able to read these as words, no more than he could read the coded messages of the Cold War numbers stations, those strings of numbers read at night by unidentified voices on the shortwave. But this didn't mean they weren't talking to him.

At the start of October the plane from the south bought Morgan a confidential letter. It was from a wartime colleague now at Cambridge University. He wrote that their radio telescopes had found a new mystery: beacons of energy, unimaginably powerful, flashing at us from billions of years ago in the deepest regions of space. These strange new objects, so little understood that they hadn't been announced yet, hadn't even been named, pulsed with their own internal rhythms, their signals rising and falling with a period of hours or weeks. "Time signals from the universe," the letter had said. "Lighthouses in space."

After he finished the letter Morgan went outside and looked up at the twilight. Stars shone in the north. In the south was the thin aquamarine band under which lived his wife and his daughter. The geodesic radar dome, raised fifty feet above the module train, glowed faintly in the dark, as if it could store and release a little of the sun that still showed itself at midday. High on the Doppler tower an unblinking red light shone over the sea. The Jamesway huts in the construction camp, now abandoned for the winter, looked like old boats overturned on a beach. Everything was covered in snow. The supply plane had come and gone, taking with it the last of the construction workers, and the silence had stolen back after it left. A windsock hung limp by the airstrip. The sea was flat and gray and oily, except close by the shore where pancake ice was forming. Morgan thought of the Heat Death: I am close to the edge, to the end of the universe. Yet up there somewhere, among those frozen stars, unspeakable fires were burning. Their frequency was much too high for the shortwave and VHF and UHF gear at Tuktoyaktuk auxiliary radar station. He would have to go south with the next plane.

That evening, when Morgan was a quarter way into his last bottle of Mackinlay's, the general alarm went off in crew quarters. Then his telephone rang. Colonel Milner, the US Air Force's sector controller, was on the radio from the main station at Cape Parry. Would Group Captain Morgan please come to the surveillance room?

Normally crewed by one or two civilian radicians, the surveillance room was now full. Two American Air Force captains,
who had been visiting for an inspection, stood at the back of
the darkened room, together with the cook, the mechanics, and the
off-duty radicians. But no one was looking at the radar, not even
the men on the screens. All eyes were on the station chief, Wollaston, who stood adjusting the dials on the shortwave receiver.

"What is it?" asked Morgan. He dreaded to hear any possible
answer.

"Shut the fuck up!" hissed a civilian radician. Then he saw
who it was. "Sorry, sir," he whispered. "But we're trying to hear."

Wollaston adjusted the volume and the room filled with a
familiar sound, the automated male voice on Station WWV in
Maryland broadcasting the time signal at twenty megahertz. Wollaston waited for the beep of the time pulse, indicating precisely
thirty-five past the hour at Greenwich, then he reached up again
and adjusted the knob by a tiny degree. "Now," he said.

At first Morgan heard nothing but his own tinnitus, the aural
scarring from thousands of hours of unshielded aero engines.
Then came the crackle and wash of the shortwave band. It was
buzzing and bright tonight: Morgan felt sure there would be a
lovely aurora. Looking around he saw bodies stiffen and faces turn
to one another, and then he was able to hear it as well: a bright,
fussy little sound, like a telephone left off the hook: beep, beep,
beep, three times a second. The men in the room looked about
them, faces slack with wonder. The beeping grew louder, then
it faded again, fuzzed out, until all that was left was white noise.

Colonel Milner's voice filled the room. They must have
patched the radio into the PA system.

"It's in space," said Milner. "The Soviets have claimed it, and
Washington confirms the claim. They say the Reds launched it at
around nineteen-thirty Zulu from the central USSR. It's in ellipti-
cal orbit between two hundred and nine hundred kilometers up."

"What does it do?" asked an American captain.

"It goes beep."

Morgan pushed to the front of the room, keyed the microphone on the main console. "Morgan here. Nineteen-thirty Greenwich is three hours ago, Colonel. With that kind of orbit it should have got to us sooner."

"It did. This is the second time it's come around on us. We didn't notice the first time. Bare Mountain had to tell us to listen out for it. *We* should be warning *them*."

"If they can shoot a transmitter into orbit," someone said, "they can shoot bombs that way too. They won't need to send planes over the pole."

There was a heavy silence in the room.

"Fuck it, boys," muttered one of the radicians. "I'm on a thousand bucks a month. We only just got here."

The American captain spoke to the mic. "What does Bare Mountain want us to do, sir?"

"Nothing. They just wanted to know if we could hear it too. Our radar can't track it. The Brits are still trying with their big new dish at Jodrell Bank."

Morgan spoke again. "What's the inclination of its orbit?"

"Bare Mountain reckons about sixty-five degrees. It should reach to just south of us here."

Morgan thought of the map he had pinned to the wall of his childhood bedroom, the world map on which he'd later marked up his ham-radio contacts.

The map had been based on the Mercator maritime projection, which, in order to faithfully depict angles of bearing between any two points on the earth's surface, progressively inflates the apparent size of land masses the closer they are to the poles. There was, mathematically, no end to this inflation: the poles themselves became infinities and could not be shown.

Instead, the upper margin of the rectangular map was a wavering white line suggesting the permanent pack ice just north of Greenland. The northern coast of Antarctica, still with a few broken lines to show remaining unknowns, formed the margin in the south. Beyond these limits, several degrees short of where the poles should have been, there was nothing. Instead, the lines of longitude marched off the map in parallel lockstep, refusing to compromise, much less converge. As if, if only, the world went on forever.

The map had been centered on Greenwich, on the zero meridian. If you needed to steady yourself you could grab hold of that.

Morgan's parents had given him a globe for his thirteenth birthday, but after waiting a decent interval he had put it in his closet where he wouldn't have to look at it. There was no art to a globe. It was too on the nose. Its poles were merely points of rotation, and it didn't matter that they were both obscured, for about eight degrees toward the equator, by the spinning brass discs that held the globe on its stand. These brass discs covered the holes that John Cleves Symmes, the prophet of the hollow earth, had predicted would be found at the poles, giving access to a warmer and gentler world within.

A globe was round and you couldn't fall off it. But a map was a map, a metaphor, full of judgments and choices and victories and regrets; a map was built on hacks and heuristics and mistakes and lies, cracks through which you might, just maybe, someday slip away.

From today the world would be merely a globe. There was no escaping from it.

"Does it have a camera?" asked Morgan. "Can it look down at us?"

"Beats me," said Milner's voice on the speaker. "If this one doesn't have a camera it's a cinch the next one will. Or the one after that."

We did our best, thought Morgan. But we knew all along that it couldn't last forever. The Magnetic Union. The Great Game. The Polar Council. Room 38. The North Warning. There would be no place to hide from the eyes of the satellites, when even great storms, born far out in the ocean, would be spotted, tagged, and sorted before they ever came ashore.

The meeting, or announcement, whatever it was, was over. Milner would talk to Morgan again after he'd heard from Strategic Air Command at Bare Mountain, Massachusetts.

Morgan went back to his room and looked about him. He had already packed most of his things for the flight south in the morning. His next escape was almost prepared. All that remained for him to pack, apart from the outdoor gear he would wear to the plane, were his sleeping things, his washing kit, and his whiskey.

No: there was one more thing of his in the room, half hidden on the desk behind the bottle of Mackinlay's: his old brass carriage clock, a white circular face on spherical feet, hands set to Greenwich time. He picked it up and turned it over in his hands, watching his fingerprints fade from the smooth brass.

Meares had given it to him at their final meeting twenty years ago, two years before the war. Like their first, it took place at the Angela Hotel. Old Captain Rant had recently sold up and the food and the service weren't what they had been, but Meares was, in his decline, a man of fixed habit.

It was Morgan's first visit to the Angela since his messenger days; walking up that familiar path he asked himself where thirteen years had gone. He still wore a blue uniform, still felt he should use the back door.

Meares waited in the lobby just where he'd sat when Morgan first saw him. His face was a dull shade of yellow, and so were the whites of his eyes.

"My health was ruined by that blasted trip to the Yukon," Meares said. They both knew that he was lying. "I should have known I was too old for another winter journey. I should have left that whole business to you."

Morgan noticed how Meares's hand shook as he picked up his whiskey.

"You had to go," Morgan said. "Johansen was your man. It was up to you to bring him in. You never even told me who he was."

"He was his own man. Bess Magids found him in Alaska. I never knew who he really was either. It was Bess who gave him his false name, Hjalmar Johansen. She made quite a point of it. I've no idea why. The police got it wrong anyway."

"I'd never have managed up there without you. What do I know about sled dogs?"

"We were too late anyway."

"Too late for poor Johansen. But you got what you sent him to find."

Meares drank heavily all through dinner, alternating swigs of Mackinlay's with sips of wine. When they were done he produced a wooden box and put it on the table.

"I want you to have this. I won't need it anymore. It's time for me to move on."

Morgan picked up the box. "Where are you going? Back to England?"

Meares grinned at him, the savage grin he had first seen the day Meares caught him snooping. "Somewhere like that. Perhaps a bit warmer."

Morgan opened the box. "Is that your old chronometer? The one you lent Johansen so he could hunt down that map reference?" He held it up to the light. The clock's mechanism, housed in a metal cylinder as wide as it was deep, had been removed from the square, glass-topped wooden housing in which it used to sit with its dial facing upward. The sides and bezel had been gilded, and four little round feet were screwed to the bottom of the case.

A handle was fixed to the top. The name on the dial had been artfully altered from "Arnold" to "Reynolds."

"You've changed it," Morgan said.

"I had a jeweler in England do it. It's a carriage clock now. There's not much call for those old chronometers now that you can wear a small one on your wrist. Plus, that clock is stolen property. It belongs to the Greenwich Observatory. Better it learn to go in disguise."

"I doubt if anyone is looking for it."

"Maybe not. But it could be looking for them. I happen to know that it has a strong homing instinct. No matter where you send it, it always finds its way back."

Meares had died two months later. Morgan kept the clock running for the sake of his memory: chronometers were no longer used much in aerial navigation, thanks to all the technologies developed in the war.

And someday soon, Morgan thought, finding himself back in his room at Tuktoyaktuk, there'll be satellite navigation too. Even our maps will one day be redundant.

He put the chronometer down, then looked out the window. He'd been right. The night had brought a spectacular aurora. It trembled and shimmered across half the sky, waves of green and blue and purple streaming past the stars. If those lights ever failed then the planet would die: they showed how the earth's magnetic lines of force, emanating from the poles, repelled the solar wind, that stream of charged articles that would, if it could, ionize the earth's atmosphere and lick it off into space.

Some day, very soon, Morgan thought, man will go into space and see those lights from above. He will drag them down from heaven and pin them to the dirt.

To the south, the lower camp melted in a creeping layer of ground mist. The flare path at the landing strip was extinguished and the passenger terminal, an old air force bus on blocks by the apron, was unlit and lifeless. Then it too was swallowed by fog. There would be no arrivals tonight, nothing to disturb the silence except the hum of muffled generators.

One last round of listening, thought Morgan. If you're ever going to talk to me, talk to me now.

The bottle of Mackinlay's fitted under his parka without showing an outline. He was halfway out the door when he remembered the clock. You should never leave it sitting out like that, he thought. It was like in the war, back in Castle Archdale: some bugger might swipe it.

He wrapped the old clock in a sweater and shoved it deep inside the bag.

The main exit was next to the loading bay. Morgan was adjusting his buttons, putting on gloves, when the external door opened and a man came in from the night. Morgan recognized one of the meteorologists. He must have been out checking the Stevenson screen.

"You going out now, sir? There's a fog coming in off the sea. It'll soon be a whiteout."

"I know my way around."

The man shook off his wolfskin mittens and wiped snot from his nose with the back of a glove-liner. "One of the guys from the airstrip said they had to call the bear warden today to come deal with a bear. When he showed up all he had with him was a single-shot twenty-two. So now there's a bear out there with a really sore ass and a deep sense of grievance."

"I have a gun." And he did. It was in the waistband of his flight pants. An old Webley service pistol, pitted with spots of corrosion, which Meares had given him on that flight to Aklavik. Because as Meares had said to its previous owner, you just never knew.

"You want me to tell the comms room you're outside, sir? So they can look for you if you get turned around out there?"

"Don't bother. I could be out there for a while."

PART NINE

Cape Flyaway

Inuvik, Northwest Territories

Nelson woke on the couch and remembered that there was no food in the apartment, no milk in the fridge. He made black coffee and knocked on the bedroom door.

"I was thinking," he said, "just before I fell asleep. If that letter from the map people was put in the wrong mailbox, then Bert must have a right mailbox. Right?"

They found it in the hall of the apartment building, just inside the front door. They had walked past it several times without noticing. One of the keys on Bert's ring fit the lock. As soon as Nelson turned it the door sprung open, impelled by the weight of the backed-up mail within.

One letter stood out from the junk mail and bills. It had been sent express and its envelope was marked with the name of a TV company.

Toronto
January 3

Dear Mr. Nilsson,

Please excuse me for writing to you by mail, but I have sent several emails to which you have not replied.

I regret to tell you that the results have come back from the genetic laboratory and they show that, based on comparisons to your own DNA, there is no realistic possibility that your great-uncle Arthur was the same man as the so-called "Mad Trapper of Rat River."

I cannot say how sorry we are to have to tell you this. We know how much work you put into this cold case. The parallels you drew between the appearance and behavior of "Albert Johnson" and the photographs and life story of your missing relative were astonishingly close. If your case hadn't been so compelling we would not have agreed to arrange for the DNA test; we considered our investigation closed several years ago, after our original documentary could reach no conclusion about the true identity of "Albert Johnson."

I hope this disappointment is not too upsetting for you. When you get this letter please give me a call or an email and I can answer any further questions you may have.

Yours sincerely,

Regina Dawson

Senior Producer

"So you had a long-lost uncle."

"Yeah."

"How very romantic of you."

"He was my granddad's big brother. He came with them from Norway to Wisconsin. He joined the peacetime US Army, but they kicked him out. They say he was a bit crazy—liked to live out in the woods by himself. Last thing they heard, he was prospecting alone up in British Columbia. That was all they ever told me. They didn't talk about him much."

"And he was called Arthur Nilsson?"

"Sure. So was I. That's what they christened me too. Arthur." Then he saw that she had something more. "Why do you ask?"

She picked up one of Bert's books, leafed through it, then showed him a page. "It says here that when the police tried to identify Albert Johnson after he died they heard of a man who sounded just like him. A loner and backwoodsman who vanished from the Yukon at exactly the same time that Albert Johnson arrived in the Northwest Territories. No one knows where he came from before that, or where he went after. But he called himself Arthur Nelson."

Nelson thought about his grandfather. He had moved up from the States at a time when half of western Canada was going the other way. He had logged and mined in the Rockies until war broke out. Then he joined the Corps of Signals. "I had to volunteer for the Canadian army," he used to say, "to dodge the American draft." After the war he had settled in Grande Cache, Alberta, still in sight of the mountains, married a local woman, and took a job down in the mine. Nelson remembered a gentle old man who walked with a limp from the shrapnel he'd taken at Hamburg. After his wife died he had come to live with Nelson's family in Grande Prairie. He was always very quiet, apart from his habit of whistling some old regimental march tune. There was also the cough that had killed him.

Bert had been close to their grandfather; they had worked together building Bert's first ham radio. What else had Granddad told Bert while they were messing about with their wireless gear?

Between the old man and Nelson there had always been a silence. Nelson was always in trouble, and the old man dreaded arguments. He would go into the corner whenever Nelson's parents confronted their son, his father yelling, his mother in tears, and Nelson, desperately seeking a way to escape, to avoid having his failings explained to him, would look around the room and see the horror and confusion on the old man's face, and Nelson would think: he can barely stand to look at me. All that he's done in his life, and this is what he gets for a grandson. At least he has Bert to make up for me.

Nelson used to think that it would have been better for the old man if Bert had been called Arthur, like his missing brother, and he himself had been Albert. Now he finally saw the truth of it: I was the Arthur alright.

Whatever happened to the first Arthur Nilsson? Had he starved to death in a remote mountain cabin? Had he frozen to death on the trail? Had he fallen in a river, been eaten by a bear, murdered by a partner, wasted by TB or cancer? Did he die in a prison or charity hospital and get buried in an unmarked grave? Or had he finally come down from the mountains to live a quiet, dull little life in some settled town or city, married maybe, maybe with kids, and had simply chosen, for reasons of his own, never to reach out to the younger brother who'd had his grandson named Arthur? The only thing that Nelson could say for sure about the late Arthur Nilsson—thanks to that note from the film company—was that he hadn't fought a running war with the police and army above the Arctic Circle in the depths of a terrible winter. He hadn't gone out in a hail of defiance on the ice of the Eagle River.

"Are you okay?"

"I never liked the name Arthur. I always said Nilsson. And then later I changed even that."

She reached across the table and put her hand on his. "It's okay," she said. "You have to live your own life."

If you really think that, he thought, then you haven't been paying attention. You haven't been joining the dots.

"Your brother must have been very upset when he got those emails from the TV company. After all the energy he'd invested in this Mad Trapper thing. Then to be told he'd been wrong all along . . . It could easily have pushed someone . . ."

She decided to leave it at that.

Fay went and stood over the desk. They had left the smartphone unplugged when they fled the apartment and its battery had died. She wondered if it had rung again after they'd left, still trying to snare them. But there was no point worrying about that now. They had unplugged the landline. What more could they do?

Bert's laptop was still fully charged. Fay could switch it on, log in as a guest user and cruise the Internet all she wanted, but Nelson's brother had set his own password-locked profile to hide his private business. Maybe, if Bert's body didn't show up somewhere in the thaw, the police would find a way to get into the computer. But Fay and Nelson could do nothing more with it.

She looked again at the large maps of the Yukon Territory and the Mackenzie delta pinned over the desk, at their cellophane overlays covered with crosses, scribbled notes, dates from the 1920s and 1930s, all written in wax pencil.

It was now obvious to her that Bert had used the maps and the surviving police reports to trace the movements of Arthur Nelson and/or Albert Johnson. The thickest cluster of crosses lay in the valley of the Rat River, centered on a place that Bert had marked in pencil: Destruction City. There, the X's were so small and so close together that they looked like dotted lines.

Fay looked at the map for a while longer. Then she picked up a blue wax pencil and began to join the X's in the order of their dates.

They made an outwardly expanding spiral, centered a few miles north of Destruction City.

Constable Carter had been right: the Trapper hadn't been running. He'd been searching for something. That's why he stayed around the Rat River valley even after he tangled with the police. It was only after he found whatever he'd been looking for that he tried to escape to Alaska.

What did my grandfather have to do with all this? Had he come north with Meares to join the hunt for Johnson? She remembered Constable Carter's description of Johnson's last moments, of the stranger who whispered in his ear, of the metal boxes removed from the dying man's pack. Perhaps Meares and her grandfather had come to help Johnson, to try and save him from the police. They had turned up just too late.

This was too big a deal for some drifter from Wisconsin.

Nelson sat on the couch, the letter still in his lap. He spoke at last. "You're wrong about Bert being disappointed by this letter. He never got it, remember? Anyway, he already knew that Johnson wasn't my uncle. Moses Isaac had told him that already . . . What I don't understand is why he was pleased when he heard that. He must have worked for years on this thing. It must be why he moved up here in the first place. And it turned out he'd been wrong all along."

"Maybe," she said, teasing it out for herself, "he started out looking for Arthur Nilsson and then stumbled across Meares instead. Maybe he saw that photograph in Eagle Plains, like we did, and used his government security access to check out the people in it, including my grandfather."

"So?"

"So maybe by the time he found out that Albert Johnson wasn't your uncle, he wasn't bothered anymore. He was already after bigger game."

"Like what?"

"Like Room 38."

"Room 38 . . . ? I thought that was the name of Bert's secret archive. Where he got all that stuff in his files. He wrote it on the covers."

"I think it was something more than that. It was mentioned in Crozier's letter, and the note to Meares from Captain Oates's diary. It sounded like something or someone they worked for in secret. Something that they had to keep hidden."

"Like a spy thing?"

"Maybe . . . Or some kind of secret society. Like the Freemasons. There was a lot of that sort of thing back then."

"A conspiracy. A bad thing."

She studied again the pattern of X's on the map. Destruction City. Jack London's story about a lost cabin in the forest, metal boxes hidden in a grave, the initials on an old pistol, F.R.M.C.

Francis Rawdon Moira Crozier had disappeared in the snow, leaving his name on a part of the planet that very few people would ever see. No one had witnessed his passing. Just like poor young Bellot, she thought. And Eskimo Joe. And Captain Oates. Roald Amundsen. And maybe my grandfather. Bert Nilsson had gone without trace. Were they all bad people? Had they vanished, or escaped?

"Whatever it was," she said, "it kept its secrets. I don't know if that's bad."

Aklavik, Northwest Territories

The village of Aklavik could be reached by car only in winter when the government plowed an ice road across the frozen delta. It twisted and wound through countless unnamed islands, humps of black spruce trees proud of the snow. On one of these accumulations of silt Lieutenant John Franklin, no longer young, had raised the silk flag sewn for him by his first wife, the Romantic poet Eleanor Porden. Already unwell by the time he left England, she had asked him to plant it for her when he reached the Arctic Ocean. He had kept his part of the deal. But by then she was already dead.

It seemed to Fay, sitting in the passenger seat of Bert Nilsson's Equinox, that if she looked through the willows on the island fringes, if she stared hard enough into the trees, it would not be at all surprising to see a scrap of bright silk hanging from a spruce pole. And if I did, she thought, should we stop the car so we could look at it? Their wheels hummed smoothly on the black-and-white ice, drawing them, she guessed, to a final unraveling.

Nelson set the car into the long smooth bends between the snow banks thrown up by the plows. There were no turnoffs, no forks, just a groove in the snow guiding them onward. A rain of fine crystals burned in the headlights, as if the car were moving through a field of drifting stars. The sky itself was silver and blue, almost ready for the sun to rise. Sometimes, crossing a sound between islands, Fay could see all the way to the southern horizon. There was a band of bright red on the mountains.

The river widened and there was Aklavik, a line of lights on a ridge above the Peel. Clapboard houses built on piles above the permafrost. Steaming stovepipes. Scrubby birches and alders. A ramp of dirty snow leading up from the river. Poles and pylons and webs of sagging wire. Two swaddled figures on two Ski-Doos—men or women, old or young, who could say?—shot down the ramp as the Equinox climbed it, each towing a toboggan loaded with gear. A shit-truck drew sewage from one of the houses, its engine running loudly to power the pump, but there was no one on the street to give them directions. They had to find the cemetery by themselves. It lay off a side street, a half-acre of crosses and headstones where alders and willows peeped from the snow.

There was a hand-painted sign by the split-log lych-gate.

Albert Johnson arrived in Ross River Aug. 21, 1927. Complaints of local trapper brought the RCMP on him. He shot two officers and became a fugitive of the law with howling huskies, dangerous trails, frozen nights. The posse finally caught up with him. He was killed up the Eagle River, Feb. 17, 1932.

"Ross River is in the Yukon. They think Albert Johnson and Arthur Nelson were the same man," said Nelson.

"Maybe they were. All we know is that Johnson wasn't your uncle. There could have been two Arthur Nelsons." Or three, she thought.

Stepping off the street's compacted snow, Nelson was suddenly in powder up to his thighs. Floundering among the crosses, he called back over his shoulder. "Imagine wading thirty miles a day in this. I guess this is what it was like to be Arthur Nelson."

You *are* an Arthur Nelson. But Fay was distracted by something across the street. It was an upright cartoon figure, a lifesize wooden cutout of a man with a pack and snowshoes slung on his back. He was holding a rifle. There was a hole where the face should be so that you could, if you wanted, stand behind the cutout and have yourself photographed as a comic book Mad Trapper. From where Fay stood, the hole framed only the blank sky beyond it.

"I've found it," called Nelson.

He had trampled down the powder snow, making it easier for her to follow him to the grave. It was contained by a rectangular picket fence filled with snow to a foot from the top. Digging with his gloved hands, Nelson uncovered a plain wooden cross. Two words were written in poker-work letters: "Albert Johnson?"

They stood together looking down at it.

"Well," said Nelson. "What did we expect?"

"It was worth having a look."

Fay turned away and took in the little cemetery. Even the undisturbed snow couldn't hide its matter-of-fact, bedraggled sense of itself. If anyone had left flowers on these graves they were deep under the snow. Plastic flowers maybe, that would bloom again each spring.

The man called Albert Johnson had cheated the grave they had buried him in. He would always be someone else, somewhere else. What an escape act.

She took Nelson's arm and drew him away, retracing their steps to the gate.

A police truck came down the street, cruising in low gear. It drove on past the cemetery, passing the spot where the Equinox was parked, and then it stopped and backed up until it was just outside the lychgate. The driver's door opened and Sergeant Peake got out. He leaned against the side of his truck and waited for them to come out of the gate.

"Let me guess," he said. "The Mad Trapper, right?"

The walk through deep snow had left Fay a little breathless. "Yes."

"Not a hard guess. I don't suppose either of you has anyone of your own buried in these parts."

You'd be more surprised than we would, thought Fay. "We're just visiting his grave."

"Distant Early Warning. The Mad Trapper's grave. There aren't a lot of tourist attractions up here. You take what you get, I guess."

Fay didn't like the way Peake was smiling at them. He seemed to be settling in for a proper conversation. Or was it something more? "I think I've seen everything now." She made an effort to smile back at him. "It's time for me to leave."

"I heard you tried to leave already. Laurie from the snowplow radioed your names in, from up in the mountains. In case you got stuck. She said you were heading south in a beat-up old Ford." He took a slow look at Bert's Chevrolet Equinox, parked at the side of the street.

Nelson spoke up. "We were turned back at Eagle Plains. Fresh snow around Tombstone Mountain."

"So then you came all the way back to Aklavik?"

Fay wondered where this was going. "We went to Inuvik first."

Peake nodded slowly, as if mulling it over. "You're staying at the Northern Villas, I think you said."

"Not anymore." Fay felt her temper rising. If he asks me where I'm staying, I'll tell him to go fuck himself. It's no business of his. But then she remembered Nelson's delicate position. She prepared herself for the question. But it didn't come. Instead, the sergeant nodded meaningfully, as if a private box had just been ticked for him. Then he pushed himself away from the side of the truck, getting ready for business.

"I'm glad I ran in to you. I'm looking for old Moses Isaac. Has either of you seen him?"

"We saw him yesterday," said Nelson. "In the seniors' center at the hospital."

"Sure. Eunice told me you'd been in to visit him. But have you seen him since? He's gone missing."

"Missing?"

"He got up and walked out of there last night. No one even saw him go. Didn't even have a coat on him, as far as anyone knows. I've come over to Aklavik to ask around, in case he's shown up at any of his relatives. But they've heard nothing. It's not looking good. They're searching the woods back in Inuvik."

"That's terrible."

"So I guess you haven't seen him since the hospital?"

"No. I'm really sorry."

The sergeant looked from Fay to Nelson, as if waiting for them to say more. "So," he said finally, "the Mad Trapper, eh?" He stamped his feet a couple of times on the ice to knock the snow of his boots, to show he was ready to go. Then a thought seemed to strike him.

"You ever hear," Peake said, looking from one to the other, "what they say about dying? That everyone dies twice: once when you die physically, and the second time, for real, when the last person who knew you passes away." He nodded toward the grave of the unknown fugitive. "Old Moses was the last living person who'd ever met Albert Johnson. If Moses is gone, then the Trapper's finally gone too. You picked a good day to come here."

Fay saw his point. But maybe, just maybe, there was more to it than that. She'd never met her grandfather, and yet she thought she could somehow feel love for him. "The thing about Albert Johnson," she said slowly, still working it out for herself, "is that nobody ever knew who he was. Which is why he can't really be dead. He got away with it. He slipped through a crack."

She would have expected the policeman to laugh or to look at her funny. Instead, he nodded his head a couple more times, digesting her words, and then he held out his hand. "You could be on to something there. If you're heading south I won't see you again. It was nice to meet you."

Fay shook his hand. Then Nelson spoke.

"Sergeant. There's something that I need to tell you."

The policeman released Fay's hand and turned to look at Nelson, it seemed to her reluctantly. "Oh yeah? What's that?"

"I'm worried about my brother. He's been missing for days."

"Your brother?"

"Albert Nilsson. He's a teacher at the high school."

Fay watched the play of expression on the policeman's face. She thought she saw several emotions. One was amusement. She did not see surprise. The sergeant settled on a smile.

"But *you're* Albert Nilsson."

"No, I'm not. You mistook me for him when we met in Tuktoyaktuk. I'm his brother. Arthur Nilsson. We look very alike. I want to report him missing."

Nelson stood with his feet slightly apart, his hands rammed in his pockets. His chin was raised just a little too high, so that he stared down his nose at Sergeant Peake. This is how he fronts up when he's in trouble, thought Fay. This is how he looked as a boy.

"Missing? Really?"

"As far as I can tell he just walked out of the apartment and left everything behind him. Even his coat. Just like Moses Isaac."

The policeman patted Nelson on the shoulder. "Thirty days of night, eh?" He turned to go. "We all get a bit squirrelly here at midwinter. We can all use a laugh."

Nelson stood his ground. "I'm not joking. I'm not Albert Nilsson."

Peake opened the door of his truck, his back half turned so they couldn't see his face. "Sure you are."

"Okay. Have it your way. I'm Albert Nilsson. In that case, I want to make a missing person report for my kid brother. His name is Arthur."

"Yeah?" The policeman got into the truck but held his door open. "You want to make a report?" He started the engine. "Okay. If you think it's urgent, come and see me in Inuvik. I'm heading back there now. But please: if it's not urgent, leave it until the day after tomorrow."

"Why?"

"Because we're flat-out busy right now. There's this search for poor Moses, and then we've also got the festival tomorrow. It's all hands on deck. There's always a few people who get a little too drunk the day before."

"The day before what?"

"The Sunrise Festival. Tomorrow's the day when the sun comes back. The place goes a little crazy."

They watched him drive off.

"Well," said Nelson, "you can't say I didn't try."

The mailman had done a bad job of posting the envelope. It protruded from Bert's mailbox by two or three inches, so they couldn't miss seeing it when they came through the hall. They wouldn't even need to fish out the key to open the mailbox: they could just grab the letter and pull it out of there. Otherwise they'd probably have left the letter where it was. They were both done now, finished, having come back from Aklavik.

Nelson made coffee while Fay looked at the white A4 envelope. It was marked with the logo of the Royal Museum in Greenwich. Several pages were nested inside it, giving it heft.

I don't care, thought Fay. But she opened it anyway.

The cover letter was from the curator of the horological workshop, the department that maintained and cataloged the precision clocks and marine chronometers that had been the stock-in-trade of Greenwich for hundreds of years.

Dear Dr. Nilsson,

It was very kind of you to send me an advance copy of your
draft paper offering a solution to the mystery of the Franklin chronometer, Arnold 294. I read it with great interest
and not a little scholarly admiration. If your paper were
intended as a work of fiction I would have no hesitation
in endorsing it. As historical research it may well contain
many fine and novel parts—although I have not been in a
position to check your rather esoteric sources for myself, I
trust your reputation. But as a solution to the mystery of
Arnold 294 I am afraid to say it is wide of the mark.

Since Arnold 294 returned to Greenwich several years
ago we have been doing our own detective work to deter-
mine how such a delicate instrument survived a lost mission to the Arctic. As it happens, we arrived at our own
conclusion around the same time that we received your
paper. Our solution is sadly less romantic than yours but
rather more straightforward: we believe that the chronometer never left Britain at all.

According to our surviving records the instrument in
question, having been built in 1807, was probably in need
of refurbishment by the time HMS *Erebus* was due to sail
for the Northwest Passage in 1845. It might therefore have
been sent back to the Arnold workshop in London for
a last-minute overhaul. However, this would have been a
mistake: old Mr. Arnold himself had died in 1843 and his
workshop was in chaos, so the navy had just ordered that its
Arnold chronometers should thenceforth be sent elsewhere
for repair.

Had *Erebus*'s navigation officer gone back to collect
Arnold 294 on the eve of sailing, and found that it was not
ready, he might have quietly resolved to come back for it

after *Erebus* returned from her voyage—no one would miss it, as the ship already had several other working chronometers on board, some of them issued by Greenwich, others the private property of officers. But of course, the ship did not return.

In the meantime the Arnold business was taken over by another clockmaker, who stated at the time that Arnold's paperwork and affairs were in disarray. If the chronometer had not been labeled as Royal Navy property it would have been regarded as part of Arnold's own stock and sold off with the rest of it. At some point thereafter it was converted into a carriage clock, probably to make it more saleable, and re-engraved with the name of the clockmakers who presumably altered it, Reynolds of London. There was, therefore, nothing underhand or criminal about the alteration of the chronometer's original appearance. It was simply a matter of commercial practice.

We ourselves recognized the little "carriage clock" as a former Royal Navy chronometer when we saw it in an auction catalog several years ago, and we duly bought it for our collection. It was only after we opened its case that we realized what a very special chronometer it was. Since then we have been able to trace its previous ownership back to the 1970s, when it appeared in an antiques dealer's catalog. How they came by it we do not know: antiques often change hands on a cash basis without any records being kept.

A full account of our findings is included in our catalog of all the marine chronometers issued by the Royal Observatory. This is not yet available online, so I shall make copies of the pages relating to Arnold 294 and put them in the post for you.

May I just say again how fascinated I was by your theory, which is quite enchanting. Let us hope that the mathematicians and physicists are correct, and that a universe exists where it is also the correct one.

Yours, etc.

Sitting at the desk, Fay turned to the other pages in the envelope, color photocopies of the catalog for Arnold 294. There were several photos of the clock itself, shown from the front and then partially disassembled. It was the first time she had seen it pictured in high-definition color, the soft glow of the brass, the white-silvered clock face. It looked so simple inside, almost austere—a scalloped case for the spring, a fine wheel for balance, a neat little chain like the chain of a bicycle. There must be more to it than that, she thought. How she wished that she could hold it in her hands again.

"This cover letter," said Nelson, somewhere behind her. "It's a copy of an email that was sent two weeks ago. The curator must have printed it out to include it with the photocopies."

"So?"

"So Bert never got that envelope. But he got the email . . . It must have killed him to find out his theory was wrong. Whatever it was . . ."

She turned the chair around. He was sitting on the couch, the letter held in his lap, looking into the light that leaked through the curtains. His desolation moved her.

"You don't know that it was wrong . . . Why would he believe them anyway? Their solution is full of supposition. And don't you think it's a coincidence that they only came up with it after he'd already sent them his paper?"

"You don't really think that. If you really didn't believe in coincidence, you'd have to believe in conspiracy instead."

Once again, he was proving smarter than she'd imagined. Once again, it angered her. "Why not? Someone called us on the phone, remember? Someone else who's looking for Bert."

"Maybe it *was* just the credit-card company. I didn't see what number it was. You did."

"So I'm deluded. And so was your brother."

"He was always half crazy. You I don't know."

She turned away from him, stung. This wasn't fair. She'd been starting to like him. Their share in this mystery had made her less lonely. And now the mystery was gone. Because whatever she said to Nelson, she too had to privately side with the experts in Greenwich.

Had Bert Nilsson believed in his mad quest himself, or had he been making it up for his own amusement? Maybe he'd been writing a story, or crafting a hoax. Or maybe both at once. So many of Bert's clues were presented in his handwriting, including the mention of her grandfather . . . As for the clock in her grandparents' wedding photograph, why did she ever think that it was Franklin's lost chronometer? It was an old black-and-white picture. There must be other such clocks . . .

Nelson was right: if she wasn't prepared to believe in coincidence she might as well go crazy and believe in a Room 38.

She put her elbows on the desk and her chin in her hands. Her eyes, when she opened them again, were caught by something on the wall, one of the many notes and photocopies pinned above Bert's desk.

This particular page was a printout of a web article about the Distant Early Warning Line. At the top was an account of how the North American Aerospace Defense Command had upgraded and modernized the DEW Line in the late 1980s. Many of the smaller stations were shut down and most of the rest were automated. The name was changed too: from then on the Distant Early Warning Line was to be known as the North Warning System. No sense of poetry: she could see why nobody used the new name.

There followed a list of the fifty-four surviving stations, a chain stretching three and a half thousand miles from Alaska to Labrador.

Point Lay. Wainwright. Point Barrow. Point Lonely. Okliktok. Flaxman Island. Barter Island. Komakuk Beach. Stokes Point. Shingle Point. Storm Hills. Tuktoyaktuk. Liverpool Bay. Nicholson Peninsula. Horton River. Cape Parry. Keats Point. Croker River. Harding River. Bernard Harbour. Lady Franklin Point. Edinburgh Island. Cape Peel West. Cambridge Bay. Sturt Point. Jenny Lind Island. Hat Island. Gladman Point. Gjoa Haven. Shepherd Bay. Simpson Lake. Pelly Bay. Cape McLoughlin. Lailor River. Hall Beach. Rowley Island. Bray Island. Longstaff Bluff. Nudluardjk Lake. Dewar Lakes. Kangok Fiord. Cape Hooper. Broughton Island. Cape Dyer. Cape Mercy. Brevoort Island. Loks Land. Resolution Island. Cape Kakiviak. Saglek. Cape Kiglapait. Big Bay. Tukialik. Cartwright.

Do we believe in these places? she wondered. Was that it? Does it matter so long as we can say their names?

Bert had circled several of these names in red ballpoint: Tuktoyaktuk, Cape Parry, Lady Franklin Point, Gjoa Haven, Hall Beach, Loks Land.

There was a footnote at the bottom of the printout, in type so small that Fay hadn't noticed it before. It informed her that on December 24 each year the North Warning radar picket, posted far out in the polar night, was tasked with a very special mission: the detection and tracking of Santa Claus as he emerged from the North Pole to deliver gifts to the children of the world. There was a link to NORAD's website where you could monitor Santa's progress on the map.

Fay wondered if Bert Nilsson had noticed this tiny footnote when he printed out his handy list of radar stations. She remembered her childish notion of her grandfather, a Santa Claus lost in the ice. Had Bert Nilsson also understood in the end, as she did now herself, that in his search for Room 38 he'd been looking for something magical, a hole in the map, an escape from dull causality, though he knew very well that it didn't exist?

"We should go for a drink," she said.

The whole town was out and about that night. There was to be traditional dancing and drumming in the high school, and people arrived on foot or in cars, double-parking on Mackenzie Road. It may have been the dancing in the high school, or all the preparations underway for the next day's events—the snowmobile parade, food fair, firework display, lantern procession, concerts, and bonfires—but the pub was still almost quiet when they went in. Mike sat at the bar with a beer and a shot. He pointed to an empty stool beside him. "You two can share that one. I'm too old to stand."

He waved his hand around the dimly lit room. "I don't normally belly up to the bar here, but it'll be crazy in an hour or so. On the night before sunrise it's a good idea to keep your supply lines short."

Mike ordered three whiskies, three beers. Fay tasted sweet beer cut with the sting of the whiskey, felt the blood pump in her head. The band—the same one as the last time—was still setting up, but the PA played country rock music. Pool players yelled wisecracks to put one another off. Buzz of voices, clink of glasses, ring of tills. Nelson bought a second round. Fay remembered that she had never paid him for the lift to Tuktoyaktuk. Maybe, she thought, as she looked around the darkened bar, I should check where I stand with him. See if I'm still on the clock.

Nelson and Mike were now watching the television, heads cocked as if trying to hear. A man in a red diving suit floated amid the kelp that grew from the timbers of a shipwreck, pointing to an old cannon that lay in the silt. From the length of the camera shot and the movements of the diver's hands, Fay guessed that the diver was providing a spoken commentary—they could do that, she thought, with the new kinds of diving gear. But because of the noise in the bar she couldn't hear. Then a caption came up, too small for her to read, and the picture changed to something else—men and women in suits in a parliament.

"So that's the end of that," said Mike bitterly. "HMS *Erebus*. They had to go and find her. They had to solve a perfectly good mystery."

They both leaned on the bar—Mike on two elbows, Nelson on one—watching the bubbles form and vanish in their beer.

Fay felt a need to comfort them. "It won't be over," she said, "until they find the *Terror* as well. She's still out there, remember?"

"They'll find her," said Nelson. "It's only a matter of time."

Fay and Nelson went out for a smoke leaving Mike to mind the barstools. Kids wandered happily up and down the street. Nelson wasn't sure how cold it was—they'd been drinking for a while—but he no longer felt that he needed his coat. Maybe he was warmed by the glow from the town; it hid the stars, obscured the aurora, if there was one tonight. Fay shivered. "It'll be alright," she said. "We'll sort everything out the day after tomorrow."

They went back inside. Fay swayed on the edge of the floor, watching the dancers. Who else might still be out there, she wondered? Who else might come in from the dark? The couples held hands and swung around in close orbits, inclinations set by their relative heights. They flashed in and out of her sight, in and out of her momentary existence.

She remembered how her mother used to take her up the steep hill through the park to the Greenwich Observatory. She would skip from one side of the prime meridian to the other, from east to west in a leap, in a heartbeat. It was like that tonight. Nothing had changed, not herself, not the light, not a flicker, and yet there was her mother, still young and pretty, still smiling down at her, a world away and close enough to touch. Who draws these lines for us? East/West. North/South. Go/no go. Living/dead.

She hadn't studied mathematics—another gift from her grandfather that hadn't been passed to her—but she liked to read articles about quantum physics. They talked about particles—which she had to visualize as tiny points of light, like the crystals that rained from the sky here—flitting instantly from one place to another, millions of miles away, as if to say to space and time, "We're not the ghosts—you are." She had always found a kind of comfort in that.

The music changed to a fast country waltz. She took Nelson by the hands and pulled him onto the floor. He didn't know how to dance, but after a few turns he had learned not to step on her feet and they could hold each other closer. She smelled cigarettes and sweat and whiskey, but she didn't know if it was his smell or hers. Opening her eyes, she watched the world turn around her like clockwork. A stocky, whiskery man danced with a dark-haired young woman who seemed delighted by his skill. A young man with short hair and calm gray eyes limped across the dance floor, heading for the door. Up at the bar, talking with Mike and watching the dancers, a thin old man with a big hawk nose polished his glasses on his silk scarf. Fay thought she saw children in the shadows at the back of the room—how did children get in here? Maybe, on the night before the sun came back, such things were let slide. She closed her eyes and let the music move through her.

"This is perfect," she said.

They stopped turning in circles, stood on the edge of the floor. "But it's time to go," Nelson said.

There was a sign where the highway diverged from the road to the airport. Nelson was sure it must be new. It was big and square and luminous, shining in the headlights: an arrow pointed left for the airport, right for the long lonely road to the outside. He couldn't have missed a sign like that if it'd been there a few days before, when he'd gone by mistake to the airport. It would have steered him away from all this. But now here it was, guiding them both to the end of the road.

Out here, beyond the edge of the town, there was no artificial light apart from their low beams and the glow of the dashboard.

The Northern Lights played their ageless games in the sky, indifferent to anyone who watched them. Would it have made any difference, Fay wondered, if I'd had children of my own? Would they have watched me from outside the circle of light in which the old drunkards were dancing?

The engines roared, yellow-tipped propellers became yellow-edged discs, the earth pushed away from the undercarriage. There was the highway, there the white slash of the river's east channel, glowing in the starlight. The forest became a dark stain on the snow. They were flying due north ahead of the sunrise. The town briefly appeared like a childhood beneath them, all red, green, and yellow and Christmas trees and snow. Then it was gone and they were drifting with the stars, those flitting points of light, holding hands in the warm darkened cabin, already falling asleep.

Epilogue

Royal Canadian Mounted Police
Inuvik, Northwest Territories
On January 26 last I was contacted by a senior RCMP officer in Ottawa who asked me to prepare this confidential report on the death of Dr. Albert Nilsson, the former government scientist whose body was found in the snow on the outskirts of Inuvik two weeks before.

The officer in question hinted that the report was for the information of the Canadian Security Intelligence Service and/or one of its partner agencies in the United Kingdom. He also asked that his own name be kept out of it.

I must state now that I found his request highly irregular, and am only complying with it because I also regard it as harmless; there is nothing that I can add to the existing official case files, which I gather have already been shared with elements outside the force—itself a highly irregular state of affairs.

The particulars: around noon on January 12 last some kids out riding a Ski-Doo found the bodies of a man and woman lying in the snow on a bluff that looks over the river. They lay side by side and there was no sign of violence.

The medical examination showed they both had elevated levels of blood alcohol. It was the coroner's opinion that they got drunk and then fell asleep in the snow, which is said to be about the most pleasant way there is for a person to go. They probably stayed up drinking then went out there thinking to watch the sun rise, January 12 being our first dawn in these parts after a month of Arctic night.

My constables found nearby a 2013 Chevrolet Equinox SUV registered to Albert Nilsson. They searched the dead man and found a wallet with a driver's license, credit cards, and various other particulars identifying him as Albert Nilsson, born Grande Prairie, Alberta. This name was also written on the label of the dead man's coat.

On further inquiries, Albert Nilsson turned out to be a former government scientist who came from outside to teach geography in the high school. His only listed next of kin is a brother, Arthur Nilsson, last known address Fort McMurray, Alberta, a drifter whom we have been unable to trace.

The dead lady had no identification of any kind on her, except that some of her clothing labels came from the United Kingdom. I myself went to search the dead man's apartment in person and there was no sign there of the lady's personal effects or documents or any indication that she had ever been there.

I also personally checked all the hotel and guesthouse registers in town but no one of that description had been checked in to any of them. We sent out her picture and data through the usual channels, but she did not match any missing person reports in Canada or the UK or the States.

I am afraid to say that stories like this are not unknown up here on the delta, which is the end of the road for a lot of drifters and suchlike.

I don't know what else I can tell you. I never met Dr. Nilsson myself, and neither of the deceased came to my attention in any way before their demise.

If the people in London or Ottawa or wherever do come up with any further information I would ask that they supply it to the RCMP through official channels and not to involve me personally again. As far as I am concerned the case is already closed. It is true that we can't find anyone to identify these people and lay them to rest, but lives don't always end like they're supposed to. Some people slip through the cracks.

Yours,
Sergeant Martin Peake RCMP

Acknowledgments

So many people helped me in the writing of this novel that I am sure to forget to thank some of them here. Sorry. Thanks.

This book received generous support from the Arts Council of Ireland and from the Canada Council for the Arts. Particular thanks go to Sarah Bannan in Dublin and to Suzanne Keeptwo in Ottawa.

My wife, Nuala Haughey, put up with several years of spiraling introversion, severe mood swings, mental absences, and poorly performed domestic tasks. Now that the book is finished, none of this will change. Bláthnaid and Iseult are already old and wise enough to expect no better.

My sister Róisín, another secret polar enthusiast, was an excellent reader when I needed one, as were Nuala Haughey, Kevin McCarthy, Maeve McLoughlin and Conn Ó Midheach.

My mother, Gabrielle Hetherington, offered much-needed hospitality in Grande Prairie and Edmonton, while Kerri and John O'Loughlin did the same in Calgary. Emmal Baker and Omar Karmi provided a welcoming refuge in London. Carol Haughey held down the Lurgan end for all of us.

Jeroen Kramer was, as ever, a wonderful companion on the road; his photographs of the Mackenzie delta were a source of inspiration whenever my well ran dry.

I am particularly indebted to Jonathan Betts and Rory McEvoy of the horological workshop at the Royal Observatory in Greenwich, who shared their precious time with me. If I have trampled on their learning it is only for artistic reasons, or because I failed to understand them.

In Dublin I was kindly assisted by Sinéad Shiels Mac Aodha at the Ireland Literature Exchange and by the libraries of Trinity College, UCD, and Dublin Corporation. Special thanks are due to Sinéad Haughey.

In Inuvik, Peter Clarkson was generous with his knowledge, his contacts, and his snowmobiles. Denny Rodgers showed us around and tried to take us curling. Onida Banksland introduced me to Peter Esau and Alice Aklauf, who were a fount of information on life in the tough old days. Heather Moses of the tourist office provided a small but vital piece of last-minute information about the non-availability of cigarettes at Inuvik airport. Olav and Judi Falsnes were informative hosts at the Arctic Chalet Resort. Thanks too to Rick Adams at the Mad Trapper Pub, the best and indeed only tavern in town.

Merven Gruben, the mayor of Tuktoyaktuk, showed us around his township and was very helpful with background. Thanks also to the Voudrach family and to Lennie Emaghok.

The Aklavik troop of the Canadian Rangers hosted us on their annual training camp in the depths of the Arctic winter. Sergeant Marcy Maddison, their regular army instructor, patiently put up with her civilian intruders. Captain Sandra Bourne and Captain Stephen Watton of National Defence Headquarters in Ottawa authorized what I would like to claim as the world's most northerly military embed. Thanks also to Edward McLeod and Frank Kasook for guiding us and putting up the tent.

Major Mathias Joost of the history directorate at Armed Forces Canada repeatedly came to my aid with information about the epic post-war photo-surveying mission of 408, 413, and 414

Squadrons of the Royal Canadian Air Force. Hugh Halliday helped me to get my hands on an invaluable copy of the newly published history of 408 Squadron.

Kristina Kwiatkowski of the Canada Centre for Mapping and Earth Observation dug into her archives to unearth priceless contemporaneous information about the discovery and naming of Prince Charles Island, Air Force Island, and Foley Island in 1948. I thank her for this, and also for having the job title of "Toponymy Specialist," which is a wonderful thing. I would also like to thank Richie Sue Allen and Sophie Tellier at Library and Archives Canada.

While researching the Distant Early Warning Line I was fortunate to stumble across the blogs of Paul Kelley and Brian Jeffrey, two civilian radicians who worked on the DEW Line in the early days. Both were then patient enough to deal with many vexatious questions.

Neal McEwen, Sid Reith, and Bryan Robinson will never have heard of me, but I have borrowed their online reminiscences of their lives as telegraph clerks and twisted them to my own ends.

The great Edith Iglauer is owed a considerable debt, both for her classic work of north-country reportage, *Denison's Ice Road*, and for the contacts she gave me in Yellowknife, including the very helpful Bill Braden.

I am grateful to author Barbara Smith for her fascinating book on the fugitive "Albert Johnson" and also for showing me the long-lost secret report on the manhunt by Constable William Carter RCMP, which she unearthed in the course of her research. John Evans of the Canadian Police Research Center gave me his insights on the manhunt.

Dr. Lorne Hammond of the Royal British Columbia Museum helped me to track down useful details of Cecil Meares's last years in Victoria, BC. My portrayal of this intriguing figure relies heavily—in so far as it is based in fact at all—on the work of Leif

Mills, whose biography of Meares is, as far as I know, the only one ever written. Mr. Mills was kind enough to send me one of his own copies of the out-of-print *Men of Ice*, which also contains a fascinating account of the deeply affecting life and death of Alister Forbes Mackay, a long-forgotten Shackleton associate who was part of the first expedition to reach the south magnetic pole.

Professor William Barr of the University of Calgary has actually been to Cape Chelyuskin and could tell me what it was like. I met him at the annual Shackleton festival in Athy, County Kildare, whose organizer, Seamus Taaffe, I would also like to thank.

Just up the road in Dunshane, John O'Loughlin, Catherine Choiseul, and Dan O'Loughlin were always good for a free meal, good conversation and a break from weekend writing. In Newbridge, Rose O'Loughlin and family lent us a retreat and a pool.

Marissa Doyle, an expert on historical dance, elucidated an important point about nineteenth-century dance cards.

Brendan Barrington of the *Dublin Review* published an essay that I wrote on the Mad Trapper of Rat River—an essay that later fed into this novel.

Dr. Lisa Goldfarb of the Wallace Stevens Society helped me to obtain the rights for the poem "The Snow Man," which is used as an epigraph. Peter Fallon of the Gallery Press was very generous following a similar request about Derek Mahon's aching "Antarctica."

He had little to do with this particular novel, but I still owe David Beresford my deepest gratitude for many other things, so I'll take the opportunity to thank him here.

Sabine Klingner, Justine Driscoll, Deborah Behan, Myra Dowling, Edel O'Connell, Aisling Sexton, Julianne Gee, Louise Dunne, Sinéad McMahon, and Nicola Brennan all provided much-needed backup when called upon. Thanks too to Audrey Magee.

Many great books and periodicals (not to mention DuckDuckGo and Wikipedia) helped to inspire and inform the writing of this work of fiction. Chief among these was Pierre Berton's *The Arctic Grail*, a gripping yet comprehensive history of the centuries-long search for the Northwest Passage. Some of Berton's elegiac *The Klondike Fever* also found its way in. The debt that a certain passage of my novel owes to the great Jack London story "In a Far Country" has to be seen to be believed.

My interpretations of the characters of Roald Amundsen and Bess Magids are drawn principally from the recent Amundsen biography by Tor Bomann-Larsen. I apologize for the many crimes that my fiction has committed against his facts.

Ralph Lloyd-Jones's fascinating paper on "The Paranormal Arctic" is at the heart of the chapter about Joseph René Bellot. Chauncey Loomis's elegant life of Charles Francis Hall, *Weird and Tragic Shores*, supplied not only an epigraph for my book but also an intriguing murder which, like all good mysteries, ought never to be solved.

To switch media, I would also like to mention the Conet Project's audio compilation of broadcasts by numbers stations, those enigmatic Sirens of the shortwave radio band. Eric Holm's *Andøya*, an album of eerie ambient music taped from military antennae in the Arctic, made an obvious mark on part of my story.

I thank my agent, Peter Straus, for selling the book, and Jon Riley of riverrun and Quercus for buying it. My editors, Richard Arcus, Jon Riley, and Nick de Somogyi, have worked long and hard to turn a self-indulgent mess of cobbled-together myth and mystery into something like a novel. Jeff Edwards made the excellent maps, with some help from Bláthnaid O'Loughlin. Finally, thanks to you, the reader, for reading it—assuming you made it this far.

Dublin, 2016

About the Type

Typeset in Bembo at 12/16 pt.

Created by the Monotype Corporation around 1928, the modern interpretation of Bembo is based on an original design by Francesco Griffo that dates back as far as 1495. The modern version has since been a popular choice for publications, due to its attractive and legible design.

Typeset by Scribe Inc., Philadelphia, Pennsylvania.